Maker's Fire
Tiffee Jasso

"Maker's Fire" is written for my son, Richard, whose artistic mind beats in rhythm to the music of life, and whose heart of gold spreads joy to those around him.

Notes for the Reader

For the sake of not treading on the privacy or intellectual property of those who own businesses in Hollywood or elsewhere, I have used fictional names for most businesses, some streets, and fashion designers. There is no deliberate connection to any real person, mayor's office, business, or brand, other than the FBI. That department does exist, but as far as I know Special Agents Vincent Windino Lopez, Ace Marvel Whittaker, Cheri Milagro Thompson, and Special Agent-in-Charge Benjamin Yost Langstrom of the Los Angeles branch of the FBI, do not. Detectives, coroners, officers, and others that appear in the Maker's Fire are fictional as well. Also at this time and place, the Washington Bureau of Psychic Investigation—BPI—and, Doctor Genie Ferguson exist only in my book and imagination.

Past conversations, foreign words, brands, books, or films that I have created, and my characters' thoughts are in italics to help you distinguish them.

Chapter 1
Frightened

A house is just a house unless those that live within are extraordinary, then it also becomes remarkable. No. 1 Hattera Lane is such a house. For Hollywood, it is a great deal like the other homes in the area, a large spacious single story home—white stucco trimmed in red brick with a red tile roof—a large swimming pool, natural stone walkways, award winning roses, trimmed hedges, and a huge glass enclosed patio. But the similarities end there, as the occupants are as different from the average citizen as a lion is to a house cat; They are more than six hundred years old.

As was her habit, Hattie Drake woke up at ten minutes to nine. Once she had showered, dressed, and combed her long tangled reddish-blonde curls, she made her way to the dining table and sat down.

Nigel Quin came through the kitchen door carrying a tray with a fresh pot of tea, toast, and a plate with two coddled eggs on it. He set the tray down in front of her. "Good morning, Hattie."

Hattie smiled at the older man who was not related by blood but had been her guardian for more than fifty years, and as far as she and her sister Marie were concerned, he was the only other family member they had. One brow went up when she saw his hair was now, red. "Morning, Nigel. I see you have changed your hair color."

"Yes I have," Nigel said, nodding his shaggy head at her as he filled her cup. "I grew irritated at myself for being born with yellow hair."

"Irritated?" Hattie asked, not mentioning his hair had turned gray from age, more than a decade ago.

"Yes," Nigel declared, putting the coffee pot down, and folding his arms for emphasis. As Hattie raised an eyebrow, he explained. "It's my brain's fault."

Both of Hattie's brows went up at that statement.

"It started last week when I was washing pans and saw my hands had shriveled up from the being in the water. You've got dishwater hands, I told myself. *And dishwater blonde hair to match*, my mind said. After that, every time I started to wash pots, that little voice in my head called me a *scummy blonde pot washer*."

"Ah. That would irritate me as well," Hattie said, working to keep a smile off her face. "I do like the red color though. I think it makes you look younger."

She said nothing about him washing pots and pans as he preferred to do the cooking and cleaning for the kitchen. Marie and her cleaned the rest of the house other than the two kitchen apartments. Nigel clean the one he lived in and dusted the other one as no one used that one.

Nigel's dark eyes, and wrinkled face lit up at her words. "I thought so too, but for me to point that out would not be mannerly."

"Maybe so, but I can say it. That is what family is for," Hattie said before she turned to butter her toast. She put the bread and knife down when the blue phone on the table rang.

"Hattie Drake," she stated once she had put the phone's receiver to her ear.

"Are you sure? The detective?" a woman's voice questioned.

"Well, unless there was an overnight change that I am unaware of that is my name. And I do a bit of detective work, yes, but only for paranormal activities," Hattie answered, more amused, than annoyed by such a question.

"Good. Then, I must see you. Something is trying to kill me."

"I will be at *Rancini's* restaurant this afternoon for lunch about two o'clock if you would care to join me there," Hattie said. "I will be wearing a *Ricky Bodenski* lavender dotted suit."

"I will be there," the woman promised with a sob.

Hattie heard the hysteria in her voice. "Perhaps, we should make it earlier, you do seem to be a bit stressed.

"Oh, could you? I am so frightened!"

"I will be at *Rancini's* within the hour. Meet me there," Hattie said, and waited for the woman's reassurances that she would be there before the she ended the call.

"What was that about?" Marie asked, overhearing the phone conversation as she walked up and sat down.

Hattie looked up at her twin sister. The only real difference between the two of them was hair length. Her hair was shoulder length and Marie's reddish-blonde curls were cropped short. They both had deep green eyes, and were the same height—five feet, five inches tall.

"She did not say, but she is scared, and says *something* is trying to kill her."

"Did you get her name?"

"I do not need her name to know she is in danger. The fear in her voice was palpable," Hattie responded. It was her opinion that names were not important when one's life was in jeopardy. It was the woman's use of *something*, and not someone that had her worried.

"Then I am going along with you. I dreamed a foul dream last night, and you know what that means," Marie stated, her emerald-colored eyes daring her sister to try and stop her.

It was Hattie's turn to frown. "Yes, but I wish I did not. Sit down and join us. Nigel and I need to hear about your dream."

Marie made a face of irritation as she thought about having to relive the dream, but nevertheless, she sat down in the chair next to Hattie.

Nigel was quick to set a cup in front of Marie and fill it with tea before he sat down at the table. He too, wanted to hear about the dream.

"I found myself back at the castle. It was the day of the purge, and as you well know, death was everywhere. We were in our room hiding under the bed when Uncle Terin came in and told us to follow him. As we made our way downstairs, we found Mother and Aunt Marie lying dead in the hallway. Before we could stop and mourn for them, Uncle pulled us into the library room. "I have to get you out of here or the same will happen to you," he told us as he opened a hidden doorway by the fireplace. He then took us to a burial room below the castle that he called the sanctum. There he explained that he would be leaving us behind, but another would come along and take care of us. Before we could question him, we were caught up in a blue light, and when we woke, we were lying in a field outside of London."

"Which was a miserable place to be at the time," Hattie commented.

"Yes, if it hadn't been for Lord Grakeland's carriage driver finding us, I imagine we would have ended up either in a workhouse or as bonded slaves," Marie put in.

"From what little I heard you say, Grakeland was a good man," Nigel said, trying to comfort them. He knew more about the history of the women than they did. For in his many roles, he was Uncle Terin, Lord Grakeland, Tom Risnor, and the list went on throughout the years. Today, he was Nigel Quinn, the ladies' latest guardian, and had been for the past five decades.

"Lord Grakeland was a dear man, indeed," Hattie agreed.

"Anyway, back to my dream," Marie said when Nigel remained silent. "My eyes felt tired, and I closed them. When I opened them, I found myself in that same meadow, but this time alone. The fog was thick, and I could not see but a foot or two in front of me. I heard a noise, and then felt a cold draft of wind upon my face. I shivered as a dark figure landed before me. When he swept his cape back, and I saw the face, I cried out, waking myself up. It was Vladimir, Hattie. Older, of course, but it was him," Marie whispered. "If my dream concerns this woman, then it probably has to do with him."

Both Hattie and Nigel looked at Marie with shock on their faces.

Hattie shook her head. "Surely not Vladimir, Marie. He is dead and long gone. He has to be. It has been too many years for him to still be *alive*."

"Remember, we are still alive, Hattie. He was or is Aunt Marie's son which makes him our cousin."

"Yes, I know that, but he is the reason everyone in the family, but us, died that day. How could he have survived?" Hattie protested.

"That remains to be seen, but I have no doubt that we are on our way to meet a woman who might hold the answers to some of our questions, even if we do not know what tempest is brewing outside fate's window," Marie said dramatically.

Nigel did his best to reign in his emotions. He had no doubt Marie's dream was an accurate depiction of things to come, he had never known her psychic sense of the future to be wrong. His boy was alive. Seeing him should not have frightened her. *So what did frighten her?*

"Well then, let me go slip on some sandals, and then Nigel can drive us to *Rancini's*," Hattie said. "That way, he can seat himself at a different table, and keep watch to see if anyone is following her or has any interest in her."

"Or in us," Marie added.

"This is Hollywood, Marie, once we enter *Rancini's*, we will in effect be on stage. I can guarantee you someone will be interested in us. There will be reporters, photographers, and film people there looking for their next story."

"Is that why you are wearing that ostentatious outfit? You look like an advertising for purple bath bubbles," Marie stated, her short, cropped curls dancing about her head as she laughed at her own joke.

"I know you do not care for this suit, Marie, but I think you go too far when you compare it to bath soap."

"I was simply voicing my own opinion, Hattie. I consider large dots on women's clothing to be unflattering, but I am sure there are those like *Bodenski*, an obviously you, who think it *tres chic*."

When her sister continued to stare at her in disapproval, Marie added, "Then, consider this, what if we need to get out of there in a hurry. Dressed as you are, a blind man could follow us."

"Okay. You have made your point, but when I dressed this morning, I had planned on a simple meal at my favorite restaurant. I am somewhat of a celebrity since I have solved the mystery of the haunted building at the film studio. People expect someone like me to dress flamboyantly."

"Yes, I suppose they do, but I am wearing this black dress. I don't care whether it fits your role or not," Marie said as she stood and picked up her handbag and slung it over her shoulder.

Hattie laughed. "Black or not, Marie, every woman who sees you will know you are wearing a *Maddi Jam* original, and that handbag of yours was not bought at a bargain center, nor were your *Christletoe* shoes."

"Maybe so, but I can blend in with a crowd if needed."

"And with my polka-dots, I can create a diversion. Together we make a team."

"*Touche!* my dear," Marie said with a wave of her hand. "Just ignore me, I did not get much sleep last night."

Hattie's face softened as she stood and put her arm around her sister. "I am sorry you have these dreams, Marie. Next time, come get in bed with me. Then we both can lose sleep, but we will do it like we do everything else, together."

"You know, I think I will do that. At least then, I won't have to shiver in the dark all alone."

"That settles it, you are moving into my room until this matter is settled," Hattie stated.

"Nigel, when we get back from *Rancini's*, find Rudy, and get him and his grandson to move Marie's bed to my room."

"Rudy is out back working on the rose bushes, I saw him a few minutes ago. I will go let him know, and then get the car out of the garage, and meet you two at the front door in ten minutes," Nigel said, before he turned and hurried off to find their gardener.

"We are moving my bed today?" Marie questioned.

"Yes, in case you have another nightmare. Then I will be just a few feet away," Hattie answered. "I am not going to let you go through another night of fear. Why have you not told me how frightened you are by these dreams?"

"I have always been disturbed by them, but never *frightened*. Not like I was last night. It was so real, the cold wind on my neck, the noise his cape made as it flapped in the wind, and an overwhelming sense of dread," Marie said with a shudder.

"Come, we both need to go get something to eat," Hattie said, pushing her sister ahead of her, as she headed to her bedroom to change her slippers for heels.

* * *

As Nigel drove to *Rancini's*, he wondered where Vladimir had been all these years. Hattie, Marie, and him had lived mostly in London or Paris over the years, until Marie decided to move to New York in 1902. As the girls never aged beyond their thirtieth birthday, they were forced to move every two to three decades, regardless of where they lived. Fortunately, New York had turned out to be the perfect place to hide. For the most part, no one paid the slightest attention to anyone else, so they only had to move twice in eighty years.

When the time came to venture elsewhere, Hattie chose to move to Hollywood, and Marie agreed as film stars fascinated her. A New York realtor had found the house for him. And though it had cost over three million, back in 1982, as it sat on five acres, it was the perfect place for them. They would never have to worry about neighbors wondering why the girls never aged. The estate across the street from them had to be twenty or more acres and was all but hidden by the huge oak trees that surrounded it. The north side bounded a storm channel. The wall at back of the property skirted an exclusive golf course. And the block wall on south side separated another home similar to theirs. That property had sold last year for forty-two million to one of the movie moguls.

Nigel guessed their property was probably worth a similar price in today's real estate market. The house, counting the two kitchen apartments was over twelve thousand square feet. With a swimming pool, screened in patio, and eight bedrooms, one of which had been turned into Marie's painting studio. It was a comfortable home to live in. Though they had five available guest rooms, in all the time they had been here, only one guest ever came to stay, Marie's friend from New York. A retired CIA agent who now lived in Arizona, Oscar Jabber.

Chapter 2
The Flying Man

We might as well order. After all, we do not know if she will actually show up or not," Hattie said, once they had been seated, and they were waiting for the waiter to bring them hot tea.

"You will get no argument from me, I am hungry," Marie said as she looked at her menu. "The French omelet does sound appetizing. And since we are having a late breakfast, and an early lunch, we can stop and get one of those yummy chocolate cheesecakes at *Luzette's* to take home for an afternoon snack. That should tide us over until dinner."

"You always find a logical way to break the rules, Marie. Omelet and cheesecake, it is."

Out of the corner of her eye, Hattie saw a young woman with blonde hair, wearing a pair of white capris and a blue tank top moving toward their table. She waited to see if the woman would stop at their table.

"Are you Hattie Drake?" the woman asked.

"I am, and you must be the one that called me this morning. I did not catch your name?"

"Jennifer. Jennifer Parker."

"This is my sister, Marie Drake. Please join us, I hope you like hot tea as that is what I ordered for you."

Jennifer nodded at Marie.

"I could use a cup of tea. I ran out of the house as the first rays of sun lit up the horizon, and have not stopped since," Jennifer said as she sat down in the only other chair at the table.

"We are having omelets. Would that suit you, or would you rather have something else?" Hattie asked.

"An omelet sounds good, but you should know, I have no money with me." As the two women looked at her, Jennifer rushed to explain. "I am sorry, but I ran out of the house without my purse, and I was too frightened to go back and get it. Fortunately, I had my phone in my pocket, so I was able to call you. And I apologize for being late, it has taken me most of the hour to get here."

"You walked here?" Hattie asked, startled by the young woman's statement.

"Yes, I have yet to buy a car," Jennifer said, fighting back tears.

Marie reached over, and patted Jennifer's hand. "Do not worry about money, my dear. I have more than enough to pay for our lunch."

Hattie turned her attention to the waiter as he walked up. "Henri, we are going to have three of your French goat-cheese omelets with wheat toast. Also bring one of your jam trays too, please. And we will need another pot of tea as well."

Henri gave a Hattie a nod of his head and a toothy grin before he walked away.

Marie studied the young woman as she drank her tea. She reminded her of someone, but she could not match up the face with anyone in particular. She looked to be in her mid-twenties, and was very pretty with large brown eyes, and shoulder length, hair that had some curl to it. She was wearing no make-up, but at her age, one hardly needed make-up to look good. She was also taller than her and Hattie were by two to three inches.

As they finished their meal, Hattie asked the question Marie had been dying to ask. "Tell me, Jennifer, what has you so frightened?"

The young woman's face paled as she looked at the older woman. She swallowed nervously, and then began her tale. "Three nights ago, I was awakened by a noise. I looked around, but it was dark, and I saw nothing. But every once in a while, I heard something move. Not so much toward me, but toward my window. Then as a car passed the house, the room lit up enough that I saw the form of a man go out the window and fly off. I pinched myself hard to make sure I was awake.

"I was awake all right, see the bruise," Jennifer said, holding her arm out, so Hattie and Marie could see the dark blue spot on her forearm.

"Once I determined that it was not a dream, I waited until another car came by before I got up and locked the window. Actually, I went around and checked the locks on every window in the house, and the doors as well. Needless to say, I did not get much sleep that night. People cannot fly, and I swear that is exactly what the man I saw did."

Neither Hattie nor Marie commented. They both knew Marie had seen Vladimir fly in her dream.

"You say that was three nights ago, so what happened last night that frightened you?" Hattie questioned.

"He came again, this time when I opened my eyes, he was leaning over my bed looking at me. His eyes looked into mine, and I found I could not move. I screamed, or at least I think I screamed. I am not sure whether any noise came out or not because he kept looking into my eyes, like he wanted me to tell him something. When I screamed again, he did straighten up, and despite having checked the lock on my window before I went to bed, it was open again, and he flew out of it."

"By the time, I got over my hysteria, it was almost daylight. I hurried and got dressed. When the first rays of sun hit my windows, I ran."

"Why didn't you call the police?" Hattie asked, waiting to see the woman's reaction to her question.

Jennifer shuddered. "And tell them what? Some man came into my house and flew out my window. They would have tested me for drugs or sent to the psycho-ward. Who would believe such a story?"

"I would," Marie said.

"As would I," Hattie agreed.

"That is why I called you. Because when I searched for paranormal help using my phone, your name came up."

"Ah, that answers that question. Do you have any family that you can go stay with? Hattie asked. "I do not want you going back to your house, not even for your handbag. He could be waiting there and follow you to wherever it is you are going to stay."

Jennifer looked around the room in panic.

"We have someone watching to see if anyone followed you. Since he has not called, I assume no one has."

"I only have my mother, but she lives in Seattle, and is ill. I cannot burden her with this," Jennifer said, shaking her head. "If she saw the state I am in, it could kill her."

Marie felt the girl's desperation as she spoke of her mother. "Then you will come stay with us, until Hattie can find who or what has been paying you visits," she offered. "But first, we will go shopping," her face lighting up at the thought of visiting all those grand stores on Rodeo Drive. "You will need several outfits, nightgowns, shoes, and all the other things a woman needs to be comfortable."

"I told you; I don't have any money. And even if I did, I would not be able to afford more than one outfit, and some underwear," Jennifer protested.

"You don't need money, my dear. I have cards, lots of cards, and an accountant that pays the bills for me," Marie said.

At Jennifer's look of confusion, Hattie explained. "She is correct, she does have a lot of credit cards, and she loves to shop."

"I will pay you back when I find a job," Jennifer promised.

"A job! How opportune is that? Only this morning, I told Hattie, we need to find someone to come help with the house. Hattie and I are not all that good at housework, and

Nigel is getting too old to work as hard as he does. Of course, do not ever let him hear you say that. He is a very proud man. It is a live-in job, and we can pay a thousand a week, plus room and board. Can you cook and clean?"

Hattie raised a brow at her sister but made no comment.

"Of course, I can clean," Jennifer replied. "However, I will have to study books for cooking, but I am a fast learner."

"Oh, never mind that part, Nigel can teach you what you need to know. He likes puttering in the kitchen.

"Then, the job is yours. Instead of a guest room, you can have the maid's apartment. It is on one side of the kitchen, and Nigel's apartment is on the other side. As for the clothing and such that we buy today, you need not pay me back for them. The money I am going to spend is mine to spend."

Jennifer's eyes went from Marie to Hattie and back to Marie, a questioning look on her face.

Marie gave her a reassuring smile before she explained. "Hattie and Nigel will not allow me to spend a dime of my painting money on the house, so it sits there in the bank doing nothing but gathering dust."

"She is right about that, Jennifer. We were left a nice trust fund that takes care of our household needs. When Marie's paintings started selling in New York, I told her to put that money in her name and use it for the good of others. Now, let us finish our lunch and go shopping, which is good for all of us. I could use a new outfit, some comfortable walking shoes, and a new bathing suit. You will need a couple of bathing suits as well, my dear. We get our exercise in the pool. It is much more private than running down a public road or path, don't you think?"

"I don't know what to think or say. Thank you, hardly seems enough," Jennifer said, her eyes moist as she looked at her newfound friends.

Chapter 3
Jennifer's Apartment

Hattie bid Marie goodnight, and then went to her office. Now that everyone had settled down for the night, she wanted to see if she could find any reports or sightings of a man flying around Hollywood.

After using every key word she could think of, but the one she did not want to use, she found nothing helpful.

Okay... it seems I am left with little choice, she thought, and entered a new search with the key words she had been avoiding, *I saw Dracula.*

Several thousand posts popped up, most concerning films. She found the colorful language used by the posters had more bang to it than did the threads on vampire movies.

After looking at several hundred, she began to think it was a waste of time. Then she saw one post with a few comments, mostly negative, but it was exactly what she was looking for, and the date was right.

I know you all are gonna think I am stoned, or lying, but I am not. Tonight... I saw Dracula. It was not at the movies either. I was walking on Theodore, and he dropped right out of the sky, and landed in front of me, his cape flapping in the wind. He gave me a look that froze me to the bone, and then flew to the house across the street, and went inside one of the windows. It took me awhile to unfreeze my body. But when I did, I ran until I got such a pain in my side, I could not run anymore.

I set down on the sidewalk, and cried until a man came along, and ask me if I needed help. He did not have a cape on, but he was wearing a black suit, and it scared me.

I jumped up and ran the rest of the way home. Once inside, I locked my door, checked all my windows, grabbed my laptop, a blanket and a pillow, and took refuge in the steam room. It has no windows, and there is a steel lock on the door.

You all need to know that for a few seconds, I saw death's shadow hovering over me. My blood still quakes, and my hands are shaking so bad I am having a problem holding onto my phone as I dictate this. Tomorrow, I am going to have my therapist use hypnosis on me, and erase what happened from my mind. I cannot live with this kind of fear inside me.

The girl's last statement gave Hattie further proof that she had seen whatever it was Jennifer had seen. She sat back in her chair. Vladimir had the ability to freeze people with his mind. He had often teased her and Marie by making their body freeze. But that she could recall, he could not fly. Too bad, there was no one left to ask what he could or could not do, Marie and her, were the last of their family.

She made a mental note to ask Jennifer for her address. Tomorrow. She and Nigel would go fetch the girl's belongings.

* * *

It was almost daylight when Vladimir Romanov entered the house. The young woman was not there. He saw her handbag lying on the bed and picked it up. He did not need to look in it for her name, he had found that on a utility bill on the dining table—Jennifer Parker. However, he did want to see if he could find more information about her. As he looked through her wallet, he found a Washington State driver's license. He would have someone check that address tomorrow. He noted the wallet held only three one dollar bills, and one bank card which meant she had very little wealth. There was a receipt for rent, but no photos. According to the driver's license, she was twenty-five years old.

And Bella went missing twenty-five years and six months ago, he told himself.

With a sigh, Vladimir put the purse back on the bed. He admitted, if only to himself, he was tired.

He went to check the other rooms and found a back porch off the kitchen. He was more than pleased when he found a large stuffed armchair on the porch facing the screen door. He would rest while he waited for her to return. She would have to come home sometime. He would then explain why he was here. Maybe then, he would find out what had happened to her mother.

* * *

Vladimir heard voices, and then a key being turned in the lock. He quickly moved to stand beside the screen door, leaving himself room to watch the front door. He used his mind to block out his presence, and all thoughts, whether they be hers or his. If the girl was who he believed she was, she might be able to sense him. He did not want to frighten her again nor use his telepathic power to freeze her mind.

A man and woman came in, but not the girl. He frowned in irritation, but then his mouth dropped open with surprise as he saw the gold amulet the woman wore. He had not seen Hattie or Marie since the purge, and at the time they were just girls. He had believed them to be dead. He had hunted for them before he left the castle, but never did find their bodies.

When the woman raised her arm to point the man toward the bedroom, he saw the scar and smiled. It was Hattie. She had gotten that scar when she fell off her first pony.

He hoped his ability to hide himself from others would be enough to keep Hattie from sensing his presence.

The questions he had now: How was the girl connected to Hattie? Was Marie alive? And the most important one of all, was Bella living with them? Vladimir thought about confronting her but was not sure whether he wanted her to know he was alive. Hattie and Marie most certainly blamed him for their mother's death, and he could not blame them. Everything had been staged to make it look like he was to blame for the deaths of the women. Which is what had prompted those in the village to rise up and kill everyone in the castle. Finding him hiding in this house would probably condemn him even more. Memories of the day of the purge filled his mind.

"By putting the blame on you, boy, I have destroyed your family, and have taken my revenge on your Maker," the beast had shouted at him as he used his stone hard fists to beat him senseless in a room beneath the castle.

He had woken up the next day on the floor of a hidden crypt, Bella had dragged him into it to hide them from the villagers. She had evaded the purgers' swords and scythes, by hiding in a hidden cave off the root cellar.

The villagers had set the castle on fire, but for the most part it was made of stone and so, other than some of the furniture and drapes on the first floor, the rest of his home was not harmed. And fortunately, because of the fear of the beast, and the fact that Count Dracul still lived, there had been no looting of the castle.

Vladimir used his mind to blot out the pain and forced himself to get to his feet. He then used the secret stairways Papa Terin had shown him to get to the upper floors to gather up what he deemed they would need to survive: gold and silver coins, jewelry, warm clothing, scarves to hide Bella's blonde hair, and blankets. He was greatly relieved when he found a half dozen leaves of kado grass in an envelope with his name on it in Papa Terin's room. He carefully wrapped them in a handkerchief and put them in his bag.

They then waited for it to get dark, so they could leave. On their way out, they stopped at the kitchen, and took what food they could fit in their packs. They carried all the supplies to the winter meadow where the horses were kept. He picked out four of the best horses, and they began their trek to the Ottoman Empire. Traveling at night for the most part, so as not to be discovered by soldiers, bandits, or slave traders.

Vladimir waited for Hattie and the man with her to leave before he made his way to the front window. He wanted to see what kind of car they had come in. His brow went up when he saw the license plate. He used his phone to call his secretary and told her to get the address for who owned a blue Cadillac with the California Palm Tree license plate HATTIE D. Then he told her to send somebody out to pick him up at the corner of Marbleton and Theodore. He could hardly fly back to his apartment in broad daylight.

Chapter 4
Origins

It was a quarter to ten when Hattie heard her phone in the dining room ring. She put her book down and went to answer it. That it was ringing at such a late hour did not surprise her, most paranormal events took place at night.

"Hattie Drake," she answered.

"Hello, Hattie, it's Vladimir."

Hattie remained silent.

"We need to talk, Hattie. I am in trouble."

"Where are you?"

"I am here in Hollywood. Can you meet me at *Pedro's* on Sunset?"

Hattie hesitated as she considered his request, but then she realized it would be more prudent to find out what he wanted. "Yes, I can be there in thirty minutes," she answered.

"Then, I will see you there."

"You are not going without me," Marie insisted when she found out why Hattie was putting on her coat. "Let me put on some clothes on, and I will go with you."

"While you do that, I will leave a note on the kitchen counter in case Nigel wonders where we have gone. Then I will bring the car around to the front door. Just make sure to wear your amulet," Hattie said as Marie started to get dressed.

"I take it off only when I shower. If he is alive, I may not even do that," Marie responded.

Hattie nodded.

Hattie had not been in *Pedro's* before, but other than the large fancy Mexican hats that decorated the wall behind the bar, and female barmaids wearing colorful skirts, it was akin to any English pub in size and atmosphere. She looked around and saw Vladimir waving to her from a table at the back of the room.

"Follow me," she told Marie.

"Ay, *mamacita*, come sit down, and have a drink with me," a man said as Marie passed by his table.

"Maybe later, *amigo*. Right now, I am with family," Marie replied smoothly.

"Then I will wait for you," the man replied with a grin as he raised his beer in toast.

Vladimir's body tensed as he watched the encounter between Marie and the drunk at the table. When he heard her use the Spanish word for friend, he realized she was probably more comfortable with her surroundings than he was.

Hattie greeted Vladimir, and then sat down.

"You look well, Vlad," Marie said as she sat down, and looked at her cousin who looked to be no older than Hattie and herself. The only difference between them was his hair was dark and so were his eyes.

"So do you, Marie. You too, Hattie."

Hattie continued to stare openly at him.

"You both have a right to resent me, I know that. And I am sorry I had to call you out in the middle of the night, but I am anxious to find out about the young woman you are acquainted with."

Both Hattie' and Marie's faces hardened as they frowned at their cousin.

"It is not what you think," Vladimir said stiffly. "It's much worse than that."

"Bring us two glasses of red wine," Hattie said, forcing her attention on the girl who had just walked up to take their order.

"I will take another beer," Vladimir stated, then waited for her to walk off before he added, "She is my daughter, and I need to know where her mother is."

"What!" Marie practically shouted, then ducked her head in embarrassment when she saw several people turn to look at her.

"How can that be?" Hattie asked, making sure to keep her voice down, though she was just as surprised by Vladimir's statement as Marie was.

"I don't know. That is the problem. Twenty five years and six months ago, Bella disappeared. I have searched the world for her, but to no avail until last week when I passed that girl on the street, and sensed she is my child which means she has to belong to Bella."

Hattie felt a strange sensation and looked around. There was a man sitting a table staring at them. When his eyes met hers, they slid away, but she recognized him. He was a reporter. *This is not good*, she told herself.

"How did you get here, Vladimir?" she asked.

"I moved here ten years ago."

"No, I mean how did you get here to *Pedro's*?"

"I walked, why?"

"I think we should talk about the weather until we finish our drinks, and then have this conversation in the car as we drive you home. It would be more private. I would invite you to the house, but Jennifer is there, and she is frightened of you."

"Yes, I know. I saw her face when she woke up and saw me standing over her."

"I love New York, but Hollywood is my home," Hattie said, changing the conversation for the sake of the girl who set their drinks down.

Hattie chatted about New York and Paris as she took several small sips from her drink. When Vladimir had drank a good portion of his beer, she motioned with her head it was time to go, and without words, rose from her chair and headed for the door.

Vladimir waited for Marie to get to her feet before he followed her.

"*Mamacita*, where are you going?" the drunk asked, putting his hand out as Marie approached his table.

"Sorry, I have to go. My sister is ill," Marie said, artfully dodging the hand that reached out for her.

As the man started to rise from the table, Vladimir stopped and stared at him with his gold flecked eyes for a second or two before he moved on toward the door.

The drunk sat back down, shook his head, and looked around with blank eyes, until he spotted the drink in front of him. He picked it up with a smile on his face. All memories of the woman, gone from his mind.

Marie had stopped to look back, worried that the man would follow her. She saw Vladimir stop at the table for a few seconds, a friendly smile on his face, and then move on toward her. "*Well done*, she thought as she turned and made her way through the front door, and outside to where Hattie waited for them.

"My apartment is a couple of blocks from here," Vladimir said, pointing up the street as he got into the back seat. "They have valet service, so you can just pull up in front of the building. Turn in where you see those blue lights."

* * *

"Nice," Hattie commented as they walked into a spacious front room decorated with modern furniture.

"Is that a Monet?" Marie asked, moving over to look at a painting on the wall.

"Yes, I picked it up some years back in France when they were more affordable," Vladimir answered.

"And, I see you have one of Marie's paintings," Hattie said, moving over to look at a still life of a vase with flowers.

"Marie's? No, I bought that in New York, last year. It is by the artist..." Vladimir words trailed off as he turned his head to stare at Marie, "Juliana Drake."

Hattie nodded, a grin on her face.

"Ah, no wonder it appealed to me," Vladimir said. "The painting reminded me of the flowers that Mother kept on the table. When I saw it, I had to have it."

"I did an entire series of paintings based on my memories of that vase, and the flowers in it. One for each month, beginning with Spring and April, and ending with her Winter vases of twigs and ribbons for January, February, and March. The last one, I kept for myself. It is in our den or office as Hattie calls it," Marie said. She chuckled as she looked at her signature on the painting before she added, "I use my middle name, Juliana, so that I am not hounded by reporters, or those who want to commission me to paint what they want to see. I paint only what I want to see."

Vladimir stood looking at the painting. It meant a lot more to him now that he knew the history behind it. He turned to look at the women. "I will fix us a Martini, and we can catch up," he said, moving over to a bar set into the opposite wall.

"You know, until yesterday, I thought you both dead," Vladimir said as he mixed ingredients.

"And until, day before yesterday, we thought you were dead," Hattie said.

"I buried our mothers in the sanctum below the castle. I hid them in a secret crypt, so no one would find them, and desecrate their bodies. I know it is hard for you to hear this, but I also know, if it was me, I would want to know."

"Yes, thank you, Vlad, we have always wanted to know what happened to them," Hattie agreed.

"We saw them dead in the hallway, but Uncle Terin dragged us off to the sanctum, stating we would die too if the villagers found us," Marie added.

"He was right. They would have killed you. Bella was the only other one to escape. She got away by hiding in a root cellar. She found me in the sanctum, unconscious, dragged me into an ante room behind one of the crypts. I had tried to stop the beast from killing a young girl he had stolen from the village, and he beat me with his fists. Thankfully, Bella had brought some vegetables from the root cellar for us to chew on, and a couple bottles of wine.

"To tell you the truth, I was more scared of him finding us then I was of the purgers. I was afraid he would kill Bella, and I knew I was not strong enough to defend her. Me, he did not want to kill, he wanted the villagers to do that."

"I looked for you both as we gathered what we needed, but you were not in the castle. I thought the purgers had burned you both, along with some of the others they killed. We laid the girl, the beast killed in the same crypt with our mothers."

"Where is Bella?" Hattie asked, looking around the room, and noting there were no signs of a female presence.

"Gone," Vladimir answered as he set the tray of martinis down on the table. He then sat down in the stuffed chair that faced the sofa before he continued. "Twenty-five years, six months, and eight days ago," he continued emotionally. "She just disappeared in Vancouver one day. I have hunted the world over and found nothing. It was not until that young woman walked past me last week that I found a clue. I knew instantly, she was my child."

"How could you know that Vladimir?" Hattie questioned.

"Think, Hattie. If I were to hide twenty women in twenty rooms, and then ask you to tell me which room Marie was in, what would you say?"

"I would know which room, no matter where you put her, we are connected."

"Exactly! That is how I know she is my child."

"Well, that explains why I thought she looks like someone I once knew," Marie said. "But why would Bella hide her from you?"

"I don't know the answer to that. If I did, I might be able to sleep without waking up every time I hear a noise, thinking she has come home."

"What do you do for..." Hattie paused and swallowed nervously before she added the last word, "*blood.*"

Vladimir laughed. "I don't need blood to survive. I never did. That was all part of the beast's plan to create havoc among the villagers and cast the blame on me. Those poor wretches that had their throats ripped out, were killed by him, not by me or Bella. In truth, he bit both me and her. At the time, I was too afraid of him to confess what he had done. Then when the virus he infected us with turned our skin the color of stone, everyone assumed it was as he said, we were children of the devil that needed blood to survive. He used his mind to tell some of those in the village to kill us all if they wanted the killings to stop."

"You are not gray now, Vladimir," Marie said, looking at him closely.

"No, thankfully, Papa Terin gave us some *kado* grass, and we began to heal. By the time we reached the Ottoman Empire, Bella and I regained our normal skin color. Though we both still have scars from where he bit us."

Vladimir undid the buttons on his shirt's cuff and pulled it back as he turned his arm over, so the women could see the two black marks on his wrist.

"Why is it that we all have lived so long, Vladimir?" Marie asked. "A normal human would have died six hundred years ago."

"Papa Terin never told you?"

"We never saw Uncle Terin after that night," Hattie answered. "When we woke up, we were in a pasture outside of London. A man named Lord Grakeland came by and took us in to live with him. He told us Uncle had sent him a letter."

Vladimir ran a hand of frustration over his face. With a heavy heart, he decided to tell them what he knew. "You both were about two years old, and I was ten when we were brought to the castle. Mother picked me to be her son. Your Mother picked you two to raise. I never said anything to you because Mother explained the less people that knew where we came from, the better it would be. She then went on to explain she had used the story that when our birth mothers died of the fever epidemic, we were brought to the homes of our father. At the time, it was a common practice for royalty to take in their *woodland children* and raise them as servants. However, we never were treated as servants.

"We are bastards?" Marie questioned sharply.

Vladimir shook his head. "No, you are my sisters, and we were brought from another world to save our kind."

Marie began to cry. "All this time, I have been angry with you for something you did not do, Vladimir. And now, I find out you are my brother. I always wanted a brother," she said brokenly.

Vladimir rose from his chair and moved to comfort her by patting her on the back. "I am sorry, Marie. Mother had planned on telling you someday, after you grew old enough, but that day never came."

Hattie wiped tears from her eyes as well. When she saw the concern on Vladimir's face as he comforted Marie, she realized he was as much a victim of fate as they were. "And Bella, who is she?" she asked.

"Bella is not our sister, but she was brought with us, as was her brother Charles, who died the following year after we were brought to the castle. Supposedly, of a fever, but I now believe he was murdered."

"Murdered?" both women questioned, a look of shock on their faces.

""Have either of you ever been ill with a fever?" Vladimir asked. Hattie and Marie shook their heads. "Bella and me, have never been ill either, other than from the bites the beast gave us. No, I believe Uncle Josef poisoned him. He took him on a hunt. When he returned he said Charles came down with a fever and died the next day. They buried him in the forest."

"Why would he do that?" Hattie asked.

"I imagine, it was to make sure he would not inherit the estate if Count Dracul did not come back from the crusade. He did not bother to poison Bella. She was female, and therefore was no threat to him as she could not inherit the title or the land."

"How awful," Marie murmured.

"How can you fly, Vlad? That I know of, Marie and I cannot fly," Hattie questioned.

"I spent several decades studying with a mystic in Cairo. He was able to use his mind to levitate objects. Over the years, and with lots of practice, I learned to levitate objects, and later, myself. The cape I wear, I bought off an old magician in Istanbul, who needed money for his family as he was dying, probably with what we call cancer. It makes me invisible against a dark background. and at the same time, if someone does see me, due to the tales of Dracula, they run the other way. When I add my ability to erase someone's memories, or freeze their body, I have become a pretty good magician myself."

Chapter 5
Who Came First?

It was only the third week in March, and eleven o'clock in the morning, but the sun was warm, and Hattie wore a hat to shade her head as she cut roses for the dining table. "Just think, Marie, if this was New York, we would still be treading on icy patches of ground, and there would be no flowers, only concrete."

"Yes, I suppose so, but when you think about it, one always has to deal with the weather no matter where you live. Summers here are downright hot."

"Yes, and that is why they invented air conditioning," Hattie responded happily as she put another rose in the basket Marie held.

"When are we going to tell Nigel about Vladimir?" Marie asked.

"After lunch, he is driving me to the market. I will tell him then. We cannot risk Jennifer overhearing any conversations about Vladimir. Not only would it frighten her, but it could cause her to run. If that happens, we may never find her again."

"I think I will ask her if she will let me paint her. If so, that will occupy both of us for the afternoon, and I can get to know her better."

"What a great idea, Marie. While you are it, try and find out more about her mother. That might help us figure out if it is Bella."

"If it is, Hattie, she may not want us to find her. I mean, she must have left Vladimir for a reason."

Hattie frowned as she looked at her sister. "His love for her, and his grief at losing her are genuine, Marie, I felt them both."

"I loved Michael. You know that. But there were times, I would have loved to chuck him out the window. It is one of the reasons why I chose to never marry again. That, and the fact that I am fated to watch any mate I take, grow old and die while I never age a day. I think, toward the end of his life, Michael hated me for that."

"Why have you never told me this before, Marie?"

"Because it is my own private pain to bear. That is why."

"If you had only told me, I could have told you that what you believe is not true. The day before Michael died, he told me how blessed he was to have found you, and how he loved that your beauty never wilted."

"He said that?" Marie asked, swallowing painfully as she tried to reign in her emotions.

"Yes, do you think I would make something like that up. Wilted is not a word I would use to describe your beauty. Eternal or glorious, maybe, but certainly not *wilted*. However, I can say that after watching Michael die slowly of age, and then losing Etienne to the plague, like you, I don't think I ever want to go through the heartbreak of burying another husband."

Marie faintly heard Hattie's last words as her face lit up with joy, knowing Michael had truly loved her.

* * *

Hattie waited until they pulled into the parking lot at the market before, she told Nigel about their meeting with Vladimir. "It has to be Fate that brought Jennifer to us, or why else would she have found us?"

"You could be right," Nigel said without conviction. His instinct told him it was all too fortuitous to be simply coincidental.

"You don't believe Vladimir's story?" Hattie asked, picking up on Nigel's skepticism.

"No. Him I believe," Nigel said. "It is Fate, I don't trust."

"Why?"

"I am not sure, Hattie," Nigel said as he idly watched a mother put her child into a shopping basket, and then go on into the store. "My mind tells me it is kind of like that chicken and egg thing everyone talks about."

"Whatever do you mean by that?" Hattie asked, completely baffled by his statement.

"Who came first, Jennifer or Vladimir?"

"Ah, I see what you mean. The answer chronologically would be Vladimir, but since we did not know he was alive at the time, then the answer would be Jennifer."

"Yes, it would seem so, but when you consider she was driven to you by him, then the question reverts back to who came first?"

"Then, what do you suggest we do?" Hattie asked.

"Do nothing, for right now. Most certainly do not tell Jennifer about Vladimir, until you acquaint yourself with her mother. If it is Bella, we need to find out why she left?"

"Exactly what Marie said, but for an entirely different reason."

"What reason would that be," Nigel asked.

"One that had to do with her marriage to Michael ages ago, and really not relevant to the present problem. But since you both feel this way, who am I to question it?"

"Jennifer has told me her mother is ill. Why don't we invite her to come here to Hollywood. We have plenty of guest rooms waiting for guests, and they do have wonderful medical facilities in this part of America," Nigel suggested.

"What a brilliant idea. However, I know Jennifer has no money, which means Bella probably does not have any either. They may not want or take our offer to help."

"Jennifer loves her mother. Between, you, Marie, and myself, we should be able to convince her that we only wish to help. We can work on that at dinner. Right now, let's go shopping. We need to get back home, so I can put the roast in the oven," Nigel said as he opened the car door.

* * *

Hattie waited until everyone was almost finished with their dessert before she signaled Marie to go ahead with their plan.

"Jennifer, I have been thinking about your mother. What is wrong with her?"

"The doctors do not know, her skin has turned gray, and she is weak."

Nigel's interest perked up considerably when he heard the symptoms. He was fairly sure Jennifer's mother was indeed Bella.

"That sounds awful. Why not bring her here?" Marie asked. "There are several medical facilities in this area that may be able to help her."

Hattie watched Jennifer's face turn red before she lowered her face to stare at her plate. "Is it because you do not have the financial means?" she asked. Hattie ignored Marie's frown. "I am sorry if I am making you uncomfortable, but I really need to know the answer, and so does Marie."

Jennifer raised her head and looked questioningly at Marie. When she saw her nodding encouragingly at her, she answered the question. "Yes, but I am hoping with my new job, I can soon afford better doctors for her."

"Exactly! my dear. That is what I needed to know," Marie said. "I want you to bring her here to live with us while she seeks treatment. I can use my painting money to pay for the doctors, and whatever else she may need."

"Why would you do that?" Jennifer asked, "You have not even met her."

"Perhaps not. But in the cosmos of all things, we are women, and therefore, we are family at heart if not in body. I have already told you that I use my painting money to help others. Your mother is in need, so please do set your pride aside, and let me help her."

"It is not like we have to move things around to make a place for her. We have five empty guest rooms to choose from," Nigel put in.

Jennifer's swallowed painfully when she realized the gift, they were offering might save her mother's life. "I will call her and see if she will come."

"Let her know you are not sleeping well and are worried about her being alone. When she hears that, she will come," Hattie said. "Then tell her Nigel, and I will be flying up tomorrow. We will help her gather up what she needs to bring with her."

Jennifer sat there looking at Hattie with shock on her face.

"You cannot travel right now, my dear. It is much too dangerous. So Nigel and I will go fetch your mother. If we get an early start, we can be back here by dinner."

"Do tell her not to worry about her apartment, all I need is a name and address, and my accountant can take care of any rent fees," Marie said.

Jennifer's eyes got moist as she looked at the two women. "Thank you, but she owns the home she lives in. Grandfather left it to her. And now, with the salary you are paying me, I should be able to pay the rest of the bills."

Hattie smiled and nodded at the girl. She knew that Jennifer needed to feel she was able to help her mother financially, but she also knew that if was Bella, Vladimir was more than capable of taking care of them both.

"Why don't you use the phone in the kitchen. That way, you will not have to worry about the connection getting dropped," Hattie suggested.

Jennifer rose from her chair. "Thank you. I will go call her right now and insist that she come."

Hattie waited for Jennifer to disappear into the kitchen before she spoke. "Nigel, see if you can get us an early morning flight to Seattle, and then get three tickets for our return trip. I do not intend to take no for an answer. Bella will be coming back with us."

"Then you believe it is Bella?" Marie asked.

"Yes, I do. When Vladimir told us the other night that his skin turned to the color of stone. I remembered when that happened. At the time, you and I were scared we were going to turn gray too."

Marie closed her eyes and searched her memory. "Vaguely," she said as she opened her eyes.

"Then we can hope you are right," Nigel said, pretending he knew nothing about the disease. "Now, if you will excuse me, I will go make the call for the tickets in the office."

"We will wait here for Jennifer to finish her call," Hattie told Marie. "In the meantime, I think I will have another small piece of cheesecake. It is delicious."

"And I will have another cup of tea," Marie said as she lifted the teapot and filled her cup.

Chapter 6
Seattle

Hattie met Vladimir by the airport's front entrance. "Bella might refuse to come, and from what Jennifer tells me she is very ill. Her description of what is wrong with her matches the same illness you both had when you were bitten by that creature."

Vladimir's face paled visibly at that news. "Call me the first chance you get, and let me know that it is indeed, Bella. Please, Hattie, I need to know," he added.

The desperation in voice did not go unheard.

"I will call you before I leave Seattle which will be around three. We get back to Los Angeles around six. How about I stop by your place tomorrow morning? By that time, I should know about the woman, and her medical condition."

"I will order us breakfast from the kitchen. Say about ten?" Vladimir responded.

"Yes. That sounds good. Marie and I will be there barring some unforeseen misadventure."

"Why do you say it that way?" Vladimir asked, frowning at her.

"Because lately, we seem to have nothing but misadventures. I mean, if anyone had told me last week that I would find a long dead relative—*alive*, travel to Seattle, and have two more lost relatives move into my house, all in one week, I would have said they were crazy."

Vladimir chuckled at her remark.

Hattie's phone beeped.

"Gotta go, Vlad. Nigel says our plane is boarding."

* * *

Nigel opened the cab's door for Hattie. Once they both were seated, he gave the driver the address for 34th Avenue South. "How far?" he asked.

"Probably not more than eight to ten miles south of here," the gray-haired woman answered. "We may have to make one or more detours as some of the streets are flooded. We had a storm go through last night, and it dropped several inches of rain."

While Nigel and the woman had a lively conversation about the weather, Hattie leaned back and enjoyed the ride. She noted that it did not take long for them to leave the congested city and enter the quieter residential streets. The driver stopped in front of a small home that could have used some new paint. She noted there was a carport, but no car. She again, had to wonder why Bella had left Vladimir to live in what amounted to poverty.

Nigel paid the cab driver, and then handed her a hundred dollar bill as a tip. "If you could come back in two hours, I would appreciate it," he said.

"Thanks. I will be here," the woman promised as she put the bill into a pouch hanging off the belt around her waist.

When the door opened, Hattie knew immediately, they had found Bella. Her beautiful honey-colored hair was now white—like her face—and she was terribly thin, but there was no mistaking those honey colored eyes with green flecks.

"Hello," she said. "I am Hattie Drake, and this is Nigel Quinn, my uncle."

"I am Sally Parker. Come in! Jennifer said you were coming, though I told her I do not need help."

"Perhaps you do not, but Jennifer does." Hattie put in. When she saw Bella open her mouth to protest, she hurried to explain. "She came to us lonely and frightened. When we found out she was worried about your health, we decided you should come to stay with us. By we, I mean Jennifer, my sister Marie, myself, and Nigel."

"We have a guest room that is in need of a guest," Nigel said, giving her a warm smile. He longed to embrace his lost child, but he dared not let either woman know how pleased he was to see her.

Sally reached for the corner of a chair and held on as another wave of dizziness caused her legs to buckle beneath her.

Nigel moved to her side and grabbed hold of one of her arms. "Here, let me help you sit down."

Hattie got on the other side of Bella and helped get her into the chair. "Are you in need of medication?" she asked.

Sally shook her head. "No, there is no medication or doctor that can help me. I have seen them all. It is why I sent Jennifer away."

"We will find a way to help you, Bella, I mean Sally," Hattie said, correcting herself. She flushed when she saw Bella look at her strangely.

"Who are you?"

"Sorry, but you look a lot like my cousin Bella," Hattie replied.

"My name was once Bella. That is the only thing I could remember when he found me hiding behind a box on his boat. He took me to a doctor, then brought me here, fed me, and gave me a home."

"A man found you?" Hattie questioned, shocked by her statement.

"Yes, Robert Parker. He found me injured and hiding on his boat in Vancouver. He brought me to Seattle, and took me in."

"You never looked for your family?" Hattie asked.

"No." Sally replied, shaking her head. "I have no memory of a family, only vague memories of being beaten by someone which over the years, have diminished. After a few months when I did not recover my memory, Father told everyone I was his long lost daughter, Sally Parker. He died last January from pneumonia. The doctors think the loss of losing him set off an autoimmune disease with my body, but they have not been able to find a cure."

Tears flooded Sally's eyes as she struggled with her grief. She put a hand to her eyes to try and hide them. When she looked up, she saw the man and woman staring at her. "Forgive me, my mind seems to wander lately. It is like I am losing my grip on this world and spinning off to another."

"All the more reason for you to come with us to Hollywood," Hattie said, doing her best to keep the tears out of her own eyes.

"When did you last eat?" Nigel asked.

"I did eat a bit of dinner last night, and then packed a few things. They are in that carry-on by the door," Bella answered. "However, I cannot travel in my robe. If you could help me get to my room, I will change clothes."

"First, you need to eat, it might help the dizziness," Nigel said, then hurried toward the doorway where he could see part of a kitchen stove.

"Would you like some water? I can go get a glass for you," Hattie said.

Sally nodded. "Yes, please, I am thirsty."

Hattie hurried toward the kitchen. She saw Nigel had found some eggs and was whipping them with a fork. She grabbed a cup from the dish drainer and filled it with water.

"What do you think?" she whispered.

Nigel shook his head. "Not good, Hattie," he whispered back as he continued to whip the eggs.

Hattie got her emotions under control before she took the water to Bella.

Sally managed to eat most of the eggs, and a bite or two of her toast before she leaned forward and set the plate on the coffee table. "Thank you, for the lunch, Nigel, I am feeling much better."

"Think nothing of it, my dear," Nigel said as he picked up the plate, and headed for the kitchen to wash the pan and dishes he had used.

While Hattie helped Bella dress, Nigel put what little food there was in the refrigerator into the trash and took it out to the can that sat at the back alley. He then checked all the outside faucets to make sure none were leaking. He found the mailbox was full of mail, and brought that in. He took it all to the dining table and sorted through it. The advertisements, he put to the side. The bills, he put in his coat pocket. He would see they got paid. There was one personal letter, and he waited until Hattie said he could come in to give it to Bella.

"It's a get well card from my friends at *Airplante*, where I worked until I got sick," Sally explained when she saw all the greetings her friends had sent her.

Nigel heard a horn outside and went to look. He saw the cabby had returned. He went out to talk to her.

"I know I am early, but I wanted to make sure you knew I was here," she said as she stepped out of the car.

"Good. I think we may be ready to go a few minutes early too, as there was not much packing to do. My niece has been ill, and we are hoping the doctors in LA will be able to help her."

"I hope they can too," the cabbie murmured politely.

I have a hat with a veil on the top shelf of my closet, and a pair of long silk gloves in the top drawer, if you would get them for me, I would appreciate it," Sally told Hattie. "People tend to be afraid of me when they see my skin.."

"Yes, it probably is a shock for some, but this is not the first time I have seen someone with the same kind of illness you have," Hattie said.

"Where was that?"

"In Paris or Brussels, it has been so many years ago, I have forgotten which one," Hattie lied smoothly. "I had better go get them, and we can get on the road. It takes time to get through the x-ray machines at the airport," she said before she turned and headed back to the bedroom. While she was getting the hat and gloves, she reminded herself to be careful of what she said.

Hattie saw a jewelry box on the dresser and opened it to make sure Bella had packed her jewelry, but there were only a few earrings and bracelets in it. None appeared to be gold or silver.

"I see you packed your good jewelry," she told Bella as she helped her with the gloves.

Sally laughed softly. "I only have a silver cross and a pin that I value. Both were Christmas gifts given to me by Father. I put them in my handbag last night."

* * *

"It is Bella, Vlad, but she is painfully thin, and truly ill. It is all she can do to sit up without falling over. Nigel paid one of the airport employees to take us on his electric cart through the lobby and check point stations. When we explained Bella was ill, they got a wheelchair. We used that to get her to boarding gate. She has also lost her memory. She remembers nothing but being beaten by a man. Fortunately, another man found her, and took her home with him and cared for her. That is how she got the name Sally Parker. When she did not get her memory back, he told everyone she was his long lost daughter. He died a little over a year ago, and left her the house she lives in, and about twelve hundred a month from his pension account. As for the trip back to Hollywood, we should be just fine as we only have one carry-on to deal with, and the airline has already made arrangements for someone to meet us with a wheelchair when we arrive in LA."

"One carry-on! There could not possibly be more than a gown and a couple of outfits in it," Vladimir practically shouted. He recalled the three one dollar bills in Jennifer's wallet. "I will send someone by tomorrow to get her measurements. I cannot have my wife looking like a scarecrow left out in a field."

"I know this is hard for you, Vladimir, but how will I explain someone showing up to take her measurements?" Hattie protested.

"Blame it on Marie," he said hoarsely. "She said she loves to go shopping, and so did Bella before she lost her memory."

"I am sorry you have to go through this, Vlad, but right now, we need to be more concerned about her health than with her having gowns to wear."

"You are right, of course, Hattie. Forgive me, I – I just feel so helpless."

"There is nothing to forgive," Hattie said emotionally. "I cannot begin to imagine the pain you have lived with all these years."

Hattie saw Nigel waving at her. "I have got to go, Vlad. They are getting ready to take Bella on the plane."

"Yes, go! I will see you in the morning."

Hattie slipped her phone into her handbag, and then hurried back to where Nigel was waiting with Bella. She was just in time to board the plane.

Chapter 7
The Truth Is...

"Nigel and Jennifer are taking good care of Bella," Hattie said as she sat her coffee cup down on the dining table in Vladimir's apartment. "She needs to rest today. The trip was hard on her."

"Hattie, has it occurred to you that I may the only one who can help? Bella not only lost her memory, she lost me. Somewhere in the back of her mind, she knows that, and grieves for me as I have grieved for her. If I did not have my memories, and the job of hunting for her, I would probably be in the same condition she is in."

Hattie chewed on her lip as she considered his words. "You may be right, but right now Jennifer is frightened of you, and we have no idea of how Bella will react to you."

"Why not bring her here tomorrow morning for breakfast?"

"She is not up to dining out, Vlad," Hattie said, shaking her head.

"Then I will go to your home to see her."

Hattie's brow went up. "That might work, but we will have to get Jennifer out of the house first."

"Nigel and I are taking Jennifer shopping tomorrow after lunch for gowns and robes for Bella. You could come by then," Marie put in. "But be careful. Seeing you, could send her into shock."

"I will be careful, Marie. First, she will see me as I enter the room. If she does not seem alarmed, Hattie can introduce me. If she starts to get agitated, I can erase my presence from her mind, and leave."

"That should work," Hattie said as she reached for her purse. "In the meantime, I have something to give you." She took out an envelope, opened it, and handed him the amulet Nigel had given her.

"Why would I need this?" Vladimir asked when he saw the necklace.

"To protect you should the beast come back. You might as well know, Vlad, he might have been the one that attacked Bella as all she can recall is her name was once Bella and being beaten with fists."

Vladimir's swallowed painfully at that news. "How is it that you have extra amulets, Hattie?" he questioned as he stared down at the pendant.

Hattie did not want to reveal it was Nigel who had given her the amulet. It would have taken too much time to go through the list of guardians that had taken care of them over the years. "I don't recall where they came from, but we keep them in a box that has been with us since London." *Which is the truth,* she thought. *The last time she had seen them they were in the little silver box Lord Grakeland had given Marie on her fifteenth birthday.* "I have already given one to Jennifer and told her to never take it off because it would protect her from the flying man."

"Sorry," Hattie apologized with a quick shrug when she saw Vladimir's face flush, "but I had to make sure she keeps it on as I could hardly tell her why she really needs to wear it."

"What about Bella, she is more vulnerable than ever?"

"I had Jennifer give her one of the amulets as a gift. Bella prizes it, no doubt about that as I have seen her several times put her hand on it and rub it with her fingers. Which reminds me, make sure to wear your amulet beneath your shirt when you come to the house. It would not do for her to see you wearing the same amulet the rest of us are wearing."

Vladimir nodded before he put the amulet around his neck and fastened it. He then pulled his wallet out of his pocket and took out a credit card.

"Here," he told Marie. "I had the bank make a card with your name on it. Use it to pay for whatever Bella and Jennifer need."

Marie took the card and smiled at him. "Just so you know, I like to shop, and I have my own credit cards."

"I know you do, but Bella and Jennifer are my responsibility, and I have waited twenty five years to find them."

Marie heard the pain in his voice, and impulsively, wrapped her arms around Vladimir, hugging him tightly. "I am so sorry, Vlad that you have had to go through this," she said tearfully.

"Me too," Vladimir said, hugging her back.

"I want in too," Hattie said as she put a hand on Vladimir's arm.

Vladimir opened his arms and put them around both of his sisters. "You know, by film standards, we are the perfect Hollywood family," he said with a grin on his face.

"Why do you say that, Vlad?" Marie asked, looking up at mystified by his statement.

"Because it took six hundred years for us all to be reunited, and yet, here we stand, arguing over who pays for a shopping trip to Rodeo Drive."

Hattie burst out laughing.

Marie chuckled, nodding her head.

* * *

It was late, and Hattie was on the internet looking at the local news to see if any odd or unusual sightings, or events had occurred. She checked the young woman's Dracula post, but true to her word, the girl posted nothing else about that night. Her latest posts were mostly of flowers or rainbows.

She was surprised when Nigel came in. Normally at this hour, he was in bed.

"When I went through Bella's mail, I found these bills. Now, I don't know what to do with them. At the time, I thought I would just open them and pay them, but I cannot do that. I mean, the letters belong to her, not me."

"Lay them here on my desk, I will give them to Jennifer tomorrow, and suggest she give them to you to pay, so as to not burden her mother with them," Hattie said. "That way, you can in all good conscience, can open them and pay what needs to be paid. Also, I will let her know that she needs to put in a change of mailing address for herself, and for her mother. In the meantime, you can go ahead and hire a gardening service to take care of the yard once a week. I don't think we need to ask permission for that. I will talk to Vladimir and let him find out what else needs to be taken care of, like insurance and taxes."

Nigel nodded at her. He wanted to say more, but to do so would break the silence he had kept all these years. Something bad was coming their way, he could feel it. Since Hattie and Marie now, knew they came from another world, he could not help but feel the wall of secrets he had built to keep them safe, might do more harm than good in this day and age. Before he could decide whether to tell her or not, Hattie's next question cracked the dam.

"Nigel, tell me how you came by the box of amulets?"

"Why do you ask?"

"Vladimir asked me where I got mine. I did not tell him it came from you. I just said we kept them in a box that we had since London, which in a way is the truth. The last time I saw them they were in a box Grakeland gave Marie. I just did not tell him how many years it has been since I last saw that box."

Nigel sighed before he went and sat down in one of chairs by the fireplace. "Now, you are wondering how I came by the box?"

Hattie nodded.

"Then go get your sister. It is a long story, and she needs to hear it as well."

Once Hattie explained why she needed to wake up, Marie rose and put on her robe. With bare feet, she followed Hattie to the office.

Nigel had turned the gas fireplace on, and its warm glow was a welcome sight to Marie, who was regretting not putting on her slippers. Despite the plush carpet, her feet were cold. She grabbed a folded lap robe from the bookshelf, and sat down on the small sofa that faced the chair Nigel sat in. She pulled the foot stool closer, put her feet up on it, then covered her legs with the knitted blanket.

"I am ready," she said when she realized Nigel and Hattie were waiting for her to get settled before the meeting began.

"This is going to difficult for you to hear, but I want you girls to understand why I have done what I have done. Please keep in mind, I have always done what I have had to do to protect you. Now that Vladamir has explained to you that you came from another world, it is time for you to hear the rest of the story."

Hattie and Marie both leaned forward to better hear what he had to say.

To make a long story short, I am Nigel Quinn, but I am also Uncle Terin, Lord Grakeland, Count Rison, Belter, and all the others who have been with you throughout the years."

"What!" Hattie and Marie exclaimed in unison, sitting up straighter in their chairs.

Nigel held his hand up. "Let me tell you the story. Then you can ask questions."

"What you do not know, is that you did not travel in a spaceship to get here," he continued. "We all are from another dimension."

"No!" Marie cried.

"Sorry, child, but yes. We came from another dimension that sometimes connects with this one if you know what to look for. I brought you two, Vladimir, Bella, and her brother Charles through a portal which was destroyed on the other

45

end after we came through. I left you children in a nearby cave and went to see about getting housing. When I was questioned by the guards in the village, I pretended to be a doctor, and so was brought to *Castle Dracul* to treat the cook. She had a fever.

"Which reminds me, in addition to the feuds and wars being waged around the country, there was also an influenza outbreak. Without proper medication, many died. Fortunately, one of the *Dysonisan* healers had filled a bag with *kado* grass and gave it to me to take with us. I made a pot of tea using the grass, and had the cook, and several others who were ill, drink it. Their fever was gone by morning.

"Lady Marie asked if I would stay on as they had no one to help with the sick and injured. Most of the healers were with the militia. I told her I would take the job, if she would take in the five orphans that I had brought with me. When her sister Anna saw you two, she fell in love with you both. Marie of course, picked Vladimir. She had lost her only son to disease some years back. Your aunt Hattera, took in Bella and Charles."

"I am not sure which woman came up with idea that they would claim you were woodland children from their husbands whose mothers had died of fever. Since the men were off on a crusade, no one argued against it, and you all were accepted by those in the castles, and those in the village. Though I imagine, even if your stepfathers had come home, they would not have questioned it either, as Lords of castles often had female servants accompany them when they traveled or went off to fight wars."

"Why did our real parents send us away?" Hattie asked.

Our home world was invaded by a race of beasts that need blood from humans to survive. This world calls them vampires. On our world, they are called *jogeths* or *beasts*. By then, your parents, Bella's parents, and my family were dead.

"Dysonians were always a peaceful people, mostly farmers, musicians, scholars, and priests. We had no crime or enemies and were ill prepared to defend ourselves. We humans were called the Maker's children and there were only several hundred of us. Though we did not age or die from disease, few children were born. Within a short time, you all were the only children of our kind left. When the Tribal Elders decided we would not survive the invasion, they appointed me as your guardian, and sent us here using a portal. I assume they destroyed the portal as I lost contact with them shortly after we arrived."

"But you are not like us, are you? You have the ability to alter your appearance," Marie stated.

"Yes, instead of never aging, like you two, I regenerate every six or seven decades. There were only a few of my kind among the Maker's Children. None left by the time I was chosen to be your guardian. Also, I can read minds like Vladimir. Your father was telepathic as well, and that is why Vladimir is able to do what he does with his mind. It is also why you were able to find who was really responsible for the fiasco going on at the film studio, Hattie. And you, Marie, have your dreams."

"If your people had a portal that led to Earth, why did they not use it to escape?" Hattie asked.

"Because we were the only Dysonians with human features left. Most Dysonians have blue skin, silver wings, and a tail. Those on Earth would have considered them demons and would have killed them on sight.

"Who is the Maker?" Marie asked, now worried that she was a clone.

"God, the Light, the Creator, or however one wants to call him," Nigel answered. "Our kind knew him as the *Maker*."

"Vladimir told me that the beast killed the villagers, not him. Where did it come from?" Hattie asked.

"Somehow, the beast found a portal, and followed us to this world. How I do not know, but I saw him once standing outside Dracul castle. A few weeks later, he caught Vladimir and Bella when they went to feed the horses and bit them. They both fell ill with the same illness that you now see in Bella."

"After he bit them, the murders ceased for a time, and I was hoping someone had killed him. But he returned and began killing young women again. Then he began to leave the bodies of his victims outside the castle to make it look like Vladimir was the murderer. He used his mind to tell several villagers that they needed to destroy everyone connected with the castle."

Nigel paused long enough to take a drink from his water bottle before he continued his story. "On the day of the purge, I could not find Vladimir, nor Bella. I went back the next day to look for them but did not find them. I believed they had perished along with the others."

"How did we do that? I mean, go to London?" Because I do not remember traveling, only waking up in the field," Marie questioned.

"I put a sleeping potion in the biscuits I gave you. When you were both asleep. I had already established an estate there. If you recall, I was often absent for several days at a time as I went about healing those afflicted with one illness or another. Much of that time, I spent in London setting up the Grakeland estate. I was planning on take you all there before you girls came of age to be betrothed.

"Betrothed?" Marie questioned. Again, shocked by one of his statements.

"Yes. By the age of fourteen to fifteen, any lord of the realm could petition your mother for your hand in marriage. She would have had no choice but to grant the petition. I could not allow that to happen."

"What about Bella? She must have been of the age to be betrothed?" Marie questioned.

"Bella was betrothed to Vladimir, so there was no problem there."

"What happened to the beast?" Hattie asked, swallowing nervously as she thought about such a creature.

"Once I had you settled in at Grakeland, I went back and killed him," Nigel answered.

"Then he cannot return if you killed him?" Marie asked.

Nigel shook his head. "He is not a living creature such as we are. I put a wooden stake through his core or heart as some would say. Though in truth, the beast does not have a beating heart as we know it."

Marie shuddered at his words.

"I sealed his body in the sanctum, but now that I think about it, I should have burned it on a pyre for I believe that might be the only way to kill him," Nigel added.

Chapter 8
First Attack

"Sally, this is Vladimir Romanov, the gentleman I told you about. He believes he has seen your illness before. He may be able to help you," Hattie said as she introduced Vladimir.

"Nice to meet you," Sally said, looking up at the man with a frown on her face.

Vladimir's throat and mouth were dry due to emotion, and his eyes felt uncomfortably wet. He forced himself to give a slight bow before he sat down in the chair Hattie pointed at. Though Hattie had warned him Bella was ill, he was not prepared for the emancipation of her body, nor for the lack of light in her eyes.

"Have we met before, Mr. Romanov, your name seems familiar?" Sally asked.

"Not that I recall," Vladimir said, swallowing painfully. "But call me Vladimir, and I will call you Sally. After all, I intend to be around quite a bit to help you get well."

"Thank you," Sally said as she reached out to hold onto the arms of her chair as a wave of dizziness washed over her. When it passed, she looked over at Hattie. "I am sorry, but I just need to rest for a bit, she said, leaning back in her chair and closing her eyes.

"While you rest, dear, We will go see about getting some hot tea made," Hattie said as she motioned for grabbed a small lap robe laying on the sofa and covered Bella with it. She then motioned for Vladimir to raise the chair's foot up.

"She is worse than I allowed myself to believe, Hattie," Vladimir said as he watched her fill a tea kettle with water, and then set it on the stove.

"Her condition is a shock for us all, Vlad."

"She is dying, Hattie. I can feel her life force leaving her," Vladimir said hoarsely.

Hattie put a hand over her mouth to help reign in her own emotions. They had just found Bella. To lose her would be devastating. "Perhaps we can find a doctor," she said emotionally.

"I doubt the doctors can help her. The disease comes from a creature not of this world. If only I could find Papa Terin."

"Why Uncle Terin?" Hattie questioned.

"He saved us the first time when he gave us some leaves of grass to chew on. Only then did we begin to heal.,"

Hattie pretended to watch the tea kettle, so Vladimir would not see her face. Nigel had asked her and Marie to keep his secret between the three of them. Without his permission, she could not tell Vladimir that his Papa Terin still lived.

"I know the name of the grass," Vladimir continued. "Or at least the name Papa Terin used, but I do not know what they call the plant in this world, or if it even grows here."

The kettle began to whistle. Hattie turned the burner off.

"There is a tray in that cabinet," she said pointing opposite of where she stood. "Could you get it out while I get the cups and saucers out. While you are at it, put some of those napkins on the tray. I will add some biscuits too. Hopefully, Bella will eat one."

Vladimir waited until she got everything ready, then picked the tray up, and followed her back to the living room.

Bella's eyes were closed, but she opened them when she heard the tray being set down on the table in front of the sofa.

"Here, dear," Hattie said as she placed a half-filled cup of tea and a raisin biscuit on the table beside her chair.

Like everyone else in the house, Bella drank her tea black.

"Have you seen my disease before, Vladimir?" Bella asked after she took a couple of sips, and then set the cup down on the table beside her chair.

"Yes, I believe so—in Egypt. Of course, I don't pretend to know what medicine the doctors used, but I did see progress in those that were being treated. I will make some phone calls tonight and see what I can find out."

"Perhaps, there is a glimmer of hope for me after all," Bella said. As another wave of dizziness struck her, she added. "Now, if one of you could help me up from this chair, and excuse me, I need to go back to my room."

Vladimir took both of her hands and gently pulled her to her feet. When he saw her sway as he let go, he took her arm. "Let me help you to your room." When Bella stumbled, he smoothly picked her up in his arms, and looked at Hattie, who had gotten to her feet. "I will follow you," he said.

Vladimir discreetly moved to the door while Hattie helped Bella get into bed. He felt his throat constrict painfully when he heard her apologize for being such a burden.

"Never think that, Bella," Hattie protested. "You would do the same for me if I was sick. Now, try and get some sleep. I am going to have a wheelchair delivered tomorrow. You are far too weak to walk parking lots and hallways to get to the doctors, and—."

"You called me Bella again," Sally whispered.

"Yes. Sorry, but you remind me of my cousin, Bella," Hattie said.

Sally's eyes searched Hattie's. "Where does she live?" she asked, but before Hattie could answer, her mind drifted off.

"I don't know, she disappeared twenty-five years ago," Hattie said softly. When she realized Bella had not heard her, she heaved a sigh. *So close*, she thought.

"She's asleep," Hattie said once they were back in the front room.

"I will have a chair sent out tomorrow and hire some nurses to help take care of her," Vladimir said. When Hattie stared at him, he added, "To help for a few hours in the morning with bathing, dressing, and whatever else she needs. You, Marie, and Jennifer, are not nurses, and right now that is what Bella needs."

Hattie motioned for him to sit down in the chair opposite to the one she sat in. "You are right, we could use a nurse or two, but at the same time, we do not want the health authorities taking a closer look at her. The more that see her condition, the more threat of that happening. That could create a whole new set of problems. Bella has Jennifer to help take care of her, and who would be here right now, other than we made sure she was out of the house. As for a wheelchair, yes, we could use one of those."

The look on Vladimir's face was bleak as he forced himself to admit she was right.

"Perhaps it is time to tell Jennifer who you are, Vladimir," Hattie suggested. "At least that way, you would not have to hide your visits. I am sure that once she gets over the shock, she will be glad to see you."

Before he could answer, Vladimir heard Bella cry out. He jumped up out of his chair and ran back to the bedroom. Hattie was right behind him.

Bella was sitting up in the bed, her eyes wide with panic. "The beast!" she cried out. "He said he is going to kill me!"

Vladimir rushed to the window, found it open, but saw no one. He closed his eyes and used his mind to search for the jogeth's presence but found nothing out of the ordinary.

He locked the window and turned to check on Bella who lay shaking in Hattie's arms. He longed to ask her more about what happened, but he did not. Now, was not the time to try and force her to recall her past. The shock could kill her.

"I think it would be better if we moved you to the sofa in the front room—Sally. That way, should he come back, I will be here to protect you," Vladimir said.

"What about Jennifer?" Sally asked.

"Jennifer can stay with Marie and me, in our room tonight. I do not think any of us should be alone until we can determine what is going on," Hattie said.

Bella struggled to sit up.

"Here, let me help," Vladimir said, sweeping her up in his arms again before heading for the door.

Hattie grabbed a pillow and a blanket and followed him. She did not want to be left alone in the room either.

Vladimir put Bella on the sofa, and started to sit down, but stopped as he heard the garage door open.

"Ah, the others have returned," he said. "While you tell them what happened, Hattie, I will go and make those calls to Egypt. Where would be the place to do that?"

"The office. That door over there," she said, pointing at the oak door across the room.

Vladimir nodded. Then turned and hurried across the room. He had barely closed the door when Jennifer came rushing in to go check on her mother. When she saw her on the sofa, she stopped and headed that way.

"What's wrong?" she asked as she saw her mother's tear stained face.

"I am not sure, but someone may have broken into her room," Hattie said. "I am glad Mr. Romanov was here, Marie. It made me feel safer."

"It was the beast," Sally stated.

Marie's face lost its color when she heard that.

"Vladimir's presence makes me feel safer too, Hattie. Where is he?" Sally asked, having forgotten that he had gone to make calls to Egypt.

Jennifer raised her head and looked around the room.

"He is in my office making some phone calls," Hattie replied. "I need to go tell Nigel about the break in. Perhaps you could take that tray into the kitchen, and make us all a fresh pot of tea, Jennifer. It looks like it is going to be a long night. Marie will be here if your mother needs anything."

"Yes, of course, Hattie," Jennifer said.

* * *

"**We have** a big problem, Nigel," Hattie said as she found him in the garage, putting away some of the things he had bought.

"Did Bella have a bad reaction to Vladimir?" Nigel asked, putting a new wrench into the long metal tray he kept on a shelf for wrenches.

"Worse, she claims that the beast was here this afternoon, and told her he was going to kill her. Vladimir is in my office and is planning to stay the night to guard her. I don't blame him. If you had seen the terror in her eyes, you would stay with her too. The time has come to tell Jennifer who she is, and who Vladimir is."

Nigel blew a breath of frustration. He folded his arms as he stood there trying to figure out what impact this latest incident would have on them. For the first time in many years, he worried about his children's very existence.

He unfolded his arms before he spoke. "I hoped we would have more time, but you are right. Jennifer has to know, and so does Bella. We cannot let them blindly proceed without they understand, where they come from, and what it is that is after them," he said.

Hattie's face winced at his words. "Then we had better get to the kitchen. Jennifer is there making tea."

Jennifer had just set the kettle on the burner when Nigel and Hattie came through the garage door. She noted Nigel locked the door behind him.

"Mother is now having hallucinations, and I do not know what to do," she said, swallowing painfully as her eyes teared up.

"Sit down, Jennifer!" Hattie commanded softly. "It is time to tell you what is wrong with your mother."

"Some of what we have to tell you is going to sound so bizarre that you will have trouble believing it all, but at the same time, it will solve some of the puzzles you have experienced throughout your life. For I am sure you have noticed you are not quite like those around you," Nigel said.

Jennifer blushed. When she twelve, she began to hear other's thoughts, but she had never told anyone that, not even her mother for fear of being thought of as mentally ill.

"I think I will begin the story with our going to pick up your belongings at your apartment," Hattie said. "The man that scared you was there. Oh, we did not see him, but he saw me, and recognized me. He then called me. His name is Vladimir Romanov."

"He is your father," Nigel said when Hattie paused.

"What!" Jennifer cried.

"Yes, he is your father, but there is more that you need to know," Hattie rushed to explain. "When your mother disappeared almost twenty-five years ago, he did not know what happened to her. He has searched all these years for her. A couple of weeks ago when you walked by him, he felt your presence, and realized you were his daughter. Instead, of introducing himself as he should have, he tried to find out where you came from."

"By scaring me?" Jennifer questioned.

"True, it was not the right way to do that, but he worried that you would run away, and he would not be able to find you again. You have to realize he was desperate to find your mother. Nigel then told her about her parents.

"Of course, there is much more to the story than I have told you, but all that can be told some other time," he finished.

Jennifer pinched herself and yelped in pain. "Well, this is not a dream, is it?"

"No, dear, it is not," Hattie replied.

The tea kettle began to whistle.

Nigel got up and poured hot water in the tea pot, and put the infuser in.

Hattie rose and fetched the tray for him. Then she put the cups, saucers, and other items on the tray, making sure to add a cup for Vladimir.

"Jennifer did not move.

"Are you coming?" Hattie asked.

"I need a minute or two. Even if he is my father, I am afraid of him."

"While Nigel serves the tea, I will go get Vladimir, and introduce you to him. I know this is a lot for you to sort through, Jennifer, but realize the threat is real. If the beast has found us, then we all are in danger until it can be dealt with."

Jennifer nodded. "I will be there in a minute, once I have had a good cry. I never thought I would ever see my father. Mother said she didn't know who he was as she has no memory of him."

"No, and she still does not, and I am not sure we can tell her. She is too ill to battle her past, let alone this present day crisis," Hattie said, looking at Nigel.

You are probably right, Hattie. We can discuss it later in the library."

"Who will keep watch on Mother, if we all go into the Library?" Jennifer asked.

"If that beast comes within a hundred feet of the house, I will know," Nigel said. "No jogeth can hide their presence from me. Not even the one they call Dracula in this world."

Jennifer shuddered at hearing the dreaded name spoken out loud. She rose from the table. "I will cry later," she said "Right now, I want to go sit by mother's side. I want to see if she is okay with this man you call my father," she said.

Good for you," Hattie said. She then motioned for Nigel to go ahead of them.

Chapter 9
Catching Up

Hattie introduced Vladimir to Jennifer, and was glad Bella was looking at him, and not at her daughter's face as she would have seen the fear on it.

Vladimir smiled as best he could and gave a nod of his head in greeting. He then sat down.

"Now that we are all here, tell them what happened, Sally," Marie said.

Bella looked at her in confusion. "What happened?" she asked.

"Someone threatened you. Do you not remember that?" Hattie asked. "You called him beast."

Bella's face went blank as she searched her memories. "Yes, but it was just a dream. I have them all the time. He bit me a long time ago. See," she said, holding her wrist up.

Vladimir flinched as he saw the two black dots on her arm. It was those same bite marks that were killing her.

As a bout of dizziness struck, Bella let her arm fall. She lay back and closed her eyes.

"Are you all right, Mom?" Jennifer asked.

"Just tired. I think I will rest for a bit, but you go on and visit with each other. It is nice to hear other voices in the room."

"I think we will all go into the office, Sally. There are plenty of chairs in there for us. We will leave the door open, and you can still hear the murmur of our voices, and we can keep an eye on you at the same time," Nigel said.

Bella did not answer as she had drifted off into the world between sleep and consciousness, due to the illness that ravaged her body.

"Let me say first that I am so happy to have you for a niece, Jennifer," Marie said.

"Niece?" Jennifer questioned.

Nigel slapped his forehead. "Forgive me, dear. In all the excitement, I forgot to tell you that your father is Hattie's and Marie's long-lost brother."

Jennifer looked around the room at all the smiling faces, but she did not smile back at them. Instead, she concentrated on resisting the urge to jump up, and run out of the room.

"I forgot something too," Hattie said. Things have moved so fast I have not been able to ask you, Nigel, but do you have any more *kado grass*? Vladimir believes it is what cured him and Bella, the last time they had the disease."

Nigel saw the confusion on Vladimir's face. "Today, I am Nigel. You knew me as Terin, and yes, I do have some of the grass left, and have already given Bella two doses of the tea."

"Then there is hope," Vladimir said before he turned and gave Hattie a raised brow look.

"I only found out last night that he was Uncle Terin," Hattie explained.

Vladimir's eyes narrowed as he looked at Nigel. The man did not look anything like his Papa.

"I need to go get into something more comfortable, and get these shoes off my feet," Marie said making a face. "They are new, and I am fairly sure I have a blister on one of my little toes."

"I will go with you, Marie. I would like to slip into something more comfortable as well," Hattie said, not wanting Marie to go their room, alone. "Which reminds me, Jennifer. You will bunk in our room tonight. Marie and I can share my bed. After all, it is a king size bed. There is safety in numbers."

"I was going to keep watch on Mother," Jennifer said.

"No need. I intend to watch over her tonight," Vladimir said. "My mind will alert me if the beast returns."

Jennifer opened her mouth to object, but then realized, he was the better choice when it came to her mother's safety. "Thank you," she murmured stiffly.

Vladimir nodded. "You are welcome to come check on her at any time during the night. You will not disturb me. I intend to use meditation to keep watch and get my rest too. It is something I learned to do when your mother and I lived in Cairo."

"What about you, Nigel? Your apartment is isolated from the rest of the house. You should use the guest room next to Bella's room," Hattie suggested.

"Yes, please do, Nigel. I know I will sleep better. If that beast does come back, we will need your help," Marie said as she saw him start to shake his head.

Nigel quit shaking his head. "You are right, Marie. You will need me if he returns. Now, I think I will go make more tea for Bella. Vladimir, perhaps you can join me while Jennifer keeps a watch on her mother. We have not had time to catch up with each other's lives."

Vladimir rose to follow Nigel but stopped as he saw Jennifer fingering the pendant around her neck. "You need to know that amulet around your neck is to prevent the beast from attacking you, Jennifer. Do not take it off, not even to shower," he warned. "It is undoubtedly, what saved your mother today."

Jennifer's hand let go of the amulet as if it had burned her. She looked up at the man who was her father, and swallowed nervously, but nevertheless nodded.

* * *

Hattie has told me how you and Bella escaped the purge, and went to live in the Ottoman Empire, Vladimir, but where have you lived for the past hundred or so years?" Nigel asked once he had returned from his bedroom with a blade of *kado* grass in his hand. He washed it at the sink, and then put it into a yellow teapot that set on the counter.

"We lived in Paris from about 1870 through the late nineties," Vladimir began. "From there we went to Prague. Stayed there only a few years because of political unrest. Bella and I then moved to Montreal, just in time to miss World War One. We lived there until the early fifties. Then New York. It was a nice place to live in those days. In the eighties, we moved to Vancouver. That is where I lost her. About a dozen or so years ago, I moved here to Hollywood. Fortunately, it will be another forty or so years before I need a new identity. Though with the invention of computers and data bases, it is going to be a real challenge to establish one."

"Yes, I know what you mean. I am working on that problem myself," Nigel said. I will have to change identities within the next few years or sooner if this body begins to fail."

"What do you mean by that?"

"Instead of never aging as you, Bella, and your sisters do, I am one of the Dysonians that has to regenerate every so often. I generally change my appearance and name. Over the years, I have used many names," Nigel answered.

The pot began to whistle, and Nigel rose to turn off the burner. He then poured the hot water into the yellow teapot.

"That needs to set for about ten minutes," he said as he sat back down.

"I find it interesting that you were in Paris, and New York about the same time as we were, and that of all the places in America, you chose Hollywood for your new home. Hattie says you live only a few miles from here."

"Yes, I have a nice top-floor apartment."

Nigel smiled. Marie and Hattie had told him about Vladimir's penthouse. "Marie says you own a Monet as well as one of her paintings."

"Actually, I own more Monet's. I met Claude in Paris, and we became friends. I bought several of his paintings at the time. Both because Bella and I liked his art, and it helped him out financially. One was stolen years ago in Paris, and long before his paintings became valuable. Of course, I imagine the thief did get a few thousand francs for it at the time. I have three left: The one Marie and Hattie saw, one in my bedroom, and one that hangs in my office."

"Office? You have a business then?"

"I do have a business downtown, but by office, I mean the room in my apartment that I call my office. Any Monet, as you well know is valuable in today's world, and I keep them close. I own the building I live in, though most do not know that as I have my own security company managing the building. As far as the tenants are concerned, I am just another wealthy Hollywood eccentric, surrounding themselves with armed guards, cameras, and motion sensors."

"I think it is time we have cameras and motion sensors put in here," Nigel said, looking toward the patio doors. "Before today, I never worried about someone breaking in."

"Then I will have my company on it tomorrow morning. They can install the cam screens and control center wherever you decide would be best. Which reminds me, we will also need to install a back-up generator system in the garage as well. That way, if the power goes off or gets cut off, your security system is covered."

"Your company?" Nigel questioned, not hiding the surprise on his face.

"Yes, I own Romanov Security."

"Ah, it does my heart good to find you have done well for yourself, Vladimir," Nigel said, his face lighting up with a smile.

"And I am glad you all are doing well too," Vladimir returned. "I never thought I would ever see any of you again. Of course, you don't look like the Papa Terin I remember."

"No, but I have all the same knowledge and abilities that I have always had. However, I am not able to fly like they say you can."

"You might with practice. First, I learned to move a feather, and then progressed to larger items. It took me nearly two centuries practicing levitation before I could lift myself into the air, and several more decades of practice to actually fly."

"Nevertheless, it is an amazing feat. "Perhaps in my next lifetime I will work on it. Nigel said rising out of his chair as the timer on the counter went off. "Come. It is time to take Bella her tea. Hopefully, we will see some improvement in the next few weeks."

Chapter 10
We Need Help

Hattie was buttering her toast when she heard Marie gasp. She put her knife down.

"What's wrong?" she asked.

"There was a murder last night in an alley, just past Hollywood and Vine. A young girl had her throat ripped out," Marie answered.

Hattie looked around to make sure they were the only ones in the room. "Let's go show it to Nigel while Jennifer is helping Bella with her bath. I would prefer she not see that paper."

"We cannot hide something like this from her, Hattie," Marie protested.

"Hide what?" Nigel said as he came in with his plate of eggs and bacon.

"A young girl was murdered last night, Nigel," Marie answered as she waited for him to sit down before she handed the newspaper over.

Nigel made a face as he saw the headline. He then read the article very carefully. When he came to part that stated her wounds looked to be from some type of animal, rather than a person, he put the paper down. "Well either Goff has somehow, survived, or another jogeth has been loosed upon this world."

"How could that creature come back, Nigel?" Marie asked. "You said you drove a stake through his heart."

"Aye, that I did. And I have been thinking about that, and realize, I failed to take one thing into consideration. Over the years that wooden stake could have rotted away, allowing for the beast to wake. Once awake, it would not have taken him long to figure a way out of the crypt."

"Well now that he is back, what are we going to do about it?" Hattie asked. "We cannot leave him to prey on others."

"You and Marie are no match for a jogeth, Hattie. Don't even think about going after him. This is not a mystery to solve. We already know the who, the what, and the why of it all. No, it will be up to Vladimir and myself to track him down, and this time, destroy him forever."

"I realize I am ill prepared to battle the devil himself, Nigel, but what if he attacks us while you are out hunting for him? Marie and I need to be taught to defend ourselves," Hattie countered.

Nigel realized she was right. The beast would eventually find them or worse, if Bella did see him yesterday, he already knew where they were.

"I will be right back," he said, jumping up out of his chair.

"Don't you think that was strange? I mean, he didn't answer your question.

"Maybe he left something on the burner," Hattie answered.

Marie gave her sister a look of irritation. "Now you are doing it," she accused.

"Doing what?" Hattie asked irritably, flinging out her hand that was holding the toast.

"Avoiding the question."

"Not deliberately. I have no idea why he hurried off, but knowing Nigel, he must have a good reason. Other than that, I am hungry," Hattie replied before she took a bite of her toast.

Marie was silent as she used her spoon to pick the pieces of banana from her cereal and eat them.

Hattie sighed and put her toast down. "I am sorry, Marie. If I had answers I would most certainly give them to you."

"I know," Marie murmured. "I am just out of sorts from the dream I had last night."

"You are supposed to wake me when you have a dream."

"I know, but it was an awful dream, Hattie. I could not share it with you because then we both would not have gotten any sleep."

"Tell me about your dream, Marie. You know I cannot help unless I know what is bothering you."

Marie swallowed emotionally before she answered. "I saw myself lying on the floor dead. Then I heard gunshots, and when I opened my eyes, I saw you standing there on fire."

Hattie felt tears spring to her eyes as she looked at her sister. "If you opened your eyes, then were not dead."

"No, probably not," Marie admitted tearfully. "But you were. No one could survive what I saw."

Nigel came in and saw both of his girls hunched over the table, crying and holding hands. "What is wrong?" he asked.

Hattie told him about Marie's dream.

Nigel gave a sigh of relief. "Oh, thank the Maker," he said.

"What!" both women exclaimed, shocked by his words.

"When a Dysonian dreams of someone on fire it is a good thing," Nigel soothed without giving them an explanation.

Both Hattie and Marie looked at each other with surprise on their faces. Before they could ask why it was a good thing, Nigel gave them another surprise.

"I just came from Rudy's. I told him to take Rocky and go on vacation until I tell him it is safe for them to come back home."

"You told him about that beast?" Marie questioned.

"No, of course not. I told him someone had made death threats against Hattie, and I wanted to make sure he and

Rocky were safe until the man can be caught. They will be leaving for Florida this afternoon. It was not hard to talk them into going on an all-expenses paid vacation in Florida."

The doorbell rang.

"That must be the security people that Vladimir said he would send over this morning. We are getting floodlights, cameras and motion sensors put in today," Nigel said as he stood.

"Well, I don't know if that is good news or bad news," Hattie told Marie, once Nigel was out of the room.

"Why do you say it like that, Hattie?" Marie asked.

"The good news is we will know when the beast is outside, and the bad news is we will know he is outside. I mean, we have no way of defeating him. Not on our own."

"Then we need to hire those that can. Jabber has a group of Marine veterans that hire out as bodyguards."

"Jabber is an old man, Marie. He walks with a cane."

"Yes, but I talked to him last week. He and his team had just returned from a job in Virginia."

"Even if Jabber has some Marines that can help us, where would we put them? We only have four bedrooms left, and we would need at least a dozen men," Hattie protested.

Marie's mouth opened, but she shut it as she realized she had no answer. "Regardless, Hattie, I think it is a good idea. I doubt even Nigel's beast would take on a dozen armed men," she said as she glared at her sister.

"It is a good idea, Marie. Just the thought of that many armed men between us and that creature Nigel has described would make me feel safer. And thinking about it, those bedrooms are good sized rooms with their own bath area. If we take out those giant California beds, we could easily put three bunk beds in each room, and a couple of extra armchairs. I mean, soldiers are used to hard beds, aren't they?"

Marie nodded in agreement. "I would think so. It has to be better than the ground they sleep on when they are out in the field."

Neither woman realized that the kind of work Jabber and Bravo Team did in today's world came with lavish bedrooms in a mansion or a penthouse suite in a Five Star hotel.

Marie's face lit up as it occurred to her that help was only a phone call away. She jumped up from her chair. "While I call Jabber, you call the movers, Hattie. Once the rooms are ready, we both can go pick out the new furniture."

"Shouldn't we wait and ask Nigel?" Hattie asked.

"No, let's surprise him," Marie said with a sly grin on her face. "That way, he cannot say no."

* * *

When Nigel opened the door, he was not surprised to see three trucks parked outside, and three men standing at the door. Two with Romanov Security patches on their shirts, and one holding onto a wheelchair with a big red bow on it.

He signed for the chair, and then turned his attention on the two security men. "Best you have a look around, and then come in by the back patio doors. We can sit and talk at the kitchen table. Vladimir ought to be back by then."

Nigel started to go back in the house to take the wheelchair to Jennifer, but stopped as a silver Mercedes came up the drive and parked behind one of the security trucks.

"Morning, Nigel," Vladimir greeted as he got out of his car. "Glad to see the chair got here."

"Yes, me too. Come on in. Hattie and Marie are in the dining room.

"And Bella? Is she any better?" Vladimir asked.

"It is too early to tell. We will just have to wait and watch for signs of improvements. Since she has been ill for more than a year, I imagine the healing process will take time as well. In the meantime, I will keep giving her the *kado* tea. We won't run out any time soon. I still have more than half of the basket left."

"You are right, Papa. I remember it took us weeks to fully recover, and we were never as sick as she is now. By the time we arrived in Constantinople, the gray scales had disappeared from our bodies."

"It cannot have been easy to travel such a distance, and in such turbulent times. It is a miracle that you both are alive."

"We had some narrow escapes all right. Without my telepathic abilities, we probably would have been killed several times over," Vladimir agreed as he followed Nigel into the house.

Nigel stopped when he reached the front room. "Have you seen this morning's paper?" he asked as he turned back to look at Vladimir. When he saw him shake his head, he added, "Have Marie show it to you while I take this chair and set it outside Jennifer's door. The shower bench I ordered arrived earlier, and she is helping Bella get a bath."

Vladimir found Hattie and Marie in the dining room. He looked around but did not see a newspaper. "Nigel said you would show me what's in today's paper."

"I have it here," Hattie said as she pulled the paper off her lap and slid it across the table. "We do not want Jennifer to see it."

Vladimir sat down. One look at the headline, and he realized why they were hiding the paper from Jennifer. He read the article, and then laid the paper down. He felt a tightness in his chest as he realized how close he had come to losing Bella yesterday. When the message beeper on his phone chimed, he pulled it out of his pocket.

"I better go check on my men. We need to get the cams installed as soon as possible," he said as he rose from the table.

Vladimir started for the kitchen, but stopped as Nigel came up. "Tom has the camera sites tagged. I will need you to approve them before they can start the installation. Also, you need to let us know where you want the cams screens and control center set up?"

"In the office," Nigel answered, turning to point toward the office door. "We can move the books and shelves and use the library section."

While Marie made her call. Hattie waited for Nigel and Vladimir to leave before she hunted for the piece of paper, she had written the phone number of the moving storage company. When she found it, she used the blue phone on the table. Once she explained what she needed, the woman put her on hold while she checked to see if she could arrange for a truck to come in the afternoon.

"Miss Drake?"

"Yes, I'm here," Hattie said when she heard the woman's voice come back on the line.

"The van can be there around four this afternoon, if that is suitable?"

"Perfect timing," Hattie responded, knowing Nigel would not be here as he was taking Rudy and Rocky to the airport.

"That will be seven hundred and sixty-five dollars which includes the first three month's storage fees. If you can give me your credit card number, I will process the order."

Hattie reached for the card Marie kept beneath the napkin holder and gave the necessary information. She then gave the woman instructions on how to find the house. Hattera Lane was not on any maps. It was a private road that led to only to their home.

She had just hung up the phone when Nigel returned.

"Where's Marie?" He asked.

"Making some phone calls," Hattie answered truthfully. Before Nigel could ask any questions, she added, "How is the job outside progressing?"

"The floodlights will be operational by tomorrow, and the cameras and motion sensors within the next two or three days. They have to run wiring through the overhead attic space. In the meantime, I need to remove the books and desk from the library room, and put them in storage, so there will be room to put the monitors on the wall, and a work counter below."

"Let Marie and me take care of the books. We can stack them in that wheeled cart in the garage. Perhaps, Vladimir can spare a couple of men to move the shelves and desk into the guest rooms. If all goes well, we should have the books out of the way by the time you get back from the airport," Hattie offered.

***

Hattie was starting the dishwasher when Marie came sailing into the kitchen, a big smile on her face as she looked at her sister. "Jabber has found us some Marines. They are called Bravo Team. There are five of them, plus Jabber. He is coming too as he is the team's leader."

"Do you think that will be enough?" Hattie asked.

"Jabber explained there will be three on duty most of the time. And in case of emergency, they all can be operational within two minutes if the need arises."

"How much do hired guns get these days?"

"A thousand a day, plus room and board," Marie answered.

"For all of them?"

"No, of course not. We will be billed five thousand a day for Bravo Team. Jabber states he doesn't want any pay and is looking forward to seeing us both again."

"What's he going to say when he finds that we have not aged a day, Marie?"

Marie sighed and looked at her sister. "Years ago, I confided our story to Jabber, Hattie. He knows all about us. But you don't have to worry, he will not repeat it to anyone."

Hattie nodded. She knew Marie cared more for Jabber than anyone else who had touched their lives. She also understood the isolation they lived in. It was one of the reasons she had taken up solving paranormal mysteries. It got her out of the house, and out into the real world.

"Well if that be the case, there is nothing we can do about that, but don't tell him about Nigel. That is his secret, not ours."

Marie's face fell.

Hattie rolled her eyes. "You already told him, didn't you?"

Marie looked at the floor. "Yes. I felt he needed to know what he is up against."

Hattie moved over to her sister and gave her a hug. "You are right. He does need to know. I am sorry if I was sharp with you. Now, go get your sneakers on because we have work to do, and then meet me in the library."

Chapter 11
A Lesson in Disappointment

Nigel and Jennifer had spent most of the morning shopping for groceries and other items for the house. As Nigel came up the driveway, he saw a furniture truck, and two men carrying a mattress through the front door. He was curious but was more concerned with getting things ready for dinner than he was with looking at new beds.

Marie and Hattie supervised the setting up of the new beds, the placement of the armchairs, tables, throw rugs, and the new writing desks. Instead of bunk beds, they had bought five half-sized beds. Three for the larger bedroom, and two for the smaller bedroom. Jabber would stay in the room he always stayed in when he came to visit.

After Hattie had signed the delivery receipt, she looked around the bedroom.

"That king-size bed must have taken up a lot of room, Marie. Even with three smaller beds in here, and the new sitting chairs, the room looks roomier."

Marie did not say anything as she stood there with her lips pursed, looking at the beds.

"What's the matter?" Hattie asked.

"With all our furniture shopping, Hattie, we forgot to buy new bedding. The sheets and blankets we have, will not fit these beds."

Hattie's blinked with surprise. "We can make a quick run to the mall tomorrow and buy what we need."

"There is one more thing we also forgot," Marie said. What's that?"

"We need more help. Jennifer has her hands full taking care of Bella, and even with our help, we cannot expect Nigel to cook for six more visitors."

"Then, we need to hire some help, Marie. We will need cooks, housekeepers and someone to do the laundry. Between all the showers and the pool, I imagine just the towels will take two or three tubs a day. Which reminds me, we had better buy more towels. While I go call *Sunset Livery Service*, you make a list of the bedding, towels, and whatever else you think we might need."

"Make sure they all have background checks," Marie called out before she moved over to the new game table and sat down to make her list.

Nigel, back from the market, finished putting the groceries away, and decided he would go to his room and change into his loafers before he started on dinner. He was just entering the bedroom when he spied Hattie coming out of the farthest guest room.

When he finished changing shoes, he went to take a look at how the bookshelves had worked out. Nigel was not surprised to find Marie sitting at table writing in a notebook, but was surprised to see the new beds.

"Three beds?" he asked, moving over to where Marie sat.

Marie jerked with surprise at hearing his voice and looked up at him.

"Uh, yes. Uh...." she stammered, her face turning bright red.

"It's all set, Marie," Hattie said as she walked into the room. "I ordered two housekeepers, two cooks, and..." Hattie stopped speaking when she saw Nigel. "And one additional person for the laundry. She is the niece of one of the cooks," she finished.

"Come in and sit down, Hattie," Nigel said softly as he seated himself in one of the chairs at the game table. He waited for her to sit before he spoke. "I am disappointed that you girls did not think enough of me to include me in your plans."

Marie' and Hattie's faces fell at his words.

"I am sorry Nigel. I came up with a plan and—"

"No, *we* came up with a plan, Marie," Hattie interrupted, not wanting Marie to take all the blame.

"But I am the one who said we should not tell you, Nigel. I did that because I was afraid you would say no if you knew we were hiring Jabber's Marines to come help us," Marie stated, keeping her head down as she spoke to hide the tears of shame in her eyes.

"Now that we have established blame, would you mind telling me about your plan?" Nigel said, looking from Marie to Hattie, and then back at Marie.

Marie explained about Bravo Team, and Hattie filled him in on the help she had hired for the house.

Nigel sat back in his chair and looked at them. Hattie was right to state they had no way of defending themselves against the beast. While he might be able to hold his own against Goff, the girls were just a vulnerable as any other human that lived in this world. And if Jabber was bringing his own team, he knew the men were former Marines with combat experience. *Hopefully, they are younger than Jabber*, he told himself.

"Good plan. Hiring extra help is also good, but I reserve the right to replace them if I feel they are not working out," he said."

"Absolutely, Nigel. Maybe, you could set up the payroll accounts with Chester, as well. You know more about those things than Marie and I do."

"I am paying for Bravo Team," Marie put in. But Chester will need to do the payroll and make out the checks. You know I am no good with accounts,"

"How much are you paying for these men, Marie," Nigel asked, letting her know he would accept her offer to pay.

"A thousand dollars a day each, plus room, board, and whatever else might be needed to get the job done," Marie answered. "However, Jabber does not want any money for his services. He says being with all of us again is payment enough," she added.

"When will they get here?"

"Jabber said they will be here Sunday afternoon," Marie answered.

"And the housekeepers and cooks?" Nigel questioned.

"One cook and one housekeeper start tomorrow. They work Friday through Monday. The relief cook, and housekeeper start Tuesday, and work through Thursday. That way, we should have at least one cook and one housekeeper on duty, nine to five, most days. The laundry girl works ten to four, Monday through Friday," Hattie answered.

"What wages will we paying them?" Nigel asked as he began mentally began adding up the costs.

Hattie handed her notes over to him. I have it all written down here, including weekend hours. They get more for those. They are not expected to work on Holidays, but that should not be a problem as there are few Holidays this time of the year. The agency guarantees their employees have full background checks and are bonded. Which reminds me, we also need to pay the employment agency twenty-four hundred for their services."

Nigel nodded. He was familiar with agency fees as they used one for their pool service contract. "Call the agency, and have them fax over a list of names, resumes, hourly pay, and a copy of their bill. I will look it all over, and then fax it to Chester."

"I am truly sorry for putting this added expense to the household, without talking to you about it first, Nigel," Marie apologized. "You can tell Chester to bill my account for the cooks and housekeepers as well."

Nigel shook his head. "No. House staff needs to be on the household account. To tell you the truth, I am glad for the help. Jennifer has a full time job taking care of Bella, and it is a full time job for me trying to keep up with the meals. Now, what else is needed?" he asked.

"I believe only the bedding for the beds, and more towels need to be bought," Marie answered. "We already have a supply of bath soaps, shampoo, and such. Hattie and I will go to the mall tomorrow, and get what else we need," Marie replied, noting that he was not smiling at them.

Nigel took a card out of his shirt pocket. "Here. Vladimir gave me this. Call this woman and tell her what you need. She is a professional shopper," he said, handing the card over to Marie. "She will go out, buy it all for you, and have it delivered by tomorrow afternoon."

"What an interesting career," Hattie said, looking over at the card Marie held in her hand.

"Yes, there is that, but the good news is she will be billing Vladimir," Nigel said with a grin. "Now if you ladies will excuse me, I will go get dinner ready."

"We are fortunate to have Nigel with us, aren't we, Hattie?" Marie said.

"Yes, but from now on, we are going to tell him if we come up with anymore plans. I never want to see that look on his face ever again. We hurt him, Marie."

Marie nodded. "I know," she whispered emotionally. "I will apologize to him again, later tonight."

"As will I," Hattie said, patting her sister on the shoulder to comfort her.

Chapter 12
Bravo Team

Nigel noted it was fifteen minutes to nine when the doorbell rang. He went to answer it. A man and a woman stood at the door.

"Hello, I am Isles Manning," the man said offering his hand. "I am a certified chef. This is my wife, Kate, and she is a housekeeper. We are from *Sunset Livery Service*," he said as he handed the employment cards with their information to Nigel.

"I am Nigel Quinn, and your employer," Nigel said as he shook hands with the couple.

The man was a few inches taller than his five feet eight inches, and so was the woman. Both had blue eyes, short dark blonde hair, were pleasant to look at, and dressed for work. According to their resumes, they were in their early forties, but both looked younger.

"There are a few things you need to know about the job before you commit," Nigel told them without inviting them to come in. "Right now, we have five living here, and a sixth that comes and goes as he pleases. Beginning Sunday, we are adding six more guests. Security guards as my niece has some fame as an artist and has acquired a stalker. You should be safe enough as he only comes around at night," he added, using the story they had come up with to explain Bravo Team's presence on the premises. "If that will be problem for you, you may quit now, and I will see you get your day's pay, and any fees you may owe the agency."

Isles looked at Kate. She shrugged. "Since it is not us, he is looking for, I have no objection. Having guards on duty will make me feel safer," she said.

Isles nodded. "We are staying," he said.

"Then come on in, we can start with the kitchen," Nigel said, inviting them inside. He stopped in the foyer to point at a door across the room. "That is one of the guest bathrooms, the other bathroom is in the kitchen. You may use either one. That opening over there is the entrance to the hallway that leads to the bedrooms. There are two apartments between the kitchen and patio. I am using one, and Jennifer uses the other one. Though right now, she is staying in her mother's bedroom most of the time."

As they trekked through the dining room, Nigel pointed out the main dining table, and told them he would be adding another dining table on the patio, and a smaller table in the kitchen for anyone who wanted to use them, including staff.

"There will be another cook and housekeeper starting Tuesday. By then, you should have most of the kitchen routine down, Isles. And you, Kate, should be familiar with what needs to be done in the rest of the house."

Both Isles and Kate nodded.

"Good. I would appreciate it if you both would also come in Tuesday, just for this week, and train the new cook and housekeeper. I will see that you both get a cash bonus for your time and trouble, plus your regular hours."

"We would be glad to work an extra day," Isles said.

Kate nodded.

"You may find yourself helping out in here in the kitchen at times, more than tending to the rest of the house, Kate. I hope that is all right with you."

"Makes no difference to me what part of the house I work in, sir. I have worked with Isles in the kitchen on most of our jobs."

"Good. You can call me Nigel. I live here with my nieces Hattie and Marie Drake. Recently, my niece, Bella, and her daughter Jennifer joined us. Bella is ill." When Nigel saw them look at each other, then back at him, he added, "Nothing contagious. She was exposed to radiation at her job, and is not only weak, she also gets confused as to who is who. Jennifer takes care of most of her needs. Of course, her room will need cleaned, and her bedding changed daily. As for changing the rest of the beds, they can be done on Saturdays for you Kate, and Wednesdays for the other housekeeper. The linen closet is the first double doors on the left once you enter the hallway. We also will have someone to do most of the laundry. Should you need to wash something, the laundry is that door there with the window."

Nigel looked at his watch. Marie and Hattie were already up and about and would want breakfast within the hour. He decided he had better get the logistics out the way first.

"Isles, the pantry is through that door. We keep the pans in the cupboards below that section of the counter," He stopped to point to the stove area. "The dishes are in those cupboards," he said, waving a hand at the opposite wall. "The silverware is in those drawers. Serving bowls, trays, platters, and such are in those cupboards below the island workstation. Most of the food supplies are in the pantry, and there is a cold storage walk-in at the back of the pantry."

Nigel pulled out a drawer beneath the island counter. "I keep a notebook and pens in this drawer," When you find we are low on something, write it down in this notebook, and I will add it to my list. Also, if you have some favorite spices or other food that you often use, but don't see, write that down too. If for some reason, I am not here, stick to a basic three course meal for dinner. In most cases dessert is not needed as we generally have biscuits or cookies as you probably call them, later with our tea."

"Thank you, Nigel. That will make my job go smoother," Isles agreed.

"Right now, I would like you to make six cheese and olive two egg omelets with chopped green onion, and a plate of French toast to go with each. No syrup, we use jam. Bella and Jennifer will be eating in their bedroom. Fix those two plates first!"

"I will let them know you are bringing their breakfast, Kate. Turn left into the hallway, Bella's room is the second door on your right. The other meals are for us who will be eating at the dining table that we passed on our way in."

"Kate use that cart over there to put the teapots, dishes, and plates when Isles has them ready. We have four different jams, and I use those blue sauce bowls stacked over there to serve them. Right now four bowls will do. When the security team gets here, we all will be eating at different times. You might want to ask them whether they prefer jam or syrup."

Kate nodded, and then without being told, she went to the refrigerator and got out the eggs."

"That yellow teapot on the counter has a special medicinal tea that is used to help Bella heal. Please do not use it or move it. Olives are in that green jar in the refrigerator door. The cheese is in the cold storage section of the pantry. This morning, use sharp cheddar for the omelets, Isles. The grater is in that cabinet," he said, pointing toward a cupboard. "The onions are in the vegetable section of the pantry."

"We generally drink hot tea throughout the day, and without sugar or cream," he said as he got out the tea box. However, I imagine when our new guests arrive, they will be wanting coffee. "All the makings for both are in this cupboard. Creamers are with the dishes. Kate, you will need to put a pitcher of ice water on the table at every meal, and a glass of orange juice with breakfast meals."

"Now, I will leave it to you to set the table and serve breakfast this morning. Feel free to wander around and familiarize yourself with cupboard, drawers, pantry, and the rest of the kitchen, as well as the rest of the house. I am going to go tell Hattie and Marie you are here."

Figuring, he had given enough instructions, Nigel left his kitchen to the new cook. Once breakfast was served, he would know whether the man was a keeper or not.

Bravo Team's blue king-cab truck pulled into the driveway early Sunday afternoon, and right on time.

"Oh, Jabber, I have missed you so much," Marie said, giving her silver-haired friend a hug, once he had climbed out of the truck.

"And I, you," Jabber said, giving her a kiss on her forehead, his dark eyes damp with emotion.

After some seconds of staring happily at her, Jabber stepped back and greeted Nigel, "Let me introduce you to Bravo Team. You too, Marie, he added. "This is Louie Crosshatch," he said, putting his hand on the shoulder of a man who looked to be in his late thirties, brown-skinned, dark hair, and darker eyes. "He's Navajo, and of course, a former Marine. He runs the unit. If you have questions or need help? He is the one to ask."

"Nice to meet you, Louie," Nigel murmured as he shook the man's hand.

"You must let me paint you while you are here, Louie," Marie said, fascinated by the turquoise jewelry and belt buckle the man wore. I will do one painting for me, and one for you."

When Louie continued to stare at Marie, not sure whether to make a comment or not, Jabber intervened. "I would take her up on the offer if I were you, Louie. She is quite famous for her paintings."

Louie's face remained blank, but nevertheless, he nodded at Marie.

The rest of Bravo Team eyed the woman with a bit more respect.

"This here is, Lee Skidmore, part time peacekeeper, and part time cowboy," Jabber said, introducing another man with a deeply tanned face, who looked to be in his mid-forties as his hair—what was left of it—was beginning to turn gray. "He and I have a small ranch in Sedona. You would like it there, Marie. God's land, it is."

"Mam. Nigel," Skidmore greeted.

"Nice to meet you, Lee. I look forward to hearing more about your ranch," Nigel said, shaking hands with the dark-haired man.

"Me too," Marie said.

"Next up, Jack Pratt," Jabber said with a grin as he introduced the youngest of the group. A tall, slim black man in his late twenties, wearing goggle type glasses. "He just finished up his second tour of Iraq and is battle fresh. He is a whiz at computers, but not nerdy about it. And to top it off, he can outrun the rest of us."

Everyone laughed at that statement.

Jack rolled his eyes, but the grin never left his face. He was used to getting ribbed by rest of the team. It came with the territory when you joined a new unit.

"This is Earl Farber. He works at the ranch when he not on a Bravo assignment, or on the rodeo circuit riding bulls. That is why he's so bowlegged. He can also shoot the wings off a fly at five hundred yards."

Marie cocked her head to the side, and imagined what the young man with blue eyes, and ragged blonde hair would look like wearing a cowboy hat and chaps. She hoped he had brought some of his rodeo pictures with him. She would like to paint him as well.

Jabber waited for the humor to die down before he introduced the last, but not the least, of the bunch. "This here is Oxford Knottingham, best known as Ox. He is a race car mechanic when he's not working for Bravo Team. One look at his size, and you can see why he is called Ox. He is also a sharpshooter, and the best of us at hand-to-hand combat."

"Nice to meet you, Ox," Marie said as she looked at the tall husky man who appeared to be in his mid-thirties with green eyes, and brown curly hair

"Nice to meet you too, mam," Ox greeted.

"Now that we have all met, I need to make sure you understand why you are here," Nigel said. "It is not a man you will be defending us from. It is a beast or vampire as most would call it that has returned from the dead. I know it sounds unbelievable, but believe me when I say he does exist, and he is dangerous. He is after those who live in this house, but he will not hesitate to kill you too. It is my job, and yours, if you choose to stay and help us rid this world of him.

"If he comes around, do not hesitate to shoot. The head would be the area to aim at. That could disable him. Shots to the body will slow him down, but they will not kill him—he has no heart. If you decide this is more than you bargained for, and want to leave? I will see that you get a ticket back home, and five thousand for your time and trouble."

No one said anything, but the men looked at Jabber. They had believed he had been exaggerating when he told them they were going vampire hunting. They now knew he had spoken the truth.

"Damn, I knew I should have brought my leather collar," Jack quipped, holding a hand up to his throat.

"You can borrow, one of my silver chains," Louie offered with a grin on his face.

"I am here to stay," Ox said.

Earl and Lee nodded at Nigel.

"Good, but you will not need chains around your neck. I have amulets that will keep the beast from attacking you. You are to wear them at all times, even in the shower."

When Nigel saw the grins on their faces, he added, "I am not joking. The amulet is the only thing between your throat and him. They are gold, and they are yours take with you when your return to your homes. There is one more thing you need to know. Bella is very ill, but her illness is not contagious. She suffers from a rare disease. She also has no memory right now that she is Bella, as she was attacked by a man years ago, and lost her memory. She believes herself to Sally Parker. The household help has been told she is ill from radiation exposure, but I want you to know the truth."

"Oh, I almost forgot. The help believes you are here because someone is stalking Marie. I would like you to keep an eye on them as they come and go to make sure nothing happens to them. They should be in no real danger in the morning as the beast you hunt, generally, only moves about after dark."

"What about in moonlight?" Earl asked.

"He can move about anytime, day or night, but sunlight or any bright light causes him pain. On stormy days, we all will need to be more vigilant," Nigel answered.

Chapter 13
Unexpected Harmony

Hattie had risen early and sat at the patio table with a cup of tea sat watching Ox go through a vigorous exercise routine. Jabber had told her the man was good at hand-to-hand combat. She could see why. Despite his size, he was all muscle and no fat. He was also lightning quick with his movements.

When he finished, he came into the patio, nodded at her, and then went on into the kitchen. She heaved a small sigh of disappointment. She had hoped to find out more about him.

She was surprised when he came back with a towel around his neck, and a bottle of cold water.

"You have a nice home, Miss Hattie, mam," Ox said as he sat down at the table.

"Thank you, I like it here too, Ox. And please, call me Hattie. I am well past the age of Miss."

"Hattie it is, then," Ox said as he leaned back in his chair and looked around. His eyes stopped on the big blue swimming pool, and he smiled.

"I like it here," he said. "In Arizona, we have miles of empty land. Closest neighbor is a mile or two away which suits me fine. And though I know I am sitting here in the heart of a big city; it doesn't feel that way. Other than a few cars passing by, and some hollering over that way," he paused long enough to point toward the back fence that skirted the country club's golf course, I still have a sense of privacy."

"To be truthful, Ox, I have never looked at it that way. We moved here from New York. It was never quiet there, not even at night. When we came here, I used to set out here in the evenings and wish for a parade of people."

"Why?

"With no people, we had no stories," she replied.

"Stories?"

"Yes. In New York, Marie and I would sit out on our balcony, and pick out someone walking along on the street below. We then invented a life for them by the way they dressed. We got quite creative at it. Marie even started doing sketches. She always been good at art, you know. In a way, our stories were more entertaining than anything on television."

"Now that I can understand," Ox said. "When I was a boy, I went on cattle drives with my father. The best part was the evenings sitting around the campfire listening to the older men tell about the good old days of going off to fight in one war, or another, falling off horses, getting snake bit, and eating burnt beans. To me, that beat anything on TV," he finished with a grin.

"You do understand," Hattie said, smiling at the man. "Well, as you can see, we have no people walking by on a street. So, it was not long before boredom set in, and we found ourselves for the first time in our lives with nothing to do. We started going to the theaters that play those older black and white films. Somehow, the characters in those films were a lot like our stories. Real, but at the same time, compared with today's world, not real."

"Never heard loneliness stated any better than that," Ox said, smiling at her.

Hattie turned her head and looked at him. "You surprise me with your insightfulness, Ox. Yes, now that I think back on it, I guess one could say we were lonely. Anyway, after a time, we quit going to the movies. Marie took up painting and has done very well with it. I write a bit, and have had a few articles published here and there, but I do it for my own enjoyment, and so, few know my name. Then, last year, I got into the paranormal detective business by accident."

"Paranormal? You mean like ghosts?" Ox questioned, surprised by her choice of profession.

"Yes. Though I have yet to see a real ghost. Most of the unexplainable can be explained if you know where to look."

"Glad to hear that. The one thing that might scare me would be a real live ghost. Or maybe I should say, a real dead ghost. Which somehow, doesn't quite sound correct when you think about it."

Hattie laughed, and so did Ox.

"What's so funny?" Jack asked as he joined them.

"We just found out ghosts are oxymorons," Ox answered, a grin on his face. When Jack scratched his head, he added, "You had to be here, kid, but basically, what it comes down to, is a ghost alive or dead?"

Jack chewed on his lip for a second or two as he thought about that. "Well, it could be neither one as a ghost is an ethereal being," he said with a pleased look on his face.

Ox chuckled as he looked at his friend. "Good answer. You just provided a third option that could be debated."

"We're not going to be fighting ghosts too, are we?" Jack asked, swallowing nervously.

"Why would you ask that question?" Ox asked.

"Because vampires don't exist either, yet we are here to fight one," Jack answered.

"No. Hattie is a paranormal detective, and we were discussing her job," Ox said.

Jack's brow went up as he looked the woman who was now his boss. "I thought those only existed on TV, or in the movies," he said.

"There are a few agencies here in the United States, but there are many more paranormalists working in Europe. London, Paris, Rome, Madrid, Prague, and other cities that have all seen centuries of human occupation," Hattie said. "Mysteries, like life, happen, and some are quite strange. Do ghosts exist? I have yet to see one, but I do not rule out the possibility. Last October, Marie, Nigel, and I went to a Paris conference for paranormal investigators in Europe. It was enlightening. After talking with several paranormalists, and listening to their tales, I have concluded that while most stories and sightings of ghosts are either tricks of the mind or staged by others, there is a certain percentage that are not. Do ghosts exist? Yes, I believe they do."

"Well, I hope I never see one," Jack said with a shudder.

"There is no need to fear a ghost, Jack. Have you ever heard of anyone being actually murdered by a ghost?" Hattie asked.

"Well...," Jack said as he chewed on his bottom lip, thinking about the question. "No, mam, I guess I never have. Not in real life."

"Exactly. Nothing to worry about," Ox said as he checked his watch. "Who's minding the cams this morning?" he asked changing the subject.

"Earl just relieved me. Nothing but birds moving about this morning. I saw a nice white-face barn owl fly by just as the sun was peeking up over horizon. He was headed for those trees that line the back fence," Jack answered. "I used the roof cam to zoom in on it."

"Interesting, I did not know we had owls around here," Hattie said.

"That's because they do most of their flying at night," Jack replied.

"In that case, I may have to take a turn at watching the cameras too. But for now, my tea is cold, and I am getting hungry. I think I will see if Isles can fix me some oatmeal and toast," Hattie said as she rose. "Nice talking with you both."

"You too, mam," both men said in unison.

Hattie was not surprised to see Jabber sitting at the breakfast table with Marie. The two would probably be inseparable while he was here. That thought made her smile. She sat down across from them.

"Morning, Jabber."

"Good morning to you too, Hattie," Jabber responded, looking up at her.

"Jabber and I are going shopping this morning, Hattie. Would you like to come with us?"

"No, but I thought, Nigel had an appointment with Chester to go over the first payroll."

"Oh, he does. I called Bernie and hired one of his cars and a driver for the day. You know I am not comfortable driving in traffic, and Jabber does not drive anymore due to his failing eyesight. But, even if he did, he has no idea of where to find the stores."

Hattie nodded. "While you are out shopping, see if you can find a couple of sets of deluxe unbreakable type glasses, cups, plates, and trays for the patio and pool area. It will prevent someone from getting their feet cut on broken glass."

"Put that on our list, Jabber," Marie said.

Jabber picked up the pen by his plate, pulled a notebook out of his pocket, and wrote the letters PD beneath beach towels.

The doorbell rang.

"That will be our car," Marie said as she rose from her chair. "See you later, Hattie. Call me if you think of anything else."

"Will do!" Hattie called out as she watched them walk off.

She had just finished her toast when Nigel came in. "Good morning," she greeted, and then frowned when she saw his face. "You don't look well, Nigel."

"Probably not. I did not get much sleep last night," he replied.

Before Hattie could ask what was wrong, Vladimir joined them.

Vladimir nodded at Hattie. As he sat down, he greeted Nigel.

"I was just asking Nigel why he looks so haggard this morning?" Hattie told Vladimir.

Vladimir turned to look at Nigel.

"I did not get much sleep last night," Nigel repeated when he saw them both staring expectantly at him.

"Why? we have guards on duty now to keep a watch on the house," Hattie asked.

"While Jabber's men are no doubt good at what they do, they cannot sense what I can. Goff was here last night. Not close enough for the motion sensors or for the cameras to pick up, but close enough for me to sense him. I spent most of the night watching the camera grid, but Louie and I never did see him."

Hattie felt a shiver go down her spine. She would not have slept either had she known the beast was out there.

"What do we do now?" she asked.

"Sit here and wait for him to get close enough to see him," Nigel said.

Vladimir shook his head. "No, we can do better than that. I bought a dozen special field cameras used by the government with field matrix capability last month. They are more computers than cameras, They turn the terrain into a matrix field. If anything moves, the camera sends out an alarm, and begins tracking the movement by size, speed, and range."

"Good!" Nigel exclaimed. "That might help even up the odds of spotting him before he gets to one of us."

"Oh, I intend to see we have more than a chance, I will not lose Bella again," Vladimir said. "I have asked Jennifer if I can use her apartment to sleep in. With you on one side of the house, me on the other, Bravo Team, and a field matrix camera cluster on the roof, he should not be able to get past us."

Nigel nodded but made no reply. Not with Hattie sitting there. Though he knew, she understood the beast had to be killed, he doubted she fully understood what it would take to kill the jogeth.

Isles came in with Nigel's breakfast. "I did not know you were here, Mr. Romanov. What would you like for breakfast?" he asked.

"I've already had breakfast. This cup of tea is all I need," Vladimir answered.

"Isles and his wife seem to be settling in nicely," Vladimir told Nigel once the chef went through the kitchen door.

"Yes, they are. I am hoping our other help will as good."

"I don't think we are going to be disappointed," Hattie said. "The cook is a woman who was born here in Hollywood. Her name is Connie Garcia, and she makes tortillas, and other Mexican dishes."

"I do like Mexican food," Vladimir said.

"Me too," Nigel agreed.

"The other housekeeper's name is Myra Gleason. She came yesterday afternoon to meet us and get the lay of the house. She seems quite nice. Bella was quite taken with her. They chatted for several minutes."

"They chatted?" Vladimir asked, curious as to what Hattie meant by that statement.

"Yes, she is only person, other than Jennifer, that I have seen Bella take any interest in. Of course that could be because Myra has a British accent."

"Hmm. Interesting," Vladimir murmured. "When will she be on duty?"

"Tomorrow," Nigel said. "She works Tuesday through Friday."

"Then, I will make sure to be here. I want to see what she looks like," Vladimir said.

"Looks like?" Hattie asked with surprise.

"Yes, there must be something about the woman that Bella recalls from her past. Though she may not know that, I will. I can recall every friend or housekeeper we have ever had."

"Ah, good point. Which remind me, I have yet to visit with Bella and Jennifer this morning, and so I think I will go check on them." Hattie said as she rose from the table.

Chapter 14
"You are my father!"

After lunch, Hattie went to visit Bella. She found her sitting in one of the armchairs, a book in her lap. Jennifer was sitting at the desk, looking at her computer.

Hattie went and set down in the chair by Bella.

"I am glad to see you are up and reading, Sally," Hattie greeted.

"Yes, Myra says I need to be moving around more. Though this is not moving, it is the best I can do right now."

"I also see you are reading Longfellow," Hattie said when she saw the title of the book she held in her hands.

"Vladimir brought it to me. He said I would enjoy reading it, and he was right. It is one of my favorite books. I remember when he used to read it to me..." Bella's voice broke off as she recalled a scene of Vladimir reading Evangeline to her by lamp light, a Christmas tree by the window. Her face paled as she saw the blue ginger jar on the fireplace mantle. She remembered that jar.

Her face lit up as she recalled Vladimir had given her that jar on the anniversary of their marriage when they lived in London—*together*.

A rush of anguish filled her mind as she remembered the lost years, and the one who had attacked her. She cried out, and putting her hands to her face, she began to weep.

Jennifer jumped up from her chair and ran to her mother. "What's wrong, are you in pain?"

Bella shook her head, and continued to weep as her memory of the night she was attacked filled her mind with shame.

"I had better go find Nigel," Hattie said, rising out of her chair and heading for the door.

She ran to the dining room, and then panicked when she saw it was empty. She continued on into the kitchen. "Isles have you seen Nigel or Vladimir?"

"They just went out garage door," Isles answered.

Hattie did not see either one of the men, but the garage door was open, and she hurried outside. She found them standing by Vladimir's car. "It's Bella, she needs help!" she cried out as she rushed toward them.

She did not need to elaborate, both men hurried toward the front door. Hattie followed them.

Vladimir was the first to reach the bedroom. He dropped to his knees and took her hands from her face. "What is wrong, my dear?" he asked.

Violent sobs racked Bella's body as she looked at him. "I am sorry, Vladimir. I-am-so-sorry," she said between sobs."

"There is nothing for you to be sorry for, my sweet," Vladimir comforted as he patted her hand.

"Oh, my God!" Jennifer exclaimed hoarsely. "You are my *father*."

Vladimir's body stiffened as he heard Jennifer's words, but he kept his eyes on Bella.

Bella looked up at her daughter with shock on her face. She opened her mouth to confirm that Vladimir was, indeed, Jennifer's father, but her illness caught up with her, and her body went limp as she fell unconscious.

Vladimir caught her as she slumped forward. "If you will turn down the covers, Jennifer, I will move your mother to her bed," he said.

Jennifer ran over to the bed and pulled the bedding down.

Vladimir picked Bella up and laid her on the clean white sheet. He then straightened up and looked at Jennifer and Hattie.

"What happened?" He asked.

Jennifer shrugged. "I don't know. She and Hattie were having a conversation about the book she is reading.

Vladimir looked over and saw the book on the floor. He bent down and picked it up. "It is one of her favorites," he murmured.

"Yes, that is what she said," Hattie said. "Then she said, 'I remember when Vladimir used to read it to me,' and stopped there. Her face lit up for a second or two before she began to cry. When Jennifer could not console her, I went and found you and Nigel."

Vladimir gave an audible sigh. "For many years, I have read Evangeline to her every Christmas Eve while we sat in front of the tree, waiting for midnight," Vladimir said looking down at Bella, and tenderly brushing her hair out of her eyes. "She must have remembered that."

"If you could move for a minute. I would like to examine her health," Nigel told Vladimir.

"Do you think we should call a doctor?" Vladimir asked as watched Nigel put a hand to Bella's forehead.

"No, her fever is down. And thanks to Longfellow, she may have her memory back. I think the excitement of recalling her past overwhelmed her senses. Right now, sleep is the best healer."

"Jennifer, call us if your mother wakes or there is any other change. In the meantime, the rest of us should get back to whatever it is, we planned to do today, and let her rest," Nigel said.

Reluctantly, Vladimir turned and followed Nigel out the door.

Hattie decided she would go to her office, and search the internet for recent unsolved murders, but changed directions when the doorbell rang.

There was no need for her to wonder who was at the door, a camera screen had been installed by the side of the door, as well as an alarm button. She opened the door to a man wearing a construction belt.

"Yes?" she asked as she opened the door.

"I am here to do the measurements," the man answered.

Before Hattie could ask, what measurements? Nigel came up behind her.

"Just in time, Rick. Follow me, and I will show you what I want."

Hattie watched them walk off, wondering what Nigel was up to now, but since he had not invited her, nor explained why the repairman was here, she decided she might as well go on with her plan of searching the internet. She would ask him at lunch.

Chapter 15
The Heart Weeps

When Bella woke up late in the afternoon, she sat up and looked around. She saw Jennifer sitting in a chair, looking at her, a book in her lap.

"What are you reading?" she asked.

"The book you were reading earlier."

Bella closed her eyes and swallowed painfully, willing herself not to start crying again, even if most of the tears were joyful ones.

"Are you all right, Mother?" Jennifer asked.

Bella opened her eyes and nodded.

Jennifer saw a light in her mother's eyes that she had not seen for a long time.

"It was not a dream, was it?" Bella asked.

"No, he is here. Well, not exactly in this room right now, as he is outside helping the security team put in some new type of camera."

"How did he find us?"

"He found me, but it is a long story," Jennifer answered. "How about I help you get up, and into a chair before I tell it to you."

"Yes, please, but I need to make a trip to the bathroom first," Bella answered.

Jennifer rose and brought the wheelchair around.

"No," Bella said when she saw the chair. "Just help me walk, I have to get stronger."

Jennifer smiled as she saw the look of determination on her mother's face. "You are getting stronger, Mother, but even such a small trip will tire you out. For now, use the chair. I have a long story to tell, and I would like you to be able to stay awake long enough to hear it. Also you missed lunch. You can eat while I talk."

Bella chuckled as she scooted herself to the edge of the bed. She motioned for Jennifer to stay back as she stood up on wobbly legs. She then sat down in the wheelchair with a sigh of relief.

"You are right, Jennifer. I need to save my energy. I am not ready to do much walking."

"But you soon will be. Your fever is down, and Nigel says you are starting to heal."

Bella nodded. She knew in her heart, she would get better, now that she knew Vladimir was alive.

* * *

It was past nine by the time Jack and Vladimir had the new camera up and working. Once that was done, Vladimir decided it was time to eat. He found several pieces of baked chicken and some noodles in white sauce in the refrigerator. He used the microwave to heat the food.

"I was wondering when you were going to come in and eat," Nigel said as he came in.

"Other than the few minutes I took to go check on Bella, there was not time to eat," Vladimir said as he removed the plate from the microwave and headed for the table.

Nigel grabbed the fresh pot of tea he had just made and took it to the table. He then sat down, After, he got the biscuit tin opened, he said, "Jack told me the new camera is working."

"Yes. If anything out there moves about tonight, even a mouse, we will know it," Vladimir said.

"I will rest much better knowing that. You notice, I said rest, not sleep. I don't get much of that anymore."

Vladimir nodded. "Me neither, but now that I will be staying here in Jennifer's apartment I can at least lay down on a bed."

"Where have you been sleeping?" Nigel asked, upset with himself for forgetting to offer Vladimir a bed to sleep in.

"Last night, in the recliner in the front room. The night before in my car, after hearing you say you sensed the beast's presence, I decided I needed to be inside the house, and not outside."

"He was out there somewhere beyond our grounds. I only got faint vibrations of his presence, but there was no sleeping after that," Nigel said.

Vladimir nodded, and then fell silent as he ate his dinner.

Nigel waited until he moved the plate aside before he asked, "Does Bella know who you are?"

"Yes. I am hoping that when she wakes up tomorrow, she will not have forgotten me."

"Get her to talk about herself. The more she recalls, the better it will be for both of you. However, do not push her to tell you what happened to her. That could cause her to shut down again. Whatever happened to her was traumatic enough that her mind closed the door on the both the deed and her past life. From what Hattie told me, we can assume it was a man that harmed her."

"Yes, I believe he robbed her as well," Vladimir declared grimly as he stared into his cup of tea. "When she disappeared, she was wearing her ruby and diamond wedding ring, a gold chain with a diamond studded heart pendant, and diamond earrings. Hattie told me Bella had no jewelry other than two pieces of silver jewelry given to her by Parker."

"Jennifer calls him grandfather and has nothing but good things to say about him. If you look at the timeline, you will see that Bella fell ill right after he passed away. I believe the shock and grief of his death to her system, revived the disease."

Vladimir raised his head. "You are probably right about that. I think I will go check on her before I call it a night," he said as he rose from the table.

When he started to reach for his plate, Nigel stopped him. "I will clean up. You go see Bella."

* * *

Bella was sitting up in bed waiting for Vladimir. She knew he would come check on her before he went to bed. She willed herself to stay awake, and not slip back into the darkness that plagued her lately. She had something she needed to tell him.

Vladimir looked around for Jennifer but did not see her. He sat down on the side of the bed. Without speaking, he took Bella's hand and held it as he looked into her eyes. "I have missed you," he said.

Bella smiled sadly. "I am sorry I cannot say the same, Vlad. I do remember grieving when I found I could not remember who I was or where I came from. But at the same time, I was relieved to find that I was not pregnant by the man that hurt me."

"You were raped?" Vladimir questioned, rage filling his mind.

"Robert found me hiding on his boat. I was injured. The first thing he did after he made port in Seattle, was to take me to a doctor. In addition to the head injury, I had other cuts and bruises on my body. It was the doctor who told me I was three months pregnant," Bella answered, not able to bring herself to say the word rape in reference to herself. "I want you to know what happened to me before you commit to taking me back. And I will understand if you never want to see me again," she whispered brokenly.

Vladimir pulled her into his arms, tears in eyes as well. "You are my beloved, Bella. Yesterday, today, and forever," he said. "If you sense anger in me, it is because of the pain you have had to endure all these years."

"And now I have passed that pain on to you," Bella said, tears leaking from her eyes.

"I have lived through worse," Vladimir consoled.

"Worse?" Bella questioned, not comprehending how anything could be worse.

"Yes," Vladimir answered. "For me, the pain of losing you all those years is more than the pain of finding out you were attacked."

Bella put a hand on Vladimir's cheek, her honey-colored eyes looked into his, and she smiled. "You have always known how to heal my heart when it cries."

Vladimir smiled back at her and laid her gently on her pillow. He could see was exhausted.

Bella closed her eyes, only to open them a second later. "I do not want Jennifer to find out, Vladimir" she whispered. "It shames me."

"The blame is not yours, Bella. Never think that. If this had happened to Marie or Hattie, would you think less of them?"

"No. My heart would weep for them."

"And that is why we will not tell them. It would only bring them pain. I cannot undo the past, but when you are rid of this illness, and it is safe to do so, I will erase the memories of the attack, and you will never have to live with them again."

Bella tried to nod but found herself falling back into the dark oblivion of exhaustion from the disease that had tried to destroy her body.

Vladimir sat there holding her hand until Jennifer came in.

"She is sleeping," he said as he laid Bella's hand atop the blanket, and then rose to his feet, and faced his daughter. "I am sorry I was not there to take care of you, Jennifer."

"Me too. And I am sorry I did not believe your story until I saw Mother's face today. I also realize that if you had not found me when you did, she would already be dead.

Worse, she would have died alone because I..." Jennifer's voice broke off as she swallowed back tears, "did not know she was dying."

Vladimir put a hand on her shoulder. "This is not your fault, never think that. She will get well now. Papa will see to that."

"Papa?" Jennifer questioned.

"Forgive me. It has been a long day. I meant Nigel," Vladimir replied, not wanting to reveal more about his past until his daughter had time to get to know him.

Chapter 16
Special Agents

FBI Special Agent Vincent Windino Lopez—Latino heritage, in his mid-forties, and a good four inches shorter than his partner Special Agent Ace Marvel Whittaker a tall, blond, California born man in his early thirties—stood looking at a drone's aerial footage of the house in question.

"You can see they have cams mounted around the house. That silver square with glass insets mounted to the antenna frame on the roof should be the MS-2 Matrix Scanner, according to the data file the boss gave us," Lopez said.

"They also have an armed guard carrying an assault rifle," Whittaker put in as he spotted a man coming out the back door. You have to wonder what has them so spooked?"

"Yeah, I see him. According to the file, two women in their mid-thirties, live there with an uncle who is sixty-seven. Research could not find any known political or social media activity, other than Hattie Drake has a website for a paranormal detective agency. Nor have they filed any complaints about threats or harassment with the local PD. The only other item of interest, is Marie Drake is a high-ticket artist selling under the name Juliana.

"Paranormal activity attracts crazies, you know?" Whittaker stated.

"Enough to spend half a million on a *MS-2 Matrix Scanner*?" Lopez asked.

Whittaker shrugged. "As you well know by now, Vincent, rich people do things the rest of us never even think about."

Before Lopez could comment, the footage showed another armed man coming out of the house and walking toward the one with the rifle.

"There is also a man in the pool, and he does not match the description of the gardener nor his son. He is not only younger, but he is also black." Whitaker said.

A phone rang.

Whittaker flipped open his phone. "Whatcha got?" he asked when he saw the call was from Research.

"Well, we now know who the men are," he told Lopez once he ended the call. "Suzy states she has identified the man with the rifle. He is a hired gun from Arizona, and part of an outfit known as Bravo Team."

"Which is ran by former CIA agent Oscar Jabber. You would think, the man would have the decency to retire by now—or die," Lopez said sourly.

"You know him, huh?"

"Yes, I met when I was working out of Phoenix," Lopez answered.

"Good."

"What's good about it?" Lopez snapped.

"We won't need an introduction," Whittaker stated.

"That was more than two decades ago, Ace. It was my first year working for the Agency. He shoved me out the way just before a sniper put a hole in my head. Then chewed my head off for being stupid."

"Were you?" Whittaker asked with a grin.

Lopez glared at his partner before a grin broke out on his face. "Yeah, now that I think back on it, I guess I was. I almost got us both killed."

"Seems to me, you owe the man,"

"Don't remind me," Lopez said gruffly as he turned back to watch the rest of the drone's footage.

He paid special attention to the roads, buildings and trees in the vicinity. From what he could see, there was only one way into the property by vehicle. The fence at the back of the house belonged to the golf club which had its own security personnel and cameras. The estate on the south side of the property was secure enough, as it was guarded by a half dozen trained rottweilers that ran loose on the grounds. On the north side of the property was a concrete storm channel which was at least a twenty foot climb.

* * *

The doorbell rang, and because Marie, Hattie, and Nigel had gone to town, Jabber went to see who was at the door. When he saw the two men flashing badges at him, he shut the door behind him.

"What brings you to this patch of paradise, Lopez?" Jabber asked, giving the man a smile that did not go up to his eyes.

"Got word, you deployed a *MS-2 Matrix Scanner*, yesterday," Lopez answered.

"As far as I know there's no law against that," Jabber answered, keeping the surprise off his face as he wondered why the matrix scanner would interest the FBI.

"It's a government thing, Jabber. Damn few civilians have one or can afford one," Lopez replied. "Nor do they hire someone like you, and your team. We would like to know why? You, expecting visitors?"

Jabber looked at the man with Lopez. "How long you two been partners?" he asked.

"About ten years," Whittaker answered.

Jabber nodded before he turned his attention back on Lopez. "I could lie, Lopez, but I won't. You know that person who has been tearing folks throats out around town?" He waited for both men to nod before he continued. "Well, he was here last week. The only thing that saved the woman was her husband was in the house at the time."

"Is the husband here? We need to speak with him. No one has any description of this killer. It would help to get a BOLO out on him," Whittaker said.

"I doubt he can help you. The beast was gone by the time he got to the bedroom. Right now, he's resting as he spends most of his night watching the cam screens."

"Yeah, I can relate to that. The only difference is he will be sitting in a comfortable chair, and not the front seat of a car like we will be."

Jabber's eyes narrowed. "Does that mean, you are going to be running a surveillance op on this house?"

Lopez nodded. "Until the Boss says different, we're stuck with watching what goes on at this house."

"Then I suggest you join us in our cam room for night duty, it will be safer for you." As Lopez and Whittaker shook their heads, Jabber frowned. "Either of you got any idea what it is you are up against?" Both men shook their head again. "Then I will tell you, but first, I am going to remind you of what I told you once before, Lopez, I don't lie about life or death. Never have, and never will."

"I remember," Lopez said.

"What these folks are afraid of, and what the killer you are looking for, are the same thing. And as hard as it is going to be for you believe what I am going to tell you—believe it! It is not a man you are looking for. It is what most folks call a vampire. Bullets may slow him down, but they won't kill him because he is already dead."

Lopez's face visibly paled.

"What did I tell you, Lopez? Paranormal and crazy go together," Whittaker scoffed.

Jabber cast the man a look of disappointment. "Folks like you, are the reason I quit working for the CIA. Poor vision and shallow-brained."

Whittaker's face flushed at the insult. His hands curled into fists.

"He's got a point, Ace. It makes sense when you think about it. There's a half a dozen dead women, all murdered the same way. No blood left in their body, and not one clue or witness. No one ever sees anything, even if they are standing but a few feet away at the time the crime was committed."

"What! You believe that dead people are walking around, Lopez?" Whittaker protested.

"Don't think of it as a person," Jabber warned. "It is a beast. We already know it can move faster than we can, and it can control minds. That is why no one recalls seeing it."

Lopez opened his mouth to speak, but Jabber beat him to it. "You both can sit in your car, or you take me up on my offer to come in and watch the cameras. It's your choice. I've given you warning, so my job is done. Now, if you have nothing else to say, I got things to do."

Jabber turned and opened the door.

"You can expect us around eight tonight," Lopez said, surprising Whittaker.

Jabber pulled his wallet out of his pocket and turned around. "Here's my card," he said, handing it to Lopez. "It's got my phone number on it. Though there's no need for you to call tonight. The cams will spot you the minute you enter the property. Try and get here as early as you can. The creature only hunts after dark."

Chapter 17
Mouthful of Teeth

Lopez and Whittaker came back around eight, and joined Jabber, Louie, and Jack in the cam room. Like any stakeout op, it was a boring job for the most part, but Louie and Jack welcomed the two FBI agents, and the new stories they had to tell. When Vladimir came in around midnight, and introductions were over, Whittaker decided he would take a cigarette break out on the patio.

"I'll go with you. I could use a smoke too," Jack said.

As the two men walked out, Vladimir sat down in Jack's chair. He checked the matric scanner, and saw several alerts, but all were small animals.

"Look at this!" Louie said, entering the code for replay. They all watched as an owl swooped down and grabbed a field mouse.

"Interesting. When this is all over, I will have to invite Tom Esselmeyer over to take a look at this. He's a professor at UCLA," Vladimir said. "This type of camera could easily be adapted for use by the academic world to study birds and other animals."

"You are probably right about that, but the word from upstairs is that this camera was made for government projects only," Lopez said.

Vladimir nodded politely as he made a mental note to order a half dozen of the cameras tomorrow before they disappeared off the market.

"Why would this camera be regarded as a security issue for the government?" he asked.

Lopez shrugged. "I have no idea, but someone is keeping tabs on those who buy one, or otherwise, Whittaker and I would not have gotten the assignment to check it out."

"It smells like a DEA or AFT Ops, if you ask me," Jabber said. "Whoever buys one of these cameras has lots of money. So they send agents like you to find out why someone is so interested in the security of their establishment. In most cases that would be someone in the business of drugs, guns, diamonds, or money laundering."

"You are probably right about that, Jabber," Lopez agreed.

The matrix scanner alert started pinging.

"We got something bigger than a rabbit this time. It is human in shape, but look at the speed it is moving," Louie said as he watched the figure come from the back of the house and head toward the patio.

"You stay here and keep watch, Jabber," Louie said as he jumped up out of his chair and ran out the office's door.

Vladimir and Lopez followed him.

Louie did not slow down until he got to the patio. He saw Jack standing there with his mouth open, but he was not moving.

The tall figure that had a hold of Whittaker turned when he heard the men running toward him. His sharp teeth were extended as he was about to feed. He growled at them, and then turned back to rip into the man's soft throat.

Goff's growl froze Lopez but did not freeze Vladimir or Louie as they wore the amulet.

Louie did not reach for his gun. There was no way to shoot at the vampire without hitting Whittaker. Instead, he switched the pistol to his left hand, pulled his hunting knife from its scabbard, and threw it, hitting the creature in the middle of the back.

A screech rent the air as the knife buried itself to the hilt in the middle of the vampire's back.

The beast let Whittaker fall to the grass, and then moving at a speed not possible for a human, ran toward the storm drain wall, jumped over it, and disappeared.

Louie ran over to where Whittaker lay. When he saw the man was not bleeding, he heaved a sigh of relief. He then spat out a curse as he realized he had just lost his favorite knife.

Vladimir waved his hand in front of Jack's face, but the young man remained frozen. He looked at his neck for the chain that held the amulet but did not see it.

"What's the matter with them?" Louie asked.

"The beast is able to paralyze their bodies with his mind. Had you and I not been wearing our amulets, we would have been frozen as well," Vladimir said.

"But Jack has one of those necklaces. Why did he freeze?" Louie asked.

"He may have one, but it is not around his neck," Vladimir replied.

"Damn fool, kid!" Louie exclaimed.

"Help me throw him into the pool. The shock of the water ought to bring him out of it," Vladimir said, grabbing the young man by one of his arms.

"Stay right where you are!" Louie said when Jack came up out of the water sputtering.

"We're going to toss Whittaker in the water first, then Lopez. You make sure neither one of them drown."

Jabber had watched the entire event on the patio's cam screen. He called Nigel and let him know that they had just had an encounter with the creature on the patio, and that Louie and Vladimir were helping Jack, Lopez, and Whittaker at the pool.

Nigel already knew Goff was on the grounds. He had sensed the jogeth when it approached the house. He was standing in front of Hattie's and Marie's door, praying that he would be able to battle the beast with his mind should he get inside the house, and go after the women.

When Nigel saw Louie and Vladimir helping Whittaker and Lopez out of the pool, he grabbed some towels from the cabinet, and went over and handed them out to Jack and the FBI agents.

"Sorry about throwing you in the pool, but we were left with little choice," Louie said. "That creature froze you with his mind just like Jabber said he would."

"No need to apologize," Whittaker said with a shudder. "I saw everything that was happening, but I was not able to move. Those salivating teeth will haunt me for the rest of my life."

"Me too," Jack said, shivering beneath the towel.

Louie turned and frowned at the kid. "You are supposed to be wearing the necklace, Jack. What happened?"

"Well-uh, I took it off while I showered, and forgot to put it back on," Jack said.

"I guess you won't be doing that anymore, will you?" Louie asked.

"No, sir." Jack stated. "I am never going to take that necklace off again for the rest of my life. In fact, you can bury me in it."

"I did not bring you here to bury you. Remember that when you think about taking that necklace off again," Louie said. As angry with himself as he was with Jack. He too, had thought Jabber and Nigel were exaggerating the danger.

"Why is it you two were not affected by his mind control?" Lopez asked.

"We are wearing these necklaces," Louie said, holding up a dollar sized gold pendant with a compass star pattern impressed into it for Lopez and Whittaker to take a look at it. Nigel gave them to us."

Both FBI agents turned to look at Nigel.

"I have faced this type of supernatural being once before in Europe," Nigel began. "At the time, there was a man who knew how to fight it. He gave me a pendant that protects the wearer's mind from such a creature. With all the deaths that have recently happened I realized that we could yet be facing another of those beasts. I had a jeweler copy my pendant, and then handed one out to each person in the house. You and Whittaker are welcome to have your own amulet, but if you are not interested in keeping it around your neck, then don't bother asking me for one."

"I will take one," Lopez said, shivering from cold as he wrapped the towel around his body.

"Me too," Whittaker said. "And, I won't be taking it off." The FBI agent turned to look at Louie. "Thanks for saving me, man."

"You would do the same," Louie stated.

Whittaker shook his head. "No, I wouldn't. I don't know how to throw a knife like that. I probably would have gone for my gun and shot the both of you."

"Yeah," Louie said, putting a hand to his chin as he thought about it. "You probably would have at that. However, you would have saved me from having my throat ripped out by a vampire. So, in my case, if it ever comes down to the both of us, do not hesitate to shoot."

Whittaker nodded and turned to look at Lopez.

"I would rather you learn how to throw a knife, Ace. I am in no hurry to die," Lopez said, shaking his head with a grin.

Everyone chuckled at those words.

"Come let's go into the house, and get you guys into some dry clothing," Nigel said.

"Jack, you probably have something that will fit Whittaker," Louie said. "And Lopez, you look to be about my size. Jack, get one of my sweat suits out of the closet and give it to him. I am going to stay here in case that creature comes back."

"Follow me, gentlemen," Jack said.

"I am going to fix us some tea and coffee to take to the office. It will help warm those who went into the water," Nigel told Louie and Vladimir.

Vladimir helped Nigel fill the cart with mugs, sugar, cream, and a couple of biscuit tins.

"He is faster than we realized, Louie," Vladimir said as he filled the cream pitcher. "He came from the back of the property, and it did not take him more than ten seconds to get to the pool."

Louie nodded. "Yeah, I know. It probably took us that long to get from the cam room to the pool.

Nigel stopped filling the infuser with tea leaves as an idea occurred to him. "What we need is something equivalent to a moat," he murmured.

"What?" Louie asked, not understanding the reference.

"Something to slow him down until help can arrive," Nigel answered. "The beasts do not like iron, it burns their skin. If I put iron bars on all the windows and entrances, and steel door frames on the front door, bedrooms, and office door, it may stop him long enough for you to get a shot at him."

"You know we were lucky tonight. If it had not been for Louie, Whittaker would be dead, and maybe the rest of us as well," Vladimir said, still shaken from the encounter.

"And if it had not been for your cameras, we would not have known he was out there in time to save Whittaker," Louie pointed out.

Vladimir made a face, but nevertheless nodded.

"He spoke to my mind tonight," Vladimir said, forcing himself to state what had happened between him and the beast.

"But you are wearing the amulet," Louie protested.

"Maybe so, but I still heard him."

"What did he say?" Nigel asked.

Vladimir's face hardened as he repeated the beast's words, "*Watch! This is how you will die.*"

Nigel's face paled. "It will remain to be seen whether he has gained enough power to get past the amulet's power or he has taken a special interest in you, Vladimir," he said choosing his words carefully.

Vladimir gave a slight nod of his head, letting Nigel know he understood that they could not speak of him being bitten by the beast in front of Louie.

"Well, the amulet worked enough to keep that thing from paralyzing me tonight, and that is what is important," Louie said.

"Yes, you are right, Louie," Nigel said as he filled two teapots with hot water, and put the infusers in. "Now, if you will put the coffee pot on the cart, Vladimir, we can go to the office."

* * *

With Louie's knife in his back, Goff blindly ran up the storm drain to get away. When he could no longer run, he stopped to pull the knife from his back. He then sat down and rested.

When the first light of dawn began to light up the sky, he knew he needed to find shelter, and started off again, but stopped as he spotted a brick building with no windows, inside a gated fence. He went through the unlocked gate and approached the building and read the bronze letters over the door "Grey Family Mausoleum."

Perfect, he thought as he ignored the layer of cobwebs covering door. He twisted the padlock until he heard a snap. He then tossed it over the fence into a patch of weeds and went inside. He found the building was empty except the brick stairs that went down into the crypt. He turned and bolted the door from the inside. Once that was done, he slumped down on the steps, and leaned against the door. He needed to sleep to renew his body.

Some hours later he wakened, not refreshed, but he had recovered enough to use the stair s. He found the vault was more than adequate to meet his needs. No more tree copses or sheds for him. He found it curious that the vault was carpeted, contained a sofa, a sitting chair, and two tables with oil lamps on them. The leather book with a cross that lay atop one of the tables was just as dusty as the lamps, and the rest of the furniture. *Yet another sign, the vault does not have many visitors*, he told himself. He found only one of the crypts had been used—the date of 1937, told him why no one had recently visited the vault. This world was now counting their years with two thousand, not nineteen.

Goff did not worry about being discovered. If someone did come visit the grave, he would simply use his mind to erase all knowledge of his presence.

He used one of the lacy mats that covered the tables and wiped the dust and webs off the sofa. Once that was done, he gingerly laid down. Before he fell asleep, he plotted his revenge on those who had hurt him. Not tonight, but soon, he would pay another visit to Terin's house. This time he would go through the front door. Then he would take one of the women. He knew where they slept. He would not take Bella. She had *scrang disease* from the bite he had given her. He should have killed her and the boy all those years ago, but at the time, he needed and wanted the villagers to believe it was those within the castle that were killing the young girls. Now, all he wanted was revenge. He would make Terin pay for trapping him in that underground vault. When he woke, he had been covered with webs. He hated spiders.

I will take one of the two sisters that he watches over, he gloated with a sneer on his face. *And when I have finished killing everyone in that house, I will then feed on Terin's blood.*"

Chapter 18
Iron Bars

Hattie heard someone calling her name and opened her eyes. She groggily looked up to see Nigel standing there looking at her. She glanced over at the clock on the nightstand, and saw it was ten after six. She sat up. "What's the matter?" she asked.

"Nothing at the moment, but I need you both to get an early start this morning as I plan on having work crews in here by eight o'clock," Nigel answered.

"Doing what?" Marie asked as she removed her eye mask and glared at Nigel.

"They are going to be putting bars on the windows, and steel doors and frames on the bedroom doors."

"Why?"

"Because we found out last night, we are not going to be able to stop the beast from attacking those inside this house unless we do more to protect ourselves."

"He was here!" Hattie and Marie exclaimed in unison, sitting up in bed.

"Yes, he attacked one of the FBI agents. If Louie had not been here, the man would be dead."

Nigel held a hand up when both women started asking questions. "We can discuss it over breakfast. Right now I need to go wake Jennifer and Bella."

That said, Nigel turned and walked out shutting the bedroom door behind him. Once he was in the hallway, he stopped and pulled out his phone.

"Rick, it is me, Nigel Quinn. I need the doors and frames put in as soon as possible. I am also going to need iron work installed outside on all the windows, but with a certain design. Do you have someone that can do that?"

"Yes, I believe I do. When do want us to start?" Rick asked.

"Yesterday, would have been good, but I will take today," Nigel answered.

"The doors and frames will not be a problem as I have a local supplier," Rick said.

"What about the window bars? I need those as soon as possible too."

"Joe Garcia does all my iron work. He has his own shop and is good at what he does. A custom design should not be a problem. I will give him a call and have him meet us at the house. You do realize that it may take him several weeks to finish all the windows and entrances. There is sixty feet of glass windows and doors just in the patio area," Rick said as he looked at the figures on his notepad.

"I know," Nigel said. "Hire however many men you need to get the job done. Tell Joe there is a five grand bonus in it for him to get the windows in two of the bedrooms done by tomorrow. That ought to get him moving."

"You do realize this is going to up the estimate I gave you. If I have to pay bonuses, and overtime, that adds up in a hurry," Rick said.

Nigel knew the estimate Rick had made a few days ago was not going to pay for the job that he was now requesting.

"I will give you a check today that should cover most of it, and a separate check to cover whatever Joe estimates will be needed. If you need more, let me know. Otherwise, you can give me a final bill when you finish."

"Thanks, Nigel. I appreciate that you understand the costs involved for the project."

Nigel ended the call, turned around, and knocked on the bedroom door to wake Jennifer.

* * *

Hattie ate her toast and sipped on her tea as she listened to Nigel tell them what had happened last night. "I want to watch that footage myself," she told Nigel.

"Just so you both know, it is disturbing to watch," Nigel warned.

"Marie and I, need to see the beast for our self, so we know what we are up against, Nigel," Hattie declared.

"Yes, you are probably right about that. I will have Lee get it ready as he is working the cam screens this morning. We can watch it together, but we will do it after lunch as I have a meeting with the contractors in a few minutes. Just keep in mind, any questions that you have will have to wait. We cannot discuss the beast nor the past in front of the others."

Nigel saw Marie cast a quick glance at Hattie. He knew that look. "What have you done this time, Marie?" he questioned.

Marie sighed. "Sorry, Nigel. I told Jabber all about us years ago when we all lived in New York. That is why he came when I told him we were in danger." When she saw Nigel frowning at her, she added, "Jabber is not only my best friend, he is family, Nigel. I love him dearly. And he loves me back. I know that because just before he left New York, he told me that even though, I am years older than him, I will always be the daughter he never had."

Nigel heard the emotion in Marie's voice. "I see. In that case, I will invite Jabber to our meeting. If something happens to me, you will need him."

Both Hattie and Marie were shocked by his statement.

Nigel held his hands up to quiet them. "Like you, I am old, but in this body, even older. That limits my ability to battle Goff. I am hoping Bravo Team will be able to take him down enough for Vladimir and me to rid the world of him.

119

Now, sit here, and finish your breakfast. I will go find Jabber and let him know what's up."

"But, Nigel, you have not told us where the meeting will be?" Marie questioned.

Nigel turned around and smiled sheepishly. "Yeah, I guess I forgot that part. How about we have it in Marie's studio?" We will not get interrupted there."

* * *

After breakfast, Vladimir went to his penthouse apartment to get some clothing, and other things he would for need for his stay at Hattera Lane. He then went downtown to his office to check on his own security teams and sign the never ending flow of paperwork that his business produced.

It was past noon when he returned to Hattera Lane, he was not surprised to see several construction trucks blocking the drive. One was loaded with metal doors and frames, and one with ladders, toolboxes, and assorted other gadgets for construction. He passed four pickup trucks before he found room enough to park his car but did not complain. He knew the men who came in those trucks were here to make the house safer for the women.

He found Bella in the living room, sitting in a recliner reading a book. He walked over, leaned down, and gave her a kiss on the cheek. "I did not know you liked mysteries," he said when he noted the book's title.

"It is a book that has a cat who narrates the story, and who helps his mistress find the murderer. Hattie brought it to me. She says she has four books of the same series. Also the setting is London in the 1960s, my favorite time and place."

"In that case, I may have to read it as well," he said as he sat in one of the chairs that faced hers.

"I hope you do. It is an enjoyable tale."

"Where's Jennifer?" Vladimir asked.

"She went to the market with Hattie and Marie. They should be back anytime. Nigel has been keeping me company, but one of the construction men came got him a few minutes ago. Kate has been in here twice asking if I need anything," Bella answered. "I am well taken care of."

"A bit noisy with all the hammering going on inside," Vladimir said, wincing as a power saw powered on inside the house.

Bella grinned at the sour look on Vladimir's face. "It reminds me of the time, we had the parlor remade when we lived in Paris."

Vladimir chuckled at her words. "Yes, I think you had them move the fireplace three times."

Bella laughed. "At the time, it seemed the thing to do. Now, thinking back on it, I was a bit daft about it, wasn't I?"

"Yes, you were," Vladimir replied, grinning at her.

When Bella went back to her book, Vladimir sat back in his chair and watched her read. He smiled as he noted Bella's cheeks had some color in them.

"Why are you looking at me like that?" Bella asked when she looked up from her book.

"Just grateful that you are healing so well. Two weeks ago, you could hardly stay awake, and now, here you are, sitting there reading with the sparkle back in your eyes."

Bella laid her book down, nodded, and then yawned. "That said, I think I am ready for a nap."

Vladimir rose from his chair and took the book out of her hands. "I will sit here and read this while you rest."

"Don't you have more important things to do?"

"Nothing is more important than being here with you," Vladimir said as he tucked the lap robe beneath her feet.

"Thank you, my feet were feeling a bit chilled," Bella murmured as she closed her eyes.

When Vladimir saw her face relax as she fell asleep, he sat back down in the chair and opened the book.

* * *

Earl set in front of the big screen watching the footage of last night's attack. Like Jack, he had believed the talk about a vampire hunting people was a joke. He would not make that mistake again. He had kept the necklace around his neck at all times, even when he took a shower, but that was not due to fear of being attacked. No, he did it because Louie told him to keep it on twenty-four seven. He had learned in Iraq, discipline made all the difference in whether you lived or died. That was the second rule he lived by. The first rule, was always carry a weapon, which he did.

He watched the scene again. The creature turned to look at Louie and Vladimir with a sneer of disdain on its face as they ran toward it. Then it opened its mouth and started to take a bite out of Whittaker's throat. Louie, in one fluid motion, switched gun hands, grabbed his knife, and threw it as he ran past Jack, and did it all within the blink of an eye.

Earl watched the knife sink in the creature's back, all the way to the hilt. He knew, anything living would have died right then and there, but it was plain to see, the creature did not die. Instead, it gave a high pitched scream, dropped Whittaker, and ran off. The knife did not seem to slow it down any either as within a few seconds, it made it to the flood wall, jumped over it, and disappeared.

Like the rest of Delta Team, Earl had a knife hanging off his belt. But when he asked himself if he would have figured out to use it in time to save the FBI agent? He knew the answer was negative, and made a sour face at that thought.

"What's the matter?" Jabber asked as he came walking in and saw the frown on Earl's face.

"Just thinking that I am never going to be as good as Louie, when it comes to defensive moves."

"Well, if it makes you feel any better, you are wrong about that. You got your own set of skills that none of the rest of us have. Together, we make a team."

"I am not scared of a fight. You know that, Jabber. But, the thought of ending up as vampire food scares me."

"If you didn't feel scared, I would start to worry. Face it, Earl, we are dealing with something completely unnatural. Something that comes from another time and place. And something that will not hesitate to kill anyone and everyone. We are at war, son, whether the rest of the world knows it or not."

"Thanks, Jabber, but if I do get killed, I want to be cremated. Then I would like you to put the amulet and a cross inside the box with my ashes, and bury me somewhere, on your ranch. I don't want to come back as something unnatural."

Jabber was both surprised and saddened by Earl's words. On every op Bravo Team accepted, they stood a good chance of dying—that came with the job. As for the Afterlife, he had learned many years ago to leave that part up to God.

"Good point. I would hope you all will do the same for me if it comes down to that. However, dying nowadays, takes paperwork. I think I had better go find Nigel. We need a lawyer to put all that in writing. Otherwise, the only say a person has when someone dies, is to tell them goodbye."

* * *

Marie changed into her one of her painting outfits—an older pair of black pants and a red t-shirt stained with paint—and headed for her studio. She was working on Louie's portrait.

Hattie followed along behind her. She wanted to see the painting. She had caught Marie staring at the man several times when she thought no one was looking. There was no mistaking the look on her face. Her sister was falling for Bravo Team's leader.

As she stood before the painting looking at the glint in the one eye Marie had finished, she asked the question she had been wanting to ask for several days. "Has Louie ever said anything about his wife?"

"I am not married," Louie said, overhearing Hattie's question as he entered the room. "Had a wife once. But on my first tour in Iraq, I got one of those Dear Louie letters, and the divorce papers a few months later. I signed them and have never looked back."

Hattie turned around and grinned at the man.

Marie's cheeks flamed in embarrassment as she pretended to hunt for a brush.

"I'm sorry. I mean, about prying into your life, Louie. Well, I guess, I am sorry about your divorce too," Hattie added, doing her best to look contrite.

"No need to be sorry, Hattie. I am not. It was the best thing for both of us," Louie said, his eyes on Marie.

"Well, I know Marie is anxious to work on her painting, so I think I will go check on Bella. I have not had time to talk with her today," Hattie said, noting the look on Louie's face as he stared at Marie.

This could get interesting, she thought with a satisfied smile on her lips.

Once Hattie left the room, Marie turned to look at Louie. "I apologize if she embarrassed you, but I don't apologize for her. My sister often thinks she needs to protect me, and of course, I often let her."

"No apologies needed. I got one just like her at home. Should I take you there, she would be asking the same kind of questions. That is what sisters are for," Louie said as he took his place in front of the white screen, Marie was using for a temporary background.

Marie nodded but did not reply. Instead, she picked up her brush and dabbed it in the splotch of burnt umber she had put on her palette. She then swiped a bit of rose madder, yellow ochre, and white into the mix. She adjusted the colors until she got the skin tone she was looking for, and then put a tender brush stroke just above the eye she was working on to put some depth into the eyelid.

Chapter 19
Tin Foil Hats?

"The walls are a mess, but the steel doors are in place on all the bedrooms, and there are temporary bars installed on Bella's and Hattie's bedroom windows. Joe suggested they do that while they make new panels with the amulet design on them. Of course, the house will have to be repainted, inside and out when they finish the job," Nigel told Vladimir who was sitting on the other side of the kitchen table, eating another late dinner.

Vladimir nodded but said nothing.

Nigel stared at the man he had helped raise. "You want to tell me what it is that is bothering you."

Vladimir started to shake his head, but then decided if anyone else needed to know Bella's plight, it was Nigel. He could die before he could erase Bella's mind. He set his fork down.

"Bella was raped when she was attacked," he said, doing his best to ignore the pain the words caused him.

"Ah! I am sorry, lad. For the both of you," Nigel said, his own eyes growing moist at the thought of the violence one of his children had suffered.

"Yes, it pains me too, Papa," Vladimir said, reverting to the name he had used as a boy for the man sitting across the table.

Nigel too emotional to speak, nodded.

"Anyway, I promised to erase it from her mind when she gets well enough to do so. But as life is precarious right now, and I may not be here when the time comes. I would like you to take care of it for me if that happens."

"I give you my word, it will be so," Nigel said.

"Can you do it without her knowing that you know? She does not want others to know."

"Aye, if it comes to that, I will remove that part of the attack from her memory, and any other memories associated with the rape, but leave the actual attack of the robbery and beating, so that her memories of her subsequent life are not destroyed."

Vladimir's face showed his distress.

"What's wrong?" Nigel questioned.

"I had planned on just wiping her memory of the entire event. It did not occur to me what problems that would cause."

Nigel sighed. "How many times have you had to erase something from her memory?"

"None. Why?"

"Be glad. I have had to erase a couple of things from Hattie's and Marie's memories to protect them. And each time I did, I worried whether it would cause more harm than good. Erasing memories can have dire consequences. That said, I can also wipe your mind of the memory as well."

"I thought about asking you to do that, but should she have residual problems in the future, I will need to know what happened to her to better understand how to help her."

Nigel nodded. "A wise choice."

Vladimir rose from the table. "I think I will go lay down for a bit. I am tired," he said.

"I think I will go sit with Whittaker and Jack. They are manning the cams tonight. By the way, Whittaker has decided he might give up smoking as it could kill him sooner, rather than later," Nigel said, his eyes sparkling with humor as he picked up a bag of beef jerky lying on the table.

"Yes it could, being you have to go outside to smoke," Vladimir agreed.

"That is why I am taking him something to chew on."

* * *

Hattie read the headline, then sighed heavily. "Another young woman was killed last night. 'Hollywood Vampire' is the headline," she said, showing Marie the newspaper's front page.

"How many does that make now?"

"Thirteen in the past two weeks, And, not one witness or clue, according to the reporter," Hattie said as she passed the newspaper over to Marie.

The blue phone on the table rang.

Marie put the paper down and looked at Hattie. "Don't answer it," she said.

Hattie gave her sister a shake of her head before she picked up the phone. "Hattie Drake," she said.

"Miss Drake, this Police Commissioner Harris Burbank. I was hoping I could stop by your office today and talk to you."

"I do not have a public office, Commissioner. I work out of my home. However, I can you meet you at *Rancini's* for lunch. One o'clock would be good for me."

"A little too public for me, Miss Drake. Everyone knows who I am, and most know who you are. They would be sure to put two and two together and come up with the desperation I am feeling right now."

"In that case, I could stop by your office about eleven, and then go on to *Rancini's* for lunch," Hattie said. "My sister will be with me as she is the intuitive one. My expertise is more a psychic one."

"Right now, I will take all the help I can get. I will see you at eleven," Burbank said.

"Right. We will be there," Hattie replied before she hung the phone up.

"Who was that, and where are we going?"

"That was Police Commissioner Harris Burbank," Hattie answered.

"Hmph!" Marie exclaimed. "So, now I am intuitive, huh?"

"Among other things," Hattie replied, "You always have been. It is why you have your dreams."

"Ah, I never thought about in that light. You could be right, but there is no stopping that beast by dreaming, he can control minds."

"I have been thinking about that. We use the amulet to protect our minds. But what else could be used to block his ability to control minds?"

When nothing came to mind, Marie shook her head. "I don't know."

"Neither do I, but I do have an idea, and with Vladimir's help, I should be able to find out if it works," Hattie said, reaching for her smart phone.

Vladimir listened to Hattie's theory, and how she wanted to test it.

"I can do that, but you will have to take off your amulet as it may block my mind.

"Go get the aluminum foil, Marie!" Hattie commanded softly.

"Oh, the things one must do when related to a sleuthing genius," Marie said as she rose from her chair, raised a hand to one brow, and looked off into the distance, mimicking one of her favorite silent film stars.

Vladimir laughed at her antics as he walked up. "You should paint that pose, Marie."

"Yes. You should," Hattie agreed. "But right now, go get the foil so Vladimir can test my theory."

Hattie gasped when she felt Vladimir's mind take control of hers.

"You must keep in mind, Hattie, that I can just as easily slip into your mind, and erase any knowledge that I was ever there," Vladimir explained as he released his hold on her.

"Oh!" Hattie exclaimed. "I had forgotten how that feels."

"Yes, it is invasive. I now, only use my ability as a defensive weapon, and I make sure to erase all memory of my presence."

"Isles found the tin foil for me," Marie said as she came back from the kitchen. She laid the box of foil in front of Hattie.

Hattie reached for it and unrolled several feet. She then began wrapping it around her head. When she finished, she decided it was not enough, and wrapped another long sheet around her head.

"Now, Vladimir. See if you can take control of my mind."

Vladimir was surprised to find he could not. It was the first time anyone had blocked his abilities. "You are brilliant, Hattie! I cannot break through the foil."

"Good. Now that we have determined this, I need you to come with me to the Commissioner's office and conduct the same experiment on him."

"I cannot do that, Hattie," Vladimir said, shocked she would consider exposing him to the rest of the world. He shook his head. "No one, but family can know about my abilities."

"Yes, I know that. But in this case, you will go as my telepathic friend *Professor Albert Bolshek*, from Prague. With your abilities to control minds, you should be able to have the Commissioner, and anyone with him, see you as an elderly man with bushy gray hair, and a beard, wearing thick glasses."

"You could use the old man in my painting for a model," Marie offered, pointing at one of her paintings. "Just add the beard."

Vladimir looked at the painting she pointed to and nodded. "How's this?" He asked as he gently entered Marie's mind and altered his perception of him to that of the old man in her painting with a beard and glasses.

When Marie gasped, he grinned.

"That's incredible!" she exclaimed. "Hattie's plan might work after all."

"Of course, it will work. Or elsewise, I would not have thought of it," Hattie stated with a grin as she rose from the table. "Which reminds me, we will need to stop by the market on our way and pick up a new box of tin foil. Now, I need to go get dressed. Meet you back here at ten o'clock, Vladimir. That should give us time to stop at the store, and still get to Commissioner's office by eleven."

"Make sure you wear something flamboyant, so the entire office will focus on you, and not on Vladimir," Marie called out.

Marie laughed when she saw Vladimir looking at her with a puzzled look on his face. "Hattie completely changes character when she goes into detective mode," she explained. "I was just making light of her habit of wearing outfits with polka dots or flowers that can be seen a half mile away."

"You two, continue to amaze me," Vladimir said with a chuckle as he gave Marie a fond look.

"Hattie always amazes me with her detective business. She often comes up with bizarre answers, or at least, ones I would never have guessed—like the tin foil. But she is right, you know? The foil does seem to work."

"Yes, apparently it does," Vladimir agreed.

* * *

Marie studied Harris Burbank. She had seen his face many times in the newspaper or on the TV, but none of that had prepared her for the inner strength she felt when he shook her hand. He was obviously, in his mid-fifties, but his gray hair and mustache made him look distinguished, not old.

"You cannot be serious," Burbank said when Hattie finished telling him of her plan.

"I expected you to be skeptical, Commissioner. That is why I invited, Professor Bolshek to come with me.

Fortunately, he had some free time before his plane leaves for Paris. He is telepathic and will give you a demonstration."

Burbank looked at the elderly gentleman sitting on the other side of his desk.

"First, you must realize that in Europe, Commissioner Burbank, we have dealt with creatures of this nature several times over the span of a half-dozen centuries," Vladimir said. "The film industry in America has made it all look like a myth, but I can assure you, the vampire does exist," "Why just last year, in Europe there were dozens of similar murders in a half dozen different countries, including Transylvania, the original home of Dracula."

"Dracula!" Burbank scoffed. "Good God, man! You cannot expect me to believe that he existed in real life."

"In life, no," Vladimir countered, raising a hand for emphasis as he was starting to enjoy his role. "He is not a living creature like us. It is believed that he comes from another world. You can shoot him, but only a wooden stake can stop him or so they say. No one living has been able to claim victory against such a creature."

Hattie allowed Burbank to sputter a protest before she interrupted him. "Commissioner, I am fully aware that what we are telling you, and what we propose you do to stop the beast, sounds incredible. But do keep in mind, you have asked for my help. The least you can do, is to allow the professor to demonstrate what happens to the victims and witnesses at the time of the attacks."

"All right, you can run your test, but I want a couple of my deputies in here to witness what it is you do to me."

Hattie smiled sadly at the man. "You may bring in as many people as you like. It will make no difference for the test."

Burbank flipped a switch, and told his secretary to send Yanno and Sievers in.

When the two police officers had been apprised of the situation, and were ready to witness the test, Burbank gave the elderly professor permission to start.

Burbank tried to move when he felt the other man's mind inside his brain but found himself paralyzed. He made a small noise of relief when he felt the presence leave, and he was able to blink again.

He looked up at his men. "What did you see," he asked.

"Nothing, Commissioner. You just sat there staring at us."

Burbank looked at the box of tin foil. "Oh, what the hell!" he exclaimed as he opened the box and pulled out a several feet of foil.

"Best you put one more sheet around your head, Commissioner. That is how I did it," Hattie said.

Burbank tore another large sheet from the roll and wrapped that around his head.

"Again, professor," he said irritably once he had wrapped the second sheet around his head.

This time Vladimir found himself blocked from the man's mind. He strained as hard as he could and found he could not penetrate the Commissioner's mind. He was glad he had previously placed a command in Burbank's mind that he was an elderly professor. He sat back in his chair and shook his head. "I cannot reach your mind," he said.

Burbank tore the aluminum off his head. "Now, see if you can get inside my head."

Vladimir nodded, and smoothly slipped inside the man's mind. "*I am here with you,*" he said, speaking with his mind as he used his power to freeze the Commissioner's body.

He held the man frozen for a few more seconds before he left.

Burbank felt a cold shiver run down his spine as he realized everything Hattie Drake had told him was true.

"I thank you, Miss Drake for your information. However, I have no clue as to how to get the citizens to wrap their heads in tin foil."

"That part is simple. Have your department and your officers start wearing military hard hats made of metal, like the soldiers do in combat areas. Then have them line the inside of the hat with tin foil as an added layer of protection. That will protect your officers. For the people, you will need to go on one of the morning shows and tell everyone why you have done so."

Burbank's eye bulged as he looked at the woman. "That is not going to happen," he stated emphatically. "Why, it would cause pandemonium, if not a stampede. Also, you have to realize they would put me in a straight jacket before I could get back out the studio's front door for being psychotic."

"Commissioner, I do not have the time to stay here and convince you of the monster you are dealing with. However, a short visit to Miss Drake's house, may help you understand. She has something you need to see. It is an attack on an FBI agent, night before last, on her patio. It may help you in the days to come," Vladimir said.

Burbank frowned at the trio sitting there looking at him, with disappointment on their faces. He found himself nodding his head, but only because he wanted to head off a possible leak to the press by Hattie Drake. He looked at his calendar. "I can stop by tomorrow around ten, if that is suitable for you?"

"It is," Hattie said before she gave him instructions on how to find the house.

The Commissioner waited for his guests to leave before he looked at his officers. "Not a word of this to anyone! I will have your badges, understand?"

Both men nodded.

"Yanno, go tell Ford I want to see him! Not one word as to why I want to see him."

"Yes, sir," Yanno said, stopping long enough to eye the tin foil before he went out the door.

"Sievers, I want you to go through every report for the last three weeks. Look for any witnesses, drunks, addicts, or anyone that made bizarre statements about what they saw. We might be able to find a pattern in the deaths. Have Nora go over them with you. She is good at seeing what others do not. Let me know what you find. Tomorrow, both you, and Yanno will go with me to see that film."

"You might want to keep in mind, boss, that film can be faked," Sievers said.

"Yes, I know that, but I intend to talk to the FBI agent involved. If he is real, then we can assume the footage is real."

Sievers swallowed nervously at the thought of vampires actually existing, but confirmed he would have the car ready.

Chapter 20
Live Bait

Once the Commissioner had seen the film, and finished talking with Whittaker and Lopez, Nigel escorted him and the officers to the door.

"I wish to thank you, and your niece, Mr. Quinn. I think her idea will save lives, once I figure out the best way to use the tin foil to our advantage."

The two officers with him did not say anything as they followed their boss out the door.

Nigel noted the haunted look on all their faces. Goff's attack was bad enough to watch on one of the small grid screens, but on the office's big screen TV, it was a shock to the senses to see that mouth open wide, and those sharp teeth protrude as the jogeth prepared to rip Whittaker's throat out.

Nigel made his way back to the office where Hattie, Marie, and Vladimir sat in silence.

"You have passed the word along. You have done all you can do without jeopardizing your own lives," he consoled. "But Burbank is right when he says he cannot make a public statement about the killer being a vampire. No one would believe him."

Hattie looked toward the camera room. She saw Ox sitting there. She turned back to Nigel, a helpless look on her face.

Nigel saw the problem. "Marie, I would appreciate you showing me your painting of Louie, Hattie is quite impressed with it. Have you seen it, Vladimir?" he asked.

When Vladimir shook his head, Nigel invited him to come with them as well.

Once they all were in the studio, and the door locked, so that no one would overhear their conversation, Nigel told them to find something to sit on.

"Now, what was it you wanted to say, Hattie?" Nigel asked.

"Marie and I feel that we are partly responsible for the deaths, Nigel. For if we were not here in Hollywood, that beast would not be here," Hattie replied.

"You are wrong to think that. For no matter if you were in New York, Paris, London, Prague, it would make no difference. He would find us as he hunts for a way to go back to his kind. He believes I have that knowledge. So—the guilt is mine, not yours."

"Why do you say it that way, Nigel?" Marie asked.

"I do not know how he got here to this world, but I do know he believes I can open a portal that will allow him to bring his kind here."

"You have the ability to open a dimensional portal?" Vladimir asked.

"No, I did not open the portal by myself. The Dysonian elders helped me. I can only open jump portals which can take me short distances, like London to Paris, and back again. There is no going back to our home world."

"Then we need to find a way to lure him into a trap, Hattie said. "If I were to take my amulet off, would he come for me, Nigel?"

Marie gasped at the recklessness of her sister's question.

"The risk is too great, Hattie," Nigel answered. "You saw how fast he can move. He could grab you and be gone within seconds. There would be little we could do to stop him, without killing you too."

"Well, that answers that question," Hattie said as she saw them all gaping at her. "It was an idea, okay. It is not like I was not looking forward to using myself as bait."

"Bait!" Marie exclaimed angrily as she stood up and glared at her sister, tears in her eyes. "This is not a fishing contest, Hattie. This is a vampire that we are facing. Don't you dare get yourself killed!" With a sob, Marie ran out of the room.

Hattie was stunned by Marie's outburst. She swallowed painfully as she looked at Nigel and Vladimir. "I need to go talk to her," she said as she stood.

Both men nodded and watched her walk of the room.

"Her idea is a good one, Nigel. With a few adjustments, it could work," Vladimir said.

"I will not risk your life either, Vladimir."

"No, but I will. To begin with, I doubt he can control my mind, amulet or no amulet. I have had years to improve my abilities in that area. I can also levitate myself. That we have seen, he cannot fly. When he is within a few feet, I will simply fly off, and Bravo Team can open fire."

As Nigel opened his mouth to protest, Vladimir held up a hand. "I know what I am doing. I have faced the beast before."

"And lost," Nigel put in.

"Yes, but I was young and unprepared. This time, it will be different. He can no longer control my mind. I am confident of that. Also, I will be wearing a vest and body armor. That should protect me from bullets. If I cannot get away from him, Louie and the rest of them can shoot for the chest area. While it may render me unconscious, it will not kill me."

Nigel sat there thinking of all the things that could go wrong, and there were a lot of them. "I think we need to put the idea before Louie and Jabber," he said. "Combat is their field of expertise, not ours. They are the only ones who will truly know whether you can survive being shot at."

Vladimir nodded his head in agreement, then could not help but grin at Nigel's next statement.

"I just hope, they don't freak out when they find out you can fly."

* * *

Hattie found Marie in their bedroom, sitting on her bed, using a tissue to wipe away her tears. "I am sorry, Marie. I did not mean to upset you."

Marie put her hands over her face and began to cry again.

Hattie went to sit on the bed beside her. "What is wrong, Marie? It is not like you to cry like this."

Marie nodded. "I know, but..."

"But what?" Hattie asked when Marie did not continue.

"If something happens to you, Hattie, I will be alone."

"Nothing is going to happen to me. And if by chance it does, you will still have Nigel, Vladimir, Bella and Jennifer."

"They are not you." Marie wailed. "Every day since I can remember, you have been here with me. No one knows me like you do. You are the half of me that shines, and I am the half of me that basks in your light. Take that away, and all I have is darkness."

Hattie swallowed painfully. "As would I, if I were to lose you, Marie. Yet we both know that no one lives forever, do they?"

"I guess not, but maybe we ought to ask Nigel. Have you ever considered what will happen to us once we die, Hattie?"

"Before all this happened, never. Now it occupies my mind on a daily basis," Hattie answered.

Marie looked at her sister, grief on her face. "What do you think will happen if one or both of us die?"

"I try not to think about that."

"Have you asked, Nigel?"

"No."

"Why not?"

"Fear, I guess. The answer could change everything I know and think about my life, and this world."

"Why do you say it like that?" Marie asked as she felt the sadness in Hattie's mind.

"We have lived through life, death, famines, wars, and the death of our husbands, Marie, and yet, very little in our life changes, but the address. Death has always concerned someone else, not us. I have grown used to that. I don't want to learn at this late date, there is no afterlife for us here," Hattie said emotionally.

Ox had showered and was on his way to the kitchen when he passed by Hattie's room. The door was open, and he stopped as he saw the women sitting on one of the beds, holding on to each other. He could see they had been crying.

"Knock, knock," he said as he moved into the room. "Anything I can do to help?"

Marie saw Hattie's face brighten up as she looked at the man, and it brought a smile to her face. "I am just having a bad day," she said. "Hattie as usual, has been doing her best to cheer me up."

"Then, how about we all go out for lunch? My treat," Ox said.

Marie looked at Hattie, who was nodding her head.

"Good. "I will go see if Jabber wants to come with us. He could use a change of scenery as well. You girls can meet us at the door in about twenty minutes. How's that work for you?"

"Sounds good to me," Hattie said.

Marie nodded.

Once Ox was gone, Hattie rushed over to close the door. "What should I wear?" she asked, turning around to look at Marie.

"Hopefully, something a bit more sedate than that flower dress you wore to the Commissioner's office," Marie suggested with a grin.

Hattie laughed. "Okay, just because you are not feeling well, I will humor you. How about my white capri outfit with my jeweled sandals, and that little gold clutch I bought in Paris?"

"Good choice. I will wear my white capri outfit too, but with a red scarf, shoes and handbag."

"Then we had better get dressed," Hattie said as she reached into her closet for the capri set.

Chapter 21
An Evil Minded Visit

Lee stood at Nigel's side watching the men install the wrought iron panels in front of the patio windows. It felt good to be standing outside and feeling the sun's warmth on the back of his shirt. Without warning, the hair on the back of his neck rose. "We got company, he told Nigel."

"Yes, I can feel his presence also," Nigel said, looking toward the country club's trees that lined the back fence.

Lee used his comm unit to ask Earl if he was seeing anything on screen.

"Nothing moving on the matrix scanner or the cams," Earl said.

"Better get Louie and Jack up! He is out there, and if he moves in, we need to be ready," Lee said.

"Aye, I will let them know," Earl said.

"You say you can sense him?" Nigel questioned.

"Yeah, anytime, danger gets close, the hair on the back of my neck rises," Lee answered.

"Interesting."

"It has saved my life, several times over the years."

"Yes, I can see how it would," Nigel said as he looked around at the men working on the wrought iron panels.

He looked at his watch. It was a little after one. He walked over to where Joe stood holding onto a panel that was being welded.

"I know this sounds strange, but if I tell you, and your men to go inside the house, please do. As you well know, the reason we are installing these panels is because Marie is being stalked. We just got word the stalker was seen in the area."

Joe nodded, then hollered in Spanish for one of him men to bring another panel. The idea of a stalker in the vicinity did not bother him. Most celebrities had a fanatical fan or two. It was why business was good.

"If you need help, Nigel, my men can help you escort him off the property or sit on him until the police can get here," Joe said.

"Thanks, Joe," Nigel said. "The offer is appreciated, but Lee and the rest of Bravo Team are here to take care of trespassers. That is why I hired them. As you have seen they are armed. I just want to make sure, you, and your men are safe if it comes down to a fight."

"Ah, I see. Then as you say, we will go wait in the kitchen if you deem, we need to go."

Nigel next called Vladimir, who was downtown at his office.

"We have not seen any movement on the matrix screen, but he is somewhere in the trees behind the club's fence."

"Tell Jennifer to lock down their room. I don't want Bella wandering around. He may be able to communicate with her, regardless of the amulet she wears because, like me, she has been bitten by him."

"Hmm. You may be right about that," Nigel agreed.

"l will get there as soon as I can," Vladimir said, ending the call.

"Stay alert, Lee. I will be right back," Nigel said.

Jack and Louie passed Nigel in the kitchen. Both packed semi-automatic rifles and had ammunition belts slung around their shoulders.

Nigel found Jennifer sitting in a chair in the living room reading a book. He explained what he needed her to do.

Jennifer's face paled. "Mother is in the kitchen. Didn't you see her?"

Nigel turned and ran back into the kitchen. "Isles have you seen Bella?" he asked when he did not see her.

"Not since lunch," Isles answered.

"Earl!" Nigel called out, using his headpiece. "Do you see Bella anywhere on the cam screens"

"Yes, she is sitting on the steps at the front door. No, wait, she just got up, and is walking toward the side of the house."

Nigel turned and ran back through the house. Jennifer ran after him.

He went out the front door and saw Bella standing on the sidewalk looking off into the distance.

"You need to come back in the house," he told her as he took her arm.

"Nigel, I am so glad you are here. Jennifer wants me to go look at the roses she found growing out back by the gardener's cottage, but I don't seem to have the strength to get there. Maybe, you can help me."

"That is not Jennifer speaking to you, Bella. It is the beast."

Bella's eyes rolled upward, and she fell against him.

Jennifer cried out when she saw her mother begin to fall. She ran to help Nigel. Between the both of them, they managed to lay her gently on the grass.

Nigel got on his headphone and asked Jack to come help them. He then sent Jennifer to get the wheelchair.

"*She is very weak, Terin. Why is that?*" Goff asked.

Nigel stiffened. "*She may be ill, Goff, but I am not,*" he replied.

"*Yet, I note the stress in your mind. Good. That tells me that you fear me.*"

"*I do not fear you, beast. Show yourself, and I will put you to sleep again,*" Nigel taunted.

"*You will not conquer me so easily this time. I know your abilities, and you will not be using that trick on me again.*"

"*And I know all about you, as well,*" Nigel countered.

"*Yes, and now that we have that settled, I need to go and get my rest. I have a lot to do tonight.*"

Nigel felt Goff's presence leave his mind.

Jack bent down and picked up Bella. She was so thin he could feel her ribs. He wondered what she was doing outside but did not ask. When he turned around, he saw Jennifer hurrying toward them with the wheelchair. He shook his head. "I will carry her back to your room. It will better than trying to get her in and out of that chair. Since she is unconscious and cannot tell us if we bend her the wrong way," he explained.

"I will go open the door," Jennifer said as she pushed the chair over on the grass and left it there. She then ran to open the door.

Nigel stayed where he was. He knew Goff would not attack them this afternoon. He also knew Vladimir would be here shortly, and he wanted to talk to him privately.

When he saw Jabber's king cab pickup enter the driveway, he sighed. He was going to have to tell Hattie and Marie the jogeth had once again visited them.

When the truck stopped, Louie and Jabber both got out with weapons in hand. Nigel realized Earl must have alerted them to Goff's presence.

"It is safe for the moment. I believe he is gone," Nigel said.

"Why are you here outside, alone?" Hattie asked.

"The beast got to Bella. She came outside, but thankfully was too weak to walk toward the back fence. Jack just took her back to her bedroom. I am waiting for Vladimir. He should be here anytime."

"We had better go see if we can help, Hattie. Jennifer will be upset," Marie said.

"Thank you for lunch, Ox," Hattie said.

"Yes. Thank you for taking us to lunch, Ox. It was nice to get out. Jabber I will see you later," Marie called out as she hurried to catch up with Hattie.

All three men stood and watched the women enter the house.

When Ox saw Jabber put his gun away, he slipped his pistol back into holster he wore around one shoulder. "Life around here must never be dull," he murmured. "One a painter—one a detective—and both beautiful."

Jabber saw the look on Ox's face and grinned but said nothing. Love was not a subject he joked about.

"You got that right, Ox," Nigel said, watching Hattie and Marie enter the house.

He did not see what Jabber saw. Ox was falling in love with Hattie.

"Well, we had better go check in with Louie, and let him know we are back," Jabber said, slapping his friend on the back.

"Yeah," Ox agreed as he walked over and grabbed hold of the wheelchair. "I will take this back in. Bella will need it."

"Looks like Vladimir has arrived," Jabber said, turning his head to look at the car moving toward them. "I will be in the cam room if you need me, Nigel."

"Thanks for taking the girls to lunch, Jabber."

"That was not my idea, Nigel. Ox was the one that planned the outing when he found Marie and Hattie sitting in their room. They had been crying."

"Ah, yes, there was a misunderstanding this morning between the girls."

Jabber looked at Nigel, his brow going up.

"Hattie had an idea to use herself as vampire bait."

"Ah, I can see how that would upset Marie," Jabber said.

"Yes, but Vladimir has decided the idea has merit, and now wants to be the bait," Nigel added.

Jabber shook his head at that news. "Then, I will go on inside, and give you time to try and talk him out of it."

Nigel turned off his comm unit before he told Vladimir what had happened to Bella.

When Vladimir started to go inside," he put an arm out to stop him. "Jabber, Hattie and Marie have gone to check on her. We need to talk as there is more you need to know. While I was standing here waiting for you to arrive, Goff spoke to my mind."

"I guess the amulet does not stop him from communicating with us," Vladimir stated.

"Yes, it seems so. Though in both cases, he was not trying to control our minds. He tricked Bella by pretending to be Jennifer."

"What did he tell you?" Vladimir asked.

"He bragged about how he would beat me the next time we meet."

"And?" Vladimir asked when he saw Nigel was avoiding his eyes.

Nigel sighed. It was time had come for him to confess. He turned his comm unit back on. "Earl, I will be back in about an hour. Vladimir is taking me to the market," he said before he turned off his headphone again.

When he saw Vladimir looking at him, Nigel shook his head. "Walls have ears," he said, keeping his voice down.

Nigel waited until they were on the road before he spoke. "I have told you that I can change forms, but what I have not told you is that when I defeated Goff, I changed into a jogeth, and battled him with all the strength of his own kind. Even so, I barely won, but he does not know that. Now, he states that he will be ready for me this time. What he also does not know, is that I am unable to repeat that ability. It almost killed me to regain human form. That is why I am relying on Jabber's team to take him down."

Vladimir kept his eyes on the road as he listened. "Then it is more important than ever for us to go ahead with the plan of using me to lure him in."

"Yes, the plan is a good one, but I will be the bait. He has challenged me, and he expects me to confront him."

When Vladimir protested, Nigel raised his hand. "One of us, must remain alive to take care of the girls.

"If we both go out there, Bravo Team will save at least one of us, Nigel. I have that much faith in them. Think about it, if the beast goes for you first, I can levitate. When that distracts him, you fall to the ground, and let Bravo Team do their work."

Nigel thought about that. "Yes that could work. I will stand at the far end of the pool, and you stand at the other end. That way, he has to choose one of us. He does not know you can levitate, and it is sure to startle him long enough for me to fall on the ground. He will not be expecting that. If for some reason, he does go for you, first, I will send an energy burst at him, and he will think that I am once again, changing form. That should distract him long enough for you to get airborne, and for me to fall on the ground."

"An energy burst?"

"Yes, it would be similar to a telepathic shout."

"When this is over, you will have to teach me that trick."

"Will do. You can pull in at that bakery. We only need bread."

"Good because I would like to get back home, and check on Bella," Vladimir said.

Nigel smiled as he realized Vladimir had called Hattera Lane *home*.

Chapter 22
A Wax Job

Louie was not enthusiastic about the plan. "That creature can move fast," he said. "Fast enough to tear out your throat before we can get a shot at it. From what I saw, the only thing that saved Whittaker was the fact that the vampire believed he could freeze us like he did Jack, and therefore, he felt he was in no danger. He now knows his mind control does not work on all of us. He will not hesitate next time, and that makes him all the more dangerous."

Nigel made a face. "What would you suggest we do?" he asked.

"What we need to do is go to the nearest wax museum," Jack blurted out.

"This is no time to be funny, Jack," Jabber scolded.

"I am not trying to be funny. I was thinking, if we could get the museum to make a wax dummy of Nigel, we could set it out by the pool instead."

"What the hell do I know about wax dummies?" Jabber sputtered when he saw everyone in the room was looking at him.

"We had them make us a wax figure to use as bait for a serial killer, last year," Whittaker said.

"Did it work?" Jabber asked. When both Lopez and Whittaker nodded, he added, "Then it might be worth a try, since we need to get him close enough to shoot him without Nigel being in the line of fire."

"I will need to be within a few feet of the dummy," Nigel said. "The jogeth can sense a mind even if he cannot control it."

"Your pool has a surge pit. I saw the pool man open the door on it yesterday," Ox said. "There is probably enough room for you to hide in there. The dummy could go into a chair placed on top of the door. The rest of us can hide behind the construction debris."

"That might work for me, but it will not work for you," Nigel said. "Goff will sense your presence."

"Not if they wear tin foil hats on their heads," Vladimir said, recalling his visit with Commissioner Burbank.

"We brought our armor helmets," Earl said, as he went to one of the cabinets, and brought out a helmet.

"Put it on and I will see if it works," Vladimir said.

"Are you some kind of mind reader?" Earl asked as he stuck the hat on his head.

"Something like that," Vladimir answered as he used his mind to enter Earl's.

"Damn! That was eerie," Earl said with a shudder when Vladimir released him.

"Let me go get some tin foil," Nigel said.

"We got some here," Jabber said, walking over to another cabinet. "When Marie told me about the tin foil trick you used at the Commissioner's office, I bought a dozen boxes in case we needed them. Of course, you know that the foil is actually made of aluminum nowadays, despite what we all call it. I looked it up on the internet, and aluminum foil does block radio waves. I guess we can now include telepathic communication as well."

Jabber grabbed a box of tin foil and opened it.

Once Earl had lined the helmet, he stuck it back on his head.

Vladimir tried to enter the man's mind but found himself blocked. "The foil works, Nigel. I could not sense his presence or enter his mind."

Louie eyed the box of foil in Jabber's hand. "I cannot believe I am going to have to wear aluminum foil wrapped around my head, like that *damn fool* alien hunter that ran around Sedona, a few years back," he complained.

"You have seen worse," Jabber said.

"What could be worse?" Louie questioned, flinging his hands out in disgust.

"Well, it is not a hundred and twenty degrees outside. There is no sand or scorpions in your boots. And your pay grade is way above a hundred dollars a day."

Louie opened his mouth to argue the point, but shut it as he realized Jabber was right, Afghanistan, and Iraq were worse. "Okay, you made your point, alien hunter it is" he conceded as he took the box of tin foil out of Jabber's hand. "I will go line my helmet. I suggest the rest of you do too," he stated gruffly before he walked out the door.

* * *

Nigel had never been to a wax museum before and was surprised by the lifelike appearance of the mannequins that were on display. However, he was amazed by the work that was going on in the studio where the various statues were created. Several women were inserting strands of hair, one by one, on the molded heads of a famous rock group. Another was bearding the face of what appeared to President Lincoln.

"Last week, a man used a pair of scissors to cut Lincoln's beard off," Christopher—the young man with brown curly hair that was going to make a mold of Nigel's head—explained when he saw Nigel watching the repair job. "You would be surprised at some of the problems we have with visitors. Despite all the signs that tell our visitors not to touch the exhibits, they still wreak what havoc they will."

"How long will this take?" Lopez asked, looking away from the woman repairing the beard, and back at Christopher.

"To get a mold of the face, takes about three hours counting the set-up," Christopher answered.

"Ace and I will go check in with Langstrom, and turn in our reports, Nigel. We will be back here around four to pick you up," Lopez said.

"Good. I would like to get back to the house before it gets dark," Nigel said. When he saw Christopher was looking at him questioningly, he added, "I want to take a good look at the work the construction people did today."

Whittaker noted the reference to the dark and was in full agreement. It made for a long night, having to stay inside once the sun set, but Nigel had given them a room to stay in, and so they did manage to grab a few hours of sleep between watches.

"Normally, we take several hundred hours to make a figure. However, in your case, we are going to use just your face, and put it on one of the figures we have in the back room that matches your size," Christopher said he took photos of Nigel. "To make sure everything is a perfect fit, I recommend you send over the chair you are going to use, and an outfit that you are often seen wearing. We can put the clothing on the figure and rework it so that it sits in the chair with a natural look."

Christopher put the camera down and picked up a tape measure. "Let me get your measurements, and then, we will start on the mold."

Once the measurements were done, Nigel found himself in a chair with a neck rest that tilted backwards, and a section that rose up to hold the legs like a recliner.

Christopher kept up a running dialogue as he put a plastic cap around Nigel's hair and rubbed a layer of Vaseline on his face.

"This keeps the plaster from sticking to your skin," he explained as he put ear plugs into Nigel's ears. "Fortunately, we have an overhead TV that you can watch while you are setting here. Is the news channel, good for you?"

Chapter 23
Keep the Boss Happy

Special Agent-in-Charge Benjamin Langstrom had spent the past twenty-five years working for the FBI. When he had been promoted to head the Criminal Division in Los Angeles, he had considered it a highlight in his career. Today, not so much.

Langstrom's gray brows needled, and his intense blue eyes narrowed as two of his field agents entered his office.

"Have a seat, Lopez! You too, Whittaker!" he commanded.

Neither Lopez nor Whittaker had time to sit before the questioning began. "What the hell is going on?" Langstrom snapped, glaring at the source of what was irritating him. "I sent you two to find out why someone in Hollywood bought a pricey government surveillance camera, and you send me a report that you were attacked by a vampire."

"I know it's sounds crazy, boss, but that is exactly what happened," Lopez said.

Langstrom cursed. "You boys tired of working for the FBI?" he asked.

"No, sir!" Lopez and Whittaker said in unison.

"We brought footage of the attack, boss," Whittaker said, taking a flash drive out of his pocket. He then leaned forward to lay it on the desk.

Langstrom pushed a button on his phone. "Thompson, get in here! I need you to put up some intel on the big screen."

Special Agent Cheri Milagro Thompson a tall, brown-skinned beauty of Creole descent with blue eyes—born and raised in New Orleans—rose from her desk and headed for her boss' office.

Langstrom waited for Thompson to join them before he turned his attention back on Lopez and Whittaker. "This had better be good, or you two are going to find yourself transferred to our Death Valley office."

"I didn't know we had an office in Death Valley," Whittaker said, walking straight into the trap.

"We don't, but it might be time to open one up."

"Oh, right," Whittaker said as he handed the flash drive over to Thompson. His face flushing red as he noted the grin on her face.

Thompson walked over to the wall computer and inserted the USB drive into one of the slots.

All three men pretended to watch the screen as they waited for the footage to begin, but their eyes could not help but appreciate the young woman's slim figure.

Langstrom's eyes went wide when he saw a tall man with a mouthful of sharp teeth, holding Whittaker by the lapels on his jacket, while his other hand pulled his victim's head back in preparation to rip into his throat. Before Langstrom's mind could react to that, a knife buried itself in the back of the attacker.

Thompson shuddered as she watched the attacker run away. She now knew what was killing all those women in Hollywood. "Do you want to see it again, Boss?" she asked.

"No. Once is enough," Langstrom answered. But you might as well sit down and hear what else Lopez and Whittaker have to say. Once I kick this upstairs, I might need you as a witness," Langstrom stated.

Thompson made no reply as she went and sat down in the only chair left.

"Okay, you two have my attention," Langstrom said, once Thompson was seated. "Now, what are you doing to apprehend that maniac?"

"We are helping Bravo Team set up a trap to lure the creature in close enough, they can get a shot at it," Lopez answered.

"I do not want to know about Bravo Team. I want to know what you are doing?" Langstrom snapped.

"We are helping to set the trap, sir. That is about all we can do at this time. That, and sit in the ops room and watch the cam screens," Whittaker answered.

Langstrom scratched his head as he looked at his agents. "There is no intel here on the residents of the house, other than their names and occupations. Have you thought to question why they have an ops room, and what it is about them that attracts this thing *you call* a vampire?"

"We call him a vampire because that is what he is. He is not human, boss. No one could run like that after having a military grade knife sink into their heart," Lopez defended.

"You are still not answering my questions," Langstrom thundered as he smashed his fist against the top of his desk for emphasis.

"In respect to the ops room and Bravo Team, sir, it comes down to money. The owners of the home are wealthy. So, is Vladimir Romanov, who is the brother of Hattie and Marie Drake. His wife and daughter are staying in the house too because his wife is ill," Whittaker explained.

Langstrom picked up a piece of paper on his desk. "Vladimir Romanov placed an order for six more MS-2 scanners. Do you know why?"

"Probably because the MS-2 scanner works, and he is in the security business. I know that without that computerized camera, Whittaker would be dead as we would have had no way of knowing the vampire was there until the actual attack. He moved that fast," Lopez said.

"That's not in your report," Langstrom declared.

"I did not realize the MS-2 abilities were relevant at the time, boss," Lopez said.

"Everything about this case is relevant. You got that?" Langstrom declared as he glared at them.

All three agents nodded their heads.

Langstrom rubbed a hand over is face as he thought about his next question. "Why is the creature targeting the people in that house? I mean, he has killed more than a dozen women in the past two weeks, but as far as it is known, they have nothing in common, other than they are female. Now, we find he has taken an interest in those at Hattera Lane."

When Langstrom saw Lopez and Whittaker shaking their heads at him, he pursed his lips. "Then find out. Those people know something they are not telling you, and I want you to find out what that is."

"Thompson, I want you to do a background check on the residents of that house, and Vladimir Romanov. If they have visited the doctor for a cold in the past five years, I want to know about it. For now, we will skip Bravo Team, as we already know who they are and what they do."

Langstrom saw Whittaker flush, and then glance over at Lopez. He knew that look. "What is it that you are not telling me?" he asked.

Lopez sighed. "Nigel Quinn gave us an amulet to wear. He says it keep the creature from controlling our minds. Don't ask me how it works, but I will tell you from firsthand experience, it does work."

Both Lopez and Whittaker pulled their amulets from beneath their shirts.

Langstrom leaned forward and peered at the necklaces. He sat back in his chair before he spoke. "We live in the age of electronics, machines, and infinite knowledge via the internet, and you two, somehow, have reverted back to the dark ages, and are wearing charms to protect yourselves. What the hell is going on in that house?"

"With all due respect, sir, I would like to say there is nothing in the book that prepares you for dealing with a mythological creature. And that is what a vampire is. Those teeth, will haunt me for the rest of my life," Whittaker answered. "These amulets work in that they keep the beast from controlling your mind and paralyzing your body. Jack

Pratt, Lopez, and me all ended up frozen. We could see and hear everything going on around us, but we could not move or act to save our own lives, let alone anyone else's. Vladimir and Louie both wore their amulets, and they remained free to act. Of course, it was Louie Crosshatch's combat training that saved me. It took him no more than a second to react to the situation and throw that knife."

"Which I am grateful for, Whittaker, because now I do not have to make a speech at your funeral."

"Thank you for the thought, sir," Whittaker murmured.

Langstrom shook his head. Sarcasm always flew right over Whittaker's head. "I have only one more recommendation before you leave this office," he said raising his head. "Never—and I repeat, *never*, put anything in your reports about those charms you are wearing or that you are chasing what you believe is a vampire. You can refer to the subject as being delusional in that he believes and acts as if he is a vampire. Those teeth are obviously false and made to scare people. Also, make sure you bring your prior reports up to date before you leave on assignment. Understood?"

"Yes, sir," Lopez said, rising from his chair.

Whittaker nodded as he too rose to leave.

Once they reached their cubicle and desks, Lopez looked at his watch, then turned to look at his partner. "We got twenty minutes before we need to head back to Hollywood and pick up Nigel. You take the last two reports and fix them. I will take the first two. That should keep Langstrom happy."

"But we will be lying," Whittaker protested.

"No, we are not going to lie, Ace. We are just going to omit some of the relevant facts—for now."

"Tough break, guys," Thompson said as she stopped at the cubicle's entrance. "If it makes you feel any better, I believe you."

"Thanks," Lopez said.

"Whatever you do, Cheri, do not go out to Hattera Lane after dark," Whittaker blurted out, knowing she often brought them coffee and donuts when they were on a stakeout. "It is too dangerous. Being inside a car will not protect you. That *thing* can seize your mind, tell you to step out of the car, and you will do what it says. Understand?"

Cheri nodded and then whispered, "Gotta go," as she saw Langstrom step out of his office.

Chapter 24
A Week Later

After Isles put the roast in the oven and got the vegetable trays ready to be put in the oven later, Nigel sent him and Kate home. The wax dummy of himself had arrived today, and he did not want them to see the work being done to prepare the trap they were making for Goff.

Nigel found that if he used a cushion, he was able to sit down a on small ledge above the pool's heater frame. It was warm inside the small concrete space, so he had Jack bring him one of the extra fans from the garage.

They had piled construction debris just outside the patio doors for Louie, Ox, and Earl to hide behind. With the foil lined beanies, Jabber had fashioned, the beast would never know they were waiting for him.

* * *

It was close to the midnight hour when Goff left the crypt and went toward the city to hunt for food. He preferred females as he liked: Cutting off their screams with his mind as he grabbed them. Feeling their heart pound inside them as they saw his mouth open, knowing they were going to die. The refreshing warmth of their blood as their minds cease to exist.

* * *

By two o'clock, Nigel could not hold his eyes open any longer, and so dozed with his head leaning against the wall. He woke up twenty minutes later when he sensed the beast's presence. He picked up the book in his lap, and began to read, forcing his mind to stay focused on the words in the book, and not the trap.

He heard a loud crashing sound, and within seconds, another crashing sound. Before he could figure out where the noise was coming from, he heard high-pitched screams. The book fell to the floor as he jumped to his feet. He had no doubt the screams were coming from inside the house. He heard Louie holler for Ox, telling Earl to stay where he was, then more screams.

Nigel climbed the ladder and pushed on the surge pit's door. He found it was too heavy for him to lift with the dummy and chair sitting on top of it. Tears of frustration ran down his cheeks as he struggled to open the door above his head. He longed to call Vladimir to come let him out, but he realized Vladimir might be the only thing that could stop the jogeth. He dared not distract him.

Once Goff entered the bedroom, he found he could not control either woman with his mind as both were wearing a Maker's amulet around their necks, but that did not stop him. He grabbed Hattie, picked her up as if she were a child, slung her over his shoulder, and ignoring her screams and kicking, dashed back through the house toward the front door.

While this was going on, Hattie felt something stir in her mind. Something that had always been there, but she had never needed to use it—the instructions a wrinkled-faced woman with blue skin, silver hair, and wings had whispered to her as she waited in line for the portal to open to the new world—she whispered *Omay*, and she began to glow.

Whittaker had rushed out of the ops room, gun in hand. He stopped when he heard the sound of another door being ripped off its hinges. He started forward as he heard the screams, but stopped when the creature with Hattie slung over its shoulder came running out of the hallway. He cursed as he realized there was no way he could take a shot without the risk of shooting the woman too. "Here, hold this," he said, shoving his gun at Lopez.

As the vampire turned into the entryway, Whittaker ran to tackle the creature, hoping to get the beast to let go of the woman.

However, the jogeth heard Whittaker behind him. Without hesitation, he spun around, and back handed the man in the chest. Whittaker went flying through the air and hit the wall with a thud.

Vladimir, who was right behind Whittaker, tripped over his own feet as he tried to get around the FBI agent.

Goff had turned to look at Whittaker and saw Vladimir fall and laughed. However, his laughter stopped short as a white light surrounded Hattie's body.

He roared as the light began to burn his eyes and skin. He threw her down and ran out of what was left of the front doorway.

His figure disappeared off camera as he went behind the gardener's cottage. Then within the blink of an eye, it appeared again as he moved toward the back wall and jumped into the storm drain. He was gone before anyone could get past Hattie's blinding light, and out the door.

When Louie gave the word the vampire had gotten away, Lee went and helped Nigel out of the surge pit.

"What happened?" Nigel asked, physically exhausted from trying to get the door open.

Lee shook his head. "I don't know. Louie says the vampire is gone, but he needs you as there is problem with Hattie. She is shining like a star."

Nigel hurried as fast as he could to the front room. When he saw Hattie, he knew exactly what she had done, but he did not know how she had achieved such a state without training. He found himself blinded by the light.

"Do not look at her!" he shouted to the others.

"Nigel! I do not know how to turn it off," Hattie cried out when she heard his voice.

Vladimir is going to help you," Nigel called out.

"I need you enter her mind and reassure her that there is no danger. Tell her she can now put the light out," Nigel told Vladimir.

Vladimir kept a hand over his eyes, and his head down as he gently entered her mind. *"You are safe now, Hattie. Nigel says you do not need the light anymore."*

As Hattie's fear receded, she recalled the last instruction given to her by the blue woman. *"Ortay!"* she whispered. The light around Hattie's figure begin to fade, and then winked out.

Hattie raised her head to thank Vladimir but stopped as she saw Louie and Lopez kneeling down beside Whittaker, who was not moving.

"He's breathing, but barely," Lopez said as he checked his partner. "Someone, call 911, and get an ambulance and the paramedics out here! Tell them there is an FBI agent down. That will get them moving faster. Also, make sure to give them instructions on how to get here because Hattera Lane is not on the map. Tell them I will be at the front gate with my flashing lights on."

Nigel dialed 911. He repeated Lopez's instructions and gave the dispatcher details on how to find Hattera Lane.

"I am going to take the car down to the front gate and wait for the ambulance. I would appreciate it, Louie, if a couple of your guys could go with me in case that thing comes back."

"Ox, you, and Jack go with Lopez!" Louie commanded. "Take your AK-47s with you. Earl, you and Lee cover the back entrance, but stay inside! Vladimir, you and Jabber can watch the cam screens. Thompson and I will cover this entrance. "Marie, you help Hattie to the office. Jennifer, you and Bella need to go to the office as well. That will leave us only the one room to guard."

Marie nodded, too emotional to speak. She went and got Hattie by the hand, and gently pulled her along as she motioned for Jennifer and Bella, who were standing nearby, to come with them to the office.

Louie waited until the women were in the office, and the door shut before he gave his last order. "If that SOB comes back, go for a head shot! There is no way we are going to be able to take him down hand-to-hand," he murmured into his comm unit as he stood there looking at the twisted steel frame on the front door.

* * *

"**How did** you do that, Hattie? I mean, shine like that?" Jennifer asked, once they were all seated, and the office door was shut.

Hattie shook her head. "I don't know. I just remembered what the old woman told me when we were standing there waiting for them to open the portal to come to this world."

"And what was that?" Marie asked sharply, upset that Hattie had never told her about the woman.

"She said I was born with a gift that could save me from the jogeths. She then gave me instructions how to use it if I was attacked. I had forgotten all about it, until her words filled my mind as the beast was packing me out the door."

"I would say it is more than a gift, Hattie," Jabber called out from the cam room. "I would call it a weapon. It made that creature run the other way, and that is doing more than any of us were able to do."

Bella was staring openly toward the cam room. She realized Jabber knew the truth of where they came from.

"It is not your fault, Jabber" Marie defended. "No one expected the beast to come through the front door. He was supposed to go after Nigel in the back yard."

When Marie saw the look on Bella's face, she nodded. "Yes, Jabber knows who we are, Bella, and where we came from. That is why he came to help us."

"We saw him on the matrix scanner when he came over the drain wall," Jabber said. "He came straight toward the swimming pool and Nigel, then at the last minute, veered off behind the gardener's cottage. We lost sight of him for a couple of minutes. Next thing we knew he was coming through the front door. By the time Whittaker and Jack got up, and out the door, he had already grabbed you, Hattie. No one dared take a shot after that."

Hattie shuddered as the raw courage she had been using for the past ten minutes, evaporated. That is when she felt the pain in her left arm. She winced as she tried to move her shoulder.

"What's wrong?" Bella asked, the only one in the room who had seen the grimace on Hattie's face.

"I just realized my shoulder is hurt," Hattie said, as she fought off an attack of dizziness.

Marie jumped up and went to take a look. "Why didn't you say anything? Did he bite you?"

"No. I don't think so. I think it happened when he threw me down," Hattie answered. "But I can no longer move my arm because it hurts."

"I will go get Nigel. He will know what to do," Marie said as she straightened up.

"No need for you to do that, Marie. I just told Nigel on his earwig that he needs to come in, and check on Hattie," Jabber said.

Marie turned and went into the cam room. She sat down in the chair next to Jabber as she did not want the others to hear the question, she was going to ask.

Hattie and I have never been to see a doctor before, Jabber, she wrote on the notepad in front of her. *Will they know we are not from this world when they examine her?*

Jabber reached for the notepad. *Probably not. You told me Bella saw a lot of doctors. None of them ever saw her as anything but a sick woman.*

"Thank you," Marie mouthed.

Jabber nodded as he tore the sheet out of the notepad, then put it in his pocket. Later he would tear it up and flush it down the toilet.

Nigel came through the door and hurried over to take a look at Hattie.

"Why didn't you tell us, you were hurt?" he questioned when he saw how pale Hattie's face was and felt how clammy her skin was.

Hattie started to shrug and then, cried out in pain as she tried to move her shoulder.

"Don't move!" Nigel commanded. "I will be right back. We are going to need another ambulance if the paramedics cannot take you along with Whittaker to the hospital."

"I do not want to go to the hospital," Hattie protested.

Nigel turned to look at her. "You obviously have a broken bone or internal injuries, Hattie. This is not something *kado* grass can fix. It can help you heal but right now, you need x-rays and a doctor."

Hattie made a face but did not protest. The pain was taking over everything else.

* * *

The pain medicine made Hattie drowsy, but she opened her eyes for a second or two when the paramedic halted the gurney before loading her into the ambulance. She gave Ox a happy—I am not feeling any pain—smile when she saw him staring down at her.

"Lopez and I will be following along behind you," Ox said as he took her hand. "I will see you at the hospital once they get you a room. I am not family, so they probably will not allow me into the emergency room."

"Tell them you are my husband," Hattie suggested with a giggle. "That should get you in the door."

Ox chuckled, and let go of her hand as they moved to load her into the ambulance

Hattie smiled sweetly at him before she closed her eyes, and drifted in and out of consciousness as the ambulance began to move.

* * *

"**The paramedics** tell you anything about Whittaker?" Ox asked Lopez.

"Nothing much, other than he is breathing on his own. I guess in their world that means he's alive, not dead," Lopez answered as he turned on his roof flashers and pulled out onto the main road behind the ambulance.

"I hope Hattie doesn't have any internal injuries," Ox murmured.

"If that light came from inside her, it is a wonder she is still alive. I could feel the heat of it from where I stood," Lopez said.

"Oh, I don't think the light hurt her. That is part of her psychic abilities," Ox said. "No, I think either the beast crushed her with his arm as he carried her, or she was injured when he threw her on the floor."

"Psychic abilities? Who told you that?"

"She did," Ox lied smoothly, trying to satisfy Lopez's curiosity, so he would not make a big deal about the light when he got around to writing up his report of how Whittaker got hurt. "It runs in the family. You know, like Vladimir can read minds. Well, Hattie has other abilities. That is why she makes a good detective when it comes to paranormal activity."

"I don't believe in ghosts," Lopez stated gruffly, shaking his head for emphasis.

"Neither do I," Ox agreed with a shrug. "But then I did not believe vampires existed either before I came to Hollywood. But both you and I have now seen one—twice."

Lopez's brow went up as he thought about Ox's statement. "No argument there, but if a ghost does come through the wall, try not to step on me."

"Why would I step on you?"

"Because I will be passed out on the floor," Lopez said, a grin breaking out on his face.

Both men broke out in laughter.

Chapter 25
New Partner

The sun was just rising when Nigel stepped outside. *Right on time*, he thought as he saw the white truck coming up the drive.

"I appreciate you coming out here, Rick, on such short notice, Nigel told the contractor.

Rick did a double take when he saw the door. "What the hell did that?" he asked, looking at the twisted steel doorless frame.

"If I told you, you would not believe me. And if you did believe me, you then will wish I had kept the information to myself. It is enough to say, I need new a door and frame here, and one of the bedroom doors looks just as bad as this one does," Nigel answered.

"Did anyone get hurt?"

"Unfortunately, yes. Agent Whittaker and Hattie are in the hospital. He is in intensive care. She should be okay once they get through with their tests and put a cast on her arm. That is one reason I need the doors done today. I don't want her to see the mangled frame to remind her of what happened. There is no need to hurry fixing the damage to the walls. You can take your time on that. Which reminds me, make sure to take all the twisted metal with you when you leave tonight. Just looking at it makes me angry."

"Sure thing, Nigel," Rick said. "I will get three of my men on it right away. They can rip out the old frames, do what reinforcement is needed, and get the wall casing ready for the new doors. While they are doing that, I will go to Torrance, and get the new doors and frames. If all goes well, I can be back here about noon, and the doors should be in place by quitting time. Tomorrow, they can start on the interior walls, and the stucco out here."

"Good. Here's a check for the doors and extra labor," Nigel said, pulling an envelope out of his jacket pocket, and handing it to Rick. "You can bill me for the rest."

"Thanks, Nigel. I appreciate it. Now, I had better go make a few calls, and get my men over here."

Nigel turned to go back in the house but stopped as three trucks parked behind Ricks. *Might as well get this over with*, he thought as he waited for Joe and his crew to get out of the trucks and come take a look at what was left of the front door.

That thought reminded him that he still needed to call Isles and tell him that they had the day off as he was having work done on the house. He did not want them to see the mangled door frames either, they might quit. He did not want that to happen.

* * *

"**I want** to know what happened at that house?" Langstrom told Lopez once his agent had seated himself.

"I got footage of most of it," Lopez said as he took the flash drive out of his pocket. "You will have to see it to believe it, sir," he said as he handed the drive over to Thompson who was sitting next to him."

No one spoke as the action on the screen began. First thing they saw was a black matrix figure running.

"The matrix scanner tracked him moving at 72 miles per hour," Lopez explained.

"No human can move at that speed," Langstrom declared.

"Exactly, sir. Also, that is a new steel door installed in a *new* steel frame. It did not take him more than a second or two to bring it down. Then probably only two or three more seconds to take out another steel door in one of the bedrooms, and grab Hattie Drake."

"By the time, Whittaker and I could get out of the cam room and to the front room, the vampire was coming straight at us on his way back to the front door with Miss Drake flung over his shoulder. We could not shoot at it without risk of hitting her, so Ace decided he would try and tackle the beast."

Langstrom saw Whitaker hit the wall, Romanov stumble and fall, and the vampire laughing, but then the film went white. "What happened there?" he asked.

"Miss Drake lit up like a sun, and blinded not only the camera, but everyone in the room. We all had to keep our heads down. The light is what made the beast throw her to floor and run off. That is when she got hurt."

The white screen disappeared as movement came back on the screen.

Langstrom saw Whittaker and the woman on the floor. He also saw she was glowing, not bright enough to blank out the camera, but nevertheless, shining like a light bulb. Behind her, he got his first good look at the twisted steel frame where the front door had been.

"How did she light up like that?" he asked.

"She has psychic abilities. That is why she is a paranormal detective. However, she did not know how to turn the light off. Her brother Vladimir Romanov had to help her."

"He lights up too?"

"No, he read minds," Lopez answered, shaking his head.

Langstrom snorted, then ran a hand through his hair as he considered what he had just heard and seen.

"Thompson, you are now partnered with Lopez. You will go with him tonight and see for yourself exactly what is going on out there."

"Yes, sir," Thompson said, not sure whether to be happy she had finally graduated to the level of field agent or worry that she might get killed by the vampire.

"We will be staying inside the house, sir, as we cannot risk being outside after dark."

"Inside the house?" Langstrom questioned.

"Yes. Nigel Quinn gave us one of the guest rooms to stay in when we are not watching the security cams. It is not safe to be outside or sitting in a car after dark. A car door will not stop that creature, and guns will not kill it either."

"Then how can it be killed?" Langstrom snapped.

"They are going to blow its head off, literally, sir. That is, if they can get a clear shot at it without someone being in the line of fire. Then they are going to burn the remains. That part will not be in the official report as anyone who has not seen the footage firsthand would not understand."

"By them, you are referring to Bravo Team, right?" Langstrom asked.

"Yes, sir. They have the fire power and training to do it, but like I said, they have yet to get a clear shot."

"Lopez, you go and finish your written report, I will need it for reference when I make my report to Headquarters. Also, you can now use the word creature, as this latest footage has established it is not human."

"Yes, sir," Lopez said, nodding at Langstrom before he turned to look at his new partner. "We will need to stop by your place, so you can pack a few things to take with you, Thompson. You can use Whittaker's bed and closet." When he saw her brow go up, he added, "Don't worry, that bed is in an alcove."

"Thompson?" Langstrom questioned when she did not answer.

"Sorry, sir. I was mentally sorting through the paperwork on my desk. I believe Tucker can take over most of it. He is up to date on the cases we are working on, other than what we just saw."

"Then you are good to go, Lopez," Langstrom said, dismissing the agent with a wave of his hand.

"Now, Thompson, you can replay that footage again! If you see anything unusual, let me know." When she turned and looked at him with a frown on her face, he added, "You know, anything other than all the weird stuff we have already seen and discussed."

"Yes, sir," Thompson said as she pushed replay, and went back to her chair to watch the footage again.

After Langstrom dismissed Thompson, he pulled out a bulletin he had received last summer and had stuck in his bottom drawer. He then made his call.

"I would like to speak to Doctor Genie Ferguson," he said, asking for the Director of the *Bureau of Psychic Investigation* in Washington. When she answered the phone, he told her what he had seen and learned.

Ferguson tried to keep the excitement out of her voice as she listened to the head of LA's FBI unit state his agents were dealing with a creature that they believed was some type of vampire, and he had film of the incidents.

"I will be there tomorrow, Agent Langstrom. Give me your number, and I will have my assistant text you with the time of our arrival. You can have someone pick us up at the airport."

"I will have my driver pick you up and bring you here. I am sure you will want to see the footage, and the reports of those who we believe are this creature's victims."

"Definitely. In the meantime, could you email the files to me?"

"I can email you the victims report, but right now, the footage of this vampire thing can go no further than this office, until it can be determined what we are dealing with," Langstrom replied.

"Then I will see you tomorrow," Dr. Ferguson said before she hung up.

Chapter 26
The Failing Heart

Nigel opened the car door and helped Hattie into the car. The cast and sling on her right arm reminded him of how close she had come to dying. That thought gave him a sharp pain in his chest, and he gasped aloud.

"Are you all right, sir," the nurse asked when she saw his body stiffen, and his face lose color.

Nigel wanted to shake his head but found himself falling into a dark hole. He would have fallen heavily to the sidewalk had the nurse not caught hold of his arm. Instead, he went down slowly as she struggled to hold onto him.

Two ambulance attendants, who happened to be waiting for a patient, heard Hattie's cry, and ran to help.

After determining that Nigel was unconscious, one of the attendants rushed back to the ambulance for a gurney. The other attendant notified his dispatcher to let the hospital know they had a man down at the checkout entrance and were bringing him around to the ER on a gurney.

Hattie used her good arm and hand to dig in her purse. She got out her phone and called Vladimir. When he answered the phone, she started to cry, and could not get out the words to tell him what was wrong.

"Here, let me help," the nurse said as she took the phone out of Hattie's hand, and explained the problem to the man on the phone.

"I will be right there," Vladimir told her. "Please take care of my sister as well. I don't think she should be left alone."

"Yes, of course. I will put her back into the wheelchair and take her to the waiting room in the emergency department. That is where they are taking Mr. Quinn."

"Good. Tell her I will be there as soon as I can get there."

Vladimir went to tell Jabber and Marie what had happened. When he saw Ox coming out of the office, he asked him if he would go with them, and bring Nigel's car back.

* * *

"Hattie!" Marie called out as she saw her sister sitting in the wheelchair, her eyes red and puffy from crying.

"I will go see about Nigel," Vladimir said, once he had greeted Hattie.

Hattie started to cry again. "I don't know what's wrong with me," she said between sobs as Marie bent down by her chair. "All I want to do is cry."

"That is due partly to the trauma you have been through, and in part to the pain medications they have given you, Hattie," Ox said as he knelt down beside her chair. "It happens to the best of us when we have suffered traumatic injuries."

Hattie nodded as she wiped at her eyes. "Thank you, Ox. I needed to hear that."

Ox nodded as he handed her more tissues from a box on the one of the tables.

"I am going to see what Vladimir has found out," Marie said. "I will be right back."

Ox moved Hattie over closer to the lounge chairs and sat down in one. He then took hold of her hand and gave her an encouraging smile.

An hour passed before Marie came back with a bleak look on her face. "They say, Nigel has had a heart attack. He is unconscious. They are taking him to intensive care. Vladimir wants Ox to take you home, Hattie. You need to rest. I am going to stay here as I am the only one that can answer any questions, they have about him."

Hattie nodded as she fought back more tears. "Call me if anything changes," she said emotionally.

"I will. When they get him settled in, Vladimir and I will be home. The nurse told us that once he is in ICU, we will not be allowed in to see him for the first six to eight hours while they stabilize him. So I guess it will be tomorrow before we get in to see him."

Hattie's face paled at Marie's words.

"Tell Vladimir I will call him when we get home, Marie," Ox said, rising to take hold of the handlebars on Hattie's wheelchair.

"Oh, I almost forgot. The nurse told me that one of the ambulance attendants left Nigel's car outside in the emergency parking lot, and the keys are at the nurse's station," Hattie told Ox. "We need to stop by and get them."

"Then I will leave you two to do that, and I will go check on Nigel," Marie said, patting Hattie's good shoulder before she turned, and hurried back up the corridor.

* * *

"**I imagine,** you wish you had stayed in Arizona, Ox. It most certainly would be the safer place to be," Hattie said as they made their way through the normal rush hour stop-and-go traffic.

"If you were with me, Hattie, then yes, Arizona would be nice. Otherwise, I am perfectly happy to be here with you, dangerous or not," Ox said.

"Even with my weepy red eyes, huh?" Hattie teased.

"Weepy red eyes and all," Ox replied, glancing over long enough to give her a quick nod of reassurance before he turned his attention back to the car in front of him.

He swallowed nervously before he said what he had been trying to work up the courage to say for the past week. "Hattie, in case you haven't noticed, I... I care for you—a lot."

Hattie's eyes teared up again. "And I care for you, Ox, but for reasons I cannot explain, I—

"I know how old you are, Hattie, and where you come from," Ox cut in. "Jabber told Louie and me last year about you and your sister when he had surgery for cancer."

"He has cancer!" Hattie exclaimed, all thoughts of age difference between her and Ox, gone from her mind.

"Yes. He told us that in case he did not survive the surgery, he wanted to make sure that should you and Marie need help, we would be there for you. Thankfully, he survived, and is doing better than expected."

"He did not tell Marie about the cancer."

"I know, he does not want to worry her."

"You do know, I am going to have to tell her. We do not keep secrets from each other, and Jabber is dear to her heart, and mine too."

"I think she should know. The time might come when he needs more help than the doctors can give him."

"You mean, nursing care?" Hattie said emotionally.

"Yes, something like that, but also the love of a family. He loves Marie as much as any father would love his natural born daughter."

Hattie sat quietly thinking about Jabber. Marie would be angry and hurt when she found out he was ill, but most of all, she would be scared of losing him.

Then thoughts of Ox caring for her returned. "You do realize that as you grow older, I will not. You could resent me for that," she said.

"Never. I am worried that you will not want to look at me when I grow old and wrinkled."

Hattie smiled as she looked at the man behind the wheel. "Ox, I will never tire of looking at your face, wrinkled or not."

"Then will you marry me, Hattie Drake?" Ox blurted out, almost as surprised by his words as she was.

Hattie's mouth dropped open.

"Sorry. I know it is not the right time or place as we are in the middle of a traffic jam, and worse, a real nightmare of a case, but my heart, and mind needs to know."

Hattie felt the barriers she had put around her heart fall away as she looked at him. "Yes. I will marry you, Ox. But I would rather we keep it between ourselves until Nigel is well, and that beast is gone."

"Good. Then I have time to woo you."

Hattie chuckled. "Woo me? Wow! I have not heard that word used for a very long time."

* * *

Lopez noted the palm tree decoration in the cathedral shaped recesses on the new double doors of the house's front entrance. *Nice*, he thought as he rang the doorbell.

It was Jack that opened the door. Lopez grinned as he saw the young man's face light up when he saw Thompson.

"Jack, meet Special Agent Cheri Thompson, my new partner. Thompson, this is Jack Pratt, a member of Bravo Team," Lopez said.

"Uh, nice to meet you Cheri," Jack said, sticking his hand out to shake the woman's hand.

Thompson smiled as she shook his hand. "Same here, Jack" she said.

"Come on, Thompson! I will show you where our room is located," Lopez said as he moved past Jack, who had motioned with his head for them to come in as he smiled at Thompson.

"I am in love," Jack said as he joined Lee and Jabber in the cam room.

"With who?" Jabber asked, not bothering to hide the surprise on his face.

"With Lopez's new partner. Wait until you see here. Her name is Cheri Thompson."

"She is just another GS, Jack. Make sure you keep your mouth shut when you are around her."

"What do you mean by that, Lee?"

"She's a government spy, that's what. And worse, if something does go wrong here, it will be our fault. Lopez, and Thompson are not our friends, Jack. Right, Jabber?" Lee asked, looking toward the older man.

"In part, you are right. They are here to keep an eye on us, but that does not mean we cannot be friendly. They are just doing their job. I have known Lopez since he was about Jack's age, Lee. He is a good man."

Lee spat out a curse as he rose from his chair and scowled at Jack. "Maybe so, Jabber, but I don't trust him or her. I think I will go and grab a snack and then get some sleep. You know I do not like crowds."

"Sit down, Jack!" Jabber said when he saw the frown on the young man's face. "This is not your fault. Lee had a bad experience with the FBI a few years back. They arrested him by mistake. It took Louie and me, close to a month to get the matter straightened out and get him out of jail."

"What did they arrest him for?" Jack asked as he sat down.

"For murdering an FBI agent in New Orleans," Jabber answered.

"Fortunately, we all happened to be in Connecticut working on a job there at the time the murder was committed, but the Agency would not accept our statements. It was not until the Senator we were guarding, made a deposition that stated Lee was guarding him that night that they dropped the charges, and released him. If the Senator had not intervened, Lee would be serving life without the possibility of parole. The FBI does not like hired guns like us, Jack. I told you that when you hired on."

"Yeah, I recall you saying that, but I did not realize why. I will be careful what I say in front of her or Lopez."

"Good idea. If you believe there is something they need to know, let me know, and I will pass it along to Lopez," Jabber said, rising from his chair. "Now, I am going to take a break as well. You cover the cams. Sound the alarm if that thing comes back. In the meantime, I suggest you let Lopez explain the camera set up to the new agent. That is part of his job."

Jack grinned at the older man, and waited for him to leave the room before he moved over to the center chair. *Now, she will have to sit next to me while Lopez explains the camera setup*, he told himself.

Chapter 27
Dr. Genie Ferguson

Langstrom had his driver drop him off at the airport, and then told him to circle the drive while he went and found the doctor. He had looked her up on the web and had studied her photo. She looked to be in her early forties with short blond curls, blue eyes, and was thin. Too thin to suit him, one could see her rib bones sticking out against the fabric of the blouse she wore. When he saw her coming toward him, he gawked a bit because the photo did not prepare him for her height. She barely topped five feet, and then only because she was wearing two inch heels. *I bet she doesn't weigh ninety pounds*, he told himself.

"Agent Langstrom, I presume," Genie said, as she stuck her hand out.

Langstrom nodded as he shook her hand. He saw she was carrying a large handbag that matched her light blue pants, but no carryon.

"I will help you get your luggage, Doctor."

"No need. Peggy, my assistant, is taking care of that. She went to secure the hotel room and will wait for me there. I am anxious to see the film you have and wish to go straight to your office."

"Good. I have my driver circling the drive. Shouldn't take us more than hour to get back to the office."

"I suppose your traffic is as bad as that in DC," Genie said.

"At this time of day, probably worse," Langstrom replied as they made their way out the front entrance.

* * *

Langstrom had Lopez make an appointment for Dr. Ferguson and himself with Hattie Drake. He wanted to see for himself what kind of people attracted vampires. He was not impressed by the size of the house nor the amount of land surrounding it. There were many such estates in Hollywood, due to the film industry, and the wealthy seeking a warmer winter climate.

Marie answered the door and invited them into the front room.

"Have a seat. Any chair will do. Lopez told us you were coming. I am Marie Drake, this is my sister Hattie Drake, and that is my sister by marriage, Bella Romanov," Marie said as she pointed toward Hattie and Bella who were sitting on the sofa.

Langstrom nodded, seated himself and then introduced himself. He started to introduce the doctor but closed his mouth when she beat him to it.

"And I am Doctor Genie Ferguson, head of the Bureau of Psychic Investigation. Special Agent Langstrom has invited me to come and help with the current situation. Please, call me Genie."

Hattie's face lit up. "Though we have not met, Genie, Marie and I both were at the Paris for the Psychic Phenomena Convention last fall, and heard you give your speech on the Salem witch trials in seventeenth century America. I found it interesting that the deaths of innocent people were allowed to continue until the Governor's wife was charged with being a witch. He then put an end to the trials."

Genie looked at Hattie with interest. "Ah, I see you did hear what I had to say. Yes, beyond the ignorance and superstition of the people that I stated, there was the underlying factor of those who believed themselves to be above those being accused. I left that aspect out of my speech as it has more to do with social hierarchy, than paranormal behavior."

"There were witch trials in England as well," Marie said, recalling firsthand the havoc such trials caused. "I find it odd that those accused went helplessly, weeping to the pyres or gallows. I mean, if one actually has magic, would they not use it to escape those trying to kill them? I most certainly would."

"As would I," Genie agreed. "Of course, we are not up against a witch this time, or even a paranormal event. A vampire is a supernatural creature. It does not exist in nature as we know it."

"Does that make a difference?" Langstrom asked.

"For the vampire, no. For us, yes, as we must find a way to defeat it using something other than bullets," Genie answered.

"Bullets might work," Marie said. "Bravo Team has a plan, but they need a clear shot, and so far that has not happened."

"Bravo Team?" Genie questioned, pretending not to recognize the name.

"We hired six former Marines to help us kill Goff," Hattie explained.

"Goff? You know the creature's name?" Langstrom asked, looking at Marie.

Marie blushed as she realized she had just created a situation.

Lopez was leaning against the office's doorframe listening to the conversation. His eyes narrowed as he recalled Nigel stating he was familiar with such a creature but did not say he knew this vampire thing by name. He walked across the room to find out more.

Louie who was standing off to one side, also listening, heard her remark and winced inwardly. When he saw Lopez moving toward Marie, he went and sat down by her. "Goff is the code name we have given the creature," he said smoothly.

Genie noted Marie's red face, and the two men frowning at each other. *Ah, it appears both men have fallen for the fair maiden*, she mistakenly thought.

"Dr. Ferguson I would like you to meet Special Agent Lopez," Langstrom said when he saw Lopez had joined them."

Lopez extended his hand out to the doctor. "Glad to have you on board, Dr. Ferguson," he said shaking her hand.

"Glad to be here, Agent Lopez, but please call me Genie."

"And this is Louie, Louie Crosshatch," Marie said. "He is head of Bravo Team."

"Nice to meet you, Genie," Louie said, a smile breaking out on his face.

Genie nodded. "Likewise, Mr. Crosshatch, or should I call you, Sergeant?" she said, letting him know she had read the FBI's file on him.

"Just call me Louie. Bravo Team is a private unit, we do not use rank."

"Then, Louie it is. Perhaps you could give Agent Langstrom and me, a tour of this camera room I have heard so much about and brief us on how you intend to kill the vampire," Genie said, rising to her feet.

Louie gave Marie's hand a quick squeeze before he rose to his feet. "Come on, Lopez, you can explain the cameras better than I can," he said with a smile.

Lopez did not return the smile. He had not failed to notice Louie's intervention, and ready explanation. "Follow me," he said stiffly.

"I need to change outfits before Ox takes me to the doctor, and I will need your help to get dressed," Hattie told Marie. "When I get through at the doctor's, we are going to the hospital to see Nigel."

"First, let me go tell Isles there will be three more for lunch," Marie said, relieved that she would not have to answer any more questions about Goff.

"Three more?" Hattie asked, wondering who else was coming to the house.

"Yes, there is another FBI agent outside. "I have already told Jabber to make sure he gets invited to lunch.

"Good. Now that that is taken care of, I will call Isles on my phone and let him know there will be three additional guests for lunch. While I am doing that you can pick out what we are going to wear. Just make sure it is baggy enough to go over my arm. I have to be there at one, and it is almost noon now."

* * *

Bella saw Nigel's eyes flutter. "Papa," she whispered.

Nigel struggled to open his eyes. He saw three blurry faces staring down at him. "Bella?" he whispered.

"Yes, it is me," Bella said, tears leaking from her eyes as she took his hand in hers.

"Where am I?" Nigel asked.?

"You are in the hospital," Vladimir answered. "They say you have had a heart attack."

Nigel's vision grew stronger, and he saw the tears in Bella's eyes. "You should be at home resting, child," he scolded.

"And you should be at home with me," Bella countered. "For many years after the purge, I grieved for you because I believed you were dead. Now that I found you, I cannot bear the thought of losing you again."

Vladimir put a hand on Bella's shoulder to comfort her as he heard words.

"You will not lose me again, Bella," Nigel promised, squeezing her hand as he looked over her head at the man standing behind her.

"Vladimir, in my apartment in the top drawer of the dresser by my bedroom door, there is a box. That is where I keep the *kado* grass." Nigel paused to catch his breath before he continued. "Take Bella and Jennifer home, and then make some *kado* tea. Put it in a thermos and bring it to me." He waited for Vladimir to nod, before he continued. "It will heal my heart enough, so that they will let me go home."

"I will be back as soon as I can," Vladimir said.

Satisfied that Vladimir understood what was needed, Nigel closed his eyes. He knew that despite his promise to Bella, his cycle for this lifetime was almost over.

* * *

Langstrom listened to Lopez explain the *MS-2 Matrix Scanner*. They all watched a rabbit as it moved along the tree line. Though the screen did not state what was moving, it was not hard to guess what the matrix movement displayed by the way the creature moved as it hunted for food. He watched Thompson key in some commands, and the screen zoomed in on the rabbit. He compared the live screen with the matrix screen and could see why the MS-2 was superior. On one screen, you had a live bunny, and on the other, you had a moving patch of matrix with an estimated length of 13.85 inches that was traveling north at an estimated speed of one inch per five seconds.

"The smaller moving matrix sections are field mice or gophers," Lopez said as he pointed to the red dots that seem to be dancing around at the edge of the screen. "If you look at the screen with the roof camera, you can see the rabbit, but the mice are too small to be seen in the thick grass that grows by the back fence. That is why the MS-2 is so much better."

"Replay the matrix patterns that the creature created when he took down the front door, Jack? That will show the speed the creature is able to move," Louie said.

Jack entered the code, time, and date of the attack.

"Extraordinary!" Genie exclaimed when she saw the moving blur of a large body, and the speed the matrix camera estimated it traveled.

When Langstrom saw the numbers, he knew there was no turning back. They were definitely dealing with something not human. "Where is Vladimir Romanov?" he asked.

"He took Bella and Jennifer to see Nigel at the hospital," Jabber answered as he looked at his watch, and saw it was twelve-thirty. "I expect he will be back soon. Bella is still recovering from her illness and will need to rest."

Jabber answered a call on the house phone, then rose from his chair. "It's lunchtime," he declared, looking at the visitors. If you will follow me to the dining room, lunch is ready. Jack, you and Thompson, mind the cameras while the rest of us go eat. Lopez why don't you go invite your fellow agent standing outside to come inside. I imagine, he is just as hungry as I am."

Without waiting to see who followed him, Jabber headed for the dining room.

Chapter 28
Kado Grass

Vladimir took the thermos of tea out of the bag he carried with him. "Hope this works," he said as he handed it over to Nigel.

As Nigel sipped on the tea, he told him about Lopez's boss, and the woman who came with him. "She is from DC, and a doctor of psychic investigation. I looked it up on the internet. Turns out, there is a Federal Bureau of Psychic Investigation called BPI in Washington. The woman is the Director of that agency. Her name is Genie Ferguson."

Nigel was already beginning to feel stronger. He nodded. "I heard her speak at the Convention for Psychic Phenomena in Paris. I did not get to meet her. If we were cups, she would a demitasse one."

Vladimir grinned at Nigel's description of the diminutive woman.

"How is everything going at the house?"

"So far, so good. The beast has not come back or at least not close enough for the cameras to pick him up, but I think he was out there last night nevertheless, as something disturbed my sleep about two o'clock this morning," Vladimir answered.

"I cannot stay here any longer," Nigel complained.

"You are in no condition to battle the jogeth."

"No, but my presence here endangers everyone, Vladimir. If Goff comes within a mile of this hospital, he will sense my presence. He will come, and anyone who gets in his way will be killed."

Vladimir reached for his phone. "In that case, I had better see about finding a chair that I can sleep in as I will be staying here with you."

"No need for that, I will be going home within the hour. Call the doctor and tell him I am ready to go home."

"He is not going to let you go home," Vladimir argued.

"He will when he checks me over he will find the grass has repaired much of the damage to my heart."

"How can it work that fast?"

"Because it gave me enough energy to use my own physical abilities to help repair my heart."

"Ah, I see. Well, don't go anywhere until I find the doctor, and he confirms you have had a miraculous cure. We can hope he does not ask too many questions."

"I will tell him about the grass if he asks."

"You would tell him that?"

"Yes, the same story I tell everyone who has seen the grass' healing powers. It was given to me by an old man who lived in Peru when I was poisoned by some food I ate. When I gave the man a gold sovereign for saving my life, he gave me small basket filled with the grass. When he asks for the name of the grass, I will tell him I never got it. If he asks for a sample, I will give it to him. To date, no one has been able to come up with anything on this world that matches it."

Vladimir shook his head. "What do you intend to do when you run out of the grass? The box is half full."

"I know. That is why I want others on this planet searching for the grass. Do not worry. In the past six hundred years, I have used only half the basket. We still have enough left to get us through this crisis."

"Then I had better go find the doctor and get you out of here. I would prefer we get home before the sun sets, and not after," Vladimir said, putting his phone back in his jacket pocket.

* * *

"So tell me, Hattie, what is going on between you and Ox?" Marie questioned as she sat on her bed waiting for her sister to finish putting on her lipstick.

188

Hattie, who was having a hard enough time trying to put lipstick on her face with her left hand, jerked around to look at her sister, and ended up with a streak of lipstick across her left cheek. She turned back to the mirror, grabbed up a tissue from the box, and wiped the smear off her face. She then turned back around to look at Marie, her face pink with guilt.

"So, you are hiding something from me," Marie accused, standing up and folding her arms for emphasis.

"Not deliberately. I have been busy seeing doctors and worrying about Nigel."

"Again, you did not answer my question."

Hattie rolled her eyes. "Okay, If I must. Ox has asked me to marry him," Hattie confessed.

"Oh, Hattie," Marie squealed as she ran to hug her sister, then stopped when she saw the cast. "I never thought I would see this day."

"Neither did I. But please do not tell anyone, we are trying to keep it a secret until Nigel is better, and the beast is no more."

"But I am your *sister*," Marie protested.

"I know, I told Ox that same thing. I also told him I would have to tell you..." Hattie broke off as she realized she was about to shatter Marie's world. "Come. Sit down. There is more you need to know."

Hattie was trying to comfort Marie when someone knocked on the door.

"Come in!" Hattie called out as she handed Marie the tissue box.

"What's wrong, Marie?" Louie asked as he hurried over to where she sat.

Marie jumped up and embraced him. "Oh Louie, Hattie told me Jabber has cancer!" Marie cried, amid a new round of sobs.

"Yes, but you cannot let him know that you know that," Louie said as he held her in his arms. "He does not want you to know."

189

Marie shook her head. "I don't know if I can do that. My heart is breaking inside."

"Mine too," Louie said softly, "but to show my grief would cause him more pain."

Marie drew back and looked at the man. "You are right. This is not about my pain."

Louie nodded, but did not immediately, loosen his hold on her. She fit inside his arms and heart, like no one else ever had.

"I came to tell you both, dinner is ready," he said, looking at Hattie.

"Oh, my stars! I had better go wash my face and eyes," Marie said pulling out of Louie's arms. "Jabber must not know I have been crying."

"If he asks you what wrong, Marie, lie, and say you are worried about Nigel," Hattie suggested.

Marie's face fell. "With all the excitement, I completely forgot that Nigel is dying too. What is wrong with me?" she wailed.

"Marie!" Hattie exclaimed as she rose from the bed. "Nigel is not dying. Vladimir took him some *kado* grass, remember?"

Marie put her hands over her face, and then took them away as it occurred to her the grass was the answer. "That's it, Hattie!" she exclaimed excitedly. "We need to give Jabber some of the grass, so it can heal him."

"Only after we talk to Nigel about it," Hattie said soothingly. "Now, why don't you go wash your face, while I finish putting on my lipstick, while Louie goes tell Jabber that we are on our way."

Marie, nodded, raised up on her toes, and impulsively, kissed Louie on the cheek before she hurried off to the bathroom.

Hattie raised a brow as she as she gave Louie a knowing look.

He grinned and then shrugged before he turned and went back out the door.

Hattie finished applying her lipstick, then realized her feet were bare. She went to the closet to find a pair of sandals.

"Do I look as awful as I think I do?" Marie asked when she came out of the bathroom and saw Hattie waiting for her.

"Well, I can see you have been crying, but most won't know that. And if they do, I doubt they will question it. They all know Nigel is in the hospital. Other than that, you look fine."

Marie sighed. "Then I guess I am ready."

Chapter 29
"Send Backup!"

Vladimir gave Jack a grateful smile when he saw the young man waiting at the door with Bella's wheelchair. Nigel, despite his claims of feeling better was still weak.

"You are just in time for dinner. Everyone is at the dining table," Jack stated as he turned the chair around.

"No," Nigel said, grabbing hold of the wheelchair to steady himself before he sat down in it. "Take me to my apartment through the kitchen. I am not fit for company right now."

Jack looked from Nigel to Vladimir.

"This way," Vladimir said as he pulled out a key fob and opened the garage door.

"Oh, right," Jack said, turning the chair around to face the garage.

Nigel nodded at Isles and Kate as he was wheeled into the kitchen but did not greet them. It was all he could do to keep his eyes open.

Once Nigel was sitting in his recliner, and Jack had left. Vladimir went to see if Isles could fix them dinner as well. "Two bowls of soup, a few crackers, some English biscuits, and a pot of tea will do. Put two cups on the tray as I intend to stay with him tonight."

"Of course, sir," Isles said. "I should have it ready in about fifteen to twenty minutes as I just cooked a half dozen chickens for tonight's main course, and a pot of carrots for one of the vegetables. All I need do is combine those with some noodles."

"Hmm. Sounds good. Could you put a breast piece in my soup? A few small pieces of chicken in Nigel's bowl will do, as he is not really up to eating much tonight."

"Of course," Isles answered.

Vladimir went to check on Bella and Jennifer and found them gathered at the table with everyone else. He heard Bella laugh at something the doctor said and smiled. He rarely heard her laugh these days.

"Father," Jennifer greeted.

Vladimir gave her a smile.

"How is Nigel?" Hattie asked.

"He is better, and in his apartment, but is not up to visitors tonight, Marie," he said holding up his hand as she started to rise from her chair.

"He cannot be left there alone," Marie protested.

"He will not be alone as I am staying with him tonight," Vladimir said as he moved around the table to where Bella sat.

He leaned down and gave her a kiss on the cheek. "*I am home, my love,*" he whispered in ancient Persian.

Genie heard him. "You speak Farsi?" she asked, recognizing the word love.

"Yes, we lived in Istanbul for many years," Vladimir answered.

"And you, Bella, do you speak Farsi as well?" Genie asked.

Bella searched her mind, then nodded. "Yes, apparently I do, but I had forgotten."

"Are either one of you, able to read the language?" Genie questioned.

"I can or once could. Why?" Vladimir asked.

"I have a book. An ancient one that one of my students found in bookstore in Cairo and sent to me. The shop's owner told her the title translates to a *Manifest of Ghosts*. I really would like to know if it concerns paranormal activity."

"I would like to see it as well. Though it may be referring to what is known as the immortal soldiers, rather than ghosts."

"You may be right, but I really would like to know. I will see if Peggy can send it to me. I keep it in a drawer in my desk."

"I look forward to taking a look at it, but it could take me months to translate it. I have not read Farsi for many years. Now, if anyone needs me, text me. Unless it is an emergency, do not come knocking at the door, Nigel needs his rest," Vladimir stated, looking at Marie and Hattie.

Marie's lips pursed stubbornly, but nevertheless, she nodded.

So did Hattie, thus signaling she would also stay away.

* * *

Once Nigel was asleep, Vladimir went to the kitchen, and called Louie. "When you have time, we need to talk."

"Lopez just left to catch a nap, and I am in the cam room, alone. Jack and Thompson will be in at midnight," Louis said.

"Then how about we meet in the kitchen around midnight? That way, we can talk, and I can still keep an eye on the apartment at the same time. I cannot leave Nigel alone at this end of the house."

"Be there as soon as Jack comes in."

* * *

Goff decided he would go back to the street where young females gathered on street corners, giggling at the men as they drove by in cars. He needed more than one meal tonight as he was still healing from being burned by the woman's inner light. He would not make that mistake again. No, the next time he got within striking distance, he would just kill her before she could use the light against him.

Sergeant Nathan Horn, and officer Chris Stinson were on boulevard duty for the rest of the night. As they walked the street, they ignored the few taunts about their new beanie type police hats, and most certainly did not say a word about the hats being lined with tin foil. That would start an entire new round of cop jokes.

When they heard several high pitch screams that broke off just as suddenly as they had started up, they ran back to the corner they had just passed. They found several girls standing there with a look of horror on their faces, but their eyes were blank.

Nathan put a hand up and waved it in front of one the girl's eyes, but she just stood there as if frozen in time.

Chris tried snapping his fingers in front of another girl, but she too did not move. "We had better go check the alley. There are only four girls here, and I counted six a minute ago."

Nathan followed Chris down the alley. Both officers had their guns out. They saw a man holding a woman in his arms, and slowly moved forward.

"Freeze, dirt bag!" Chris shouted.

Goff quit feeding and raised his head to look the men coming toward him. He growled a warning, but much to his surprise, found he could not enter their minds.

Nathan turned on his helmet light, then gasped aloud when he saw the girl's bloody throat, and the mouth full of sharp teeth on the thing that stood there growling at them.

Both officers opened fire.

The jogeth screeched in pain as the bullets ripped through his body. The girl's blood began seeping from the wounds in his chest and stomach. He dropped her and was gone before the next round of bullets could reach him.

"The killer is a VAMPIRE! Do you hear me? Chris shouted into the comm unit on his shoulder strap. "We need help! Send backup!"

"We are in the alley at Sunset and Lugosi. We also need the coroner, and a couple of ambulances," Nathan put in, using his own comm unit. "We got at least one dead, and five more injured." he added as he bent down to check on the woman lying on the ground by the dead girl. She appeared to be in the same shape as the women on the street—catatonic."

When he finished with the details, he reached up, and touched the hat on his head. Though he had been the first to agree that the department was doing everything it could to make an officer's life miserable when it mandated, they wear the miserable thing, he had no doubt the foil lined hats had saved their lives.

* * *

Louie sat down at the kitchen table. It was twenty minutes past midnight, and he was tired. He also was curious to find out what was so important, it could not wait until tomorrow. He picked up one of the oatmeal raisin cookies that Vladimir and Nigel called biscuits and put it on a napkin by his cup of tea. He preferred coffee to tea, but he also wanted to get some sleep tonight, and so tea it was at this hour.

"I wanted to let you know that I have decided to go with my first plan to lure the beast in close enough for Bravo Team to get a shot," Vladimir said.

Louie shook his head. "He moves way too fast for you to get out of the line of fire."

"You forget, I can levitate. I may be within a few feet of him, but I will be in the air, and he will be on the ground. Also I can wear body armor."

Louie reluctantly nodded. "That could work, but you realize you could also lose a toe or even a foot if you are anywhere near his head."

196

"I am willing to take that risk," Vladimir said grimly.

"I am not sure I am. If Lopez is here as a witness, possibly, otherwise, gunshot wounds are subject to law enforcement investigations, attorneys, and even prison."

"Then I will make sure I have bullet proof shoes," Vladimir argued.

"That could work, and I imagine you can probably find a pair on the internet or have a pair made for you."

"Yes, and I know just the man to do that. He makes custom made vests for private cops," Vladimir said.

"You might give him a call tomorrow and find out. I think it is going to be several days before that beast comes back"

"Why do you say that," Vladimir asked.

"There was an incident a few minutes ago. I heard it on the police scanner. That creature killed again. He was also shot several times by two police officers. He got away, of course, but it is probably is going to take him a few days to heal."

"They must have been wearing foil hats," Vladimir said, a grin breaking out on his face.

"Yeah. That was mentioned by one of the officers."

Louie yawned. "If we do this, Vladimir, you need to know that getting shot is going to hurt like hell, bullet proof shoes or not."

Vladimir nodded. "I figured that. I saw the bruises on one of my men who was shot while wearing a bulletproof vest. But it would hurt a lot more to lose anyone in my family."

"I can't argue that one with you. Now, I think I will go get some rest. I am going to sleep a lot better knowing that creature won't be coming around tonight."

"Me too," Vladimir agreed.

* * *

"The beast killed another woman tonight, but this time, he got shot by the police. Seems they are now wearing tin foil caps," Vladimir told Nigel when he saw he was awake.

"He must be staying somewhere close by as I felt a faint trace of his presence for a few seconds. It woke me up," Nigel said.

"The matrix cam did not pick him up or else, Louie would have told me."

"I think he was in the storm drain. The cameras would not pick up his movement there."

"No, they would not, but tomorrow I can work on getting coverage for that area," Vladimir said, fingering his chin as he thought about the storm drain. He dropped his hand before he added, "This may be the reason we don't see him coming until it is too late. He simply jumps over the concrete wall, and then he is on our doorstep."

"Would you help me up out of this chair, Vladimir, I would like to get into my bed for what is left of the night, and I could use a trip to the bathroom," Nigel said as he struggled with the chair's footrest. When it dropped down, he rocked the recliner forward, and with Vladimir's help got to his feet.

Chapter 30
Genie's Secret

The sun was bright, and the day warm as Genie got out of the car and paid the cabbie. Before she rang the doorbell, she stopped to admire the two large cement pots full of pink azaleas that stood on each side of the front door. "You were not here yesterday," she murmured to the pots as she waited for someone to answer the bell.

Hattie was on her way to the kitchen when she heard the bell. "I will get it!" she called out when she saw Myra was busy setting the table.

"Ah, Genie. I was not expecting you," Hattie said, and then winced as she realized that had sounded rude. "I mean, I am glad to see you, it's just I was not expecting you. No. That does not sound any better."

"No need to apologize, Hattie. You are right, I was not invited. I am looking for Mr. Romanov."

"He is either with Nigel or in the dining room. We are about to have lunch. Come in and join us!" When Hattie saw the doctor hesitate, she added, "We have plenty of food, and I am really glad you came by. We did not get to talk much yesterday, and there is so much I would like to ask you."

"Thank you," Genie said as she stepped inside.

Vladimir raised a brow when he saw the doctor come trailing in behind Hattie. His eyes narrowed. He did not need to read her mind to know she could be trouble for this house. Though Bella was beginning to heal physically, her mind was still fragile. While the FBI agents did not seem curious about Bella's illness or memory loss, he had no doubt Doctor Genie Ferguson would.

He watched the woman as she stopped and admired the wall of paintings. He was not surprised when she lowered her head and studied Marie's work.

"I can see why your paintings are highly regarded in the art world, Marie," Genie said as she seated herself at the table. They resonate both beauty and emotion. The one with the homeless man on the street sharing a piece of bread with his dog, both so thin, you can see their rib bones sticking out, provokes a war upon one's senses."

"How so?" Marie asked, curious at the doctor's description of her painting.

"Your painting depicts abject poverty, but the man's face shows nothing but strength and love as he shares his meager meal with his best friend. The dog reflects that strength and love. At first glance, you are shocked by their obvious hunger, but then you realize neither of them are hungry, not for life or love. That is the magic of a good painting. It makes one step back and take another look at the world."

Marie nodded, a pleased look on her face. "I took that photo in New York in the seventies. What you describe, is exactly how I saw them that day, but you are the first to put it in words."

"Yes, we spent years gathering photos of the homeless, the immigrants, and the wealthy when we lived in New York," Hattie explained. "And it is a good thing we did because someone homeless in Hollywood is apt to be wearing a mink coat, or break dancing to a boombox on a street corner."

"Everyone at the table laughed.

"I have a painting of that break dancer in my studio," Marie said, a grin on her face as she looked at the doctor. "It was not the dancer that interested me, though he was interesting to watch. It was the rapture on the children's faces as they watched his show. "Perhaps you would like to see it after we finish lunch. I call it Street Glory."

"I would be delighted to see your work, and your studio," Genie responded, pretending she had not done the math.

Vladimir forced a smile to his face, but he was not happy. Marie had just made a major mistake. She was supposed to be thirty-four years old. When the doctor got around to analyzing what had been said, she would see the discrepancy. Marie and Hattie supposedly, were born in nineteen eighty-six, so how could they be taking photos in New York in the nineteen seventies? He rose from the table.

"If you will excuse me, I need to go check on Nigel," he said.

"Mr. Romanov!" Genie called out when she saw he was leaving the table. "I would like to interview you later today or tomorrow, if you are too busy for today."

"What about?" Vladimir asked, turning back to scowl at her.

"The vampire, your ability to read minds, and some of the events that have taken place here," Genie replied.

Vladimir pretended to look at his watch as he considered her request. "How about this evening around eight. We can talk in the kitchen. Dinner will be over by then. Of course, you will have to spend the night here as we do not come or go in this house after dark," he said.

Genie blinked with surprise but did not hesitate to take him up on his offer. "Thank you. I have an appointment this afternoon, but I will return before it gets dark."

"When you return, Marie will show you which room you will be staying in."

Both Marie and Hattie looked at each other.

"Nigel's room," Hattie mouthed.

Marie nodded. After lunch was over, she would get Myra to help her move Nigel's things."

* * *

Goff was weakened by the bullet holes in his body and slept the better part of two days. When he woke, he sat up and examined himself. The wounds were almost healed over, but his clothing stank of dried blood and his own black gore. He ripped his shirt and pants off and discarded them on the floor. He then pulled open one of the crypts he was using as a wardrobe bin, and picked out some of the new clothing he had removed from one of the stores that fronted the street that he often hunted on.

Once he was dressed, he found he was tired and sat down. *This will not do*, he thought. *I cannot go up against the weapons the people of this world use. It wears me out to have to regenerate my body.*

He then recalled the small park he passed by when he went to the city. It was always lit up at night which is the main reason he avoided it. *But.... there is a grove of nearby trees. I can hide there, and then use my mind to bring them to me.*

What about Nigel's house, they have weapons? his mind asked.

"Bah!" he scoffed aloud. "No matter the cost, they have to die."

* * *

Vladimir filled a teapot and set it on the table. He was pouring himself a cup of tea when Genie came walking in with Lopez.

"I am making a quick soda run. Hopefully, there are some chips to go with them," Lopez told Vladimir as he opened the refrigerator door.

"I saw some chips in that cabinet," Vladimir said pointing to a lidded bin on top of the counter before he invited the doctor to sit down.

"Help yourself to the biscuits, Lopez," he said when he saw the FBI agent eyeing the cookies.

"Thanks, I will," Lopez said as he grabbed a paper plate, put some cookies on it, then turned and headed back to the cam room.

"Would you like coffee or tea?" Vladimir asked.

"I prefer tea. No sugar or cream," Genie replied.

"That is the way I drink it also. Of course, I generally have a biscuit which does have sugar, among other things," Vladimir said as he helped himself to a cookie.

"Thank you. I will have one of those too," Genie said, setting her cup down, and reaching for one of the oatmeal treats, and laid it on a napkin beside her cup.

She then looked at the man sitting across the table. "I have been told that you can read minds. It that true?" she asked.

"Yes, I have been able to do that all my life. I believe I was born that way," Vladimir answered truthfully.

"Can you give me a demonstration? I have worked with the psychically gifted, but never have known one that can actually read minds."

Vladimir entered the doctor's mind.

"*Interesting,*" he told her, speaking only with his mind. "*You express interest in my psychic abilities, but at the same time you are skeptical about me.*"

"Yes, but not for reasons you would ever guess," Genie said, and then filled his mind with her memories.

Vladimir sat back and gaped at the woman. "You are right, I never would have guessed," he said when he got over the shock of finding out who she was. He used his mind to check on Nigel, and found he was awake. He told him what he had learned.

"*Bring her here,*" Nigel said, putting the book he had just started to read down. He was sure the book's story would not be near as interesting as the one the doctor would tell.

"Come with me!" Vladimir said as he rose from the table, and put the pot of tea, the tin of biscuits, and an extra cup on a tray. "It is time you met Nigel."

Genie did as she was asked, pausing long enough to pick up her cookie and napkin. She realized she had finally found what she had long been searching for, someone else who could read minds.

Once introductions were over, and everyone was seated, Nigel asked the first question.

"What is your father's name?" he asked.

"Jerico. My mother's name was Ringee," Genie replied, surprised by the man's questions.

"What happened to them?" Nigel asked, noting she used the past tense when referring to her parents.

"We were living in London during World War Two, the house we lived in was bombed. They were killed as was my younger brother," Genie replied emotionally.

Nigel swallowed painfully as he recalled his brother and his wife waiting for him to go through the portal, so they could follow.

"Your father was my brother. I hunted for months, hoping to find all of you. When I did not, I decided you did not make it through before the portal closed."

"We did make it through the portal and ended up in Canada. A Native American tribe took us in. Their chief was ill, and father cured him with *kado* grass. He then became their healer. We lived there for a long time, but mother did not age, and father did not want the people to question why that was. I think I was about twenty at the time. We lived with several tribes as the years passed. Then one day, father found out a ship was going to France. He booked passage, and we went to Paris, then Madrid, Rome, and other cities until the early 1900s when we moved to London."

Genie paused. "After I lost them, and the war was over, I came back to America."

"It must have been hard to not only be an orphan, but a poor one at that," Nigel said.

"I was not poor," Genie said, shaking her head. "It took me several days to dig through the rubble, but I was able to retrieve father's small chest of gold from the basement where he kept it."

"I wonder why it is that I cannot sense a kinship with you? I should be able to do that even in my weakened condition," Nigel asked as he mulled over all she had told him.

"Father taught all of us to suppress any sign of our Dysonian heritage. He was afraid the jogeths would be on this planet as well. I have built a barrier in my mind."

"My Dysonian name was Terin," Nigel said watching for any sign of recognition.

"I don't recall anything about you. Father never spoke about any of his family nor those on Dysonia. Thinking about that now, I imagine he did that to protect us from doing something like Marie did today."

"What did Marie do," Nigel asked, looking from Genie to Vladimir.

"She spoke about taking photographs in New York in the nineteen seventies," Vladimir answered.

"Ah, yes. I can see where that would be confusing, considering the age she is supposed to be," Nigel said.

"I found it interesting that no one else at the table reacted or tried to correct her," Genie said.

"Jabber, Louie, and Ox, know who we are, and where we come from," Vladimir explained. "And as you can see, they are very discreet about that. Thankfully, Lopez went to LA today, Jack and Thompson were on cam duty, and Lee and Earl were in their rooms. None of them know."

Alarm filled Genie's face. "Please, I do not want anyone to know who I am, not even Marie or Hattie."

"Then we will need to find some other reason to explain to Hattie and Marie why you are staying here," Vladimir said.

"Why would I stay here?" Genie asked.

"Because, regardless of whether Nigel can sense you or not, the beast might," Vladimir answered.

"He is right, Genie," Nigel agreed. "If Goff gets anywhere within a mile of you, he will know you are Dysonian, and he will try to kill you. There is no security team to protect you at the hotel. You need to stay here until you go back to DC. As for Hattie and Marie, I will leave it up to you to tell them who you are when you feel comfortable to do so."

Genie chewed on a nail as she considered her options. When she made her decision, she put her hand down, and nodded at both men. "All right, I will stay here. Not so much to protect myself, but to protect others. Maggie can go back to DC tomorrow. I do not want anything to happen to her. As far as anyone else is concerned, I am doing research for a book which is what brought me here in the first place. That will explain my presence."

"Good. Now that we have that settled, tell me what you can remember about your early years on this world," Nigel said.

"You need to rest, Uncle," Genie said as she saw him close his eyes for a few seconds. "Tomorrow afternoon, I will come sit with you, and tell you what I can remember about those days."

Vladimir agreed. "Yes, you do need to rest. Genie will be here tomorrow. You will have plenty of time to talk."

Nigel nodded. He was tired. "Give her one of the amulets. They are in the same drawer as the *kado* grass."

Genie watched Vladimir open a top drawer and pull a necklace out of a box. When he handed it to her, she recognized the pendant. "I once had a necklace like this. We all did," she said.

"What happened to it?" Vladimir asked.

"I was injured and taken to a medical facility after the bombing. It disappeared there," she answered as she slipped the chain with the amulet over her head. "When I get back to DC, I am going to have a jeweler engrave the back with the words "Do not remove this necklace," just in case I end up in the hospital again."

"Good idea. I had not thought of that. I will talk to Nigel about it when he gets better," Vladimir said.

Genie looked over at Nigel and saw he was asleep. "Best I go find my own room as I am also tired. See you tomorrow."

Vladimir nodded, and then followed her to the kitchen. It was only nine forty-five, and he decided he would have another cup of tea. As he waited for more water to heat, he took his phone out of his pocket and called Bella.

"How are you tonight, my sweet?" he asked when she answered.

"Good. Jennifer and I have been watching TV. What are you doing?"

"The doctor just left, and I am fixing myself a cup of tea in the kitchen."

"Can I join you?"

"I was hoping you would."

"I will be right there," Bella said.

Vladimir knew Bella would ask questions about Genie. He also expected Hattie and Marie would question him about the doctor tomorrow at breakfast. He found out he was wrong about that when both of his sisters followed Bella into the kitchen.

"What did the doctor have to say?" Marie asked as she sat down at the table.

"Yes, we are dying to hear what she asked you," Hattie said as she got out three cups, and brought them to the table.

"Nothing much. She wanted a demonstration of my mind reading abilities, and asked if any other member of my family could read minds. I told her no. We chatted about New York and London, and then she went off to her room," Vladimir lied.

"No, she is not in her room. I saw her go into the office. I imagine she is asking Lopez what he knows about you, Vladimir," Hattie said.

"Or us," Marie put in.

Vladimir saw the sour look on Marie's face. "I like her, Marie," he said. "She is very interested in psychic phenomena. She is writing a book on the subject."

"Well, I don't think I like that," Hattie muttered, folding her arms angrily.

"Why do you say that?" Marie asked.

"Because I don't want to be a *freak!*" Hattie snapped.

Bella's mouth dropped open with surprise.

"Freak?" Marie questioned, shocked by her sister's anger.

"Yes. We will become tabloid cover news, and worse, people will stand outside by the fence trying to get photos of us. Drones will fly over hoping to get film coverage of us on the patio or in the swimming pool. We will have to change our names and move away from here."

Marie's face fell. "I don't want to move away. I like it here."

Vladimir opened his mouth to argue, but then shut it when he realized she was right. There was no getting around reporters or photographers, not when there was money to be made. "I will have a talk with her tomorrow, and suggest she use aliases in her book to protect us."

"I don't think we should wait until tomorrow," Hattie said, folding her arms for emphasis. "I for one, cannot sleep with this hanging over our heads. Why don't you call the cam room, and invite her to come join us?"

Marie and Bella both nodded.

Vladimir got out his phone again.

Genie saw all three women were frowning at her as she sat down at the table. She wondered what Vladimir had told them. When she heard Hattie's concerns about the book she was working on, she understood.

"To tell the truth, I had not thought about what problems would arise if my subjects' identities were known as I have no plans for revealing that information. Now, I realize I had better code my notes as well to insure everyone is protected. After all, if something happens to me those notes could fall into the wrong hands."

"Thank you," Marie said. "We will all sleep better tonight knowing that."

Genie jerked in her chair and looked out toward the patio. Her face lost color.

"What's wrong?" Vladimir asked as he looked out the windows.

"For a second or two, I sensed a very strong psychic presence, but it is gone now."

Vladimir looked at his watch. It was twenty-one minutes past ten. He had no doubt that Genie had sensed the beast's presence, but he could hardly speak with her about that with Bella, Hattie, and Marie sitting at the table.

"Nigel has been wanting to meet you, doctor. If you are not too tired? I will take you to see him when you finish your tea."

Genie set her cup down. She was glad to see the women were staring at Vladimir, and not her or they might have seen the flash of surprise on her face.

"I look forward to meeting Nigel, I understand he has studied psychic phenomena for years," she replied, pretending she had yet to meet her uncle.

"Yes, he has. Give me a few minutes to take my wife back to her room, and then I will take you to meet him."

"No, need for you to do that, Vladimir," Bella said, realizing that Vladimir was trying to protect her. "I will go with Hattie and Marie when they go to their room."

Hattie eyed Vladimir and then the doctor. When she saw the worry in his eyes, she realized that what Genie had felt, could have been the jogeth's presence. In that case, the safest place for them was Bella's room. "Come on, you two. Put your cup in the dishwasher, and let's go find Jennifer. You know, we planned on watching that new *Lottie Marma* movie tonight."

Vladimir waited until the women had left before he spoke. "What did you feel?"

"Just as I said, a strong psychic presence. No doubt in my mind, it was the jogeth. For I have never felt such a presence, not even when you entered my mind."

"Then, you need to go back to the cam room where you have protection if he does decide to attack the house again. While you do that, I will go stay close to Nigel. He is in no condition to do battle with the beast. If Hattie or Marie wonder why you are not with Nigel, just tell them he was asleep."

Genie nodded, picked up her cup, and rose from the table. "I am not a fire-maker like Hattie, Vladimir, but I am very good with my mind. Though to tell you the truth, I have never used it, except the few times, I felt I was in danger. While I may not be strong enough by myself to battle him, together, we might be able to slow him down long enough for your Marines to get a shot at him."

Vladimir was surprised by her offer. "Then I suggest tomorrow we start practicing. There is one more thing about me that you have yet to learn, I can levitate things, including my body."

"You mean, like fly?"

"Yes, I started with small objects, and kept increasing size and weight. After years of practice, I could levitate myself."

"That is not something I have ever considered but would love to learn."

"Well, we can check on that tomorrow as well, and see how you do with a feather or spoon."

Chapter 31
New Defenses

After breakfast, Louie and Vladimir sat watching footage from the new solar thermographic camera that had been attached to one of the trees at the back fence to monitor the storm drain. The beast had passed by exactly at ten twenty, headed west. At a few minutes past midnight, he passed by again, this time headed east.

"You can see he is moving a lot faster on his way back," Vladimir said. "This morning's paper stated the bodies of two young girls were found in some trees by *Jinson Park* which is about a mile west of here."

Louie brought up a map screen with a lot of bright red X's on it. "That's different, considering all the others he killed were in the Sunset Boulevard area which is south of here."

"Probably because he has learned he is no longer able to control the police," Vladimir stated.

Louie nodded as he added two more red X's to his map.

He then scrolled back through the footage. "You can see, he stopped for a few seconds when he passed by the first time. When he came back, he did not stop."

"Yes, the first time, he was probably checking to see if Nigel had returned," Vladimir lied, knowing it had been Genie's presence that had attracted jogeth's attention.

"That is not exactly a comforting thought."

"Be glad he thinks the rest of us are not worth keeping an eye on," Vladimir said. "Nigel is his equal, and he knows that."

"Hattie can hurt him too. Hopefully, he will believe the same of Marie, and not come after her," Louie put in.

Vladimir shook his head. "No, it does not work that way. He is more dangerous than ever now that he knows Hattie has the ability to create the only thing that can destroy him. He won't take time to find out whether Marie has that same ability."

Louie thought about that. "How does the Maker's fire work?"

"It is a pure light given to the wielder to protect Dysonians from jogeths."

"If that is the case, then why were your people pushed into extinction?" Louie asked.

"According to Nigel there were only a few with that ability. Our mother was one of them. The jogeths found that if they separated a Dysonian with defensive powers, then all they needed was to join their own minds together to defeat that person. It did not take them more than a few weeks to kill every Dysonian with the ability to use the fire. That is when the elders decided to send us to this world," Vladimir explained.

Louie sat silent, a faraway look on his face as he mentally sorted through all the known facts. "You know, this reminds of the time I was in Afghanistan, and we had to take refuge in some rocks when we ran into the opposition. If we stayed there, we would eventually run out of ammo and die. If we ran, they would shoot us down. If we surrendered, they would behead us. So it was dead, no matter which choice we made."

"Well, you are not dead, so what did you do?"

"We called for air support, and fortunately, two stealth bombers were just minutes away from our location."

"I can see how that would work, but how does that relate to our problem?"

"Air strikes were the one thing they had no defense against. That creature has no defense against Hattie. While we might shoot him, and slow him down, she can destroy him." When Louie saw Vladimir shaking his head, he added, "Before you protest too much, I suggest we ask her."

Vladimir scowled at Louie. "No. She would probably say yes, but I will not have her risking her life."

"How about we discuss it with Nigel," Louie suggested. "He knows more about how the light works than she does."

"We can go talk to him, but I am not going to change my mind. And what you might not know is that if something happens to Hattie, Marie will never forgive us."

"Yes, I am aware of that," Louie said with a sigh. "But at the same time, I realize that we could all sit here and die, one at a time, despite all our plans and weapons, and that beast would continue feeding on humans."

Vladimir blew a breath of frustration when he realized Louie was right. "Then we had better go talk to Nigel and find out what Hattie can or cannot do."

* * *

After breakfast, Genie had gone to check on Nigel. She was sitting there listening to him talk about how they had decided to leave New York, and come to Hollywood when Vladimir and Louie came in. She rose to excuse herself, but Nigel shook his head.

"You need to stay. Vladimir has told me they are here to discuss whether Hattie can survive if she goes up against Goff."

"I know nothing about that," Genie declared.

"No, but you do have the ability to sense Goff when I cannot. You demonstrated that last night. I know you do not want your identity revealed, but the beast is now aware of your existence. It won't be long before his curiosity leads to another attack on those in this house. It is Louie's job to protect us. He cannot do that if he does not have all the facts. Also, I need you to help train Hattie. Unfortunately, you are going to have to tell her and Marie who you are."

Genie gaped at Nigel.

Louie saw Vladimir's mouth drop open as well. *Never a dull moment in this house. That's for sure*, he told himself as he fought to keep his own face blank.

Genie closed her mouth and sat back down. Her cheeks were red with anger.

Vladimir pointed to the only other chair in the room. "You sit there, Louie. I will sit on the footstool."

Genie waited for them to get seated before she turned her attention on Louie. "I imagine, you are wondering what the fuss is all about? You see, I do have psychic abilities, including being able to read minds, though I am not as good at it as Vladimir is. The reason for that is I am also from Dysonia."

Louie kept his face blank by keeping his jaw clamped down.

"You do not seem surprised. Did you already guess my origin?" Genie asked.

Louie shook his head. "No. I am surprised, but I learned a long time ago not to let that distract me from my job."

"I guess I should be grateful for that, but I really did not want to share my background with others. However, what I want does not matter, not when people are dying."

"Rest assured. Your secret is safe with me. Though I will have to tell Ox, as he is second in command in case anything happens to me," Louie said. "Like me, he will not tell anyone. However, I suggest you do not tell the FBI agents as they, by law, are not allowed to keep secrets from the government. Especially ones that concern beings from other worlds."

"Right. That what has always worried me. I do not want to end up in petri dish."

Louie nodded.

"Now that we have that out of the way, tell me what you need me to do, Uncle?" Genie asked.

"Vladimir, use your mind to find Hattie and Marie, and tell them to come here," Nigel said.

"I will tell them, but I doubt either one of them are going to like what you have to say."

"I will not let you take the blame for this, Nigel. It was my idea," Louie said.

"We best keep that to ourselves for right now. Hattie will have more confidence in herself if she believes it is my plan. No offense meant."

"No offense taken. I was not looking forward to facing Marie's wrath," Louie stated.

Nigel nodded with a grin on his face.

"Why do you need me to train her?" Genie asked.

"Because you are female, and she is going to go through changes, both physical and emotional. You also have telepathic abilities. Should she forget how to stop the fire, you can use your mind to tell her she is safe, and it is okay to put the fire out. Every Dysonian who had the ability to use the fire had a wingman, so to speak, because a fire-maker can lose track of both time and surroundings. You will be her wingman."

"Physical changes?" Vladimir questioned.

"Yes. Patterns, much like tattoos, will appear on her body when she accepts the fire. I am sure she has already noticed she is itching more than usual, but probably puts it down to stress or the pain medication they gave her at the hospital."

Vladimir nodded. "You are right about that. I picked up some medicine at the drugstore yesterday. She called it anti-itch cream."

"Good, her body has begun to accept the changes."

"What is good about it?" Genie questioned. "I would not want ink lines all over my body."

"Neither will Hattie, but the patterns will give her the power to wield the fire and protect her from the intense heat that the fire causes."

"Who will protect me from the heat?" Genie asked.

"The fire will not harm you, other than you will need to wear solar eclipse glasses while she is radiating light, and the room will heat up some. But I have never known or heard of anyone other than a jogeth being harmed by it," Nigel answered.

Hattic and Marie came in and greeted everyone.

Louie stood and offered Marie his chair.

Vladimir beckoned Hattie to come sit on the stool by Nigel.

"Girls I want to introduce you to Genie Ferguson," Nigel said.

"We have already met her, Nigel," Hattie declared.

"Not as my niece, you haven't. Genie's father was my brother. When they came through the portal, behind us, they were deposited in Canada. I had always assumed the portal closed before they could get through it. That is why I have never said anything about them."

"Why that is wonderful news," Hattie said. "

"Yes. Unfortunately, she is the only one left of her family," Nigel said.

"What happened to them?" Marie asked.

"We were living in London during World War Two, and our home was bombed," Genie explained.

"I am sorry to hear that," Marie murmured.

"As am I," Hattie said.

Hattie felt a disturbance in Vladimir and shuddered.

Marie felt her sister's discomfort within her own mind. "What's wrong, Hattie?"

"I don't know, but I think Nigel and Vladimir do," Hattie said, looking at her brother.

"Yes, we do," Nigel agreed, turning the attention back on him.

Marie turned to look at Louie. When he did not give her an encouraging smile, she turned to glare at Nigel. "Whatever it is, the answer is no," she stated.

"Have you had a dream?" Nigel asked.

Marie avoided his eyes as she shook her head.

Nigel frowned. It was not like Marie to lie. "Tell me what you saw!" he commanded.

Marie put a hand over her mouth and shook her head.

"I need to know, Marie. All our lives are at risk."

Marie dropped her hand. "I had the fire dream again."

"Where were you this time?" Nigel questioned.

Marie made a face, irritated that Nigel kept prodding her. She closed her eyes, and recalled what she could of the dream. "I don't know," she answered, opening her eyes. "The light from the flames hurt my eyes, and I had to keep them closed. Hattie was standing a few feet away from me. I was lying on the floor dead and could not move."

Louie's face lost color as he heard her describe her death.

Vladimir moved to stand behind Marie's chair. He put a hand on her shoulder to try and comfort her.

"Was Hattie in pain?" Nigel asked.

"I don't know!" Marie all but shouted.

"Put aside your fears, Marie. What you saw, is Hattie using the Maker's fire. That is a good thing," Nigel declared. "As for your being dead, you are not. Elsewise, you would not be able to open your eyes. Now, if everyone has finished with the negatives, I will tell you why I summoned you."

Nigel waited to see if anyone had more to say before he continued. "Louie has brought it to Vladimir's and my attention that he believes we are in a fight to the death.

Marie turned and gave Louie a dark look.

"He did so by stating the facts that when you are in an unwinnable situation, and facing death, you must find a new defense. He pointed out that Goff is able to kill us all, one at a time, and still be here to prey on the people of this world. He paused to let that information sink in. "There is only one thing known that can destroy the beast, so that he cannot return, and that is you ability, Hattie, to create the Maker's fire.

When Marie saw which direction Nigel was going, she shook her head. "No. I will not let you risk Hattie's life."

"They are right, Marie, and you know it. If we just sit here, and wait for his next attack, I could die anyway. Next time, I doubt it will be just my arm that gets broken," Hattie argued.

Marie looked at the cast on Hattie's arm and sighed. "You are probably right about that."

"Just so you know, Marie, Hattie will not be the bait, I will," Vladimir stated, patting her on the shoulder.

"Oh, damn! Hell! or whatever else people say around here when they are angry!" Marie shouted as she rose from her chair and ran from the room.

"I will go see if I can calm her down," Louie said. "I doubt you need me here as I know nothing about the Maker's fire, but what I saw last week."

* * *

Louie found Marie in her studio. She stood there sobbing as she sorted through her paint tubes with one hand while wiping at her wet face with a tissue with the other hand.

He went and took the tube from her hand and put it back in the empty slot.

Marie put her hands to her face. "Don't look at me, Louie. I am a mess right now," she protested.

Louie pulled her into his arms and held her. "You have every right to be upset, Marie. The danger is real."

"That is what scares me. In my mind, I keep seeing that creature grabbing Hattie, and carrying her off kicking and screaming. When I finally wear myself out enough to sleep, I dream she is on fire, and I wake up screaming."

"I know all about that. My first week in Afghanistan, our unit was attacked, not once, but three separate times in the span of twenty-four hours. We lost several men. Every time, I closed my eyes, I saw them die again. Whether you are male or female, Marie, makes no difference, we all react to traumatic events."

Marie threw her arms around him and hugged him tight. "Oh, Louie, I am so sorry you had to go through that!" she sobbed.

Louie hugged her back and held her until she quieted. "You know I could get used to holding you like this, paint smears and all," he quipped as he grabbed some tissues from the box, and wiped her damp eyes, and then a dab of paint off her cheek.

Marie looked up at him. When she saw he was serious, she smiled, "Me too," she agreed, laying her head back on his chest.

* * *

Later that evening, Bella sat in Nigel's room, listening to Nigel tell her about a house he owned in Paris. She started to ask what part of Paris the house was located in but stopped mid-sentence as an overwhelming darkness fill her mind. Her face lost color.

"*Ah, there you are, Bella,*" Goff said as he spoke to her mind. "*As always, your fear rejuvenates me. I am here to feast on the blood of your daughter.* He then filled her mind with the faces and screams of all those he had killed in the past few weeks."

"Bella!" Nigel called out anxiously as he sensed the darkness that had entered the room.

Vladimir felt the disturbance within Bella and turned to look toward the door. When he turned back, he saw the look of horror on her face. He knelt in front of her chair and took one of her hands into his. He cast Nigel a look of desperation as she began to shake uncontrollably.

Bella cried out as she saw the dead women's faces—dripping blood—circling her.

Vladimir entered Bella's mind. "*Get out of her mind*!" he commanded when he realized what was taking place. He tried putting up a mental barrier to protect Bella, but failed as Goff attacked his mind, and he found himself swirling in the darkness of Bella's mind.

Genie was in the cam room and felt the jogeth's dark presence. When she realized he was attacking Bella, she joined the battle, and found herself in the midst of horrific scenes of death. She put Bella and Vladimir to sleep, and then focused on the jogeth's mind. "*Go back to your lair, jogeth!*" she commanded. "*There is no victory to be had here.*" She then used her considerable psychic ability to counter the jogeth's attack.

Without Bella's mind to shield him, Goff quickly realized he was no match for this new Dysonian. He uttered an angry curse before he broke the connection.

Jack watched Genie with alarm on his face as he saw as a halo of green light surrounded her. "Maybe, we had better move back some Cheri," he suggested rising up out of his chair.

Thompson shook her head. "No, it is all right. I read about this. She is able to do deep psychic trances. According to the record, her body glows when she does."

"Ah, right," Jack said, nodding, but he did not sit back down.

Genie gasped as she pulled herself back into her own mind. She shook her head to clear it.

"Are you okay?" Jack asked.

Genie nodded. "Yes, but I need to go check on Bella," she said with a weak smile as she rose from her chair. "That creature just attacked her mind."

"He did that once before," Jack told Thompson as he watched the doctor hurry out the door. "He lured Bella outside. I had to carry her back to her room."

Jack sat back down, and explained in detail what he knew about Bella, not realizing Special Agent Thompson was paying a lot more attention to the details than Lopez or Whittaker had.

                                  * * *

"Come in!" Nigel all but shouted when he heard the knock on the door.

Genie entered. When she saw Bella slumped in the chair, and Vladimir on the floor, she hurried over to them.

"Wake up!" a voice commanded inside Vladimir's head.

Vladimir groaned but did not open his eyes.

"Wake up!" the voice shouted again.

Vladimir's eyes flew open. He was surprised to find himself lying on his back and staring at the ceiling in Nigel's apartment. He sat up abruptly as he recalled what had happened.

"Bella!" he cried out as he saw her leaning over in the chair, and not moving.

"I put you both to sleep to protect you," Genie said. "I will wake her now."

Vladimir nodded.

Genie gently entered Bella's mind, but then just as gently, left without waking her.

She shook her head as she looked at Vladimir. "Before I wake her, I suggest you go get your daughter. Bella needs to see her when she opens her eyes as she believes the jogeth has killed her, and the grief is threatening her sanity. Make sure your daughter knows that no matter how her mother reacts when she wakes, she is to remain as calm as possible."

Vladimir got to his feet and hurried out the door.

"Jennifer!" he called out with his mind.

Jennifer dropped the hairbrush she was holding when she heard her father's voice inside her head. *"Father?"*

"Please come to the kitchen. Your mother needs you."

"The answer is no," Genie told Nigel when she saw him fingering his chin as he looked at her.

"You haven't heard the question. And that I know of, you have not been in my mind."

"I do not need to look into your mind. The look on your face says it all. You want me to be the bait."

"No. I will be the bait. I need you to be the trap."

"What do you mean by that?"

"When he comes for me, you will capture his mind, and force him to slow down long enough for Hattie to use the Maker's fire on him or Bravo Team to get some shots at his head."

Genie sighed as she realized she had no choice but to help. She began to rub at her forehead. "I have a terrible headache."

"Rightly so. You just defeated a jogeth with your mind. If we had had even one elder with your gift when Dysonia was first invaded, we may have been able to save our kind."

"How did the jogeths invade?" Genie asked. "They do not seem the type to build spacecrafts."

"They did not come from space. They came through a travel portal, created by a Dysonian child with extraordinary powers, who wanted only to follow his father who had gone to tend the vineyards in the lower valley. Instead, he opened a portal to another world. When one of the jogeths killed him, the portal closed, but not before more than a dozen jogeths entered our world."

Genie shivered as she thought about dealing with more than a dozen of the creatures. "I cannot imagine battling that many jogeths."

"Nor could we. Dysonia had no weapons. We always lived in peace as farmers and herders. And..." Nigel's voice dropped off as Vladimir and Jennifer rushed in.

"Mama!" Jennifer cried out as she saw her mother slumped over in the chair. She knelt down and touched her mother's cheek.

Bella gave a small cry but did not open her eyes.

"You might as well get on the other side, Vladimir. She needs to see you both are all right. The jogeth filled her mind with bloody scenes of those he has killed. Once we get her awake, I suggest you or Nigel erase them from her mind," Genie said.

"I can do that," Nigel said. "I can also erase them from your mind, Genie."

"No, I will leave them in my mind for the time being as they will serve to bolster my courage for what yet has to be done."

"Jennifer take your mother's hand into yours. You take her other hand, Vladimir. Be ready to reassure her that all is well."

Tears came to Jennifer's eyes as she felt her mother's grief.

"Are you ready, Jennifer?" Genie asked when she sensed the girl's emotional struggle.

Jennifer took a deep breath before she nodded.

Chapter 32
Maker's Fire

Hattie had just finished her shower. She stood in her bathroom, and gently exercised her injured arm. The doctor had taken the cast off, yesterday. When he told her she had healed faster than anyone he had ever seen, she had answered. *"I have always been a fast healer,"* hoping it would be enough to put her miracle cure to rest. She was not about to tell him about the *kado* grass tea Nigel had given her.

As she looked down at her body, she made a sour face. She was covered with red brick colored lines on her stomach, breasts, arms, and legs that looked like tattoos. Genie told her they were there to protect her from the fire. She hoped that was true, for other than Marie, no one else was ever going to see them.

She moved to the mirror to take a better looked at the red marks, then gasped when she saw the new ones on her forehead, and cheeks.

She dressed as fast as she could, and with her hair still damp, and no makeup, she headed for Nigel's apartment.

She stopped abruptly when she saw the chain and padlock on his door. She went back through the dining room, looking for Vladimir.

"Have you seen Vladimir?" she asked Marie, who was now, sitting at the table waiting for her breakfast.

"Yes, he went to check on Bella. Why?" Marie asked, paying more attention to some photos she had taken of Louie's painting then to her sister.

"Nigel's apartment is locked up," Hattie answered.

"Yes, Vladimir told me that Nigel will be away for three or four days.

"Where did he go?"

Marie sensed the agitation in her sister and looked up. Her mouth dropped open when she saw the marks on her forehead and cheeks.

"Yes, now you know why I am looking for Nigel," Hattie snapped.

"Vladimir did not say anything to me about where Nigel went," Marie replied.

"I will be right back," Hattie stated. "When Kate comes in, let her know, I need Isles to make a couple of poached eggs and toast for me."

"Will do," Marie said, grabbing her camera, and impulsively, taking a photo of Hattie's face.

"Someday, we will laugh about this," she said.

"You, maybe. Me never!" Hattie declared before she stomped off.

Hattie knocked on the bedroom door before she went in. She greeted them all, and then waited for them to get to get over the shock of seeing the marks on her face.

"Wow! Aunt Hattie, your tattoos are cool," Jennifer exclaimed. "If you put on lots of bling, some really tight blue jeans, and a t-shirt, you would look like a rock star."

Vladimir laughed as he pictured that.

Hattie turned and glared at him, until she realized he was amused by what Jennifer had said and found herself laughing with him.

"Thank you, Jennifer, I needed to hear that," she said as she got over her mirth. "I came to invite Vladimir to breakfast as I need to talk to him. You both are invited too."

"No, you two go on. We have already eaten," Bella said. "It is Myra's day off, and she is going to take Jennifer and me shopping. She says she knows a lovely shop with a seamstress. Almost everything I have, no longer fits me."

Vladimir gave his wife a shake of his head. "Please buy new things, Bella. You no longer have to count pennies. Use those cards I gave you. That is what they are for."

"Thank you, Vlad, I might just do that. I have been wanting some pink fluffy slippers."

Vladimir bent down and kissed her on the forehead. "Leave it to you to want so little."

"Jennifer, see that your mother gets all she wants or needs, and fluffy slippers in as many colors as you can find."

"I will. I have no qualms about spending your money," Jennifer quipped, a grin on her face.

"Good. I will see you both when you get back," Vladimir said before he followed Hattie out the door.

"So, did you ever find out why Bella has taken such an interest in Myra?" Hattie asked.

"Yes. Myra reminds her of a housekeeper who lived with us for years," Vladimir replied.

"Well that answers that question."

Marie looked at her watch as Hattie and Vladimir set down at the table. Earl was going to model for her this morning, and she did not want to miss the opportunity to get some work done on her latest painting. She gathered up her photos and camera.

"I need to get to the studio. You two work out whatever it is that is bothering Hattie. If you need me, you can find me there."

Hattie watched Marie walk away. "I wish we had some place we could go sit and talk without worrying about someone coming in and interrupting us."

"When we finish breakfast, we can go to the kitchen apartment I am staying in. No one will interrupt us there."

As Hattie walked into the apartment, she looked around. "You know, it has been years since I have been in this part of the house. I had forgotten how charming this apartment is," she said as she looked at the two small green sofas decorated with magnolia blossoms, and the white wicker tables by their side."

"Yes, it is comfortable," Vladimir agreed. "I don't know whether Jennifer will stay here or come live with us when this mess is finally over."

"Jennifer will always be welcome here, Vladimir, but so are you and Bella. And even if you are only going to be twenty minutes away, I am going to miss you when you leave," Hattie said.

"I know what you mean. I feel like I belong here as well," Vladimir admitted.

"Then why don't Bella and you, move into this apartment, and Jennifer can stay in the bedroom she already sleeps in. Once Bravo team is gone, it will only leave us living here. Though Ox and Louie may come and go."

Vladimir grinned. He had not missed the looks that passed between his sisters and the two men. "I may take you up on that offer. Bella is still fragile in mind and body, and I know she feels safer when she is around Nigel."

"Which brings me to what I need to talk to you about. Where is Nigel, and why the lock and chain?" Hattie asked, as she sat down on one of the sofas.

"The time has come for Nigel to regenerate." Vladimir explained as he set down in one of the recliners. "I wrapped his bedroom in tin foil to make sure if the beast does come by it is not able to sense him as he will be vulnerable during the process. The lock is to make sure no one goes in there until he tells me it is safe to do so. What do you need?"

"I wanted to talk to him about the marks on my face. How many more am I going to get?"

"I have no idea, but Genie might. He gave her most of the details of what would happen to you in your transformation to fire-maker."

"If this keeps up, I am going to look like a clay statue that got up, and walked out of the museum," Hattie said sourly as she recalled the stone figures she had seen at the Smithsonian.

Vladimir wiped the grin off his face when he saw she was serious. "Hattie you are a beautiful woman. Those marks, only add a bit of mystery and intrigue to your physical appearance. I do recall Nigel stating that the marks are only visible when you are in the training stages, and when you use the fire."

Hattie sighed. "I hope that is true because I really do not want to wear dark glasses, tight jeans, and lots of bling."

Vladimir broke out in laughter. When Hattie did not join in, he realized she was serious. "Sorry, but it was funny."

"Yes, and I am sure I will laugh about it someday too, but right now I am not seeing the humor in it because it makes me feel ugly."

"Genie's in the office, playing a game of chess with Ox. We could go ask her."

"Why don't you call the cam room and ask her to come here. Ox too if he wants. He might as well see the marks. That way, he can bow out of his marriage proposal, if he so desires."

"Marriage proposal, huh?" Vladimir said as he got out his phone.

Hattie waited until he finished the call before she answered. "Yes, but he may change his mind once he gets a look at my face."

"The one on your forehead is the same star that is on our pendants. The ones on your cheeks look like water marks. Are the ones on your body different?

"Most of the marks are a series of repeated patterns, much like some of the pre-Columbian artifacts that I saw at the Smithsonian's Mayan exhibit. The one on my forehead is like the one on our amulets. I assume it is the symbol for the Maker."

Vladimir nodded.

"Come in!" he called out when he heard the knock at the door.

Genie came in with Ox behind her. When she saw Hattie's face, she stopped. "Good. You are progressing to the last stages."

Ox greeted Hattie and went and sat down on the sofa next to her.

Hattie searched his face for signs of rejection. "I look awful, don't I?"

Ox shook his head. "No. In Arizona we call that war paint." When he saw the tears in Hattie's eyes, he added, "I don't care if you turn blue, purple, or any other color if that is what it takes to protect you from that beast."

"Thank you, Ox, for making me feel better about myself."

Ox smiled, leaned over, and gave her a kiss on the cheek.

"Are there other marks on your body?" Genie asked when Ox straightened up.

"Yes there are lines from my toes to my neck, and the one you see on my face," Hattie answered. "That is why I wanted to see you. Nigel's gone for a few days, and I wanted to find out if you know how many marks I will get on my face, and if they will ever go away?"

"Sorry, but he never said anything about how many," Genie answered, shaking her head. Though, he did say that the marks would disappear once you finished the training, and then only appear when you use the fire," Genie answered.

"I hope so," Hattie said.

"Following Nigel's instructions, I had my secretary rent an empty warehouse," Vladimir stated. "It's a metal building with cement floors on *Haycone Drive* which is halfway across town in one of the industrial complexes. Also the eclipse glasses I ordered, arrived this morning. You will need to wear them, Genie, so you are not blinded by the light."

"What about my eyes?" Hattie questioned.

"As a fire-maker, you are protected from both the light, and the heat it puts out. That may be why that mark on your forehead is there. From what Nigel has said, the light is able to discern those who mean you harm, and those who do not. Which by the way, what you used the day the jogeth attacked you, was only the light, and not the fire."

"You mean, I will burst into real flames?"

Vladimir shrugged. "I really don't know, but a true Maker's fire, puts out enough heat to burn a jogeth to ashes."

Hattie shuddered visibly as she thought about that.

Ox looked at Vladimir. "Do you have an extra pair of those glasses?"

"Yes," I ordered three dozen pair," Vladimir answered. "Everyone here will need to have at least one pair with them at all times. It will protect their eyes. The rest will be in the cabinet in the office in case a pair breaks or gets lost."

"Then I want to help with Hattie's training," Ox offered.

Genie gave the man a grateful smile. "Thank you, Ox. I could use all the help I can get."

Hattie nodded. "Yes, me too. I will not be so scared with you there."

Vladimir heard the quiver in Hattie's voice. He entered her mind. "*Meet me here about nine tonight. I want to find out more about how the fire is affecting you.*"

"*Can I bring Marie and Ox with me.*"

"*Yes. Good idea. We all need to understand what is happening to you.*"

Genie pretended she did not hear their conversation but noticed Vladimir looking at her with a frown on his face.

"You heard me?" Vladimir asked.

"Yes. I seem to be able to pick up telepathic conversations. That is how I knew the jogeth had taken over Bella's mind. Though he must have done so from a distance, for I could not sense his presence, but I heard the conversation. Sorry, it was not intentional."

"Do not apologize. If you had not joined us, Bella's mind might have suffered permanent injury. But it is interesting what you say about him being able to take over her mind from a distance. That might explain how he was able to do so the day she was found outside. Nigel and I have been theorizing whether the amulets do not protect us if the beast is not close enough for it to sense his presence or is it because Bella was marked by him when she was young and is more vulnerable."

"Marked by him?" Genie asked.

Vladimir undid the cuff on his shirt and pulled the sleeve back from the two black dots on his arm. "Marks like these. He followed us one day when we went to take apples to the horses. He did not try to kill us. Instead, he put us to sleep, and when we woke, we both had these bite marks. We then fell ill with a fever, and our skin turned leathery. Nigel gave us *kado* grass to chew on, and we got better though it took months for our skin to return to normal. Bella had a relapse this past year due to the stress of what all happened to her."

Genie looked from Vladimir to Hattie, and then back at Vladimir. "What happened to her?"

"I will tell you in the car on our way to practice," Hattie put in when she saw Vladimir was staring blankly at the wall. "Which reminds me, we had better get going as it is getting late. Ox, you can drive us there, right?"

Ox nodded. "We will need some of those glasses, Vladimir," he said as he got to his feet.

Vladimir heard the deep rumble of Ox's voice and pulled himself back into the present world. The anger of knowing what all had happened to Bella had flooded his mind with grief. "They are in that bag on the counter," he said, raising his head to look at the man who would soon be his brother-in-law.

Vladimir got to his feet and went to the counter. He handed Ox a map. "The industrial complex is off Sunset, so

232

it should not be hard to find. You will not need a key. The lock is a digital one. I wrote the code at the top of the map."

* * *

Even with the glasses to protect their eyes, Genie and Ox lowered their heads when Hattie burst into flames so intense with light, they lit up every inch of the warehouse. Thankfully, the blast of fire did not last more than a few seconds.

Hattie shivered, not from cold, but from the adrenalin that rushed through her veins. She wrapped her arms around her body.

"How do you feel?" Genie asked

"Like a thousand ants are crawling over me," Hattie answered.

"That is normal for what you just went through," Ox said as he moved toward. "You do not have any burns, do you?"

Hattie shook her head. "I don't think so. I am not in that kind of pain. It is more like I just got zapped by an electrical shock, and my body is tingling all over."

Ox touched her with a finger. When he did not get a shock, he heaved a sigh of relief. "Adrenalin rush," he said. "It will go away in about ten or twenty minutes."

"You were incredible, Hattie!" Genie exclaimed. "Or at least what little I was able to see. When you went full corona, I had to lower my head. Nigel thought I would need to help you maintain the fire until you learned to control it, but I don't think that will necessary. You seem to be doing fine on your own."

"What did you notice about the fire?" Ox asked.

"I had no problem turning the fire on, but I was not able to keep the flames from dying," Hattie answered.

"I imagine that is to be expected. Remember, this is the first time you have created actual flames. From my side of the room, it was a mind-boggler."

Genie nodded at Hattie. "He is right about that."

Hattie looked at her watch, it was twelve minutes past twelve. "Let me try again, and then we can go to lunch."

"Ready when you are?" Genie said, putting her glasses back on, and moving farther away.

Ox put his glasses back on and went back across the room to stand beside Genie.

Hattie closed her eyes and took a deep breath. "*Omay!*" she cried out when she felt she was ready.

Her body began to glow, and then burst into flames. This time, the fire burned for over a minute before Hattie spoke the word to end it. "*Ortay!*" she commanded.

The fire went out, leaving a halo of light that dimmed with the passing of each second until only the light of the two skylights above her head was left.

"Wow! That was amazing," Ox said as he removed his glasses.

"Indeed," Genie agreed.

"Yes, for the first time, I felt I was in command," Hattie stated. "What did you see or feel?"

"Not as much I would have liked to see. You are just too bright to look at even with these protective glasses one."

"I could feel some heat, but nothing that was uncomfortable," Ox replied as he walked over to where Hattie stood and bent down to touch the concrete by her feet. "Yep, thought so. I am glad you are standing on concrete. The floor beneath your feet is probably warm enough to cook eggs. Your shoes are warm too, but not as warm as the cement beneath them."

"What would happen if I was standing on carpet?"

"I don't know, but we can bring a small rug with us tomorrow, and find out," Ox answered as he straightened up.

"Great idea, Ox," Genie said. "We can stop by one of the department stores and pick up a couple of them on our way home."

"Can we go eat now? I am *so* hungry," Hattie declared.

"I imagine that has to do with the fire. It is pure energy that you are making. It is bound to burn a lot of calories," Genie said.

Hattie's brow went up. "You mean, I might lose weight?"

"Yes, I think that would be a logical assumption, considering calories are burned by how much energy the body uses," Ox replied.

"In that case, I think I will have dessert with my lunch."

"You earned it, babe," Ox said as he offered her his arm.

"Maybe. I will have to see what the scale has to say about that tomorrow," Hattie said with a chuckle.

* * *

Genie found Ox in the cam room. "You ready?"

"Yeah, Jack and Lopez are watching the cams. I am just keeping them company," Ox replied as he rose from his chair. "Call me if you see that beast headed our way, guys. I will be sleeping with my boots on."

"You sleep in your boots?" Genie questioned, not bothering to hide the surprise on her face.

"Right now, I do. Marines, call it combat ready. Running out of your tent in your underwear and bare feet to defend yourself is something you only do once," Ox explained.

Jack and Lopez chuckled.

"Never thought about it like that," Genie said as she looked down at her feet. I will make sure I wear my flannel nightgown from now on, so if we do fall under attack, I am ready to go. Though I think I will sleep in my yellow flower Sherpa socks, and not my shoes. That way, I won't be barefoot."

When she looked up, she saw the grin on the men's faces. "You were joking?" she asked, frowning at Ox.

"No, mam. I am sleeping with my boots on which I admit is not funny, but the thought of you running around in a flannel nightgown with yellow flowered, knee-high socks is."

Genie started to protest, but stopped as she realized she probably would look something out of a storybook for children and laughed with the rest of them.

Chapter 33
Revenge

Vladimir opened the padlock, removed the chain, and opened the door. He hurried in to see if Nigel was okay but stopped abruptly when he saw him sitting in the recliner with a grin on his face.

"Good morning," Nigel greeted.

"You don't look all that different. Didn't you go through the regeneration?"

"Yes, but I chose to look like Nigel again, and it worked. It is not something I have done before, but I felt it was necessary due to the presence of our guests, and Bella's fragile condition. Most of the differences cannot be seen, other than my hair is red now, not dyed, and most of my wrinkles are gone."

"Well, I for one, am glad you are back. Hattie needs you."

Nigel's face fell. "There was another attack?"

"No, nothing like that. She is learning how to use the fire, but there is no one here who can tell her if what she is doing is the right or not. Also, she has tattoos on her face, and wants to know if they are going to go away."

"Only on her face?"

"No, she says she has them all over her body, but her clothing hides those," Vladimir answered. "What she is concerned about are the ones on her face."

"Ah. I can relate to that. I would not want a tattoo on my forehead either. Why don't you go find her, Bella, Marie, Jennifer, and Genie, and tell them I need to see them. It will not do to have them gasping in shock when they see me. Best, we get this over in private," Nigel said as he got to his feet. "On the way out, see if Isles can fix me a cup of tea and toast. You can bring it in with you when you return."

"I will go let them know. However, I suggest you put some pants on beneath that robe you are wearing. It does not hide everything."

Nigel looked down and saw the gap and chuckled. "You are right about that.

* * *

Goff had not passed by Terin's house since the new female Dysonian had forced him to leave Bella's mind. He was pleased to find there were just as many parks and streets where the young congregated, east of the crypt as there was west of it.

However, his desire for revenge had not ebbed. He decided he would go west tonight and check on those within the house. As he stood in the flood channel using his mind to see if Terin was there, it occurred to him that he should use the same trick, he had used to get the villagers to turn on those within Castle Dracul. Tonight, he would start leaving his victims at the house. Let his enemy explain how and why the dead women ended up in his yard.

Goff smiled wickedly as he thought of how angry Terin would be when the bodies were found on his land. His razor sharp teeth separated as he broke out into laughter.

* * *

"We've got movement," Jack told Thompson. "It looks like the vampire is back."

"Is he carrying something?" Thompson asked, studying the matrix screen.

"Yeah, I think he is," Jack agreed as he hit the alarm button on his comm unit, so as to alert the rest of Bravo Team.

Thompson, grabbed her phone.

Lopez jumped out of bed when he got the call. Like Ox, he was sleeping in his clothes. It took him only a few seconds to get his shoes on and grab his gun before he headed next door to check on the doctor. He started to knock, but stopped as the door opened, and Genie stepped outside wearing a robe and bright yellow socks.

"I know. He's here. I can sense him," she said.

"Yes, now we had better get to the office." Lopez motioned for her to go ahead as he added, "They are setting up a defense zone there."

Vladimir had noticed that Nigel was having difficulty with words, and decided he should stay close in case he was needed. He took over the recliner once Nigel went to bed.

"Vladimir," Nigel whispered as he came into the room.

"I am awake," Vladimir said setting up.

"Goff is near, I can feel him," Nigel said.

Vladimir came up off the sofa. "Then we had better get to the women," he said as he slipped his loafers on.

Both men rushed out the door and ran through the kitchen. They met Earl and Lee in the front room, on their way to the office. Louie and Ox were standing in the doorway with guns in their hands.

"He is out there somewhere," Nigel told them.

"Yes, Jack says he is headed for the house. I knocked on the doors as I passed by, so the women are probably up by now. Genie is in the office."

"I will get Hattie and Marie," Nigel said as he turned and ran toward Hattie's bedroom.

"And I will get Bella and Jennifer," Vladimir said as he followed Nigel into the hallway.

Louie and Ox stayed where they were.

"What's up?" Lopez asked as he entered the already crowded cam room.

"The vampire jumped the storm drain and is headed for the house. He is carrying something on his back, but we have not been able to get a closer look as he disappeared behind the gardener's house," Jack replied.

"There he is!" Thompson exclaimed as she saw a figure moving on one of the cam screens.

"Looks like he is headed for the front door again," Jack said, his voice rising with excitement as he watched the beast move across the yard.

"That is a person he's carrying" Lee said as he watched the screen that showed the beast crossing through the lit-up yard.

Goff ran past the front door, stopped abruptly, and then threw the body of the dead girl he was carrying on the front lawn, face up. He howled with laughter as he ran off.

Everyone in the cam room swallowed viscerally as they saw the bloody body lying on the ground.

By the time Lopez and Louie got to the front door, unlocked it, and got outside, the jogeth was gone.

Nigel ran in and looked at the cams. When he saw the dead woman, he knew exactly what Goff was up. He appreciated that they had FBI agents helping them. It was going to be hard enough to come up with an explanation as to why the beast brought the woman here.

"He's gone. He jumped the wall, and is in the storm channel," Jack said, turning to look at those behind him.

"You need to call 911, Thompson," Lopez said as he returned. "Make sure you tell them how to find the house. When the police get here, Louie and I will go out and meet them. The rest of you stay in the house. We don't want to be accused of contaminating the crime scene."

"Jack, I need you to make copies of the footage for both the police, and the Agency!"

"Thank God, we have it all on film, and two FBI agents as witnesses," Lee said. "Otherwise, we would all be hauled down to the police station for the rest of the night, and at least one of us, charged for murder."

"As much as I hate to admit it, Lee, you are probably right about that," Lopez said. "As it is, *that body* is going to raise questions that we have no answers for."

Lee's mouth went slack. He had not expected Lopez to agree with him.

"We will leave that for you to work out, Lopez," Nigel said. "Vladimir, you come help me make coffee and tea. Hattie you and Marie get out the biscuits and other snacks. It is going to be a long night. The rest of you ladies come along to the dining room as well. I do not want you going back to your bedrooms right now as we do not know if Goff will come back or not. Earl, perhaps you and Ox can come with us. You are armed, and we are not. You too, Jabber. I am sure Marie would be happier if you were sitting next to her. When any of the rest of you get thirsty or hungry, feel free to come help yourself. Lopez, that offer includes police officers or others that will be arriving shortly."

"Thanks, Nigel. I am sure they will appreciate it," Lopez said.

"I'm in. Coffee and cookies are the only way I am going to stay awake," Earl said.

"Count me in too," Lee agreed.

"You boys go on, I will be there in a minute or two," Jabber said.

"I think the creature did this in retaliation for me sticking him with my knife when he attacked Whittaker," Louie told Lopez, hoping to take the heat off those who lived in the house.

Lopez's eyes narrowed as he thought about that. "You are probably right about that, but at the same time, it does not explain why we are all here in the first place. I am sure the homicide detectives are going to be asking that question."

"Blame it on Marie and her psychic abilities," Jabber put in. "She is the one that dreamed about the creature, and saw it set her sister on fire. That is why she called me, and that is why Bravo Team is here. It is also why Vladimir has put up the finest security system money can buy. She was not wrong either, he has come to kill, and will not stop until he wreaks havoc on those that live here. Now, as for you and Thompson being here, you know more about that than we do."

Lopez scratched his head as he looked at his former partner. "That makes perfect sense when you know all the actors and the story, Jabber, but I am not so sure it will satisfy Homicide. What do you think, Thompson, will it fly?" he asked, turning to look at his partner.

Thompson shrugged. "We can only tell the truth. I don't see how they could think one of us killed that poor woman when there is film showing exactly what happened. Why are we here? Because we are trying to catch a serial killer. I don't think they need any more explanation than that, what with Whittaker lying in the hospital in a coma, and footage of that attack as well."

Lopez was relieved she had wrapped it up without mentioning the matrix camera. He would text her later and tell to keep that info to herself. It would just complicate matters and had nothing to with the woman's murder.

"I will mark each memory stick with a number beginning with the first attack," Jack told Lopez. "Number three is for tonight's attack."

"Good idea," Lopez said. "While he works on that Thompson, type up a list of everyone in the house by name, including us, but don't include the day help. They have no knowledge of what is going on. I imagine if they did, they would quit. I am sure Homicide is going to want to talk to each person here, including you and me. Jack can help you fill in the blanks."

"If that is the case, Lopez, then have them come back tomorrow to do that. Other than Jack and Thompson, who witnessed the act on a small screen, none of us inside this house have any information that would help them in their investigation of the woman's death," Jabber suggested. "I cannot see keeping the women up all night just so the officers can hear them say they were asleep and did not see or hear anything."

Lopez rubbed at an ear as he considered Jabber's request. "You are right about that. Make sure you tell whoever relieves you, Jack, that no one who was not in this room at the time at the time it happened, can look at the footage until after they have been questioned. It will keep them from making statements about the condition of the woman. The less everyone knows about that, the better off they will be. Now, I had better go outside, and wait for the patrol car to get here."

"Jabber, you go ahead and join the others in the dining room," Louie said. "I am going outside with Lopez."

"Thanks, Louie," Lopez said, and then grinned when he saw Louie open up a closet door and pull out an AK-47 rifle.

"Is the yard clear, Jack?" Louie asked.

"Yes, nothing is moving out there, but field mice. If he comes back, I will hit the alarm button, and let you know which direction he's coming from."

"Good. You ready, Lopez?"

"Yep."

As the two men stepped outside, they saw headlights coming up the drive.

"Probably best you set that gun down by the door, and stand in front of it, until I explain the situation, and tell them you are with me."

"Do it as fast as you can. If he does come back, we probably won't have more than a few seconds for me to grab that rifle and open fire."

Louie nodded. He moved to the curb and made sure he was in plain site with his hands at his side as the car pulled up at the curb.

Two officers got out of the car but kept their hands on their gun as they moved toward Lopez. One of the men stopped and drew his pistol when he saw Louie by the front door.

"FBI! Special Agent Vincent Lopez," Lopez called out, making sure the badge at his belt was visible. "You can put the gun away. That's Louie Crosshatch, he is with me," he added when he saw the older officer looking over at Louie.

"Jesus!" rookie officer Charlie Jones cried out when he saw the dead woman lying on the grass.

Sargent Brian Mackensie marched around the patrol car and took a look at the woman. He then used his shoulder comm to tell the dispatcher they had another victim with her throat ripped out and needed Homicide and the coroner. "ASAP!" he all but shouted before he took his finger off the talk button.

"They are already on their way, Mackensie," responded the dispatcher.

Mackensie turned his attention back on Lopez and Louie.

"We have not touched anything, nor have we stepped off the porch," Lopez said. "I suggest we all wait for Homicide to get here. They will want their own team to secure the crime scene," he added when he saw the younger officer step onto the grass.

"Who are you, again?" Mackensie barked, motioning for Jones to get off the grass.

"I am Special Agent Lopez, FBI," Lopez answered as he pulled out his ID, and showed it to the officer. "Mr. Crosshatch behind me is a former Marine, who fought in Afghanistan, and a security guard for the residents of this house. He has an AK-47 leaning up against the door frame behind him. There are security cams that cover the entire yard. If my partner Thompson, who is inside watching the cam screens, tells us the creature is back and headed our way, Louie is going to pick that gun up. I suggest you both follow my lead and get behind him. Pistols might not stop something that is already dead."

244

"What do you mean by already dead?" Jones questioned.

Louie pointed at the woman. "The thing that did that is a vampire."

Both officers gaped at Lopez before they turned to look at the dead woman again.

A new set of headlights made their way up the drive. "Hope that's Homicide," Mackensie muttered.

"Me too," Lopez agreed. "It is starting to get cold out here."

* * *

Goff was setting atop the cement ledge on the other side of the storm drain watching the cars with the red flashing lights as they made their way to the house. His teeth glistened in the moonlight as he grinned. He waited for a few minutes, but when no more cars came up the drive, he headed back to the crypt.

Unknown to him, the solar thermographic camera attached to a tree limb that jutted out over the flood channel, picked up his image as he passed by.

"The vampire just passed the TG cam, headed east," Jack told Louie.

Thompson called Lopez and let him know the creature had left the area and was headed east.

Lopez made his way back to the porch. "You heard?" he asked. When Louie nodded, he added, "He must have been waiting around to see what would happen."

"Which probably means there is a reason he brought the woman here," Louie said.

"Sure would like to know what that reason is?" Lopez murmured disgustedly.

"Nigel may have some insight as to what that is. I will ask him once things out here settle down," Louie replied.

* * *

Homicide detective Josh Ritter checked out the security cam room, and as impressive it was, it was the desk and the chairs in the office room that interested him the most. He went back outside and waited for the photographer to finish up with the crime scene photos before he joined his partner *Ben Halcroft*—who was standing by the woman's body, watching the coroner work—to tell him he had found a room inside that they could use for interrogation.

"What's the story on her, Transalle?" he asked.

"She appears to have died the same way as all the others I have examined lately. Her throat has been ripped open, and there are teeth or claw marks on her neck. The rest of it will have to wait until Forensics does their job," Transalle answered.

"Those are teeth marks doc. The security cameras caught the vampire on film. Appears he has attacked the folks in this house twice before," Ritter said.

Doctor Julius Transalle from the Los Angeles County Coroner's office, got to his feet. He looked at Detective Ritter with genuine surprise on his face. "Vampire, you say! I want to see that film too."

"So do I," Halcroft said.

"Fraser, I am through with the body. You can go ahead and take it back to the morgue now," Transalle called out as he looked over at the ambulance driver.

Fraser quit leaning against his vehicle and called for his partner to bring the gurney.

"Follow me, doc," Ritter said as he turned and started toward the porch.

Louie had heard the entire conversation, and opened the door to let them in. "You know where the office is, Ritter. I will be there in a minute and run the film for you."

Once the three men had went inside, Louie used his comm unit to tell Jack to do nothing as he was on his way in

246

and would show the footage to their guests. He then told Lee and Earl to come watch the front door.

* * *

The sun was just peeking over the horizon by the time the police and other officials were all gone. Nigel, Vladimir, and Louie were sitting at the kitchen table, drinking coffee, and discussing what needed to be done next.

"I've got Lee and Earl guarding the gates. Once the morning news gets out, there will be reporters and sightseers wanting to get a closer look," Louie said.

"They have sightseers for murders?" Nigel questioned.

"Yes. There will be hundreds that will want to come and see the murder site for themselves," Louie answered. "Some of those will undoubtedly, be fence jumpers. It is a good thing we already have the cams set up. The bad news is we are understaffed. By that, I mean we need at least one in the cam room, two at the gate, and two to catch any fence jumpers during the day. And at least four on the night shift."

"I can man the cam room during the day as I am past the age of chasing down tourists," Jabber said, overhearing the conversation as he came in.

"Thanks, Jabber. That frees up one."

"And I can help Jabber," Nigel put in.

"I will arrange for two of my security guards to come help at the gate during daylight hours. I can also help with the fence jumpers or cams at night while the others get some sleep," Vladimir offered.

"We can close up the patio. The ironwork will keep anyone from being able to get to the back door. The garage can be locked down, so they cannot get in that way. The average man cannot get past the steel door on the front of the house, and the windows have ironwork," Nigel said. "Anyone that stays out there after dark will be in grave danger, and there is little that we can do to change that."

"Maybe it is time to take Bella to my place," Vladimir said.

"No, it is not," Nigel stated, shaking his head. "Should Goff go into that area, he will sense her presence. Your security agents will be not be able to stop him, and neither will you."

Vladimir let out a breath of frustration, a pained look on his face. "You are right about that. I was not able to protect her the other night. If Genie had not come to our rescue, he might have killed us both."

"Only because he was using her mind against you," Nigel consoled. "Now that she is wearing those foil caps, he will not be able to take over her mind."

Louie's brow went up at Nigel's last words. "I thought the amulet prevented him from entering our minds?"

"I did too," Nigel replied, but after all that has happened here, I think they only keep him from taking over our minds. He has attacked Bella's mind twice. The first time, he pretended to be Jennifer and got her to go outside. Last week, he attacked her mind by filling it with those he had killed and telling her he had killed Jennifer. We also know that he has spoken to both Vladimir and me."

"That's disturbing news as he could trick or attack any of us with his mind," Louie said.

Everyone at the table fell silent as they considered that possibility.

Jabber's eyes narrowed in anger as he thought about how vulnerable they all were. "If that be the case, then we had better make us some foil lined beanies, like Bella, and keep them on at all times."

Louie winced at the thought of wearing a tin foil hat but did not voice his disapproval.

Ox came in with the morning's paper and handed it to Hattie. "I will be out at the front gate. If you need me, call," he told her as he gave her a kiss on the cheek.

Hattie smiled as she watched him cross the room, then frowned when she saw the paper's headline, "Vampire Killer Leaves Body on Paranormal Detective Hattie Drake's Front Lawn."

"What's wrong, Hattie?" Marie asked.

"I am on today's front page."

Marie reached over and pulled the paper from her sister's hands. She read the headline. "No wonder your red phone has been ringing. I disconnected it."

Hattie reached over, picked up the receiver, and put the phone to her ear. There was no dial tone. "Good. We will just leave it unplugged for now."

"Here you can have the paper back, I do not want to read any more about us or that beast," Marie said, her voice full of disgust as she handed the paper back to Hattie.

Chapter 34
Deadly Party

When Vladimir saw how many people had gathered at the gate, he called his office, and told them to send two more security guards. When they arrived, he warned them they were to leave before dark, no matter what was going on at the gate.

"The creature that is killing these women, hunts at night," he told them. "We have seen him in person and on camera, and I can tell you that by the time you realize he is there, it is too late. He can move at the speed of a jaguar."

He then introduced them to Ox, and told them he was in charge of security, and would fill them in on what their duties would be.

* * *

Isles let Hattie know they were almost out of milk, bread, and tin foil. She told him she would take care of it and went to find Nigel to see if he would like to make a trip to the market with her. She was surprised to find him and Jabber manning the cam screens.

"We are helping out," Nigel explained. "Those on night duty need their rest. Even so, Ox is at the gate, and Jack is guarding the house. Thompson and Lopez won't be back until around four. Langstrom called them in for a meeting, and Genie went with them."

Before Nigel could suggest Hattie have whatever they needed delivered, the matrix scanner alarm went off.

"Storm drain intruder, opposite the pool area," Jabber told Jack as he spotted a young man climbing up over the block fence. "Probably paparazzi or newsman as he has a camera."

Nigel, Jabber, and Hattie watched as Jack crossed the lawn, and met the man halfway. They could see Jack shaking his head as the man waved his hands in the air and pointed towards the house.

"Keep him there, Jack! Ox is sending two of Vladimir's security officers to escort him out," Jabber said, using his comm unit.

Both Jabber' and Nigel's attention focused on a new screen as the scanner alarm went off again. This time, they had a fence jumper at the front of the property. Jabber alerted Ox.

"I think it is best if we do not go out today. Look at that crowd," Nigel said, pointing toward the cam screen that showed the front gate. Call *Robarb's* and have them bring out what we need. While you are at it, order a dozen of their bake at home pizzas. Make half of them pepperoni, and the other half an assortment of other varieties, but none with anchovies. So far, only I like those, and I am not up to eating an entire pizza. Also, I need five dozen eggs, five pounds of tomatoes, and five heads of lettuce. That should get us through a couple of meals as I plan to send Isles and Kate home early. Also order a dozen or more biscuit tins, and ten pounds of assorted fruit, five cases of soda, and more juice. I opened the last jug this morning. Then, make sure they understand that we want it delivered no later than four as we want the pizzas for dinner. We don't want a delivery boy coming around here after dark."

Hattie went to her desk and sat down. She added Nigel's wants to her list before she looked up *Robarb's* number and made the call. She made sure to tell them to tell the delivery man to watch out for the tourists who had gathered at the gate.

* * *

Langstrom sat there scowling at his agents. "Did you see the headlines?" he asked as he picked up one of the

251

newspapers on his desk and held it up for them to look at. "FBI Agents Watch as Another Victim is Thrown on Their Doorstep."

"It was the front lawn, not the doorstep," Thompson corrected.

"It does not matter if she was thrown on the roof!" Langstrom thundered. "The point is you both were there and did not stop him."

Lopez's eyes flashed with anger, but he kept his mouth shut.

"With all due respect, Agent Langstrom, your agents are no match for the vampire. Had they confronted him, their bodies would be in the morgue today, right alongside the woman who died last night," Genie defended.

"I know that, and you know that. But the public does not, and neither does my boss."

"Has he not seen the footage?" Genie questioned.

Langstrom glared at her before he answered. "No, he has not. He has only seen the paperwork."

"Why is that?"

Lopez kept his face blank, but he could have kissed the doctor for asking that question.

Langstrom blew a breath of frustration. "Well, to start with, I first believed this to be hoax. Then Whittaker was injured, and I realized it was not, but due to this being Hollywood, the capitol of filmmaking, any statement or film we might make or have will be considered questionable by those in Washington."

Genie snorted. "Questionable! There are more than two dozen dead. How can anyone question that?"

"Oh, they will accept those deaths. There is plenty of evidence to back that up, but for me to state that the killer is a vampire, won't fly. I will be put on leave by the end of day, and someone from DC will be sent to investigate this entire department."

"Then I will write the report. As Director of the Federal Bureau of Psychic Investigation, they will have no recourse but to take my word that it is indeed, a vampire-like creature. You can send it with whatever footage you have collected. That should counter any doubts about what you are dealing with here in Hollywood."

Langstrom pretended to think about it for a few seconds before he nodded his head. It would not do to let her know that is exactly why he had invited her to come to LA in the first place. "Thank you for your offer, doctor. Right now, I believe you are the only person in the Country, who has the experience and credentials to make that statement without being hustled off to a sanitorium, or worse, fired. How about we all meet back here about three this afternoon. That will give you all time to go to lunch, and then write up your reports."

When no one complained or asked questions, Langstrom added, "Now, if you will excuse me, I have a luncheon appointment with Bosun from the State Department. Like everyone else, he wants to know what is going on."

Lopez was the first to rise. "Ladies, I know a great place to have lunch, and it is not far from here. We can walk," he said as he moved to open the door.

Genie bid Langstrom to have a better day as she rose from her chair before following Thompson out the door.

* * *

Jack had gotten a few hours of sleep and had just resumed his midnight till six AM watch with Thompson when the matrix scanner alarm went off.

"We have activity at the flood wall," Thompson said.

Jack flipped the floodlight switch that Vladimir had his men install yesterday, lighting up the yard a full 360 degrees. That is when he saw the vampire moving toward the back patio area on the cam-screen that covered that area.

He spoke into his comm unit alerting the other members of Bravo Team the creature was back.

The floodlights filled the bedroom with light, and Louie sat up in bed. Jack's words confirmed the worst, the beast was back. Like Ox, he was sleeping with his clothing and boots on.

Ox woke up when he heard Jack's voice in his ear. He jumped up and followed Louie to the cam room.

"He dumped another body by the rose garden, and then high-tailed it back to the storm drain," Jack called out as the two men entered the office.

"Put the call in for Homicide, Thompson!" Lopez said as he walked in.

Several alarms went off at the same time.

Every head turned to scan the screens. They saw a dozen or more sightseers had jumped the fence and were running toward the house.

Earl, you, Jack, and Lee grab your rifles, and cover the back entrance!" Louie said as the rest of Bravo Team joined them. Jabber you help Thompson man the cameras. Vladimir, you, and Nigel get the women up and bring them to this room. Lopez, Ox, and I will cover the front entrance. Do not use those guns unless it is to shoot at the vampire! Also, remember to lay rifle on the ground when the police arrive, but do not step away from it!" he commanded. "One of those fence jumpers could grab it up, and in panic shoot someone. Once Lopez explains who you are, you can pick it back up."

Louie, Ox, and Lopez no sooner stepped out the front door when they heard gunshots from the front gate area. Then several men and women were running toward them, screaming for help. Before they could respond, a blood curdling scream rent the air, and then abruptly stopped.

"What the hell is going on?" Lopez all but shouted out as he turned to look toward the gate area.

"There's a monster out there," one of the men called out as he ran up. "He is killing everyone!"

"Jabber, you better have Thompson call for reinforcements. Looks like we got more than one body out here. The beast went after those at the gate," Louie said.

By this time, several others who had jumped the fence came running up. Some were crying, others were quiet with grim faces. All appeared to be in shock. When the last straggler reached the group. Louie turned to Ox. "Escort our guests to the patio area. They can use the chairs and lounges while we wait for the police. I will let Earl know you are coming."

Genie woke when she felt the jogeth's presence. She had slept with her clothing on, and socks on her feet. She opened the door, and started to go to the cam room, but stopped when she saw Nigel and Vladimir guarding the hallway."

"What is going on?" she asked

"Besides dropping another body in the back yard, the beast also has attacked some of those who were loitering around the gate," Vladimir answered.

"Then I might be needed," Genie said as she spun around, and ran back into her room.

She quickly put on a jacket, slipped on her sneakers, and grabbed the medical kit she had set aside.

"Where are you going?" Nigel asked when he saw the bag with the red cross on it, and noted she had a jacket on.

"I have a medical degree. I might be able to help," Genie said as she headed for the front door.

"Did you know she has a medical degree?" Nigel asked Vladimir.

"No, I thought her she was a doctor of psychic phenomena, not medicine."

"I guess, I should have asked more questions," Nigel said as he watched her disappear into the front entranceway.

As Genie opened the front door, Louie spun around. "What are you doing out here?" He snapped, annoyed that she had come outside.

"Vladimir said the Jogeth has attacked some of those at the gate," Genie answered.

"It appears that way," Louie allowed. "The police ought to be here any minute, and we have called for medical backup."

"Then I need to go down there. I may be able to help."

Louie looked at the bag in her hand, and then at her. "I take it you have some background in medicine?"

"Yes, I was a field surgeon in the Army during the war," Genie answered.

"Ox, cover Lopez. I am taking Doctor Ferguson down to the gate to see if she can help with the injured."

When they were out of earshot, Louie turned off his comm unit before he asked, "Which war was that, doctor?"

"Vietnam."

"Don't repeat that to anyone but your family. Someone might start asking questions since you do not look to be in your seventies which would be expected for a veteran of that war."

"I know. I made the same mistake Marie made by referring to a past memory that does not match with my age."

"Lopez is the only one that heard that. If he asks, tell him you were in Iraq, and leave it at that," Louie suggested.

"Not to worry. I erased that last sentence from his mind."

"Good. That is one less thing for me to worry about.

Genie nodded, then stopped abruptly and put an arm out to stop Louie as she used her mind to hunt for Goff. When she could not sense the jogeth, she dropped her arm. "I believe it is safe to proceed. I cannot sense his presence."

As they passed through the gate, she could see several people lying on the ground, a couple of them lay in the road.

"Nothing you can do for these two. I will stand here with my light and try to keep someone from coming along and running over them," Louie told Genie. He then moved toward two more women that were down.

Genie hurried over to one victim that was groaning. "This man is still alive, though his arm is almost severed."

Genie dug into her medical kit for bandages to make a tourniquet to help stop the bleeding.

Louie bent down, and found one woman still alive, but breathing shallowly. She was not quite off the road, and yet, he dared not move her.

As he stood, he saw a man in a police uniform lying close to a tree. Most of his face was gone. He sighed before he used his comm unit. "We have at least four dead, and two living, but with injuries," he told Jabber, knowing the others, including Thompson and Lopez could hear him. "I can hear sirens. Hopefully, one of them is an ambulance. The two that are still alive are in bad shape. Lopez, I suggest you get down here as I need you to deal with the officers. I don't want us to get shot because we are the only ones moving about."

Lopez used his phone to call Thompson. "I need you to go help Ox at the front door."

Thompson got to her feet. "I will be at the front door if you need me," she told Jabber and Nigel.

"Where is Genie?" Nigel, interrupted.

"She's here with me trying to stop a man from bleeding out," Louie answered.

Louie covered Lopez as he made his way down the driveway. Once the agent was through the gate, he leaned the AK-47 in a shadow cast by the fence. He would leave it there until Lopez had time to explain the gun.

Three vehicles all with flashing red lights came around the curve.

Louie started waving his hand with his flashlight to let the drivers know they had reached the scene. The sirens were deafening as two cars, and one ambulance stopped a few yards away from him.

"Turn the damn sirens off," Louie shouted out as one of the vehicles' doors opened.

Detective Ritter got out of his car and turned to look at the those behind him. He ran a finger across his throat.

The ear blasting noise died.

"Thank you," Louie murmured, his ears still ringing.

Ritter took a quick look around. He then told Halcroft to move the car behind the ambulance and block the road on that end of the crime scene. He told the young officer in the patrol car to go back to the cross street and come in from the other side and block the road on that side.

While Ritter took over the crime scene, the EMTs from the ambulance ran over, and began working with Genie on the two with injuries.

"Best you get your gurneys out. These two need to be transported ASAP," Genie said. "I have done all I can do here to stabilize them."

"Are you a med-head?" one of the EMTs asked.

"If by that you mean, am I a doctor? Then yes. Though I do not practice medicine anymore. I gave that up when I got out of the Army."

Damn! Genie thought. *I just did it again.* There was no mention of her being in the army anywhere in her resume or personnel files. Though she had listed her medical degree. from Manipur. It had only taken her three years to finish a six year course. Which surprised others, but not her as she already had a British Degree in Medicine, but not for her new identity as Genie Ferguson. She reached out with her mind and wiped the last sentence from the men's minds.

"Get a hold of dispatch, and have them order up two more ambulances," Ritter told one of the paramedics. Some of those up at the house have injuries. Also make sure the coroner is on his way. You might as well tell them that he will need help. We got at least four dead."

"There is another dead woman in the backyard by house," Lopez said as he joined Ritter and Louie.

"Make that six ambulances, we have five dead, and unknown number of injured sightseers," Ritter told the dispatcher before he greeted the FBI agent. "Glad to see you are still here, Lopez. Tell me, you have footage of this massacre."

"No. We have only the front gate cam on this area. I doubt it shows much of what happened. As for being here, until we catch this killer, this is my second home," Lopez answered.

Ritter pointed toward Genie. "What is she doing here?" he asked.

"She's a doctor," Lopez answered.

"Yeah, I know that, but what is she doing here? A doctor in education is not same as one in medicine."

"She is a doctor of medicine too. I just found that out tonight."

Ritter's lips pursed in and out as he considered that information. He then scratched his head as he looked around at the dead bodies. They all looked like they had been mauled by some kind of animal, except for one woman. She had her throat ripped out in the same manner as the other women who had been killed this past month.

"There are more than a dozen men and women up at the house. I had them taken to the patio. Some ought to be able to tell you what happened here. Also, some need treatment for shock, and other injuries."

"Better send two more ambulances," Ritter told dispatch.

"It looks like they are ready to take those two to the hospital," Ritter said as he saw one of the victims being loaded into the ambulance."

"Yeah, thanks to Genie. She had them ready for transport."

Genie had followed alongside one the gurney, holding on to the tourniquet. When she reached the ambulance, she turned the job over the paramedic who would ride with the victim. She then stepped back out of the way.

She looked around and saw Louie standing with Lopez and Detective Ritter. She started that way, but stopped short as she sensed the beast had returned. She ran toward Louie.

Louie did not waste time asking her what was wrong, he ran and grabbed his rifle.

"He is somewhere up that way, close to the house," Genie said, pointing towards the storm drain.

"Ox, you and Thompson get inside!" Louie said, using his comm unit. "You can guard the front door from there. Earl, he's somewhere near the house. You and Lee, get those people off the patio, and into the kitchen. You stay inside too! You are no match for that beast."

"I hope you don't mind, Louie, but I am going to borrow one of your AK-47s."

"I take it you are familiar with the rifle?" Louie asked.

"Yeah, I spent four years in the Army."

"Use the purple ammo packs. The black ones are for extreme use only as they are armor-piercing bullets."

"Copy that. Thanks."

"You got anything, Jabber?" Louie asked."

"Nothing moving on the matrix scanner, but he could be in the storm drain. I'll check the thermographic camera."

"No one get excited," Lopez said, holding up his hands as he saw everyone was looking at Louie holding his AK-47 rifle, alarm on their faces. "He is here to help in case the beast comes back. Right now, all we know is he is somewhere in the storm channel."

"Louie, the TG cam shows he passed by the tree cam about four minutes ago, headed your way," Jabber said.

Lopez felt his heart skip a beat as a hoarse scream filled the night air.

"What the hell?" Ritter muttered as he looked up the roadway where the sound had come from. He noted the officer who was supposed to be watching traffic at that end of the road was not standing by his car. He started moving that way.

"He just killed again," Genie told Louie.

"Do not go up there, Ritter," Lopez warned as he heard Genie's words. "If it is the beast, you have no way of defending yourself."

"You two need to get out of here while you can." Louie told the paramedics.

The men looked at each other, and without words, one climbed in the back with the victims, and the other shut the door. He then went and got into the ambulance on driver's side.

A few minutes later, two more ambulances pulled up, along with two more patrol cars, and one press car from the local TV station. Before everyone could be apprised of the situation, the coroner and his assistant arrived.

"For now, I want everyone to stay within this circle of light!" Ritter told the new arrivals. "Hopefully, you all have strong bladders because right now, walking around in the dark could get you killed."

Coroner Transalle got out of his vehicle and looked around the scene. "How many dead, Ritter?" he asked.

"Four here. One up at the house, and I believe we have one more that way as the officer guarding that end of the crime scene is missing. Come daylight, or when the creature that is doing this, leaves, we will know for sure."

"Why daylight?"

"Because Agent Lopez says so," Ritter stated gruffly.

The flash from a camera blinded both Louie and Lopez as the press agent took their picture.

"So, you two have seen the killer?" Barbara Polanski, reporter for *The Daily Sky Writer* questioned.

"Get that camera out of my face before I break it," Lopez growled, flashing his badge at her.

"Just doing my job," Barbara stated as she lowered the camera.

"Do yourself a favor," Louie said. "Save that flash for the creature. He does not like light."

Barbara's grip tightened on her camera, and she nodded. "Thanks for the tip," she said before she went to see what the coroner had to say.

Barbara followed Transalle over to the body of the man across the road. She started to take a photo, but let the camera fall back to the strap around the neck when it occurred to her that if the creature did not like the camera, he might attack her for using it. She felt a shiver of fear go down her spine at that thought.

"He is gone," Genie told Louie. "At least far enough away that I can no longer feel his presence."

"Jabber, check the TG cam, and see if you can spot the beast."

"Yes, he passed by a few minutes ago, moving fast, and headed the other way."

Lopez heard Jabber's comment.

"Ritter we are clear for the moment. I suggest you get your markers up, and the bodies out of here as soon as possible. When you are finished, we can go up to the house, and you can work from there. When the sun comes up, you can come back down here."

"You heard the man!" Ritter shouted. "How long before we can move the bodies, doc?"

"Those three can be moved. Neal still has to complete the photos for this one," Transalle answered.

"You can start loading the bodies," Ritter told the ambulance drivers before he looked toward the empty patrol car.

"You are sure he is gone? he asked Genie.

"Yes, for now."

"How do you know that?"

"That why I am here Detective Ritter. I have a psychic ability to sense paranormal activity."

"Then I am going to go look for our missing officer. He may still be alive. There is an access ladder on both side of the storm drain here. I saw it on the plans Halcroft, and I studied earlier today."

"Genie and I will go with you," Louie said. "She is the only one that can tell us if the beast comes back this way."

Ritter looked at Genie, then at the AK-47 in Louie's hands, and nodded.

They did not have far to go. They found the officer's body at the edge of the storm drain, laying up against the concrete wall. There was no guessing whether he was alive or how he had died, there was a gaping hole where his throat had been.

Ritter stared at his young friend. "I have known Mike since he was in training. Good cop," he said emotionally. He stood for a few seconds, then cleared his throat before he pushed the button on the comm unit attached to his coat. "We need crime scene markers here, and the doc to come verify the body. Halligan's dead," he told Halcroft. "I want him moved ASAP. I don't want that beast to come back and feed on him."

Lopez heard Ritter's request and report as it broadcasted over the police unit's speaker box, but he stayed where he was. With both Homicide detectives, and Louie gone, the crime scene was now his job. "You, he said, pointing to two EMTs standing by the last ambulance to arrive, "get a gurney, and go help! They will need you to bring the body back."

Once that was done, he turned to other EMTs who had just loaded the last body from this crime scene. "You two might as well go ahead and leave."

When the ambulance pulled out, he realized that he was the only one left at the site. He started toward the storm drain, but stopped as a car drove up, and parked on the other side of the Detective Ritter's car.

Two men got out. He recognized one of them as a local reporter. "You are too late, Conway, the victims have been bagged, tagged, and are on their way to the morgue. Nothing to see around here but crime markers."

"Then I guess we will just film the crime markers. I see four outlines. How many victims in all?"

"There are four here. Three young people who thought they might catch a glimpse of the killer if he returned, and the police officer who tried to save them."

"Wow! What kind of killer are we dealing with?" the young photographer with Conway exclaimed.

"One that kills for pleasure, obviously," Lopez growled, pulling his pistol out as he heard footsteps coming their way.

As Genie came walking up, he put the gun away.

"How are they doing?" he asked.

"They have finished with the markers, and are getting ready to bring the body back," Genie answered, looking at the two men.

A camera flash lit up the air as the photographer took her picture.

Genie put a hand over her eyes. "Are you trying to blind me or what?" she snapped.

"Sorry, it's my job to photograph the crime scene," *Sergi Lobeck* apologized as he lowered his camera.

"I am not a part of the crime scene, and I do not want my photo on the news."

"Then what are you doing here?" Conway asked, instinctively, deciding she a was person of interest.

"Doctor Genie Ferguson, Federal Bureau of Psychic Investigation. Why else would I be here? Unlike you two, I have no death wish."

"What do you mean by that?" Lobeck asked, lowering his camera.

"It means, I have an armed guard with me, and the psychic ability to know when that beast comes our way, and...," Genie paused to put her hands on her hips before she continued, "I would bet a month's salary that both of you do not."

Lopez killed the impulse to laugh as he saw both men's mouths drop open with surprise as they shook their heads at her."

"Then it would be a good idea if you get back into your car and leave. Right now! This is no place for tourists or reporters."

"Yes, mam. I just need to ask Special Agent Lopez one question," Conway said, nodding his head at her before he turned to Lopez. "You told me there were only four victims."

"That's right. Four here, and a second police officer was killed at the storm drain entrance which makes that a different crime scene."

"All right, let me put it another way. How many total victims do you have knowledge of, Agent Lopez?"

"Six," Lopez snapped irritably. "He left another one up at the house."

"Got it," Conway said, and turned to go.

"That is an awful lot of dead people," Lobeck murmured to himself as he followed the reporter back to the car.

Lopez heard the young man's remark. "Be glad you are not one of them, kid," he called out softly.

"Looks like the last two ambulances are here," Lopez told Genie as two vehicles with flashing lights stopped in front of them. I will be damn glad when this night is over."

"Me too," Genie agreed.

* * *

Goff entered the crypt with a smile on his face, knowing he had killed several more of those who inhabited this world. For the first time in years, he felt the energy of a young jogeth.

"Fool!" he cursed when it dawned on him that he had restricted himself to the blood of the female species, simply because he preferred to see the terror on their smooth faces. Males with course hair flowing down their chins, and bad breath disgusted him. However, tonight he had feasted on both female and male. Instinctively, he knew that was what had made the difference in energy.

He sensed the sun was beginning to rise and yawned. It was time to sleep.

Chapter 35
Crossbows

Thompson woke Lopez up at noon, telling him Langstrom was on his way with a Special Agent appointed by the Director himself. "He wants to see the footage and our reports. I imagine the boys in DC are getting nervous when they found out we are calling the killer a vampire."

"Yeah, well, if it is any consolation, it makes me nervous too knowing that I am hunting a six hundred year old myth that bullets cannot kill," Lopez said.

"What about silver bullets. It seems like I read they will kill a vampire?" Thompson asked.

"They use silver bullets for werewolves. Wooden stakes are used for vampires."

"Then, how about we rig up a crossbow with a wooden arrow. I would think that would be a close approximation to a stake."

"Hmm! You might have something there, Cheri. An ancient weapon for an ancient creature. I will go ask Louie what he thinks about that, and if any of his team can shoot a bow?"

Lopez glanced at his watch. "Never mind, I imagine he is still asleep. None of us got any sleep last night. What time is Langstrom supposed to get here?"

"One o'clock. That is why I came to wake you up. I figured you might want coffee, and something to eat before they get here."

Lopez yawned. "If I am going to stay awake, I am going to need more than one cup. I was up all night. I'm tired," he complained.

"So was I," Thompson declared as she bent down, picked his pants off the floor, and tossed them on the bed.

"While you finish dressing, I will get my own cup of coffee, and then find out if anyone in Bravo Team has bow and arrow experience."

"I will be there in about twenty minutes. I need to shower and shave if the boss is coming," Lopez said.

* * *

Lopez found Vladimir in the kitchen. "Do you ever sleep?" he asked as he filled his cup with coffee, grabbed a couple of donuts, and sat down at the table.

"I do not need as much sleep as others do. Why?"

"Because I would be asleep right now, but the boss is coming with someone from DC, and I had to get up. These past two nights have been hard on me."

"Yeah, I am not looking forward to tonight either," Vladimir said. "Nigel wants floodlights put up at the gate. My men ought to be here anytime. I need to show them what we want done. Thankfully, we do not have to dig but one hole for the post, and a short ditch as the cornerstone has an electric box already installed."

"Maybe the light will discourage that beast from attacking anyone who happens to be hanging around," Lopez said.

"Humph!" Vladimir scoffed. "I doubt it. There must be close to hundred people out there right now. There is even a hotdog vendor. I have asked the police to come remove them, but so far, no one shown up."

Lopez eyed his friend. "The problem is murder scene watchers are like concert gate crashers. For everyone you chase down, ten more jumped over the fence while your back was turned."

"After last night, you would think they would realize, if they are down there by that gate, after dark, there is a good chance they are going to be killed. That is not my idea of fun and games," Vladimir complained.

"Not for you and me, but you can bet the ghost and monster hunters will be out in full force tonight, hoping to get a photo of the beast that is killing people."

"Even if it kills them in the process?" Vladimir questioned.

"The problem is they don't believe anyone actually died. Most think one of the local studios is behind it, and all the fuss is hype for a new movie. Some are looking for stardom, others for stories or photos they can sell. Right now, a photo or film clip of that vampire would bring four figures on the market, and that helps pay the rent. Any photos of a dead body posted on the internet will go viral. Money can be made that way too."

"Ah, I see your point which does not help our situation, but it does explain why they persist in hanging around."

Thompson had a good idea this morning. We were talking about how to kill a vampire, and I mentioned a wooden stake. She suggested we use a crossbow with a wooden arrow."

Vladimir leaned back in his chair as he thought about that. "That might work, at least, enough to slow him down while Hattie uses the Maker's Fire to destroy him. I will ask Nigel when he wakes up. He knows more about the beast than anyone else here."

"Good. Now, I better get to the cam room, it is almost one o'clock."

"And I think I will sit here and have another cup of tea while I wait for my men," Vladimir said as he picked up the teapot, and then filled his cup.

Once Lopez left, Vladimir pulled out his phone. He keyed in the word crossbow. He had not seen one used for centuries, but he figured the basic concept of the bow had not changed all that much.

When Hattie found Vladimir sitting at the kitchen table, she got a cup from the counter, and went and sat down beside him. "Where is Isles?" she asked when she did not see him working on breakfast.

Nigel told him not to come to work today," Vladimir answered without looking up from the phone screen.

"What are you doing this morning?" she asked.

"Right now, looking at crossbows," Vladimir replied. "Thompson suggested that a wooden arrow might stop the vampire the same way a stake would."

"After last night, I am beginning to wonder if anything is going to stop him."

"He is mortal in the sense that he can be killed by the Maker's Fire, Hattie. But he moves so fast, I cannot help but wonder if you will be able to activate the fire before he kills you."

"Kills me?" Hattie echoed.

Vladimir heaved a sigh. "Yes, my dear, despite our long levity, we are mortal. The only thing that keeps that beast out of this house right now, is he is not ready to take on Nigel. You, he will try and kill before you can light up. He has no real conception or knowledge of what Bravo Team might be able to do to him."

"What about Genie? She bested him when he attacked Bella and you."

"I imagine, he is wary of her, but does not consider her his equal."

"What do you mean by that, Vladimir?" Marie asked as she joined them.

"We were just discussing what impact Genie might have on the beast," Hattie answered before Vladimir could explain. She did not want Marie to hear Vladimir's concerns about her dying.

When Vladimir remained silent, Marie looked at her sister. "You ought to know by now, Hattie, I can tell when you are lying."

Hattie sighed. "We have been discussing the beast's vulnerabilities, Marie."

"Well, no need to repeat that conversation. I really do not want to hear about that creature this morning. The local news broadcast of the murders has been going on all morning. Worse, our house and front gate are part of a Special Report on the television. They are asking, what is it about this house that attracts the vampire killer. And I quote, "Is it Hattie Drake the paranormal detective?" *That* is what I came to tell you."

Hattie's mouth dropped open.

Vladimir put his phone down. "Good," he stated.

"What's good about that?" Hattie questioned hotly, her face turning red.

"If they think the beast is attracted to this house because of your psychic abilities, then they have found the answer to the question, and will not be looking more closely at the rest of us. As for Bravo Team, and myself, we will be seen as nothing more than security people. Lopez and Thompson have already explained their presence, and Genie's as well. So, there is no big mystery here, after all."

"I am so glad you are here, Vladimir," Marie said. "I never would have thought of it those terms."

"Back at you, sis."

"Where's Isles? I am hungry," Marie asked.

He is off for the next few days or until things quiet down," Hattie answered. "So it's biscuits or cereal this morning. I will check with Nigel, and see about ordering in some food for lunch, and dinner. I do not want Nigel using what energy he has to try and cook for us all."

Marie did not want Nigel worrying about their meals either. "In that case, we had better talk to him. You know how he is about meals. In my opinion *Rocket's* has the best catering service. I still have one of their menu sheets in my desk. I will go get it while you call him and tell him to come help us plan meals."

Vladimir stood. "I just contacted Nigel with my mind, Hattie. He will meet you here in five minutes. Now, I need to get down to the front gates. We are installing the new floodlights today.

* * *

Nigel shut the door of his apartment and walked across patio entryway to the other kitchen apartment. They had decided to meet in Vladimir's apartment because it had two sitting chairs and two sofas. His apartment had only his recliner, one sitting chair, and a foot stool. He had not bought any new furniture for his room since they had bought the house in 1982. Not because he was cheap, but because he had never needed more chairs before. No one ever entered his apartment, but him until recently.

He did not bother to knock on the door, Vladimir knew he was on his way. He greeted everyone before he sat down in the only empty chair left, opposite of Jabber.

Hattie, Marie, and Genie were sitting to the left of him on one sofa, and Vladimir, Ox, and Louie sat on the other sofa.

Once Nigel was seated, Vladimir explained why he called the meeting. "This morning, Thompson proposed that if you can kill a vampire with a wooden stake through the heart, why not use a wooden arrow."

"If that truly will kill a jogeth, then I think her idea has possibilities," Genie put in.

"It may put him to sleep, but it will not kill him," Nigel said. "I have battled Goff before and won, but I did so at a price. In order to beat him, I regenerated myself as a jogeth. It was the hardest thing I have ever done, and it was a real struggle to regenerate back to my human form. It took years to wipe the nightmare of the day I was forced to live as a beast."

"Oh, Nigel. Why did you not tell us? We would have tried to help," Hattie said.

"You were only eleven years old at the time, Hattie. It would have frightened you to know I could turn myself into such a being."

"You are right about that," Marie agreed. "I had nightmares of finding Mother and Aunt Hattera dead on the stairs for years. Still do, every once in a while."

Hattie nodded. "Yes, I know. You used to wake me up. Then we both cried together."

Marie squeezed her sister's hand.

"Anyway, getting back to Goff," Nigel continued. "I did put a stake through his chest, and an amulet around his neck, and yet as we have seen, he is back."

"Are you sure it is the same creature that you killed" Louie asked.

"Yes. He has several times taunted me. He takes great pleasure in telling me that this time, I will not beat him."

"How could he rise again if you put a stake in his heart?" Hattie asked.

"I have been thinking about that. A jogeth does not have a heart in his chest. His brain powers his body, and blood feeds his brain. My guess, is the wooden stake rotted away over the years, and he woke up. For even if someone found him, and took the amulet, they would not have bothered to remove the stake. The stake put him to sleep, but we now know it did not kill him." Migel replied. "There is more you need to know. I received a report today from a private detective I hired in France. It turns out that last summer, there were dozens of women killed in the same manner in Europe, beginning in Romania, and ending in France. There were also several deaths of a similar nature aboard a cargo ship traveling from France to Los Angeles, three months ago."

"That matches the time frame for the beginning of the vampire-like deaths in this country," Louie said.

"Yes, it does." Nigel agreed.

"I was hoping the crossbow would be what we needed to disable him," Louie said.

Jabber saw the grim look on Louie's face. "You are not responsible for that beast, Louie."

"No, but I am responsible for everyone in this house."

"Yes, and thanks to you, we all are still alive," Jabber countered.

Louie's face smoothed out as he looked at his friend. "Only because I learned to throw a knife when I was a young boy."

"Maybe so, but it was the path that fate set you on. I used to beat myself up when I failed to save everyone in the village, or in my unit. I don't do that anymore because as I have gotten older, I realize I cannot back time up, nor can I stop bullets or bombs. All I can do is my best to save as many as I can, including myself. That is my path. God takes over for those that pass on as that is a different path."

"That was beautiful, Jabber," Marie said, her eyes shining with love as she looked at him.

"No, my dear, it is you that is beautiful, and when it comes down to it, you are the brightest light on my path."

"Like Marie, I too, think it was a beautiful and a profound statement. Would you mind if I quoted you in my book, Jabber?" Genie asked, writing his words in her notepad.

Jabber's face showed his surprise. "Why I would be honored. Thank you, Genie. It gives me a sense of immortality to know my words will be in a book on psychic phenomena. But on a lighter note, if my ghost does shows up at your door one day, try not to scream."

The grin on his craggy face was contagious, and everyone chuckled with him.

Vladimir had been mulling over what Nigel has said about putting the amulet around the beast's neck. He pulled the chain with the amulet from beneath his shirt and studied

274

it. The corners of his mouth went up as it occurred to him the bow could still be the answer.

He looked over at Nigel. "What if we could order arrowheads with the Maker's mark on them? We would then have both the wood and the amulet," he said.

"By George, I think you are on to something, my boy!" Nigel exclaimed, lapsing into his British accent as he was prone to do when he got excited. "When those bows you order arrive, I will take the arrows over to Kasper. If it can be done, he will do it. He already has the amulet pattern in his files."

"Then Louie and I had better start practicing with our crossbows. I will have bales of hay and targets set up at the warehouse I rented for Hattie," Vladimir said.

Genie glanced over at Louie. "What about tonight? If he goes after those out there by the gate, what will we do?"

"Probably what we did last night. Save who can be saved," Louie answered.

"Do you think he will come back tonight, Uncle?" Genie asked Nigel.

"Yes, I do. He used the same tactics to put the blame on Vladimir when we lived in Transylvania to get the villagers to rise up and kill everyone in the castle. I imagine, he believes that he can get the same results here. It is a good thing we have Lopez and Thompson here or otherwise, one or more of us would be accused of those deaths."

"I think I had better go find Lopez and get him to insist that local law enforcement clear the gate area before dark," Louie stated, rising from his chair.

"You might want to wait until Langstrom and the FBI agent from DC that is with him leave. They might not like it if they see you and Lopez are working together, being you are what is known as a *hired gun*," Vladimir said.

"Yeah. You are probably right about that. Langstrom frowns every time he sees me," Louie agreed as he got to his feet. "I think I will go give Lee and Earl a lunch break while

I listen in on what Langstrom and that special agent from DC have to say."

"You and I, need to practice joining our minds," Nigel told Genie once Louie had left the room. "Together, we may be able to slow Goff down."

"What do I need to do?" Marie asked.

"If he attacks tonight, it will be up to you to help get Bella and Jennifer to the office. You all will be safer there. The rest of us will battle him as we can," Nigel replied.

"That I can do," Marie replied with a nod of her head.

Chapter 36
Do or Die Time

Domingo Marquez arrived at the murder scene just before dark. He was one of the younger freelance photographers making a name for himself in Hollywood. He looked around and saw a large oak tree growing in front of a fence across the street. It was just what he was looking for.

He walked to the tree and pulled a pair of chamois gloves out of the back pocket of his jeans. He then jumped up, got hold of one of the tree's lower limbs, and climbed about twenty feet up the tree. Once Dom felt he was high enough to see both the activity by the front gate, and the front of the house, he selected a nice thick branch to straddle, That done, he loosened the straps on the canvas backpack he carried and pulled it around so that he could get into it. He took out a folded foam cushion, several leather straps, and a rope with a pulley on it. He strapped the cushion to the branch and tree, so that is could not slide off. Then hung the pulley on another limb and threaded a rope through it that he let hang down to just below the first limb he had used.

When he was through making his *bird nest* as he like to call it, he went back to his vehicle to give his cousin *Felix Sanchez* instructions, and to get the canvas bag that held the water bottles, snacks, and his camera. He then opened up a box that he kept for photoshoots like this. He took out a camo cape that best matched the leaf colors of the oak tree and put it on. He started to pick up the bag, and head back to the tree, but stopped when a pickup truck from the house that he would be watching stopped at the gate.

* * *

The sun was setting as Louie drove down to the gate to pick up his crew and tell Vladimir's security guards their day was over.

"What about all of them?" Lee asked Louie as he looked around at the hundred or more people that had gathered at the scene.

"We cannot do anything for them, Lee. If they choose to ignore the warnings, they have given their permission to die," Louie replied gruffly.

"I am not sure I see it that way, Louie," Ox said. "I doubt they give their permission to be killed."

"I was speaking metaphorically, Ox. It is their choice to leave or stay. If that beast kills them because they choose to stay, then it is their own doing, not ours."

Ox, nodded. Not pleased by the thought that if the vampire came back tonight, one or more of those standing there talking, laughing, dancing, and in general, having a good time, would never see the sun rise again. He heaved a sigh of resignation before he climbed into the truck.

Earl heard Ox's complaint. He hopped back over the tailgate. "Give me few seconds, Louie," he called out before he hurried over to the front gate and climbed it.

"Hey, you all!" he hollered. "It is getting dark. I suggest you take the party elsewhere. Anyone who stays here, risks not seeing the sun come up tomorrow. I have seen the beast. I also have seen more bodies of his victims than I like to think about. He's fast. Faster than anyone here. He can also pull the door off your car before you can blink your eyes. Understand?"

"Katie!" he hollered. "I hope like hell you leave right now and come back tomorrow because I sure do like to hear the sound of your laughter," he told a young dark headed woman who was sitting on the hood of her pickup.

"Me, I am headed for the house because I do want to see the sun come up tomorrow. It is do or die time, guys, and it is completely your choice," he finished.

He climbed down from the gate and ran and jumped up on the truck's bumper. He then whacked the tailgate twice to let Louie know he was ready to go.

Ox's eyes felt gritty from lack of sleep as he climbed out of the truck. "I think I will skip dinner and grab some down time. I am going to set my alarm for midnight, but if you need me before then, don't hesitate to wake me," he told the others as he climbed out of the truck. "I will be sleeping in my boots."

"That sounds like a plan. Earl, you and Lee go grab a bite to eat, and then man the cam screens. Ox and I will relieve you at midnight," Louie said as he followed Ox into the house.

"Sure thing, boss!" Earl said, motioning with a hand for Lee to follow him. He was ready for dinner. It had been a long day.

* * *

Dom was one of those who had listened to Earl's speech. "You heard the man, Felix. You go on home, and do not come back here tonight!"

"But what about you, Dom?" Felix asked.

"I will be okay. I will be hidden up in the tree. That's what the cape is for."

"But vampires can fly, can't they?"

"I will be fine, *primo*. I borrowed one of Mom's crosses," Dom answered with a grin on his face as he pulled out the six inch wooden cross on a cord from beneath his camo cape. "If she asks you about it, tell her I needed it for a photo shoot, but don't tell her where I am or why I need a cross. She will freak out, and have your father bring her down here."

Felix looked at the cross with skepticism, but then shrugged, and nodded "Then I will be back here at daylight, unless you call me to come and get you."

"Don't worry, Felix. I will be okay. This is no different than when we are staking out a celebrity's home."

"When we go movie star watching, you don't send me away, unless it is to go get something to eat," Felix argued.

"I have given this a lot of thought, Felix. That is why I am wearing this camo cape and brown jeans. Other than the one or two that see me climb up tree, the rest will never know I am there."

When Felix continued to frown at him, Dom grinned at him. "When you come *tomorrow*, bring some egg and bean burritos from your mom's house, and a thermos of coffee. We can sit in the car and eat while I tell you what happened. Okay?" Felix nodded. "Do not call me either as I am going to have to turn my phone off. I do not want it ringing when the vampire comes around."

Felix nodded again. "*Mañana*, Dom."

"*Mañana*, Felix."

Dom waited long enough to make sure Felix was headed back home before he went around the back of the tree. He attached the saddlebags to the carabiner clip and left it hanging there while he climbed the tree. He then pulled the bags up and tied the rope to nearby branch.

Once he was settled in, he took a good look at those partying below. Just before the last light of the day faded, he changed the camera's lens to one more suitable for night scenes. He then used the camera's telescopic capabilities to look around.

Many had left after the man's speech, but several more cars full of young people arrived to take their place. He saw a couple of young actors, and one fairly well known street model. He took their photos. One never knew what would sell.

He spent a few minutes studying the house. It was probably ten times the size of the apartment he lived in with his mother, but in this part of Hollywood, all the homes were large. The only thing that made this one standout, was the fact that the original parcel of land had not been split into smaller lots, and so the house stood like a small island surrounded by a sea of grass and flowers.

When Dom got tired of watching the revelers, he pulled out the foil beanie his cop friend Brian had given him, a couple of granola bars from one of his saddlebags, and a bottle of water. When he finished eating, he leaned back, fastened himself to the tree, and closed his eyes for a short nap. Not that he expected to get much sleep, with the party going on below him.

* * *

It was five minutes to midnight when Ox and Louie came in to relieve Earl. Lee had gone to bed earlier when Thompson came in for her regular shift.

"We can take over here. You should go get some rest," Louie told Thompson.

"I can't sleep, knowing there are still so many out there by the front gate."

"I thought the police were going to make them leave," Louie complained.

"They did about, but as soon as they moved on, several more carloads took their place," Thompson explained.

Ox looked over at Hattie. "You should go get some rest too."

"I can sleep tomorrow, Ox. Tonight I might be needed," she explained. "In the meantime, I think I will go make a pot of tea."

"If you don't mind, I will join you," Thompson said, standing up and moving over to the coffee machine. "I need to wash this pot out and put on a fresh pot. It will help keep me awake."

"See if you can find that bag of coffee beans that Nigel blends himself. That is the best damn coffee I have ever tasted," Louie said.

Thompson chuckled. "Yeah, I think we are on the same channel with that one."

Ox and Louie were sitting there watching the cam screens when a heat signature tripped the thermographic camera attached to the tree at the back of the property. Four seconds later, the matrix camera picked up movement at the back fence.

"By the size, it has to be the creature," Louie said. "Looks like he has a body with him again, as there is something slung over his shoulder."

Ox swore as the matric camera went blank. "Where did he go?"

Louie checked the camera. "He appears to have jumped back over the fence.

"He is probably on his way to grab some of the tourists at the front gate."

"No. He is at the back fence," Louie said as the matrix camera's alarm went off again. "He in the brush by the fence. We will have to wait for him to come out in the open before we can guess what he is up to," he added.

"Another body drop, no doubt. I am going to go get Hattie and Thompson. It won't take him more than a few seconds to reach the house, if that is what he has a mind to do," Ox said as he rose from his chair.

Louie hit the alarm button to notify those in the house that the creature was back. His hand hovered over the floodlight switch as he waited for the beast to reappear. He pushed it when he saw the beast was moving toward the house.

Ox's estimate had been correct. The vampire was in the front yard dumping another body within the next few seconds.

Ox contacted Louie, using his comm unit. "Where is he now?"

"He threw a body in the front yard and left. No, wait! He is now headed toward the back yard, and it looks like he is carrying another body."

"We are leaving now!" Ox all but shouted at Hattie and Thompson, grabbing them by the arm, he pulled them toward the door leading to the main room.

Goff dropped the body he carried into the swimming pool. His head then went up as he caught movement out of the corner of one eye. He looked into the house and saw a man with two women disappear into another room. It pleased him to know they were afraid of him. He thought about going after them, but then as he heard the shouts of excitement down at the fence, he decided he could do more damage there.

* * *

Dom was shaking so hard he would have fell had he not strapped himself to the tree. He set the camera down on his lap. He had watched the vampire dump a body in the front yard. Worse, with his telephoto lens, he had seen the woman's wounds. He grabbed up the cross around his neck and hugged it against his chest.

His heart rate had just slowed back down to normal when someone below him began screaming. He let go of the cross, and grabbed his camera to see if he could find out what was happening. He would forever wish he had not done that as he was just in time to see vampire bite into the throat of a girl he went to school with, Lila.

He again, let go of the camera. This time, to lean over and empty the contents of his stomach. He shuddered as more screams filled the night air, but picked up his camera nevertheless, and began filming what was happening below, nevertheless.

Dom kept wiping the tears out of his eyes, but he never put the camera down. He watched the vampire leap over the fence, and chase those headed for the house. There was nothing he could do to help either the ones trying to get away or those in the house.

It took him a few seconds to realize a new noise had joined the screams, sirens.

"*Thank you, God!*" he murmured with a sob of relief.

He quickly replaced the camera's memory card. He did so because if the police found him, they would confiscate his camera, stating the film was needed for evidence. By the time, they gave the camera back to him, the investigation was over, and there was no money to be made.

He tucked the card into the hidden pocket he had made in the hem of his beanie cap, and then put the hat back on his head.

He spent the next ten minutes filming as much as he could.

* * *

When the front cam screens became active, showing dozens of fence jumpers running toward the house, Louie told Thompson to call for help. He then grabbed his AK-47 and handed another rifle to Ox. "Let's go blow that beast's head off," he told Ox.

Both men ran out through the kitchen and outside.

Before anyone could stop Hattie, she followed them.

"I had better go help her," Genie said as she hurried to catch up with Hattie.

"Sit down, Marie!" Nigel commanded when he saw her jump up from her chair to follow Genie. "You will just get in the way. I will go help them."

Marie cast him a dark look, but nevertheless sat down.

Louie saw the fence jumpers, then he spat out a curse when he saw what had spooked them. The vampire was attacking them. He ran toward the commotion.

"Fire over their heads!" he told Ox. We cannot risk a shot at him, we might hit one of the runners. Both men opened fire with their AK-47s. Screams rent the air as the gunfire erupted.

Marie, Jennifer, and Bella cried out as they heard the gunfire.

The gunfire startled Goff. Instinctively, he switched directions. Putting on a burst of speed he cleared the fence and dropped into the cement ditch. He howled with laughter to show his disdain of the shooters before he began to leisurely jog toward his crypt.

Like Dom, Louie heard the sirens, and blew a breath of relief as he saw the flashing lights round the curve. He looked down at his watch. Only twelve minutes had passed since Thompson had made the call for help. *Felt longer*, he thought as he relaxed his grip on his rifle.

* * *

Vladimir was out front helping Jack, Earl, and Lopez round up the men and women who had jumped the fence. When he heard the gunfire, he used his mind to check on Bella. "*What is going on?*" he asked.

"*The beast was in the backyard. Hattie, Nigel, and Genie are there too. So are Louie and Ox.*"

"*Stay where you are! I will go see if I can help them,*" Vladimir told her.

"*Please be careful, Vlad!*" Bella cried out, putting her hands up to her face.

Jennifer heard her mother gasp. "What's wrong?" she asked.

"Your father has gone to help," Bella answered.

Jennifer took her mother's free hand into her own. "He will be okay, mother. Louie and Ox will see that he does not get hurt."

Bella nodded, but her face was rigid as she struggled with her fears.

Hattie ran outside toward Louie. "Is he gone?" she asked when he saw him lower his gun.

"For the moment," Louie answered as Thompson confirmed the vampire had just passed by the TG cam, headed east. As Nigel and Genie joined them, he added, "Again, we were not able to get a clear shot at him."

"Maybe, not, but you saved all those here," Nigel said looking around.

"Thompson, tell the paramedics they are needed up here as well," Louie said as looked at those that were down, and not moving.

Genie ran over to the where several men and women were lying on the grass. She knelt by the man that was the bloodiest. A quick for a pulse told her she was too late. She quickly moved to another. Thankfully, she was still alive.

"Hattie, could you bring me some of those beach towels you keep in the laundry room. We got several here that are in shock," she said as she knelt down to check on another unconscious woman.

"How about everyone that is able to walk, follow me into the kitchen where it is warmer," Nigel said. "You can wait inside until the police say it is safe for you to go back to your cars. In the meantime, we have hot tea, coffee, and soda to drink. Also a bathroom and laundry room to wash up in," he added, spotting the blood and dirt on some of those standing around him. "Earl, would you like to help? You know where we keep the food."

"Sure thing, Nigel," Earl answered as he followed behind some of those headed toward the kitchen.

Nigel searched the faces of those that entered. When he saw one young man, who did not seem to be injured, he approached him. "I would appreciate it if you would open that door, and hand out the chairs that are stacked there. That way, everyone can sit down while they wait."

Hattie had counted six people on the ground, and so grabbed up a dozen towels, and carried them out to Genie.

She was not surprised to see Marie standing by Louie.

"Here!" she said, handing Marie half the towels. "Hand these out to those over there. I will take these to Genie."

Poor dears, she thought as she noted the blank faces on a man and woman sitting on the grass clinging to each other.

Once the towels were handed out, she went back to where Louie stood. "I think I had better go check on those out in the front yard, I imagine they need to be brought in as well," she told him.

"Bring them around to the back entrance. It will keep the mud and blood off the carpet," Louie told her.

Hattie nodded. "I did not think about that."

When she saw Marie shiver, she added. "If you are going to stay out here and help, I advise you to come with me, and put on an old sweater. It is cold out here."

"I will be right back," Marie told the woman who held onto her.

"Vladimir can you come help me with those who are in the front yard?" When he nodded, she added, "Grab a few towels from the laundry room, and I will do the same. Most from what I see, do not have a sweater or jacket on.

Both Marie and Hattie followed Vladimir, doing their best not to look at the body in the pool as they made their way into the house.

* * *

Doctor Julias Transalle sat in one of the patio chairs staring at the swimming pool. He was waiting for the crime scene unit to finish their job. It had taken him most of the night to examine and document the trail of twenty victims that began in the street and ended at the back of the house. The body in the pool was the last of the lot.

He frowned as he saw his assistant Neal Petroff crossing the patio.

"Well, considering the call came in about twelve-thirty this morning," he complained as looked at his watch, "and it is now half past six, what took you so long to get here, Neal?"

"Sorry, doc. They switched locations on me. A private jet slid off the runway and rolled into a cargo carrier. I came as soon as I could."

Transalle's eyes narrowed at that news. "How many fatalities?" he asked wondering if they were going to have enough room at the morgue for this last body.

"Two. The pilot, and a female passenger. I had to wait while the fire department cut them out of the wreckage."

Transalle sat back in his chair and folded his arms as he looked at the younger man. He could see he the young man was just as tired as he was.

"Well, you can sit down here beside me, and wait until they fish the body out of the water. Which by the way is victim number twenty, and as you can see, she did not drown."

Neal's mouth dropped open when he heard the count. "Again, sorry, doc. They should have called someone else to come help you when they diverted me."

"No need to apologize, Neal. It is not your fault the department doesn't have enough coroners to keep up with this *monster*."

Chapter 37
Dom Returns

It was a few minutes past eleven, and everyone that was awake sat around the big dining table eating the late breakfast that Isles and Kate had fixed for them. There was no need to guard the front gate today. The police had the road blocked to everyone, but those who lived in the area.

Earl took another bite of his pancake covered in maple sugar sauce. "These are the best flapjacks I have ever eaten," he said. "You know, I am going to miss Isles's cooking when I go home. It will be hot coffee and cold cereal for breakfast again."

"Even you could cook eggs and pancakes, Earl," Lee said.

"I probably could, but I decided a long time ago, I don't like grocery shopping and washing dishes. I either fix a bowl of cereal or a peanut butter sandwich. Sometimes I grab a bite to eat at Wonkee's Diner. That is, when I am not having breakfast, lunch, or dinner with you and Jabber."

Jabber chuckled. "Or over at Annie's. Seems like you eat there a lot too."

Earl's face turned red when he saw everyone was looking at him. "True enough," he admitted. "I like Annie. I am thinking about asking her to marry me."

"Then you better get to it, boy! I know for a fact that Harry Collins is sweet on her too," Ox said.

Earl put his fork down. "Who told you that?"

"I overheard Harry's mom talking to Mary at the Post Office," Ox answered.

Earl rose from his chair. "Tell Kate not to toss my pancakes, I will be right back."

"I bet he went to make a phone call," Lee said, a grin on his face.

"I am sure he did," Ox agreed with a laugh.

Vladimir saw Bella's face light up with amusement as she watched Ox and Lee. He smiled at her. When she smiled back at him, he took a small box out of his pocket, and set it down beside her plate.

Bella stared at the box. "You remembered," she said as she picked it up.

"Of course, I remembered," Vladimir said.

"Remembered what?" Jennifer asked, her eyes on the box.

"The anniversary of our wedding day," Vladimir answered, never taking his eyes off Bella.

"Oh, Vlad, it is beautiful," Bella murmured when she saw the ruby and diamond ring.

"I am glad you like it, my dear," Vladimir said as he slipped the band on her finger. It was as close as I could come to the one that was stolen from you."

"I love it," Bella said, her dark eyes slightly damp as she moved her hand back and forth in the light.

Vladimir took two more boxes out of his other pocket, and laid one by Bella's plate, and one by Jennifer's plate.

Both women grabbed the boxes up.

"Oh, Father, thank you, it is beautiful!" Jennifer exclaimed as she picked up the gold bracelet with a diamond pave heart charm and put it on.

Bella looked at Jennifer's bracelet before she opened her box. She was not surprised to see her bracelet was identical to Jennifer's, other than her heart charm had rubies around the edge.

"The rubies match my ring," Bella said.

"That was the plan," Vladimir said, taking the bracelet and fastening it around her wrist. He did not tell her he had brought her jewelry chest from his apartment. He would give that to her later when they were alone. He knew she would get emotional as she relived the memories of the years she had received or bought those pieces.

* * *

Jack watched the camera screen that monitored the front gate. He saw a jeep enter the driveway. "That's probably someone delivering something, Cheri," he said as he stood. "I'll take care of it. If you spot anything else, let me know."

Thompson nodded her head, her eyes busy watching the screens. "Better hurry, Jack, it would be better if they don't ring the doorbell, it might wake up those trying to sleep."

Jack moved quickly to the front door and opened it. He stayed on the front step as the man got out of the car.

"Hi, I am Dom Marquez. Sergeant Myers at the police station told me I should ask for FBI Agent Lopez or Louie Crosshatch."

"They are not available, but Agent Thompson is."

"Then I guess that is who I want to see," Dom said.

Jack looked over at the car and saw a young man sitting at the wheel. "Just you?" he asked.

"That's my cousin. He does most of the driving. It leaves me free to take photos."

"We are not allowing anyone to photograph the house," Jack said, scowling at the man.

"I did not come to take photographs. I brought film that I took of last night's attack," Dom stated.

"Are you carrying a weapon?"

"No, of course not."

"Then tell your cousin to wait in the car while you come in," Jack said as he took his phone out of his pocket and sent Louie a text.

Dom walked back to the car. "He wants you stay in the car, *primo*."

Felix nodded. He had not expected to be invited in.

Jack motioned for the photographer to follow him.

Thompson looked the man over as he was introduced and shook hands with her.

Before Thompson could ask any questions, both Lopez and Louie came in.

Jack looked at her with a grin and shrugged. He had let Louie know they had a visitor who claimed to have film of last night's attack.

Thompson grinned back at him. She had notified Lopez for the same reason.

Jack introduced Marquez to Louie and Lopez. "He says he is here to help."

Dom nodded at the men. "I understand there is a team of Marine veterans working here."

"And that interests you, why?" Louie asked, noting the man was about the same age, weight, and height as Earl; around twenty-seven, slim, and just over six feet tall. The young man also had the same color of blue eyes as Earl, despite his Latino background. He killed the impulse to smile when he saw the outline of the large cross the young man wore beneath his shirt.

"My father was a Marine. He died in Iraq in '92. I was born a few months after," Dom replied. "I figure if he was still alive, he would want me to help. I brought you a copy of the film I took last night, so you can see how that thing kills people."

"We know how he kills," Jack bragged.

Louie turned and frowned at Jack to let him know he needed to keep his mouth shut.

"Detectives Ritter and Halcroft are at the front door," Thompson called out.

"I will go let them in," Jack said.

Dom dug out the flash drive he had put a copy of the all the film he had taken and handed it over to Lopez. "Just so you know, I gave the police a copy, and I sold a copy. That's my job. I am a freelance photographer."

"Paparazzi?" Louie questioned sharply.

"No. I don't stalk people," Dom answered, shaking his head. "I mostly shoot murder scenes, fires, accidents, things like that. Of course, I do take photos of celebrities or others that are of public interest when they cross my path, or I am on assignment."

"Well then, let's see what you got," Louie said as he turned on the big screen, and motioned for Lopez to give him the memory stick.

Louie put the memory stick into the computer hooked up to the big screen TV but did not start the film. He knew the detectives would want to see it as well.

Once greetings were exchanged, Lopez told Ritter and Halcroft about the film they were about to watch. "Have you seen it," he asked.

"No, we heard about it, but we have yet to see it," Ritter replied, omitting the fact that a copy of the film had yet to reach his office.

"Some of it is pretty graphic," Dom said looking toward Thompson.

"Yes, and on this big screen it is going to be even more graphic," Lopez state grimly.

"Ritter, you and Halcroft, pull those desk chairs over here, so you can sit down and watch. Dom you can go get that empty chair out of the cam room. Lopez and I will sit on the sofa. Jack you go back and help Thompson keep an eye on the cam screens! If someone jumps the fence, it will be your job to go out and turn them around. I will remind everyone that the bathroom is straight out the door, across the front room, and is the door to the left just before you turn into the hallway in case you get queasy."

"The film is about twenty minutes long and is not edited. Everything you are about to see happened just as you see it," Dom said.

Louie went to the fridge cabinet and got out enough water bottles to go around. Once he had handed the water out, he picked up the remote, sat down in his chair, and pushed the play button.

When the screen went dark again, Lopez put his hands to his face, and rubbed his temples.

"You all right?" Louie asked.

"Head hurts. I need some coffee."

"Me too," Louie said, rising to his feet. "Let's move to the dining room, gentlemen. We can have our coffee there while we discuss what we just saw."

"We have to get back to headquarters for a briefing," Ritter said as he got to his feet. "But I would appreciate it if you could make a copy of that film for us."

"Jack, make Ritter a copy!" Louie said.

"Do you mind if I go check on my cousin?" Dom asked. "He might need a bathroom break by now."

"Where is he?" Louie asked.

"I told him to wait outside in the car," Jack answered.

"Then go bring him inside! He probably would like a cup of coffee or tea too. We will be in the dining room."

"Where was your cousin when you were filming?" Louie asked Dom as he motioned for the young man to follow him.

"I heard the speech made by one of your men yesterday, and sent him home for the night," Dom said.

"Good. I will let Earl know his speech saved at least one life."

"Oh, it saved more than one life. Dozens left. Unfortunately, dozens more came after dark."

"Yes, and quite a few of them lost their lives," Louie murmured. "Sit down! Any chair will do while I will go ask Isles to make some coffee, and a pot of tea."

Dom sat down in a chair facing the wall of paintings. He could not help but stare at them.

When Louie returned, he smiled as he saw the look of wonder on Dom's face. "Impressive, aren't they?" He said as he went and sat down across from the young man.

"Yes. I never realized just how beautiful art is. I mean, Felix has dragged me to all the local museums as he wants to be an artist. They all have paintings of course, but they are spread out across the wall. Here, they are spaced like a wall of family photographs. It is amazing."

Louie smiled. *In a way, they are family photos*, he thought. *All those in the bottom row were painted by Marie.*

Earl came in with a young man that looked to be about twenty years old. Louie could see the family resemblance: Tall, slim in nature, high cheek bones, and with the same dark curly hair as his cousin. The only difference was in the color of the eyes. Felix's eye color was black, not blue. He waited until introductions were over before he asked him to sit down.

Felix was so overwhelmed by the wall of art that hung before him, he stood there in rapture, not hearing a word that was said.

Dom reached out and pulled on Felix's t-shirt. "Real world time, Felix. Sit down!" he chided with a grin to let his cousin know he understood the lure of the paintings.

Kate came in with a cart piled with pots of coffee, tea, and other tableware. She set a plate down in front of each man, and added two more next to Louie, along with cups and saucers, and set a pot of tea down on a coaster in front of them.

"Nigel said to tell you, he and Vladimir will be here shortly," she said before she wheeled the cart back to the kitchen. Also, Isles is making sandwiches. I will bring them in as soon as he gets them ready."

"We will wait for Nigel and Vladimir to join us before we discuss the film. It will keep us from repeating ourselves," Louie said.

He saw Dom looking at him questioningly and explained. "Nigel owns the house. Vladimir is his nephew. We just work for them. They both will want to hear your story for they both are on the beast's hit list as is everyone in this house."

When Felix looked at him with alarm on his face, he added as he poured himself a cup of coffee, "We stopped him from killing Agent Whittaker, and now he wants revenge."

Nigel came in and sat down. Kate and Vladimir were right behind him, carrying trays filled with sandwiches and other snacks.

"So, Felix, Dom tells me you are an artist," Louie said, letting everyone know it was small talk until they finished their meal.

"I want to be an artist, someday," Felix answered. "So far, I am self-taught, but I just enrolled in the community college for one of their art courses. Not the best I know, but affordable."

Dom cleared his throat at that statement.

"Dom has offered to pay my tuition for art school. He is good at taking care of us, but he is saving to buy a house for his mother which I think is more important than my art," Felix explained.

"I would like to see your work, and so will Marie," Nigel said, surprising the young man. "The bottom two rows on the wall are her paintings."

Felix's mouth dropped open as he stared at the signature on the paintings. "Juliana lives here?" he asked.

Nigel nodded. "Yes, she does, but keep that to yourself. She is one of those reclusive artists who does not want people bothering her for interviews or coming to the house to see her paintings."

"Don't worry, Mr. Nigel, I keep secrets very well. I work with Dom. Most everything he does to get photographs is a secret."

Dom chuckled. "Yes, and now that is not a secret."

"Sorry, Dom," Felix apologized, a look of devastation on his face.

"I was just messing with your head, bro," Dom said, giving his cousin a quick pat on the shoulder. "No one sitting at this table is going to compromise my work."

When Felix's face remained glum, Nigel stepped in. "Do you have a sketch book with you?" he asked the young man.

Felix face brightened and he nodded. "It is in the car."

"I would like to take a look at your work. Why don't you go bring it in?"

Felix was up and out of his chair before anyone could stop him.

"Excuse me, but I had better go keep an eye on the front door," Louie said, rising, and following the young man.

Dom watched Louie leave, and then looked at Nigel with a frown on his face. "Felix won't take anything," he said, defending his cousin's honor.

Nigel shook his head. "We are not worried about that. The door will automatically shut and lock him out."

Dom's face flushed in embarrassment. "Sorry I often get defensive when it comes to Felix.."

"As you should, my boy, he is family," Nigel said, appreciating the young man's dedication to his younger cousin. It occurred to him that Felix probably had no clue what Dom had went through last night.

"Has he seen the film from last night?" he asked.

"No, and I do not want him to either. He would never want to leave me alone on assignment again, and worse, it would give him nightmares for the rest of his life. Plus, you can hear me crying in the background. I edited that out of the film that I sold but left it in for the police." Dom swallowed emotionally before he continued. "I really do not want my family to hear that. I mean, not only was I scared, but all that death was more than I could handle."

Lopez found himself nodding at the young man. "No need to apologize, Dom. I think most of us would have lost it last night if we had been up in that tree watching the massacre below."

"Thank you for letting me know that, Agent Lopez," Dom said. "I was worried that I was being cowardly."

"You are not a coward, Dom," Nigel said. "The beast counts on that fear you felt. He feeds on that fear the same as he does the blood of his victims."

Felix returned with his sketch book, a look of shyness on his face as he sat down and slid it over to Nigel.

Nigel picked up the book and rose from the table. "Grab your sandwich and cup, and let us go and sit in the kitchen, Felix, while the rest discuss last night. I was there, and do not need to hear more about that."

"*I will use your mind, Vladimir to listen to what is said,*" Nigel told Vladimir.

Dom flashed Nigel a look of gratitude.

"Tell me, Dom, how did you manage to film the creature last night without him sensing your presence, and killing you as well?" Lopez asked.

"One of my secrets is to find a large tree close to my target," Dom began, and then went on to tell them about the bird nest he made in the big oak tree across the road from your gate."

"That explains that part, but I still have to wonder why the creature did not sense you?" Louie asked. "He is telepathic and should have known you were there."

Dom's face lost color. "I did not know that, but my best bud Brian, who is a Hollywood cop, gave me a foil lined beanie, and told me to wear it anytime I was out at night. He said it would protect me from the vampire murderer. I thought he was joking, but I did wear it last night. I even stuffed cloves of garlic in my pockets."

They all chuckled at that admission.

"And the cross beneath your shirt, did you have that on last night too?" Louie asked.

Dom grinned as he pulled the cross out from beneath his shirt. "Yeah, I borrowed it from my mother's bedroom wall, though I don't think she knows that."

"Well, just so you know, the hat saved your life. However, the cross and the garlic did not stop the creature, it knows nothing of ancient superstitions."

"You call it a creature, why is that?" Dom asked, swallowing nervously. He had only put the beanie on because of the night air, and to help muffle the noise of the partygoers below him.

"Because he is one of the living dead," Vladimir replied.

Dom's eyes rounded. "You mean, he is a *zombie*?"

"No, by that I mean, you cannot kill him with bullets as he is not a biological life form like us. I am not sure what he is, but what I do know is he needs human blood to survive. I appreciate you bringing us your film, Dom. It may help us find a way of taking him down," Louie said. "However, I would like your word that you and your cousin will not come back here after dark. I do not wish to see your bodies among the dead."

Dom nodded. "You have my word. I never want to witness something like that again. Maybe, I will go to the Cannes Film Festival. That way, I can do some photo shoots of Paris as well."

"I have always wanted to see Paris," Jennifer said as she sat down next to Vladimir.

"Dom, this is my daughter, Jennifer," Vladimir said when he noticed her eyes were on the young man sitting across the table. "He is a freelance photographer."

"My name is Domingo Marquez," Dom said, not really sure why he wanted her to know that.

Jennifer gave him a bright smile before she reached for the teapot and filled her cup. "I thought about being a photographer when I went to the University in Seattle. I took several classes and ended up with a portfolio of butterfly photos."

"Perhaps I can see it one day. I have never thought of photographing butterflies."

"Sure. It is in my room. If you have time, I can show it to you today."

"I think we are about finished here, aren't we?" Dom asked.

"I think we are," Louie answered.

"I will go get my portfolio, Domingo. We can go out on the patio to look at it. The light is better there," Jennifer said as she stood. "Wait here, I will be right back."

"Do you mind if I stay and look at her portfolio?" Dom asked Vladimir.

"No, I don't mind," Vladimir replied, a bit sad that he had not known Jennifer had a University education. *I have missed so much of her life*, he thought.

"*Marie is up, and will be here is a few minutes*," Nigel told Vladimir. "*She is interested in meeting Felix.*"

"As all of you know, we cannot continue on this way," Louie said once Dom had left with Jennifer, Marie had taken Felix to her studio, and Nigel had returned. "The bodies are piling up, and we have yet to get one good shot in."

"We are not getting enough sleep either," Lee added with a yawn as he set down and joined them.

Jabber resisted the urge to yawn with him. "I agree, but I sure as hell don't know what to do about it."

Everyone at the table fell silent. They had no answers either.

Chapter 38
Death Prevails

Goff woke early with all the vigor of a young jogeth. He rose and went to the crypt he kept clothing in to get fresh socks for his feet. He put his boots on and then stood. *The iron bars on Nigel's windows will not stop me tonight*, he told himself as he went back to the bin and picked up the pair of soft black leather gloves, he had taken from the man he had killed the other night.

* * *

Hattie slept most of the afternoon and into the night. It was past ten when she finally forced herself to get up out of bed. After she showered, she made her way to the kitchen to make herself a pot of tea and a piece of buttered toast with jam.

Once she had filled a tray with the teapot, cup and saucer, and her almost, midnight breakfast, she went to sit at the dining table.

She saw the newspaper lying on the chair next to her and picked it up. She gasped when she saw the headline. Then teared up as she read the first part of the article.

Marie, Bella, and Jennifer were on their way to the kitchen to get snacks for a late movie they intended to watch but stopped when they saw Hattie crying.

"What's wrong?" Marie asked as she went and sat down by her sister.

"They are saying that my paranormal abilities attracted the vampire killer, and I am responsible for those that died."

Marie grabbed the paper out of Hattie's hand, thinking her sister had exaggerated. When she saw the headline, she swallowed painfully. It was worse. The reporter had all but accused Hattie of summoning a demon. A photograph of the beast covered a quarter of the page. She could not argue with reporter's description. The photograph did depict a demonic looking creature.

"Pay him no attention! He is an imbecile," she told Hattie, passing the newspaper to Bella.

Bella read the first part of the article, then spat out a curse in Romanian before she shouted, "*Vladimir!*" with her mind.

"Where are you?" Vladimir asked as he woke up and sat up in his bed.

"*In the dining room with Hattie and Marie.*"

Vladimir was not the only one that heard her call, both Nigel and Genie heard her as well. All three, like everyone else in the house now, slept in regular clothing.

"What is wrong?" Vladimir asked as he went to stand beside Bella.

"Read this!" Marie said, thrusting the paper at him.

Vladimir's face reddened in anger as he saw the headline. He then read the article. Without commenting, he handed the paper over to Nigel as he came up.

Nigel was stunned by the accusations made by the reporter. He handed the paper to Genie and went to sit down by the woman he had raised. He took Hattie's hand in his own.

"This is exactly what Goff wants, Hattie. To demoralize us, and make others blame us for his murderous nature. Tomorrow, all of us are leaving this house, including Bravo Team. We can no longer stay here."

"Where will we go, Nigel?" Marie asked.

"To Paris. While our home there is not quite as comfortable as this one is, and we will have to climb stairs until I can get an elevator installed, it is large enough to house us all. There is already a caretaker and his wife living there, as well as a gardener in the cottage behind the house. We will need to hire a cook, but I might ask Isles if he and Kate would like to go with us first," Nigel answered.

"Vladimir, can you have some of your men come in tomorrow, and help with crating the paintings. I do not intend to leave them here to be destroyed by the beast or stolen by vandals."

"Of course, we can store them in the underground vault at my warehouse. They will be safe there."

"Why take Bravo Team?" Bella asked.

"Because Goff could follow us when he finds we are gone," Nigel answered, knowing that the jogeth had his ways of finding him, and likely would follow them.

Hattie shook her head. "I cannot leave that beast to murder at his leisure while I hide in France, Nigel. No. You, take Bella, Jennifer, and Marie to Paris. They will be safe there. Vladimir can go with you to help protect you. Genie can go with you or go back to DC. I will stay here with Bravo Team. However, you are right about the paintings, they need to be moved. I cannot believe that until today, none of us have considered the danger they are in."

"I am not going to France, if you stay here, Hattie," Marie said. "What kind of sister would I be if I did that?"

"A sister that still breathes," Hattie said, tears leaking from her eyes as she looked around the table at those she loved.

"Hattie is right, Marie," Nigel said. "You, Bella, Jennifer, and Vladimir will leave for France as soon as we can arrange for travel. You too, Genie, if you would like to go with them. I will stay here with Hattie and Bravo Team."

Vladimir stood there looking at Bella and Jennifer. They would be safer in France, he knew that, and if they went, he had to go with them. Yet at the same time, he knew he could not leave Nigel and Hattie here to face the beast, or possibly a mob, if someone decided killing Hattie would rid of them of the vampire.

Bella saw the look of devastation on Vladimir's face as he looked at Hattie. She began to weep. "No. I am not leaving," she said between sobs. "I cannot bear to abandon any of you."

Before anyone could try and comfort Bella, the house alarm sounded.

"Everyone to the office!" Nigel shouted as he pulled Hattie to her feet.

Before anyone could move, a loud grating noise came from the side of the house, and then the sound of glass breaking.

Louie came running out of his room and spied the beast standing in the hallway. Unfortunately, he had only his knife for a weapon as he had left the AK-47 in the office. His hand went to his knife, but before he could throw it, the beast threw the door he held in his hand at him.

The steel door slammed into Louie's body, carrying him several feet in the air before he and it, fell to the floor.

Ox had been right behind Louie, but when he saw the beast in the hallway, he ran back into the bedroom to get his rifle. When he ran out into the hallway, the beast was gone, and Louie was down. He hurried over and moved the door off top of his friend. "You okay?"

"I'm alive. You go get him," Louie whispered hoarsely as he struggled to breath. Thankfully, he had thrown is arms up, and they had taken most of the impact. From what he could feel, he knew some of his ribs were broken. He hoped that was all it was. As for his arms, he could not feel them nor move them.

"He's broken in," Vladimir said as he pulled Bella and Jennifer up out of their chairs and pointed them in the direction of the office.

Marie screamed as the beast entered the front room. She turned to run to the office, but the beast moved so quickly he blocked her way.

Bella and Jennifer froze where they stood.

Vladimir moved to stand in front of Bella and Jennifer.

Ox reached the door and raised his gun but did not fire as Goff had grabbed Marie by her throat and held her up in front of him and began moving toward him.

Earl, Lee, Jabber, and Lopez had woken also, and ran out of their bedrooms, intending to help. They all froze, but not because of anything Goff did, instead, they had no place to go. Ox blocked the doorway.

Jabber saw Marie's face begin to turn blue, and tried to push past Ox, but Earl grabbed him.

"Let me go!" he hollered.

"I can't," Earl shouted back in frustration. "Ox is only going to get one shot at taking him down, and he won't be able to if you are in the way."

Jabber quit struggling, and turned to give the man who had a hold on him a dark look. That was when he saw Louie lying in the hallway. "Let go of me, Earl! I got to go see to Louie. He's hurt."

Earl spun around, and for the first time saw Louie was down. He let go of Jabber and ran to where his friend lay.

When Nigel saw Goff had Marie, he joined his mind with Genie's, and together, they began attacking the jogeth's mind.

Jack and Thompson were standing just outside the office door, both armed, and with foil lined caps, but with Marie being held by the beast, like Ox, they dare not take a shot.

"Go call for backup and medical help, Cheri!" Jack whispered as he saw Marie's face was blue.

Thompson turned and ran back to her station to make the call.

"*Omay*!" Hattie shouted, hoping everyone knew to keep their eyes turned away from her as she burst into flames and moved toward the beast.

"Keep your eyes shut!" Ox shouted out as he used one hand to take his eclipse glasses out of his pocket, and the other to keep the rifle aimed at the beast.

The jogeth growled as he struggled to free himself from Nigel' and Genie's attack. As the light and Fire began to attack his body, he knew he needed to break Nigel' and Genie's control over him, so he could flee. He began slowly moving their way.

Vladimir, like Ox, had a pair of glasses. He put them on. When he saw the beast was moving toward Nigel and Genie, he raised himself into the air, and then flew feet first straight toward the beast's back. He knew it was reckless, but he was hoping his surprise attack would get the jogeth to let go of Marie before he choked her to death, or worse, broke her neck.

He hit the jogeth with the all the force of a cannonball, and like a ball hitting a wall, he rebounded through the air, and smashed headfirst into the fireplace's brick chimney. And despite Hattie's bright light, everything for him went dark.

Goff and Marie, went flying in opposite directions. The Jogeth wall. The house shuddered with the impact. Marie ended up on the floor in the middle of the room.

Ox had been waiting for an opportunity to get a shot in but cursed his luck as he as the paintings behind the creature. "Code 9! Everyone down!" he ordered as the creature moved in front of him. He prayed everyone was on the floor as he opened fire with his AK-47, hitting the vampire in the head numerous times, hoping to disable him long enough for Hattie to destroy him.

Hattie's concentration faltered a bit when Ox started shooting, and the flames that surrounded her wavered, but she quickly recovered. She forced herself not to look at Marie. Instead, she moved closer to the beast, not realizing her body had become a raging fire that filled the room and set off the smoke alarms.

Bella did not need to get down, she was already on the floor. She had fainted she saw Vladimir lying on the floor, blood seeping from his head.

Jack pulled Jennifer to the floor when she stood there gaping at the vampire.

Cherie, the only one left in the office, got down on the floor when she heard Ox's Code Nine command.

"Here, hold this!" Ox said as he shoved the rifle toward Lee, who stood behind him. "I need to go get the fire extinguisher. She is apt to set the carpet on fire."

Lopez opened his eyes long enough to take a look when he heard Ox's words. *Carpet? She is apt to burn the house down*, he thought as he saw the flames and felt the heat.

Goff struggled to rise, but the flames pinned him down, and his screams of anger and pain filled the room. "*I will not die,*" he told Nigel and Genie. "*I will come back and kill you all.*"

"*Not this time. There is no coming back from the Maker's Fire, Goff,*" Nigel stated.

As the fire moved over jogeth's entire body, he ceased his struggles. When his mind no longer was active, his body turned to ash.

"*You can stop now, Hattie!*" a voice whispered. When Hattie did not respond, she heard it again. "*Hattie, stop the fire now! Before you burn the house down,*" Nigel commanded.

"*Ortay!*" Hattie whispered. The fire went out, and Hattie stood there shaking uncontrollably.

She was not aware the carpet beneath her feet was smoldering, until Ox rushed in, grabbed her up, and carried her to the sofa. He quickly pulled her shoes off her feet.

Hattie ignored the smoking shoes. "Marie!" she cried out as she jumped up from the sofa.

"Sit!" Ox commanded. "Genie is working on her, and the paramedics just pulled up in the front yard.

"Is she...?"

"She is breathing, but barely."

Hattie saw Vladimir lying on the floor and gave an involuntary cry of despair as she tried to break free of Ox's hold on her.

"Sit, Hattie. He is alive, but Genie does not want anyone to move him until the paramedics get here."

Hattie quit struggling, but tears ran down her face as she turned to look over at Marie, and then back at Vladimir. She did her best not to make any noise, but failed as body jerking sobs overtook her.

Ox saw she was on the verge of hysteria. "Vladimir saved the day, Hattie," he said, hoping to distract her. "He flew up in the air, and then dove straight into the vampire's back. He went one way, and the beast went the other way, but it was enough to make the creature lose his hold on Marie. Once it let go of Marie, I was able to get a shot at its head. Your fire did the rest. There is nothing left but ashes. Thanks to you, we are finally free of that creature."

Hattie looked around and saw Bella lying on the floor with Jennifer sitting at her side, crying. "Wh-what happened to Bella?" she asked, stumbling on her words as she struggled to get her mouth to move.

"I am hoping she just fainted," Ox said. "We have enough injured to fill two ambulances."

"Who-who else is hurt?"

"Louie. That creature hit him with the door from your bedroom. Jabber and Earl are with him. Looks like, he has a few broken bones, and possibly, internal damage as well.," Ox replied.

Hattie was still shaking so hard she felt like she was going to explode. She grabbed Ox's arm to steady herself.

"That's the adrenalin, my dear. You are probably going to have the shakes for the next hour or so. You lit up like a small volcano."

"I guess that is why it is so hot in here." Hattie said as she forced herself to sit back down before she fell down.

"Yes, the air conditioner kicked on just after you burst into flames. Thompson, bless her, reset the fire alarm system, and we no longer have that noise in our ears."

"Thank you, Ox," Hattie said.

"What for?"

"For helping me to believe in myself," Hattie said as she wiped at the tears running down her face.

Ox gave her a kiss on her forehead. "I would love to tell you how wonderful you are right now, but I need to go talk to Lopez and the others. If anyone asks you what happened just say you only remember him coming into the room, and nothing else." When he saw the confusion on her face, he added, "Trust me. We do not want anyone to know about the Maker's Fire or Vladimir flying, understand?"

Hattie nodded.

Ox got to his feet and hurried over to Thompson and Lopez. He quickly told them why they should tell the police that when the bullets started flying, the creature ran out of the house the same way he came in. Also that I chased after him, but he got away."

Lopez looked at Thompson. It would be her call. As far as he was concerned, no one was going to believe them if they did tell the truth.

"Unfortunately, I have to agree with you, Ox. Telling the truth will just make us all look like liars," Thompson said. "Of course, we will have to tell the boss what happened. Well, maybe, not us, I think it would be better if Doctor Ferguson tells him first, and we go from there. The good thing is Langstrom is no more anxious for the truth to come out than we are."

Lopez nodded. "I agree. Let Genie and Langstrom come to an agreement, and we will go with that."

"Jennifer, if they ask you, tell them that you saw the beast, and that is about all you remember until you heard the gunfire," Ox said, looking down at her. "Make sure you pass that along to your mother when she wakes. You never saw the fire."

Jennifer looked up at him with her tear streaked face and nodded. Like Ox, she would do what it took to protect her family.

"Good. Now, I had better go tell Nigel, Genie, and the others, so our stories match," he told Lopez and Thompson. "Oh, one more thing. Make sure you tell them Vladimir tackled the beast, and that is how he got hurt. Trying to explain that flying business to someone that does not live here, is just about as bad as the fire story, don't you think?"

Thompson nodded, agreeing with Ox's statement. She had decided some time back that most of those living in the house had gifts that needed to be protected. "You are also right about that," she said before she turned, and greeted Sargent Mackensie and Officer Jones.

"Let Jack know, Lopez," Ox said cryptically before he hurried over to Nigel and Genie. "You two meet me in the hallway in about two minutes. Do not say anything to the officers until you do. Got it?"

Both Nigel and Genie nodded.

Ox went and knelt in front of Hattie. "You stick the story I gave you, no matter who asks. You saw the beast, and then things went kind of black. When the shooting started, you heard the beast scream, and saw him run back through the bedroom. If they ask, say you saw me chase after him. Make sure you call him either beast or creature, and not by name. Okay?"

"Actually, I can truthfully say that I do not recall much of what happened until you grabbed me and took my shoes off."

"Ah, I forgot about them," Ox said looking around. When he spotted the shoes at the end of the couch, he grabbed them up. "I will put these in the closet in my room and get them out of sight. We don't want anyone asking about them."

"What about the carpet" Doesn't it show signs of burning, I can smell the smoke," Hattie said.

Ox sat back on his heels as he considered that. "Thank goodness the FBI is covering this one. By the time forensics gets around to asking questions, Lopez and I should have a story put together to satisfy their curiosity. Now, I need to go tell the others what has been decided and go check on Louie."

Hattie gave him a sharp look. "How bad is he hurt?"

"He is in a lot of pain, and having breathing difficulties, but he is breathing, and that is about as good as it gets right now," he replied as he got to his feet.

Hattie waited for Ox to go into the hallway before she got up and went and sat down on the floor by Marie. She knew her sister was alive because she could hear her labored breathing. She started to reach for her hand, then stopped herself. If Marie's neck was broken, she realized it was best not to move any part of her until the paramedics came.

Ox was glad to see Nigel and Genie were with Louie. He quickly told everyone the new story, emphasizing that they needed to claim they had little memory of what happened until the gunfire broke the hold the beast had on them. Then you saw me chase him back through the bedroom. By the way, give me the cap off your head, Earl. You too, Lee. I will put them in my room with Hattie's shoes." When Earl reached for Louie's cap, Ox added. "Leave his cap on. He won't be asked why he cannot recall what happened."

Ox took the shoes and the caps to his bedroom, put them on the bottom shelf of the closet he was using, and then went back to the front room. When he saw Hattie sitting by Marie, he walked over, and bent down. "If they ask about the carpet, tell them you do not know what happened. You recall hearing the fire alarm, but you do not know what was on fire," he whispered.

"Got it," Hattie whispered back.

Hattie held onto the back of the sofa as she watched the paramedics work on Marie. They carefully stabilized her neck before they moved her onto a board, and then to the gurney. She followed them out to the ambulance.

"Sorry, but you will have to have someone bring you to the hospital, mam. With two victims in critical condition, one of us has to stay with them which will be me," the paramedic told her before he climbed into the back of the ambulance.

Hattie nodded, too emotional to speak. She turned to go in the house as the concrete was cold, and she was still shoeless, but stepped aside when they wheeled another gurney out the door with Vladimir on it. They took him to the same ambulance Marie was in. Tears begin to seep down her cheeks as she saw he too, was unconscious. She put a hand over her mouth, hoping to quell a fresh batch of sobs that threatened to erupt as the vehicle's lights flashed on, and it started down the driveway.

She started back into the house, but stopped as another gurney was rolled out. She gasped as she saw Bella, so pale and still, she looked dead.

"Is she going to be all right?" she asked the paramedic following the gurney.

"As far as we can tell, she is in shock. Once we get her stabilized, she should come out of it," the EMT answered, giving her an encouraging smile.

Poor Bella, thought Hattie as she moved aside again as the paramedics brought Louie out. He groaned as the gurney bumped over the door's sill.

Hattie welcomed the comfort of Ox's arms as he joined her to watch Louie being loaded into the ambulance.

"You know, it is too cold for you to be out here in bare feet," he whispered.

Hattie nodded. "I know, but I needed to stay with Marie as long as I could. Then they brought Vladimir, Bella, and

Louie out. I could not abandon them either," she finished brokenly.

"No, but now you need to come inside, put some shoes on, grab a sweater, and do whatever else you need to do because we are going to the hospital. Make sure your shoes are comfortable for there is no telling how many corridors we are going to have to walk tonight. They all have different injuries which means, they will be taken to the floor that handles those type of injuries."

Hattie pulled out of his arms and hurried inside. The front room was filled with people. Some wore uniforms, others did not. She saw Lopez off to one side talking with one of the officers. Two were examining the scorched carpet. She saw Nigel sitting on the sofa, and started toward him, but stopped when a woman came from her bedroom with a camera in her hand and started taking photos of the brutalized doorframe.

She made a face of irritation, but at the same time reminded herself there was nothing sacred at a crime scene.

"Are you okay?" she asked Nigel.

"Aye. I am just waiting for Jennifer, you, and the others to get ready to go to the hospital."

"Then you need to go get dressed as well as you are still in your robe and pajamas."

Nigel looked down at his lap, and then chuckled. "You are right about that," he said, getting to his feet.

"Put on your most comfortable shoes," Hattie called out. "Ox says we may have to do a lot of walking once we get to the hospital."

Genie was crossing the room to join Nigel and heard Hattie's remark. She stopped to look down at the gray heels on her feet. "I will be right back. Don't leave without me," she told Hattie as she followed her back into the hallway.

"Thompson and I will be leaving here once forensics finish up, but we will see you at the hospital, and probably tomorrow when we come by to move our stuff," Lopez told

Ox. "I just want to say it has been a pleasure working with Bravo Team."

"We have enjoyed working with you, and Thompson too. And I am sorry that Whittaker got hurt."

"Me too, but he is awake now, and the doc says he will recover."

"Glad to hear that."

As Jabber came limping across the room with a cane, Ox frowned. "What happened to you?"

"When you get to be my age, boy, you will learn that kneeling on the floor for an hour, can cripple you up," Jabber replied sharply, slapping his hip for emphasis.

"Well, then sit down, while I go tell Lee, Earl, and Jack what to do while we are gone. When I am through with that, I will get the truck out of the garage, so we can go to the hospital," Ox said.

Nigel finished dressing, slipped a pair of his favorite sneakers on his feet, and went back to the front room. When he saw one of the forensic officers bent over, and looking at Goff's ashes, he hurried over. "That happened when I used my lighter to set a poster on fire, and threw it at the beast, trying to get him to let go of Marie," he said. "The housekeeper can vacuum it up when she comes in tomorrow."

The man turned to look at Nigel. "Thanks for explaining that. We have been wondering why the scorch marks and ashes."

"Yes, Nigel helped distract the beast long enough for Vladimir to tackle him. I will make sure your office gets a copy of my report," Lopez said as he joined them, interrupting the conversation on purpose.

"*Good answer*," he mouthed at Nigel when the forensic officer bent down to pick up the stack of evidence bags laying by his feet.

Nigel flashed Lopez a grateful look, and then excused himself as he went to check on Jennifer.

314

"Do you think the monster will be back, sir?" the forensics officer asked Lopez as he straightened up.

Lopez shook his head. "No. He went out of here with a dozen or more rounds in him, most of them head wounds. Someone will probably stumble across his body in the next few days."

"Captain said bullets won't kill him," the officer said, swallowing nervously at that thought.

"Most of his head was gone. I doubt he can recover from that. If the murders stop, then he is dead. If they don't, I go back to hunting him down, and you get more overtime."

Chapter 39
The Picture Maker

Nigel showed the men where to put the furniture as they brought it in from outside. When they finished putting everything back, he signed the invoice, and escorted the last of the carpet layers out the door. He then went back in the house and stood in the middle of the room. Rick had a crew come in and paint the walls, and so with the new muted gray-blue carpet Hattie had picked out, most of the inside work was done. Good thing too, as Marie and Louie were coming home from the hospital today.

"Ox just called. He says they are on their way," Jabber said as he came out of the office and saw Nigel.

"Good. Everything here is finished and ready," Nigel said looking at his friend. "Come. Let us go sit down and have a cup of tea while we wait. Kate just put a fresh pot on the table."

Jabber nodded and followed Nigel to the table and sat down.

He poured cream into the cup of tea Nigel handed him and stirred in a spoonful of sugar. As he drank his tea, he noticed Nigel was sitting there looking at him. "Is there something I need to know," he asked.

"I was wondering if you would stick around for a couple of weeks or at least until we know Marie is going to be all right."

"Hmm. You must be reading my mind. I was just going to ask you if I could stay until she gets back on her feet."

"No, I did not read your mind. I think it is more a case of we both care for her. You, being here will brighten her spirits, and right now that is more important than ever to her healing process."

"I would be glad to stay a while. Nothing makes me happier than seeing her smiling face," Jabber stated.

"Well, you could come live with us, you know."

Jabber looked at Nigel with surprise on his face. "Do you mean that or are you just being kind?"

"I meant every word I said. While Hattie, Marie, and I have all have been comfortable living here these past years, we also have been lonely. With you here, it will not be so lonely. In fact, we could make two of the bedrooms into an apartment for you if that would be more comfortable."

Jabber chuckled as that last statement. "The bedroom I am in has plenty of room. I have a comfortable chair to sit in, a big screen TV, and my own bathroom with a shower that has four different nozzles. Of course, I will need to pay for my room and board."

"How about you pay for some groceries, instead, and take us all to lunch once a month?"

"You sure about that?"

"Yes. Vladimir and Bella are moving into the kitchen apartment, and he is going to pay the utilities. That only leaves the food bill. The house is paid for."

"Then consider me a guest that has come to stay for a while."

"You are no guest, Jabber. You are family that has come home," Nigel stated. "And I will leave it to you to tell Marie the good news. I will let the others know once you have shared the news with her."

Before Jabber could thank Nigel, his phone rang. When he saw it was Jack, he put it on speaker.

"Hey! I thought you two might like to know. Ox just came through the front gate," Jack said as he watched the pickup come up the drive on the cam screens.

Both Nigel and Jabber got to their feet and headed for the front door.

Nigel frowned as he saw Ox bring out a wheelchair for Marie. The brace around her neck was expected, but no one had told him she could not walk on her own. "Why the chair?" he asked.

"Oh, it seems I fractured my hip bone when I fell to the floor. I also have some numbness in my legs, and the doctor does not want me risking a fall, Marie explained. Thankfully, I am not in pain like Louie is."

Louie slowly moved his head to look at her. "When I am just sitting or standing still, I am fine, my dear. Those groans you heard were due to Ox managing to run over every pothole between here and the hospital," he said as he slowly slid out of the truck, letting his feet gently touch the ground. He groaned again as he straightened up.

"Do not take another step!" Ox commanded before he went and got the wheelchair the hospital had given them.

Louie wanted to shake head in protest, but it was too painful. Then realized he would not be able to make the walk on his own. Not with both arms in a cast, and severe pain in his chest for each breath he took.

In reality, he was barely able to move, but he did not want anyone to know that.

"Now, if you all would excuse me," he said once he had seated himself, I need to go lie down."

"I will go with you and show you how to use the remote for the chair Nigel got for you," Jabber said.

"Chair?" Louie asked as Ox rolled him toward the door.

"Yes. The doctor recommended we get it for you to sit and sleep in until your arms and ribs heal. It will keep you from struggling to sit or rise."

"Thank God for technology," Louie murmured, more than grateful that Nigel cared enough to see he got the best available.

"You got you one of those chairs too," Hattie told Marie.

"Thank you for always being there for us, Nigel," Marie said, tearing up as she looked at him.

Nigel nodded emotionally as he saw the collar around her neck, and the paleness of her face.

"Come. Let me get you to your room before you pass out on us," Ox said as he saw her lean back into the truck seat, and then close her eyes.

* * *

Later that evening, Vladimir and Bella sat on the sofa watching the La traviata on the big screen, enjoying the music and the story. When it finished, Bella applauded.

When she saw Vladimir looking at her with a grin on his face, she laughed. "One should always show their appreciation for the opera," she said, leaning over and giving him a quick kiss on the cheek.

"Ah, I suspect that was a token of your appreciation for me inviting you come watch it with me."

Bella nodded. "That, and I wanted to talk to you about our future. I..." Bella faltered. She needed to tell him she did not want to move to his apartment downtown. She wanted to stay in this house, but at the same time, she did not want to disappoint him.

Vladimir put a hand up. "I have already arranged with Nigel to keep this apartment for you and me to live in. That will leave Jennifer with her own bedroom."

"I am sorry if I have caused you an inconvenience. I just cannot bear the thought of leaving here. I feel safe here with Nigel, Hattie, and Marie. I know it is better for Jennifer too. There is so much she needs to learn. Things I cannot teach her."

"No need to apologize, Bella. I like it here too. Now when I have to go out to tend to business which could mean, I might be out all night if there is breach of a client's security, I won't have to worry about you being left alone."

Bella gave a happy sigh of relief.

"I intend to start moving things out of my penthouse apartment as soon as my head, and all my bruises heal,"

Vladimir continued. "You can move your things in here whenever you feel you are ready."

"I only have a few things to move, but I think I will wait until you get someone to redo the bathroom before I move in. I do not like that old fashioned bathtub. I want a walk-in shower like Jennifer's bedroom has."

"No problem," Vladimir chuckled. He did not like that tub shower either. "I know a good contractor. I will call him tomorrow. I think I will ask Nigel if we could turn the patio on this end of the house into a couple of rooms. You need more closet space, and I need an office."

Bella glowed with happiness as she stared at him.

Vladimir moved his head closer, intending to give her a tender kiss on the lips, but was interrupted by a knock on the door.

"Come in!" He called out as he pulled back and straightened up.

Bella gave him an amused smile, and then sat back on the sofa.

Jennifer came in, excitement clearly on her face.

"What wrong?" Bella asked, asked when she saw Jennifer's face was flushed.

"You are not going to believe this, but Dom just called to ask me to go to the Premier of *Greta*, Friday."

"You mean, like in the premier of a film?" Vladimir asked.

Jennifer nodded happily. "Yes, it stars *Gloria Travis*. She portrays a widow bent on revenge."

"Sounds violent," Bella put in.

"Oh, it probably is, but then most mystery thrillers are," Jennifer said. "Dom has the job of following her around and photographing her interaction with other actors. It is more than a date as I am going to help him by carrying extra lenses, batteries, and whatever else he might need, and at the same time, study how he works. What I came to ask, Father, is there enough money on my card to buy a new dress and shoes? I don't own anything fit to wear to a premier."

"You buy whatever you want or need. That is what the card is for."

"I would like to go with you when you buy your dress, Jennifer. And, you can go through my jewel box, and pick out something to go with the dress. Or pick the dress to go with the jewelry, since some of my necklaces are antique pieces, and are no longer available on today's market," Bella offered, beginning to see why Jennifer was so excited.

"What do you think of that young photographer?" Bella asked Vladimir once Jennifer had left.

Vladimir shrugged lightly. "He seems like a good kid to me. I mean, he works hard, and from what little I heard, he takes care of his family obligations, including the support of his mother."

"Good. Then he will do."

"What does that mean?"

"According to a dream I had last year, it means our daughter has found her life mate. That was my primary reason for sending her to Hollywood in the first place, I had a dream, and was told she would marry a picture maker."

Vladimir's mouth dropped open.

Bella gently pushed his chin up with her hand. "You might want to hold off on leasing or renting that apartment downtown, considering you own the building. It would make a nice wedding present for them."

Here is where I will leave those at No. 1 Hattera Lane, until their next adventure.
Tiffee Jasso

www.ingramcontent.com/pod-product-compliance
Lightning Source LLC
Chambersburg PA
CBHW020335180626
46812CB00001B/213